THE COLD HAND OF MALICE

THE COLD HAND OF MALICE

MALICE

A DCI Neil Paget Mystery

Frank Smith

severn
House

This first world edition published 2009
in Great Britain and in the USA by
SEVERN HOUSE PUBLISHERS LTD of
9–15 High Street, Sutton, Surrey, England, SM1 1DF.

British Library Cataloguing in Publication Data

Smith, Frank, 1927-
    The cold hand of malice. - (A DCI Neil Paget mystery)
    1. Paget, Neil (Fictitious character) - Fiction 2. Police -
    Great Britain - Fiction 3. Murder - Investigation - Fiction
    4. Couple-owned business enterprises - Fiction 5. Detective
    and mystery stories
    I. Title
       823.9'14 [F]

ISBN-13: 978-0-7278-6749-0   (cased)

All Severn House titles are printed on acid-free paper.

Typeset by Palimpsest Book Production Ltd.,
Grangemouth, Stirlingshire, Scotland.
Printed and bound in Great Britain by
MPG Books Ltd., Bodmin, Cornwall.

One

Detective Sergeant John Tregalles stirred in his chair as the television screen went blank. 'What did you do that for?' he demanded of his wife. 'I was watching that.'

'No, you weren't,' Audrey said placidly as she set the remote aside and went on with her knitting. 'You were miles away; have been all evening. Hardly said a word since dinner. It's not enough that you worked all through the weekend and now you're into another week without a break and your mind's still there, isn't it? And you were quite short with Olivia when she came to say goodnight.'

'Yes well, sorry, love. I didn't mean to be. But you're right, I was thinking about work. Perhaps I should go up and say goodnight properly.'

Audrey shook her head. 'No need,' she said. 'The kids can read you just as well as I can. Olivia just looked at me and rolled her eyes as if to say "Dad's off again". She understands.'

'I'll have a word with her in the morning,' he said, settling back in his chair. 'It's just that I've been trying to work out what to do about these burglaries. I spent all day today going over everything again, but I'll be damned if I can see what else we can do. Trouble is, I'm lead on this one, and Paget phoned this afternoon to tell me he'll be in tomorrow, and he wants to see a progress report. The problem is, there *isn't* any progress, so God knows what I'm going to give him. And if Alcott decides to sit in, I'm dead!'

Audrey paused to look up and catch her husband's eye. 'I'm sure it can't be *quite* that bad,' she said soothingly. 'What is it that makes this one so difficult, anyway? I know you've been on it for quite a while and I know you've not been happy about the way it's going, but I don't know much else except what I read in the papers. Would it help to talk it through the way we used to? I used to like to hear what was going on at work, but we haven't done that for ages, and to tell the truth I miss it.

'What's it been now?' she coaxed when Tregalles remained silent.

'Must be a couple of months since all this started. How many have there been since then? Four . . .? Five . . . ?'

'Four more. The one last Wednesday makes it five altogether, and we're no closer to a solution today than we were back then at New Year. It's not so much what they take as it is the damage they do once they're inside. Its getting worse each time, and that's what worries me. God knows what might happen if an owner comes back while they're in the house.'

'So it's vandalism, then.' Audrey said. 'I thought you said they were burglaries?'

'They are burglaries, technically, according to the 1968 Theft Act,' he said, 'but you're right, they do have more to do with vandalism than theft. Although unlawful damage is also part of the act as well, so—'

'Dunbar Road, wasn't it?' Audrey broke in. She had no intention of being sidetracked into a discussion of what was or wasn't a burglary. 'The first one? New Year's Eve? I remember reading about it in the paper.'

'That's right.' Tregalles hunched forward on the edge of his chair, hands clasped in front of him. 'Broke in through the back door. It looked straightforward enough at the time. Kids or young tearaways looking for money, making a mess of the place just for the hell of it when they didn't find much. They took a few bits of cheap jewellery and odds and ends, then smashed a radio and the glass in a china cabinet in a fit of pique on their way out. Took some food with them as well; some cheese and cold beef from the fridge.

'The next-door neighbour caught a glimpse of them when they knocked over a dustbin as they nipped over the garden wall. She was out in her greenhouse setting the heat for the night, so she went straight back in and phoned us. Uniforms found several footprints at the bottom of the wall, trainers by the look of the tread, which was almost worn off. Forensic said they could get a match – if we can bring them the shoes. They'd tracked in a bit of mud from the garden, but not enough to leave any worthwhile impressions behind, so all we were left with were a few bits of thread caught on the corner of a cabinet.

'It was too dark for the neighbour to get a good look at them, but she was quite sure they were young by the way they went over the wall. Apart from that, we don't have any kind of description. Uniforms reckoned they were dealing with a spur-of-the-moment job – kids looking for drug money, probably. They took down statements, spoke to some of the neighbours, but they knew from the start they were wasting their time.

'Couple of weeks later there was another one in Abbey Road. Same sort of thing. Broke in through the back door while the owner was away at her sister's wedding in Chester. She was only away the one night, but they must have known they wouldn't be disturbed, because they stayed long enough to have a sit-down meal before they left. Took something like forty quid from a jug tucked away in one of the kitchen cupboards, but nothing else as far as she could tell. That's when Uniforms decided it could be the same pair and the case was handed off to me.'

Audrey frowned. 'And no one saw or heard anything suspicious? Didn't see them come or go? Didn't hear anything?'

Tregalles shook his head. 'Not as far as we can find out. But then it was the middle of January, pitch dark from five o'clock on, and there were no lights anywhere near the back of the houses, so it's hardly surprising that no one saw them. Which means we don't even know *when* they went in. The house was empty from the Friday afternoon until midday Sunday, so it could have been any time after dark on Friday or Saturday night.

'Ten days later there was another one in Westfield Lane. The couple there are both teachers, and they were out for the evening at a retirement party for a colleague. They left the house just before six, and came back around midnight to find the place had been broken into. Once again, nothing of any real value was missing, but there was broken crockery all over the kitchen floor. It looked as if someone had simply opened the cupboards and swept everything out, then gone through the house lashing out at anything that caught their eye. Mindless, stupid, idiotic vandalism. And to top it off they stopped to make sandwiches and drink two cans of beer before they left. SOCO's done their best, but apart from a few dog hairs that shouldn't have been there, and a few threads that might or might not belong to the villains, they couldn't come up with anything worthwhile.'

Tregalles sat back in his chair, brow furrowed in concentration. 'Number four was in View Street about three weeks ago,' he continued. 'Same sort of thing, but they did even more damage there. Went through every room. Broke good china, mirrors – they seem to have a thing about mirrors and glass – pictures, TV set. And they didn't just bash the screen in; they battered the thing to bits. One of them uses some sort of pry bar – the one they use to break in the door, flat and heavy

– while the other one uses a piece of pipe to bash things with. And, as usual, they stopped to have a meal. Took their time about it, too; a proper fry-up, which meant they had to know that the owners would be away for some time and they wouldn't be disturbed. We found more dog hair on one of the kitchen chairs, but Forensic tells us they aren't from the same dog.

'Which isn't exactly a fat lot of help in a country that's got almost more bloody dogs than people, is it?' He paused, and Audrey could hear the tension in his voice when he spoke again. 'But this latest one in Holywell Street has me really worried,' he said, 'because it looked as if the place had been hit by a tornado. The woman, Mrs Pettifer, collapsed when she saw the damage. China, mirrors, TV, chair seats ripped, and a lovely old grandfather clock literally smashed to bits. And then they sat down and ate half an apple pie. Even heated up some custard to go with it, and the only clue they left behind was – you guessed it – more dog hair, but from different dogs again.'

Tregalles spread his hands in a helpless gesture. 'I'm afraid it's got me stumped, love,' he confessed. 'When I first took on the case I thought we were dealing with a couple of kids on drugs who liked to smash things, but these two are too careful. They haven't left a single print behind, not even on the plates and knives and forks and spoons they used. In fact they washed them afterwards. About the only other thing we have are the marks made by the tools they used to get in and to smash things, but that won't get us anywhere until we catch them – if we ever do. I keep telling myself that they simply have to make a mistake sometime, or someone will spot them going in or coming out, but that hasn't happened so far.

'We've had the word out on the street for weeks, but we've had nothing back. I've had the profiler working on it, but she hasn't come up with anything, so I'm stumped. The local papers have been on our backs, as you know – not that you can blame them; people out there are worried that they could be next. And of course New Street isn't happy about all the bad publicity. They want results! Paget understands the problem, and I think Superintendent Alcott does, too, but they're getting pressure from above as well.'

Audrey set her knitting aside, got up and walked over to stand behind her husband's chair. Her strong fingers probed the knotted muscles around the base of his neck. 'I know it's serious,' she said quietly, 'but worrying yourself sick isn't going to help anyone, and it won't solve anything either. Would it do any good to have more cars patrolling the streets at night? If nothing else, it might make people feel safer if they could see a police car on their street from time to time, and they just might see something.'

Tregalles shook his head. 'They're stretched to the limit now,' he told her. 'They're twelve men short – have been for six months or more, and New Street doesn't seem to be in any hurry to replace them.' He moved his head from side to side. 'Just a bit lower on the left,' he instructed. 'Aaahh, yes! That feels good. Now you've got it.'

'Are you quite sure it's two boys or men doing all this?' Audrey ventured tentatively. 'I mean except for that woman in Dunbar Street, nobody's actually *seen* them, have they? Did she say they were both boys?'

'No. She said she thought they were both young by the way they went over the wall, but that was all. She couldn't give us a description at all. Why? What are you getting at?'

'It's just that I couldn't help wondering while you were telling me about this sort of pattern they have, especially having a meal and all, if it could be a boy and a girl? I mean, you know what it's been like with the gangs lately; it isn't only boys any more; some of the girls can be just as bad or even worse than the boys. It's probably a silly idea, but I wondered if it started out by some boy trying to impress his girlfriend and it sort of escalated so they were trying to outdo each other.'

Tregalles eased his neck back and forward, enjoying the sensation as his muscles began to relax. 'It *could* be something like that, I suppose,' he said, sounding doubtful. 'It's worth considering. In fact, anything and everything is worth considering at this stage.'

'What about the houses they choose? Any connection there?'

'Not that we can find. They're spread out all over town, and the victims are from all walks of life. They don't know each other; they have completely different jobs; they don't belong to the same church, clubs, associations or anything like that. A couple of them went to the same school many years ago, but they were something like ten years apart. We've run them backwards and forwards through every computer programme we have and come up with nothing.'

Audrey moved back to her seat and picked up her knitting. 'I'm sorry, love,' she said as she slipped a needle under a stitch and began another row, 'I'm afraid I haven't been much help, but for the life of me I can't think of anything else to suggest.'

'Nor me,' he said. 'We'll just have to carry on doing what we've been doing, I expect. Someone has to know something about these two bastards, and we'll just have to keep pounding the streets and knocking on doors until we find that someone. If only they would steal something of value and try to flog it . . .' He shrugged the thought away.

'What I would *really* like to know,' he continued, 'is where they get their information from. How do they know they're not going to be disturbed? That's the key. If we could find that out we'd have 'em!'

He rose from his chair and stretched. 'Time for bed, love,' he said, extending his hand. 'And thanks for listening. Even if we didn't solve anything, it helps to talk it through.'

Audrey finished the row. She tucked her knitting behind a cushion and took her husband's hand. 'So what will you do tomorrow?' she asked as they mounted the stairs.

'Damned if I know,' Tregalles said almost cheerfully. 'Just say an extra prayer tonight and hope to God something turns up by morning!'

Two

'And that's it, Sergeant?' Detective Superintendent Alcott demanded sharply as Tregalles concluded his report. His narrowed bird-like eyes bored into those of Tregalles accusingly. 'That is almost exactly the same as you told me last week and the week before that, and it isn't good enough. These people have to be stopped, but I didn't hear anything in your report that suggests they will be.'

They were in Alcott's office. DCI Paget was there as well. Normally Tregalles would have made his report to him, but since Paget had been out of the office on assignment for much of the time during the past few weeks, he had taken time out to catch up on whatever progress had been made during his absence.

And it was becoming very clear that 'progress' was hardly the word for it.

'Dog hair, for God's sake!' Alcott snorted. 'Are you trying to tell me that the only physical evidence you have after all this time is dog hair? Well, let me tell you, Sergeant, it simply isn't possible to go through a house doing the amount of damage they do without leaving more evidence than that behind them. Prints, man, prints! Footprints, palm prints, fingerprints. Even if they were wearing gloves, they must have had to take them off at some point, especially when they stopped to have a meal. Knives, forks, plates, the inside of the fridge, under the edge of the table, on some of the food . . .'

'All covered, I can assure you, sir,' Tregalles said evenly, heeding Audrey's caution as he was leaving for work. 'I know it might not be easy,' she'd warned, 'but you've done your best, so don't let them goad you into saying something you'll regret later.' Good advice, but not so easy to follow under Alcott's challenging stare.

'Charlie's people have been extremely thorough,' he continued doggedly. 'I doubt if there's a square inch that hasn't been examined closely and dusted for prints of every kind.'

Inspector Charlie Dobbs, universally known by high and low alike throughout the service simply as 'Charlie', was in charge of the scenes-of-crime unit. 'They found traces of talc on any number of things, which suggests that they were wearing latex gloves at all times. As for footprints, it seems they put something on over their shoes the moment they were inside the house; something that leaves no tread or trace at all. And as far as we can tell, they were careful to avoid stepping in anything they smashed.

'And believe me, sir, that would not have been easy to do. You've seen some of the damage yourself, so you'll know what I mean. On the one hand they act like drunken sailors on a mindless rampage, yet on the other they seem to maintain tight control over everything they do. It's completely contradictory; it doesn't make sense, at least not to me.

'None of the homes have alarms,' he continued, 'and the thieves or vandals, or whatever they are, always seem to know when a house will be empty, and for how long, because they're never in a hurry to leave. And that, it seems to me is the key; if we could find the source of that information, I'm sure it wouldn't take long to find them.

'And as I said earlier, sir –' he hurried on before Alcott could speak – 'we've blanketed the area in every case; gone from house to house; stopped people travelling through the area on foot, on bikes, in cars, to ask each and every one of them if they were in the vicinity around the time of each burglary, and if they saw or heard anything suspicious or out of the ordinary, and we've drawn a blank.

'We think they have a car, because the houses they've hit are all over town. We suspect they leave it some distance from their target, then simply walk in and out. If that is the case, it could explain why they never take anything they can't carry in their pockets. They've taken money, and the odd trinket or two, and yet they've never taken cash cards or passports or anything of that nature, and I think that's because they don't have a way of selling them on. They haven't even taken anything worth pawning or selling on the street, so that line of enquiry is closed to us as well.'

Alcott eyed him bleakly. 'So what do the profilers say?' he asked harshly.

'Not much, I'm afraid, sir. They believe there are two distinctly separate personalities at work here, one being led or directed by the other. The one doing the directing is a control freak, while the other is compliant and will probably do whatever the dominant one tells him to do without question.' Tregalles hesitated. 'There's even been a suggestion that it *could* be a lad trying to impress his girlfriend, and they're in this together.'

Alcott grimaced. 'Possible, I suppose,' he conceded, 'but personally I doubt it. Is that the best the profiler can come up with?'

'I'm afraid their behaviour doesn't fit any of the normal patterns,' Tregalles told him, 'and she's had a consultant in from Birmingham University as well, but he's just as baffled by the evidence.'

'And I'm sure that will cost us a pretty penny,' Alcott muttered more to himself than to the others.

His mouth was set in a thin, tight line as he sat drumming nicotine-stained fingers on his desk. He couldn't really fault Tregalles under the circumstances – the sergeant seemed to be doing everything possible – but the fact remained that there were two violent people out there who had to be stopped.

'You say the homeowners were all away from home for different reasons?' he said. 'Are you quite sure there isn't a connection there?'

'If there is, we haven't found it,' Tregalles told him. 'Mr Baxter in Dunbar Road is a single man who was working at one of the clubs on New Year's Eve. Rose Wilson in Abbey Road was away from the Friday till Sunday at her sister's wedding in Chester. The couple in Westfield Lane were out from about six till midnight at a retirement do here in town, while the Bolens in View Street were away for several days in Oxford to be with their daughter when she delivered their first grandchild. As for the Pettifers in Holywell Street last week, they went down to Cardiff for a couple of days to help Mrs Pettifer's grandmother celebrate her ninety-fifth birthday.'

Alcott blew out his cheeks and looked up at the ceiling as if seeking inspiration or divine guidance, but when that failed to appear, he fixed his gaze on Paget. 'This can't go on,' he said grimly. 'I can't afford to have you tied up with CPS and West Mercia on the Greywald case any longer. As of now, I want you to concentrate on this case. No,' he said forcefully as Paget opened his mouth to protest, 'I know what you're going to say, but I have no other choice. CPS isn't going to like it, but you've been tied up with them for weeks, and the way they're going on, nit-picking their way through every bit of evidence, you could be there for another six months. It's all very well for them, but the appeal won't be heard until September at the earliest, so they'll have to make do with someone else.'

Alcott was right; it wasn't going to sit well with the Crown

Prosecution Service, but they would have to take that up with the super-intendent. As far as Paget was concerned, he would be only too happy to return to his regular duties, even if it did mean taking on a case that seemed to be going nowhere. Certainly it would be better than what he'd been doing for the past few weeks.

Greywald Industries had been found guilty of allowing toxic chem-icals to leach into marshlands in an area covered by both the West Mercia and the Westvale forces. The poisoned ground water had found its way into wells and water systems in the area, and a number of people and animals had become sick as a result. Greywald Industries was appealing the verdict, knowing that they would be facing a string of civil lawsuits if the verdict stood. So, for the past several weeks, Paget and a repre-sentative from the West Mercia force had been working with the Crown Prosecution Service re-examining every scrap of evidence that had been collected over a period of several years to make sure it would stand up to scrutiny in court.

In fact, Paget would be only too happy to be rid of it. Spending his days answering endless – and in many cases, seemingly pointless – ques-tions by a battery of lawyers, was not his idea of a useful way to spend his time.

Alcott swung his chair around to face Tregalles. 'This is no reflection on you, Sergeant,' he said, 'but I can't let matters stay as they are. The people in this town are frightened; the press have the bit between their teeth, and New Street is pushing hard for results. You, of course, will remain on the case, but DCI Paget will be in charge of the investiga-tion.'

He turned back to Paget. 'And I want you,' he said, emphasizing his words by jabbing a finger in the DCI's direction, 'and *only* you, to deal with questions from the media. I'll have a word with the press officer about that, and I want you to make sure that everyone, including Charlie's people, understands they are to refer any questions from the media, or anyone else, for that matter, to you.'

The intercom on Alcott's desk buzzed softly. The superintendent touched a button and said, 'Yes, what is it, Fiona?'

'Chief Superintendent Brock is on line one, sir,' his secretary said. 'He said you were supposed to have called him twenty minutes ago . . .? He sounded—'

'Yes, yes, I can imagine what he sounded like, Fiona,' Alcott broke in testily. 'I'll talk to him now. Though God knows he's not going to like what I have to tell him,' he muttered beneath his breath as his hand hovered over the button on line one.

A brisk nod told the two detectives Alcott wanted them to leave as he put the phone to his ear. 'Good morning, sir,' he said cheerfully, as they made for the door. 'Sorry I couldn't get back to you sooner, but I was just discussing a new line of enquiry in this string of burglaries with DCI Paget, who is heading the investigation now . . .'

'Sorry, boss,' Tregalles said as he and Paget descended the stairs together. 'I didn't intend to land you with this, but on the other hand I have no idea what we can do that we haven't already done. There has to be a connection between these people, some common thread, but I'll be damned if I can find it. I felt like a perfect idiot in there.'

'Nobody's perfect, Sergeant,' Paget said lightly. 'Not even you.' He had never seen Tregalles so tense as he'd been in the superintendent's office, and he was pleased to see the flicker of a smile on the sergeant's face in response.

'Now,' he continued as they arrived at his office, 'what I need from you is everything – and I mean *everything* – you have right from the very beginning. I want to see the statements made by the victims, by their neighbours, and by anyone and everyone who has been interviewed. I want a list of everything that was taken and everything that was destroyed, and I want the collator's material as well as the profiler's report.

'I know, I know,' he said as Tregalles was about to speak. 'I know you told Mr Alcott that neither she nor the consultant from the university could tell us anything we hadn't already guessed, and it may be a waste of time, but I want to see them just the same. And if there is anything I've overlooked, I want to see that too,' he ended.

Tregalles blew out his cheeks. 'There's a hell of a lot of stuff,' he warned. 'It will take some time.'

'I know,' Paget told him, 'but we can start on the material from the first burglary while the rest is being put together. Now, I have a few things I must clear up here, but I want you back here with the first lot, let's say at two o'clock this afternoon.

'And be prepared to work late, tonight,' he called after him as Tregalles left the office.

Three

Paget drank the last of his tea and gave a sigh of contentment as he settled back in his chair. 'That was a delicious meal,' he said with feeling, 'and I was certainly ready for it, Grace. But you shouldn't have waited this long for your own dinner.'

'Well, you did promise to be home by eight, and you know I don't like eating alone.'

Even though they had been living together for more than a year now, Paget still couldn't believe his good fortune, and chills still ran up and down his spine when Grace came into his arms. Devastated by his wife Jill's untimely death, he'd convinced himself that no one could ever take her place, and he'd withdrawn into himself, leaving London and the Met behind for the solitude of what used to be his father's house in Ashton Prior. But he'd become restless there, and finally allowed himself to be coaxed into joining the Westvale Regional Force headquartered in Broadminster as a replacement DCI.

Those first few years hadn't been easy. Taciturn and demanding, he'd had trouble fitting in, but when chance brought him and DS John Tregalles together on a case, they seemed to click. Tregalles, originally from Cornish stock, had grown up in London, and between his irrepressible spirit and irreverent approach to life in general, he wasn't at all phased by Paget's gruff and unbending manner, and the two had gradually formed a solid working relationship.

Paget had no social life. His work *was* his life, although there was a time when it looked as if he and Dr Andrea McMillan, a suspect in a murder case, might become something more than friends, but that hadn't worked out. It had depressed him at the time, but he had cause to be thankful later on when he met Grace Lovett, an analyst with SOCO. Even then, it had taken him longer than it should have to recognize the feelings he had for her, and even longer before he allowed himself to believe that she could feel the same about him.

'Penny for them?' Grace said with a questioning look. 'There was a

faraway look in your eyes just then. I hope you're not still thinking
about the job?'

He smiled. 'As a matter of fact, I was thinking of you, and the first
time we met,' he said.

'The first time we met you didn't even notice me,' she reminded
him. 'The next time we met you took me to lunch, then told me I had
to pay for mine because I was on expenses.'

He grinned. 'Well, things have changed a bit since then,' he told her,
'and as for what I was thinking just now, I was thinking how lucky I am
to have you.'

Grace eyed him with mock scepticism as she stood up and began
clearing the table. 'They always say the way to a man's heart is through
his stomach,' she said, 'but I have the feeling that this is leading up to
something?'

'It is,' he told her as he got up and came round the table. He placed
his hands lightly on her shoulders and held her at arm's length. 'I don't
know what sort of day you've had,' he said, 'but mine's been very tiring,
so why don't we leave the clearing up till morning and have an early
night? What do you say?'

Grace's eyes danced mischievously as she pulled away. 'I'd say you
were trying to get me into bed, DCI Paget, and I suspect your inten-
tions are not entirely honourable.'

'Is that a yes or a no?'

Grace grinned. 'You don't get anything for free in this world,' she
told him. 'You should know that by now; there's always a price to pay.'

'Which is . . .?' he asked cautiously.

'We clear the table and do the washing up before we go to bed,
because there is no way I want to face this lot when I come downstairs
tomorrow morning. So, the sooner we get them done, the sooner you
can have your way with me.'

Moira Ballantyne slid the letter into the envelope and sealed it. It was
shorter than usual, but she'd found it hard to concentrate on the weekly
letter to her mother after the encounter with Laura Holbrook last night.
She'd tried to dismiss it from her mind; tried to tell herself that things
would straighten themselves out between them, but Laura's accusation
had been niggling away in the back of her mind all day, refusing to go
away.

And the more she'd thought about it, the angrier she'd become.

Laura had all but accused her of having an affair with Simon; right there in the club last night. She hadn't mentioned Moira by name, but by the way she had gone on about 'some people' getting their claws into other people's husbands, then pretending to be 'little Miss Innocent', she had made her meaning very clear, and Moira could just imagine the sort of gossip that had broken out the minute they left the club.

It would have been bad enough if it had been true, but it wasn't. Not that she and Simon hadn't had their moments in the past, she thought guiltily, but that was over long ago. It had happened at a time when she and Trevor were going through a rough patch, in fact she had given serious consideration to divorce. The work wasn't coming in the way it had; Trevor was depressed, and the more he worried about the situation the worse things became. Bills were piling up; nothing was going right, and they'd fallen into the habit of sniping at each other over the most trivial things. She knew she'd been bitchy – unbearably so, if she were honest – and Trevor had finally withdrawn into himself and wouldn't even talk to her unless it was unavoidable.

And then Simon Holbrook had asked them to design a security system for his new premises. It wasn't a big job; the premises weren't large, but it was a lucrative one, because Simon wanted the best system going. It had meant that Moira had had to spend a lot of time on site, much of it in Simon's company as he explained in painstaking detail exactly what he wanted. But with his scientific background, and being the kind of man he was, he had insisted on having every circuit explained to him in detail as they went along, and had in fact shown them how they could miniaturize some of the equipment they were using. He had also come up with some interesting and innovative ideas about where to conceal the cameras.

The new job had been a godsend. Apart from anything else, it got Moira out of the house, because she was the one who took care of the initial on-site assessment and evaluation. It was her job to work with the client, record his needs, make recommendations, and provide Trevor with the information and working sketches from which he would design the system.

Often working together far into the evening in order to meet the deadline Simon had set, it was almost inevitable that they would end up in bed together. Simon was such a breath of fresh air after the claustrophobic atmosphere at home – and he could be so damned charming when he put his mind to it.

It was all over in a matter of weeks. It was just sex – that's all it was. No regrets on either side. Except, a small voice whispered as Moira stared blankly at the envelope in her hand, that wasn't *quite* true, was it? Not if she were honest. Even now, there were times when he would give her one of those sidelong looks from those dark eyes of his, and her heart would beat a little faster, and she would shiver as if he'd touched her. She'd felt guilty about the affair, brief as it had been; she'd even thought long and hard about confessing all to Trevor, but thankfully she hadn't. It would have been the end of their marriage, and she didn't want that. Trevor might not be the most exciting man in the world, but he was a good man, and she loved him.

As for Simon, Moira had always marvelled at the way he drifted in and out of relationships as casually as he might drop in and out of a restaurant for lunch. He was like a magnet; women were attracted to him – they couldn't seem to help themselves – even though most of them soon realized there was no depth to him and he would always be moving on.

Until Laura, of course. Simon had met his match there. Moira had watched from the sidelines as their relationship developed, intrigued by the way Laura had taken control from the very beginning, first of Simon himself, and then his business.

'And now she has it all,' Moira murmured to herself as she moistened a stamp and stuck it on the envelope.

There could be little doubt that, despite Simon's unique talents and hard work, his company, Holbrook Micro-Engineering Laboratories, would have gone under if Laura hadn't come along at just the right time. Investing so much money had been a huge gamble on her part, but one that had paid off. Paid off for Moira and Trevor as well, because Simon was so pleased with the new security system that he had steered more business in their direction.

But it wasn't just the money. Without Laura's business acumen, her background as a forensic auditor, and her contacts in both private and government circles, chances were the company would still have gone under. Simon Holbrook might be a genius in his field of micro-technology, but without the ability to market what he had to offer, the business was bound to fail.

Laura had literally taken charge, and Simon had been only too happy to leave the marketing and sales side of the business to her while he went back to the bench to get on with what he and his hand-picked team did best: developing new, miniaturized products and modifying old ones.

The results spoke for themselves. In the short span of two years, the company was not only well on its way to recovery, but Simon's name and the work he was doing had appeared in at least two high-tech journals recently. Laura's doing, no doubt, thought Moira, but she had to admire the woman's drive and dedication to her work, even if she didn't like her.

Laura was a beautiful woman, and Simon was an attractive man, so Moira had never doubted for a moment that the two of them had been sleeping together from time to time, but it had taken everyone completely by surprise when he'd announced, quite casually last October, that they were married.

Simon? *Married?* Surprised? Gobsmacked would be closer to the mark!

Moira had always thought that if anyone could snare Simon it would be Susan Chase, Laura's older sister, although even that seemed unlikely after his experience of being dragged through the courts when his first wife Helen divorced him. Even so, Moira felt sure that Susan had been living in hopes, so it was ironic that she should be the one to introduce Simon to her sister.

It was hard even now to think of Simon as a happily married man. Well, he'd seemed happy enough in the beginning, but Moira wasn't so sure about now. He'd made a couple of remarks to Trevor about the amount of time Laura was spending away from home, and the way she seemed to have completely taken over control of the business. And if there *was* anything behind those remarks, it was quite possible that Simon might use that as an excuse to seek solace elsewhere.

But for Laura to accuse her — and at the club, of all places! Moira had been taken so completely by surprise that she hadn't been able to find the words to respond, so she'd been left standing with her mouth hanging open as Laura marched away. Now, reliving the scene of the night before, Moira felt the anger rising once again. If Laura really thought Simon was having it off with her, then the sooner she set her straight the better.

She looked at the time. Ten past nine. The letter to her mother wouldn't be picked up until tomorrow morning, but she could do with a breath of fresh air before bed, and Trevor and Simon wouldn't be back for at least another hour, so she might as well take the letter to the postbox at the end of the street now. At least it was better than just sitting there fuming about Laura.

The wind had been blowing steadily from the north throughout the day, but now it had shifted around to the east, which was never a good sign. It was trying to rain, and Moira kept her head down as she walked to the top of the road. Pembroke Avenue wasn't very long; eight houses on either side, single, detached, each with its own generous plot of land, screened from its neighbour by trees, a tall hedge, or a stone wall. Solid, well-built older houses, many of which had been completely renovated and modernized over the years, each with their own driveway and garage. And yet there were still cars parked on both sides of the avenue. Signs of an affluent neighbourhood, Moira thought, and wondered if that would change with the skyrocketing price of oil and the falling price of houses.

The Ballantynes' house was the last but one on the odd-numbered side, and Moira had to pass the Holbrook's house on her way to the postbox on the main road at the top end of Pembroke Avenue. She hadn't given it so much as a glance on her way there, but with the wind behind her on her way back, she paused outside the house and looked up at the light in the bedroom window.

Odd, she thought. Laura would never have the light on when she had one of her migraines, but that had been her excuse for not going to see the film tonight. Either she had recovered more quickly than usual, or she'd pretended to have a migraine to get out of going to see a film that neither she nor Moira had been keen on seeing in the first place. Not that she could blame Laura for that after begging off herself when Simon phoned to say that Laura had a migraine and had gone to bed.

Moira started to move on, then paused. Why not? she thought. If the light was on that must mean that Laura was all right, so why not go in and have it out with her right now?

Moira took out her key ring as she mounted the steps to the front door. Simon had given her a key when she'd offered to keep an eye on the house while he and Laura were away for a week just after Christmas, so she might as well make use of it now. If Laura was in bed, she might not come down to answer the doorbell, and even if she did, she might not let Moira in. No, better to take the woman by surprise and tackle her in her own bedroom. Moira stepped over the sill and closed the door behind her. She reached for the light switch, then withdrew her hand. Why put the light on and forewarn Laura? A faint light glowed at the top of the stairs, so why not just

go up quietly and walk into the bedroom unannounced? It would
surprise the hell out of Laura, Moira thought with some satisfaction
as she mounted the stairs; Laura had blindsided her last night at the
club, so now it was her turn to do the same.

Grace reached blindly for the alarm clock as she struggled to come
awake; found it, hit the cut-off bar and wondered why it continued to
ring. 'Phone,' she mumbled as she recognized the sound. Paget stirred
beside her. He opened his eyes and squinted at figures on the digital
clock. 11.28. He groaned softly as he picked up the phone and said,
'Paget.' The conversation was brief, less than a minute before he swung
his legs over the side of the bed and said, 'I'll be there in half an hour.
Let's have that address again.'

   Grace propped herself up on one elbow. 'Do you really have to go?'
she asked sleepily. 'What is it this time?'

   'Another burglary,' he told her. 'Same MO as the others, except this
time there was a woman in the house.'

   'Dead?' Grace asked, although by the look on Paget's face she was
sure she knew the answer.

   He nodded. 'Afraid so,' he said. 'Bludgeoned to death in her own
bed. Poor woman didn't stand a chance by the sound of it.'

Four

Three patrol cars, and two scenes-of-crime vans were drawn up in front of the house, and Paget recognized Tregalles's car parked a short distance away.

A uniformed constable by the name of Roberts met Paget on the path leading to the house. 'The name of the deceased is Holbrook,' he told Paget. 'Laura Holbrook. The husband is Simon Holbrook. They own that firm we've been hearing so much about lately, Holbrook Micro-Engineering Laboratories. Seems like Holbrook and a friend, a Mr Ballantyne, had been out to see a film, and they found her when they got back. It was Mr Holbrook who found her, according to Ballantyne, but I couldn't get much out of Holbrook himself. He's pretty shaken up.'

The constable consulted his notebook. 'Mr Ballantyne lives three doors down at number 15. Normally, Mrs Holbrook would have gone with them tonight, but she had a migraine and went to bed. When the two men returned, Ballantyne came in with his friend for a nightcap before going home, and when Mr Holbrook went upstairs to see how his wife was, he found her on the floor beside the bed with her head bashed in.'

The constable closed the book. 'We've had a look around, sir, and it appears the thieves broke in through the back door the same way they did with all the others. Probably expected the house to be empty, but when they went upstairs and found her in bed . . .' The man grimaced and drew in his breath. 'Well, you'll see for yourself, sir.'

'Any sign of a weapon?' Paget asked.

'No, sir, but I heard the doctor tell Sergeant Tregalles it was the proverbial blunt instrument.' Clearly shaken, the constable drew in his breath once more before trusting himself to speak. 'There was a lot of blood, sir,' he said quietly.

'Is Sergeant Tregalles inside?'

'Out the back, I think, sir. Like I said, it looks like that's the way the thieves came in.'

Paget thanked the man. The constable and his partner, first on the scene, had done a good job of calling for back-up and cordoning off the area. Even so, considering it was almost midnight, a surprising number of people had gathered in the street to see what was going on.

'Take a couple of your colleagues and get the names and addresses of those people,' he said. 'Find out if they saw or heard anything suspicious. And note down anything they have to say about the Holbrooks.'

'Right, sir.'

A uniformed constable standing at the bottom of the stairs recognized Paget when he stepped inside. 'The doctor and the photographer are still upstairs,' he said, 'and Mr Holbrook and his friend are in there.' He pointed to closed French doors across the hall. 'And watch out for the sick halfway up, sir,' he warned as Paget started up the stairs. 'Seems like Mr Holbrook spewed his guts out when he saw what had happened to his wife. Not that you could blame him; felt like doing that myself when I saw what they'd done to her. Bastards!'

'You and Roberts were first on the scene? Is that right?'

'That's right, sir. Got the call at 22.58, and we were here within four minutes—'

'Never mind that for the moment,' Paget told him. 'Come upstairs with me; I may want to ask you some questions when I've seen the body.'

'Right sir.'

The door to the bedroom was open. It was a large room, much of it taken up by heavy dark furniture, old and well-used by the look of it, but Paget's eyes went immediately to the king-size bed. The bedclothes had been dragged to the far side where the body lay half concealed on the floor.

Starkie was standing beside a bureau, filling out forms attached to a clipboard. 'Bad one,' he said without looking up. 'Come and see for yourself.' He slipped the clipboard into his case and closed it before leading the way around the bed. The photographer, who had been squatting down at the foot of the bed, changing lenses, stood up.

Paget drew a deep, steadying breath.

Laura Holbrook, dressed only in a satin nightgown, looked more like a broken doll than someone who had been a living, breathing human being a few short hours ago. It was impossible to tell what she had looked like in life, because beneath the tangled hair and crusted blood, her features had been almost obliterated by repeated blows.

Slim and firm-bodied, Laura Holbrook was quite small. Her height,

recorded by Starkie, Paget learned later in the day, was 157 centimetres
– with 5' 2" in brackets for the benefit of people like himself, who still
tended to think in feet and inches. Her hands were smooth and well
cared for, and her nails were painted a delicate metallic blue.

The bedclothes, Starkie explained, had been dragged from the far
side of the bed, and were partly covering the body when he arrived. A
bloodstained pillow lay askew on the bed, and there were more bloodstains on the sheets. A small lamp with a bell-shaped silken shade stood
on the bedside table, while a telephone, a radio-alarm clock, an empty
glass, and a small brown bottle lay on the floor beside the body. The
cap of the bottle lay some distance away, and several small white tablets
had been crushed into the carpet.

'Sleeping pills,' Starkie said as Paget bent to examine them. 'Looks
like someone trod on them. Could have been the killer or it could have
been one of your men.'

Paget turned to the constable who was standing by the door. 'Was
this bedside light on like this when you arrived?' he asked.

'Yes, sir. We didn't touch a thing except to make sure that the lady
was dead.'

'So everything is exactly as you found it?'

'Yes, sir.'

Paget studied the scene. The radio-clock lay on its side against the
wall, still showing the correct time. The telephone appeared to be undam-
aged, but the connection had been pulled from the wall, and there was
a damp patch on the carpet beside the glass.

'That lamp,' he said with a frown. 'It strikes me as odd that it remained
where it was when everything else is on the floor. Are you quite sure
that neither you nor your partner moved it?' he asked the constable
again.

'Quite sure, sir. Maybe the killer – or Mr Holbrook . . .?'

'Possibly,' Paget said without conviction. He turned to Starkie. 'I'm
assuming death was caused by the blows to the head,' he said. 'At least
until we get the results of the autopsy,' he added before Starkie could
say it himself. 'Is there any reason to believe otherwise?'

Starkie shook his head. 'There were at least five blows, possibly more,'
he said, 'and she didn't die right away. It took several blows to kill her,
possibly because the force of the blows was absorbed by the pillow
beneath her head. The killer struck again and again with considerable
force, as you can see by the pattern of blood spatters on the bed and

on the wall. Time of death was between eight thirty and nine thirty, so you won't go far wrong if you assume she was killed around nine o'clock.'

'When can I expect the results of the autopsy?'

'Depends on what I find waiting for me when I go in tomorrow morning,' he said. 'I could have something for you by late afternoon, if you're lucky.'

Tregalles appeared in the doorway. His face was grave. 'Same as the others,' he said cryptically. 'Same entry; same marks on the door; same sort of damage in all the rooms . . .' He broke off, frowning as he looked around the room. 'Except in here.' It was true; apart from what had been done to Laura Holbrook, there was no evidence of any physical damage anywhere in the room. His eyes settled on the broken figure on the floor. 'Bastards probably couldn't get out of the house fast enough after doing that,' he muttered as much to himself as to the others in the room.

Paget drew a deep breath, mentally bracing himself for what was to come. He couldn't put it off any longer; it was time to go down and talk to the dead woman's husband.

It wasn't hard to tell which one of the two men was Simon Holbrook. He sat slumped forward on the edge of a big armchair in front of the gas fire that was going full blast, elbows on his knees, hands wrapped around a steaming mug of tea.

He looked up as Paget and Tregalles entered the room. His face was pale and haggard, and he looked as if he might collapse at any moment, but Paget recognized him immediately. His picture had been in the local paper a couple of months ago – something to do with his company – and Paget recalled Grace saying he reminded her of Hugh Grant. 'He must be forty at least, but he holds his age well. He has that look about him that makes women want to take care of him,' she'd elaborated as she studied the picture – and told him he had no romance in his soul when he'd said he couldn't see it himself.

But, looking at him now, Paget had to concede that the man did have the sort of handsome-but-helpless look about him that some women might find attractive.

There was less damage in this room than Paget had observed in the other rooms on his quick tour of the house before coming in here. Shards of glass, jagged and glittering, clung to the frame of a shattered mirror above the mantelpiece, like teeth in the gaping, ugly mouth of a shark, while the rest of the mirror lay in pieces on the tiled hearth and surrounding carpet. A painting had been ripped from the wall, leaving a jagged hole in the plaster and a torn strip of wallpaper where the hook had once been. It lay on the floor, frame broken, canvas torn out and crumpled.

In the curve of the bay window, a small drum table lay on its side amid the shattered remnants of what must have been a handsome vase, and the flowers it had once contained.

Nothing else in the room seemed to be out of place as far as Paget could tell, and he wondered if the intruder had been interrupted, perhaps by his accomplice who had panicked and come running down the stairs after killing Mrs Holbrook.

The room was overly warm and stuffy, but Holbrook still wore a mackintosh, and he pulled it even tighter around himself as Paget introduced himself and Tregalles.

'Would you like to see a doctor, Mr Holbrook?' Paget asked. 'Dr Starkie is still in the house and—'

'Already taken care of,' the second man told him. 'Trevor Ballantyne,' he said as he rose to his feet. 'Simon and I have the same doctor, so I called him on my mobile phone just before you came in. My wife and I live just down the street, so Simon will be staying with us tonight. When I explained what had happened, he agreed to meet us there as soon as you let us out of here.'

Paget sat down facing Holbrook. 'I know how difficult this must be for you, Mr Holbrook,' he said quietly, 'but I would like to ask you one or two questions, if you feel up to it.'

Holbrook blinked rapidly, drew in a deep breath, then nodded. 'Yes. Yes, of course,' he said huskily.

Holbrook more or less repeated the story his friend had given to Constable Roberts. He said that Ballantyne had picked him up about ten minutes to seven; they had stopped for a drink at the Fox and Hounds on the corner of Bridge Street and Fish Lane, something they usually did before going across the road to the cinema, he explained. Time? He stared blankly at Paget as if he didn't understand the question.

'About a quarter to eight,' Ballantyne supplied. 'Film was supposed to begin at eight, but it was late starting. Ended about ten thirty, something like that.'

Paget turned back to Holbrook. 'And you came straight back here when it ended?' he prompted.

'That's right. Came inside, and . . .' His voice broke and he lowered his head to cover his face with his hands. 'I'm sorry, but I can't,' he whispered, shaking his head. 'Trevor, would you? Please? I can't do this.'

Ballantyne cast an enquiring glance at Paget, who nodded and said, 'If you wouldn't mind, sir? We can take Mr Holbrook's statement later.'

'Of course.' Ballantyne was about the same age as Holbrook, but a heavier build altogether. High forehead, fair hair cut short and neatly combed, brown eyes; a little heavy around the jowls. Avuncular was a word that came to Paget's mind.

'I came in with Simon for a nightcap before going home,' he said. 'Simon went upstairs to see how Laura was, and it was only when I came in here and saw this mess that I realized that someone had broken in. I thought immediately of Laura upstairs, so I ran into the hall and was about to go up myself when I saw Simon coming down. He looked awful, and before I could say anything, he just sort of crumpled and sat down on the stairs and started vomiting.

'I tried to ask him what was wrong, but he couldn't speak, so I went upstairs myself and took a look in the bedroom.'

Ballantyne sucked in his breath. 'I've never seen anything like it,' he said shakily. 'It was horrible. How anyone could do such a thing God only knows.'

'I understand that under normal circumstances Mrs Holbrook would have been with you,' Paget said, 'but she stayed at home tonight because she had a migraine?'

'That's right. Normally the four of us would have gone out together, Simon, Laura, and my wife, Moira, and I. But when Simon phoned to say that Laura wouldn't be going, Moira decided not to go either, so it was just the two of us tonight. As a matter of fact, I rang her as soon as I put the phone down after calling the police, because I thought if thieves had broken in here, they might have tried it on other houses in the street. I told Moira to make sure all the doors and windows were locked, and said I'd be bringing Simon home with me as soon as we were finished here.'

'This won't take much longer,' Paget assured him. 'You say you came in with Mr Holbrook for a nightcap. Do you usually do that?'

'Not every time, but Simon asked me in, and I wanted to find out how Laura was so I could tell Moira. And speaking of Moira, I would like to leave soon, because she will be worried. She isn't easily upset, but I don't like to think of her alone right now.' He looked at his watch.

'And the doctor should be there by now, so I think the sooner I can get Simon over there and have the doctor give him something to make him sleep, the better.'

'Just a couple of questions before you go, Mr Ballantyne. Did either of you touch anything or try to move Mrs Holbrook?'

Ballantyne shook his head. 'I certainly didn't' he said. 'Simon . . .?'

Holbrook raised his head and shook it slowly.

'In that case,' said Paget, 'that will be all for now. And thank you for bearing with me. I know how difficult it is. We will need each of you to come down to Charter Lane to make a formal statement, but that can be arranged later. Someone will be in touch with you to set up a time.'

He rose to his feet, and Ballantyne stood up as well. He touched Holbrook on the shoulder and said, 'Come on, Simon. Let's get you away from here.'

'I don't like to bring this up at a time like this, Mr Holbrook,' said Paget as they moved toward the door, 'but I'm afraid I must. It's a formality, but a necessary one for the record: can you confirm that the body you saw in the bedroom upstairs, is that of your wife, Laura Holbrook?'

Holbrook swallowed hard. His eyes were moist as he nodded dumbly before turning away. Paget looked enquiringly at Ballantyne for confirmation. 'Oh, it's Laura all right,' the man said gruffly. 'I only wish to God I could say it wasn't!'

Moira Ballantyne counted the strokes as the downstairs clock struck five. Beside her, Trevor slumbered on apparently untroubled by the events of the previous evening. That had always been Trevor's way. 'Put it out of your mind and go to sleep,' he would tell her when she was worried about something. 'Things always look better in the morning.'

All very well for him; that might be his way, but it certainly didn't work for her. How could you put something like that out of your mind and go to sleep?

Moira slipped out of bed and wrapped her dressing gown around her as she left the bedroom. She opened the door of the back bedroom – Trevor preferred to call it 'the guest room' – to look in on Simon. He, too, was sleeping soundly, sedated by the doctor.

Moira went downstairs and switched the fire on in the living room, then snuggled down in a chair in front of it.

They hadn't gone to bed until nearly three. It was Trevor who had insisted on ringing Susan, Laura's sister, despite the hour. 'You don't want her to hear it on the eight o'clock news, now do you, Simon?' he'd said when Holbrook had demurred. Then, 'Why don't *you* call her, Moira? She might take it better from you.'

She remembered staring at him blankly, her mind racing wildly as she made an imaginary call. *'Hello Susan. How are you? Yes, I know it's one thirty in the morning, but Trevor insisted that I ring to tell you that Laura was battered to death a few hours ago.'*

Moira drew her knees up and wrapped her arms around them. She'd made the call, but she couldn't remember what she'd said or what Susan had said in reply, except that she would get dressed and come over right away. She did remember that Susan had taken it well considering what a shock it must have been. In fact she'd seemed almost more concerned about how Simon was bearing up than how it was affecting her.

Moira had made tea when Susan arrived. She remembered listening to Susan's questions and Trevor's answers; remembered standing over the sink in the kitchen, feeling sick and wondering how she could walk back in there and carry on as if she knew nothing about what had happened before Trevor had rung to tell her.

The doctor had gone, and Simon was fast asleep in bed by the time Susan left. Moira had told Susan she was welcome to stay with them for the night if that would help, but Susan had said no, she would rather go home. There could be little doubt that she'd been badly shaken by the news of her sister's death, and yet, as always, Susan had kept a tight rein on her emotions. Her biggest concern, it seemed to Moira, had been how she was going to break the news to her father. 'To tell you the truth, I'm not even sure if I should,' she'd confided. 'Laura was always his favourite from the time she was little, but he hasn't recognized any members of the family for years, so I doubt if it would even register. What do you think, Moira?'

Susan's father, Alec Chase, was in the advanced stages of Alzheimer's disease. He'd been in a home for years. She hadn't known what to say. In the end she'd mumbled something trite and meaningless, but it seemed to satisfy Susan. She'd given Moira a hug and thanked her again for letting her know about Laura, and for the offer to stay the night.

'And do try to get some rest,' she'd said solicitously as she was leaving.

Moira stared into the warm glow of the fire. That was the sort of person Susan was, always concerned about others rather than herself.

Moira had never met anyone who didn't like Susan, and she had known her a long time. Not as long as Trevor, though; they'd been at school together, which meant that Susan must be close to Trevor's age, and he'd just turned forty. She certainly didn't look it, Moira thought with just a touch of envy. In fact Susan was older than her sister by a year or two, yet Moira had always thought of her as the younger of the two sisters. And a much nicer person all round, thought Moira coldly, remembering the way Laura had treated her at the club the other night.

Lovely girl, yet she'd never married, nor did she seem to be interested in anyone – other than Simon, of course, until Laura had come along. And the unfortunate part about it was that it had been Susan who had introduced Simon to her sister, and in doing so had killed her own chances with Simon.

Susan had been Simon's badminton partner for years. It had always been Simon and Susan versus Trevor and Moira – until that fateful day when Moira had broken her wrist, and Susan had brought Laura along the following week to fill in. Until then, there had never been any doubt in Moira's mind that Susan was in love with Simon, and if anyone was ever going to get him to the altar again, it would be Susan. But when Laura appeared on the scene, Simon had fallen for her like a ton of bricks, and it was game over for Susan. Laura had taken Susan's place as Simon's badminton partner, and Susan had become Trevor's partner.

Initially, Laura's interest had been in Simon's failing business, and even Moira had to admit that if it hadn't been for Laura's expertise and money, Simon's company would have gone under. But it soon became apparent to everyone that their relationship had gone well past that of business partners.

Even then, Susan might have clung to the hope that Simon's infatuation with Laura would pass, but it must have *really* hurt when Simon announced that he and Laura were married.

Laura! Moira closed her eyes, trying desperately to shut out the scene that had been playing over and over again inside her head. It was there when Trevor phoned; it was there when he'd brought Simon home, and it was there now. She'd washed away the blood, scrubbed herself clean, then bundled up the bloodstained clothes and stuffed them in the boot of her car. Tomorrow – no, *today!* – she must find an excuse to get away and dump them where no one would be likely to find them or connect them with her if they did.

But what she was going to do about the bloodstained coat? was still a question in her mind.

She couldn't get rid of it. It had been a Christmas present from Trevor, and he would be bound to notice it was gone, and he would keep on asking questions about it until . . .

'Moira? Moira! What are you doing out here?'

Startled, Moira's eyes flew open to see Trevor standing in the doorway in his pyjamas.

His voice softened. 'Can't sleep, I suppose,' he said. 'Too much on your mind. But sitting out here worrying about it isn't going to help, is it? Come back to bed. Things will look better in the morning.'

Five

Thursday, March 5

Grace felt a little guilty as she left the house and closed the door quietly behind her. Neil would probably be annoyed about what she'd done; he hated to be late, but it had been almost four o'clock by the time he'd tumbled into bed, and he'd fallen asleep within minutes of his head touching the pillow. He hadn't so much as moved when the alarm went off at six thirty, so she'd reset it for eight thirty before gathering up her clothes and slipping quietly out of the room. The morning traffic was hazardous enough if you were wide awake, so Grace was quite prepared to face Neil's displeasure rather than have him fall asleep at the wheel on his way in to work.

Inspector Charlie Dobbs was in his shirtsleeves, shaving, when she arrived. A tall, thin, gaunt-featured man at the best of times, he looked as if he'd been up all night.

'Hardly seemed worth the effort to go home by the time I got back here this morning,' he said in answer to her question, 'but I'll grab a couple of hours' sleep at home later on this morning, and still be back by lunchtime. I assume Neil has filled you in?'

'All I know is that there's been another burglary, and a woman was killed,' Grace told him. 'Neil was dead tired when he came in somewhere about three thirty this morning, so I didn't ask for details. He did say the murdered woman was the wife of Simon Holbrook of Holbrook Micro-Engineering, and the MO was the same as the others.'

'That's right,' Charlie said, 'at least as far as it goes. But I have an odd feeling about this one – apart from the murder itself, of course – so I've been going through the records of the previous burglaries, and I think I may be on to something. But I could be wrong, which is why I want you to go over to the house and take a look for yourself. See if anything strikes you the same way.'

'What am I supposed to be looking for?'

Charlie smiled and shook his head. 'Just look,' he said. 'Do what you do best, then come back and tell me if anything strikes you as odd or different about this one – apart from the murder itself, of course.'

It was nine thirty when Paget nosed the car into his parking slot in Charter Lane. He knew Grace had meant well by letting him sleep, but he still felt he should have been there earlier, regardless of how little sleep he'd had.

To make matters worse, Tregalles was there ahead of him, looking as fresh and scrubbed as if he'd had a full night's sleep, and it appeared that he and Sergeant Ormside already had matters well in hand. Paget had left instructions for Len Ormside to be called in early to set up the incident room and begin the task of calling people in to work on what was now a full-blown homicide investigation.

'We're pretty well up and running,' Ormside told him. 'We've got people knocking on doors throughout the neighbourhood, and we're following up on the list of names of the people who were out there in the street last night.' He pointed to the task board.

Paget studied the board, and made a mental note of the assignments, then turned his attention to the large plan of the town, and the pins marking the location of the burglaries. He studied it for several minutes, but if there was a pattern there, he couldn't see it.

'Anything new this morning from SOCO?' he asked.

Ormside shook his head. 'No, but they haven't finished yet. Charlie said there'll be someone in the house for the rest of the day at least. Also, we received a call from Holbrook's insurance agent asking for permission to have one of their investigators go in to assess the damage, but I told him he would have to wait until we'd been through the house with Mr Holbrook ourselves, and it was no longer a crime scene.'

Paget frowned. 'I would have thought that would be the last thing on Simon Holbrook's mind this morning, considering the state he was in when we left him earlier this morning,' he said.

'It wasn't Holbrook who rang him,' Tregalles said. 'It was Ballantyne. Said he was acting for Holbrook.'

'Interesting,' Paget observed. 'Which reminds me: get hold of Ballantyne and Holbrook and arrange a time for them to come in and give a formal statement.'

'Already done, boss,' Tregalles told him. 'Ballantyne is coming in this afternoon, but Holbrook won't be in until tomorrow. His doctor doesn't think he's in a fit state to talk to anyone today, but thinks he should be OK tomorrow. Was there anything else?'

'Yes, there is,' said Paget slowly, 'although I think this is something for one of Len's people,' he said, turning to Ormside. 'I'd like you to get me as much background material as possible on the Holbrooks. Were they happily married? How is Holbrook's business doing? Any financial problems? Who benefits from Laura Holbrook's death? You know the sort of thing.'

Tregalles eyed Paget narrowly. 'I thought we had this one pegged,' he said. 'I mean it's the same MO, same tools, same sort of damage. The only difference is that there was someone home who shouldn't have been because of a last-minute change of plan due to Mrs Holbrook's migraine.'

'And you're probably right,' Paget agreed, 'but let's make absolutely sure we don't become too focused on the obvious.'

'I hope you weren't too upset when I reset the alarm this morning,' said Grace as they carried their after-dinner coffee into the living room and sat down. 'I know you hate to be late, but I couldn't let you go stumbling out of here into the morning traffic with no more than a couple of hours of sleep.'

Paget smiled and shook his head. 'It's a good job you did reset it,' he told her, 'because I'd have probably slept till noon if you hadn't. Anyway, my well-trained staff had everything under control by the time I got there, so there was no harm done. How was your day? I hear you spent it in the Holbrook house. Find anything I can use?'

It wasn't exactly a rule, but they had both agreed early in their relationship that they should try to avoid talking shop at least until after dinner. Grace, who was very health-conscious and knew about these things, had made the point that it was bad for the digestion. Paget agreed, not so much because he was worried about his digestion, but because too much conversation during dinner allowed the food to go cold.

Grace wrinkled her nose. 'Not really,' she said. 'Once again we found a few strands of fibre mixed with dog hair, and a bit of dark fuzzy material that seemed to be out of place among the bedclothes, but that was about it. I don't know who these people are, but they're clever enough to avoid leaving clues behind them. Fingerprints all over the house, of course, but I'm willing to bet not one of them belongs to those two killers.

'Charlie's being a bit more enigmatic than usual, though,' she continued. 'He seems to think he's found something odd about this particular burglary, and he wants me to see if it strikes me the same way, but I'm afraid, if it's there at all, I haven't seen it yet. It has something to do with a comparison of crime scenes, but I'm not sure what I'm supposed to be looking for.'

'He didn't give you a clue?'

'Not really. Just handed me copies of the reports from all the other crime scenes, and said, "see if anything strikes you as odd about them". And that was it. I asked him again this afternoon if he could give me a bit more to go on, but he just smiled, you know the way he does, and said, "No. If it's there I'm sure you'll find it; if it's not, then perhaps it's my imagination after all."' Grace made a face. 'I don't know what he expects me to find, but one thing I have learned over the years, is that you don't ignore one of Charlie's gut feelings, so I shall go back there tomorrow and keep digging. Has he mentioned anything to you about it?'

'No, but if there is anything there to be found, believe me, I wish you luck, because we are literally grasping at straws on this one.'

'What about your day?' Grace eyed him critically. 'You seem a bit down, tonight.'

He shrugged and shook his head. 'I'm not, really,' he told her. 'Just a bit frustrated. Tregalles and I have been going through everything we have but there is nothing we can get our teeth into. Holbrook's friend, Trevor Ballantyne, came in to give his statement, but it was virtually a carbon copy of what he told us last night. I had hoped to talk to Simon Holbrook today, but his doctor wouldn't allow him to come in until tomorrow.'

Grace eyed him curiously. 'That's not a problem, is it? I mean it's not as if he's a suspect, or if there's any doubt about how Mrs Holbrook died — or is there?'

'Not that I know of, but you know the old rule of thumb when dealing with a suspicious death: look first at relatives and friends. I have to make sure that every angle is checked, even though we are ninety-nine per cent sure that Mrs Holbrook was killed by the people who broke into their home.'

Grace looked thoughtful. 'What does the autopsy show?'

'Still waiting for the results. Starkie called to say that he won't be able to do the autopsy until tomorrow morning. However, we did manage to get a commitment from Holbrook to meet Tregalles at the house tomorrow so they can go through the place together to find out exactly what, if anything, is missing.'

'What time?' Grace asked.

'That they're meeting? Nine o'clock. Why?'

'Because I think I'd like to go through the place with them,' Grace told him. 'Unless you have any objections, of course?'

'No, no, none at all,' he told her. 'I'll let Tregalles know in the morning.'

Six

Grace Lovett was already there, standing beside the wrought iron gate, when Tregalles pulled up in front of Holbrook's house in Pembroke Avenue at five minutes to nine, but there was no sign of Holbrook.

'Morning, Grace,' he greeted her, nodding toward the house. 'Is Holbrook inside?'

She shook her head. 'Haven't seen him, but it's not quite nine; I expect he'll be here soon.'

'Beautiful morning,' he observed, raising his face to the morning sun, stretching, and settled his back against the car. 'I wouldn't mind living here – except I doubt if I could afford the rates, let alone the price. Holbrook's firm must be doing all right.'

'It is,' Grace told him. 'We looked it up yesterday, and it's one of the fastest growing small businesses in the area.'

Pembroke Avenue was a pleasant little backwater. The houses were set back from the street, separated by fences, walls and hedges high enough to ensure privacy – and high enough to shield the activities of anyone trying to break in, thought Tregalles. Which might be why so many of the houses, including Holbrook's, had home security logos in their windows. Not that it had done Mrs Holbrook any good.

He pushed himself away from the car to join Grace. 'That's Holbrook,' he said, indicating a man who had just emerged from the driveway of a house three doors down. 'He's been staying with the Ballantynes.'

He leaned closer to Grace and lowered his voice as Holbrook approached. 'Looks a bit drawn,' he said critically, 'but you still wouldn't think he's over forty, would you? Looks more like one of these young blokes you see in the magazines, surrounded by birds in bikinis.'

It was true, Grace thought. She'd seen the man's picture in the newspapers from time to time, but this was the first time she had seen him in the flesh.

'Good morning, sir,' Tregalles said as Holbrook came up to them.

His face was pale, but he looked considerably better than when Tregalles had last seen him.

'Good morning, Sergeant,' he said in a low voice. 'I don't know if you realize how painful this is for me, but I suppose it has to be done. I hope it won't take too long.' His words were for Tregalles, but his eyes kept flicking to Grace.

'We do understand, sir,' Tregalles assured him, 'and we'll try not to keep you any longer than necessary. I don't think you've met Ms Lovett. She is a Scenes of Crime officer, and she will be going round with us.'

Holbrook's face underwent a subtle change as his eyes swept over Grace in a fleeting yet all-encompassing glance. He flipped a stray lock of hair away from his eyes with a practised gesture, extended his hand and said, 'This *is* an unexpected pleasure, Ms Lovett.'

His handshake was firm, and Grace felt her eyes being held by his own, and there was something subtly appealing about the look he gave her before releasing her hand. 'Mr Holbrook,' she said formally.

His eyes never wavered. 'Simon,' he said softly. 'I much prefer Simon, Ms Lovett.'

She smiled pleasantly. *Was it her imagination, or was Simon Holbrook coming on to her?*

'Shall we get on then, sir?' Tregalles said brusquely, stepping between them to lead the way up the path to the house.

A uniformed constable opened the door as they mounted the front steps, and Holbrook looked surprised. 'I didn't realize there was still someone in here,' he said as he stepped inside.

'It is still a crime scene,' Tregalles reminded him, 'so we don't want anything disturbed until everyone is finished here.'

'Yes, I see that,' Holbrook said, 'but I must say I'm not sure what it is you want from me. I told you what I could the other night.'

'About . . . about what happened, yes,' Tregalles agreed, 'but what I would like you to do now is walk through the house with me and tell me, as best you can, what, if anything was taken, and if you see anything significant about the damage.'

'What was *taken*, Sergeant?' Holbrook's voice rose. 'Do you honestly think I give a damn about what was taken, compared to what they did to my wife? And what do you expect me to see that's "significant" about the damage?'

'It's a matter of what we might be able to trace,' Tregalles said patiently. 'We need to circulate a list of everything that was stolen as soon as possible in case whoever did this tries to sell it. As for the damage, I'd like to know if you can see any pattern to it. For example: does it appear that specific items were chosen, items that perhaps meant more to you than others. I would also like to know who would have known the house would be empty Wednesday evening – or would have been empty if there hadn't been a last-minute change of plan.'

Holbrook shrugged. 'Almost anyone,' he said. 'It's been a bit of a ritual throughout the winter: Tuesday night badminton; Wednesday night a film. Not every Wednesday, you understand, because we sometimes have other commitments, but we go if we can.' His voice dropped. 'I should have stayed with her,' he said hollowly, 'but . . .' He raised his hands then let them fall to his side in a gesture of helplessness. 'But who would think that something like this could happen?' he ended huskily. 'If it hadn't been for that damned migraine . . .'

'Is there anyone you can think of who might have wanted to do you or your wife harm?' Tregalles asked. 'Anyone with whom you've had a falling out? Someone at work, perhaps? A disgruntled employee; someone with a grudge against you or your wife?'

Tregalles might have been mistaken, but it seemed to him that Holbrook hesitated for just a fraction of a second before shaking his head. 'We're like a family at work,' he said. 'There's been no trouble there. As for someone with a grudge, I can't think of anyone. But I don't see why you are asking questions like that, when this is obviously the work of that bunch of vandals who have been terrorizing people all over town. In fact, to be blunt, Sergeant, the more I think about it, the more I feel that my wife would be alive today if the police had done their job.'

'Believe me, Mr Holbrook, I can appreciate the way you feel,' Tregalles told him, 'but I'm afraid it isn't quite as simple as that. The truth of the matter is we have put a great deal of effort into trying to track them down, but these people have so far avoided leaving anything in the way of clues behind them. Ms Lovett can testify to that.'

'I'm sure she can,' Holbrook snapped, then modified his tone as he looked at Grace. 'No disrespect, Ms Lovett; I'm sure you know your job, but from what I've read, criminals always leave some clues behind, no matter how careful they try to be. Haven't you found *anything*?'

His look was so appealing that Grace couldn't help feeling sorry for the man. 'I'm afraid not, Mr Holbrook,' she said, 'which is why it is so important that you tell us what you can as we go through the house.'

Holbrook didn't look convinced, but he didn't say anything as they began the tour of the rooms. Tregalles couldn't take to the man, but he could hardly blame him for feeling as he did. He would probably feel the same if their situations were reversed.

They trailed Holbrook from room to room. He stopped every now and then to examine something and shake his head. 'Nothing missing from here as far as I can tell,' he would say, and move on. 'As for the damage, I don't know what you're looking for, but it seems pretty random to me.'

'I see you have a safe in your desk, Mr Holbrook,' Grace said when they came to the study. 'We don't think it's been opened, although it does look as if someone has had a go at the dial.' She pointed to scratch marks around it. 'Everything has been dusted for prints, so you can go ahead and open it.'

Holbrook squatted down before the safe, shielding it from them as he twirled the dial. The small door swung open; he reached inside and took out an old-fashioned cash box.

'There should be something like seven or eight hundred pounds in here,' he said, opening the lid to reveal a wad of notes held together by an elastic band. He riffled through them slowly, then closed the lid. 'Looks like it's all here,' he said.

'Do you keep anything else of value in there?' Tregalles asked.

'Nothing that would be worth anything to anyone else,' Holbrook said. 'Personal stuff for the most part. Passports, birth certificates, that sort of thing.' He sorted through the documents, then put the cash box back and closed the door. 'It's all there,' he declared as he stood up again.

Grace eyed the papers strewn about the floor. 'Could they have been looking for something specific, perhaps to do with your business?' she asked. 'I understand that some of your designs are unique in the field of laser micro-technology.'

Holbrook looked at Grace with renewed interest. 'You *have* been doing you homework,' he said approvingly. 'But, no. We do have competitors, of course, but there is nothing here to interest them, and I'm sure they know that. It might have been a different story if this had happened at the lab, but we're well protected there.'

'Speaking of protection,' Grace said carefully, 'I see you have quite a good home security system here, and yet apparently the alarm didn't go off when the thieves broke in. Did you set it before you left on Wednesday night?'

Holbrook shrugged guiltily. 'If only I had,' he said with feeling. 'Unfortunately, we couldn't see the point when one of us was in the house.'

'We found your wife's handbag open on the floor beneath the table at the bottom of the stairs,' Grace said when they came back to the front hall. 'They left her credit cards, but there was no money. Should there have been?'

Holbrook nodded. 'Laura didn't carry much cash, but she would have had something like thirty or forty pounds with her.'

'I see. Shall we go upstairs and see what . . .'

'No!' Holbrook literally turned pale at the suggestion. 'I–I can't,' he said. 'Sorry, but I just can't. Besides, there's no point; there's nothing worth stealing there.'

'What about jewellery?' Tregalles asked.

'Well, yes, I suppose there's that,' he conceded, 'but Laura didn't care much for jewellery, and what she did have, apart from the rings I gave her, wasn't worth very much. She keeps it . . .' He passed a hand across his brow and corrected himself. 'I should say *kept* it, in a rose-wood box on the dressing table.'

Grace frowned. 'The rings as well?' she asked.

The question seemed to annoy Holbrook, who shook his head impatiently. 'No, of course not,' he said. 'She wore them all the time.'

Tregalles and Grace exchanged glances. The sergeant didn't remember seeing any rings on Laura Holbrook's fingers. 'Can you think of any reason why Mrs Holbrook might have taken her rings off that evening?' Grace asked quietly.

Holbrook's eyes narrowed as he threw a questioning look at Grace. 'Why are you asking these questions?' he said. 'Am I missing something here?'

Grace spread her hands in a gesture of apology. 'It's just that everything has been inventoried, and I'm afraid there were no rings of any kind on your wife's fingers. Nor were they in the jewellery box.'

'Jesus Christ!' Holbrook looked stunned as he breathed the words. 'You mean they . . .?' He stopped, seemingly at a loss for words. 'You're sure about that?' he demanded.

'Very sure,' Grace told him, and Tregalles nodded in agreement. 'Sorry, Mr Holbrook, but I was one of the first on the scene, and there were no rings on your wife's fingers when I saw her. Were the rings very valuable?'

Holbrook grimaced. 'Just short of twenty thousand for the two,' he said. 'But it's not the money so much as the thought that they would . . .' He shook his head and shrugged the thought away as he moved to the front door. 'I'm sorry,' he said in a firmer voice, 'but I think I've done all I can here, so I hope that's it for now, Sergeant?'

'Except for taking your statement at Charter Lane, sir,' Tregalles reminded him, 'but that shouldn't take long. I'll have you back in no time.'

The look Holbrook shot at Tregalles bordered on the hostile. 'Is it *really* necessary that we do this today?' he asked irritably.

'I'm afraid it is, sir,' Tregalles told him. 'Best to do it while things are still fresh in the memory and then it's done with.' He stepped outside before Holbrook could say more.

'Oh, very well,' Holbrook muttered. 'After you, then, Ms Lovett,' he said, stepping aside to allow Grace to precede him.

But Grace shook her head. 'I still have work to do here,' she told him. 'And I do thank you very much for doing this, Mr Holbrook; I know how difficult it must have been for you, but you've been a great help and I do appreciate it.'

'My pleas . . .' he began, then stopped. 'Sorry,' he said awkwardly. 'What I *meant* to say was, if there is anything I can do, anything at all that will help you find who did this, please don't hesitate to call me, Ms Lovett.' His eyes held hers as her handed her his card. 'Any time,' he said. 'My mobile phone number is on there as well.'

Holbrook remained silent throughout the short drive to Charter Lane. He sat slumped in his seat, hands clasped loosely in front of him as he stared blankly out of the window, and Tregalles made no attempt to engage him in conversation. Instead, he went over everything in his mind that they'd talked about that morning, and wondered what it was about Holbrook that put him off – apart from the fact that the man was older than he was, yet looked about ten years younger.

He didn't doubt that the death of his wife had hit Holbrook hard, and yet there had been something predatory about the way he'd kept eyeing Grace as they toured the house. Not that Grace wasn't worth looking at – Tregalles had done his fair share of looking when their paths had first crossed – but it didn't seem right that the man should show that much interest in another woman less than forty-eight hours after his wife had been bludgeoned to death.

On the other hand, he told himself as they arrived at Charter Lane, he wasn't being very fair to the man. He'd only met him twice, both times under abnormal circumstances, so perhaps he should reserve judgement.

Before taking Holbrook's statement, he took another look at the photographs of the scene. Virtually every inch of the bedroom had been photographed, but there was no sign of Laura Holbrook's rings, either on her finger or on the dressing table. The rest of the jewellery appeared to be there, so why not the rings? The obvious answer was their value, but would vandals, who had ignored things like credit cards and items of value in other houses, know the value of Laura Holbrook's rings? And if, as Holbrook had said, his wife was not in the habit of removing the rings, that meant they had been pulled from her finger. Tregalles made a mental note to ask Starkie if there were any abrasions on the ring finger.

Like Trevor Ballantyne, Holbrook's statement varied little from what he had told them on the night of the murder – not that he'd actually told them much himself before asking his friend to speak for him. He said he and his wife had planned on going to see a film with their friends, the Ballantynes, but about an hour before they were due to leave the house, his wife had said she could feel a migraine coming on, and she had gone to bed. Holbrook had offered to stay with her, but she had insisted that he go out as planned.

'Laura preferred to be left alone when she had a migraine,' he explained when Tregalles asked him about it.

'This sort of thing has happened before, then, has it, sir?'

'Oh, yes. Laura has always been troubled with migraines, and she insisted on being left completely alone until they were over. She would take a couple of paracetamol and a herbal sleeping pill, then make the room as dark as possible and go to bed.'

'And that is what she did that evening? Did you see her take the tablets?'

Holbrook shook his head impatiently. 'No, but since that is what she usually did, I'm assuming she did the same that evening. When I went up to check on her before going out, she was in bed, the curtains were drawn and the light was out. I told her again that I didn't mind staying home if she would like me to, but she told me to stop fussing and go out as planned.'

Tregalles returned to the statement. 'You say here that when Mrs Ballantyne phoned to say they would be leaving the house in a few minutes, and you told her that your wife wouldn't be going, she decided not to go herself. Did she say why?'

'No, not really. She said something about letting Trevor and me have a night out on our own for a change, but to tell you the truth, I don't think either Laura or Moira were all that keen to see the film in the first place. Neither of them care for science fiction films, and I can't say I blame them. I mean the plots are often rubbish, but Trevor and I are more interested in the computer-generated special effects.'

Holbrook hunched forward in his seat, and for the first time since they'd met that morning, his eyes became alive. 'Most people don't realize how much work goes into a film like that,' he said earnestly. 'Some of the special effects take years of work by some very talented people. Youngsters, a good many of them, and they are good. Trev and I both have to be creative in our own lines of work – they're not the same, you understand, but the process is much the same, so we enjoy trying to work out how they achieved certain effects. And we do pick up the odd idea for our own work every now and then. You see . . .'

Holbrook stopped himself in mid-sentence. 'Sorry,' he said guiltily as he drew back. 'I didn't mean to run on like that. I was just trying to explain . . . Well, anyway, what it comes down to is, with Laura staying home, it gave Moira the opportunity to beg off.'

'I see. So you left the house at about ten minutes to seven, and went for a drink first at the Fox and Hounds.'

'That's right. We usually go there. We know the landlord, Bill Chivers, and the pub is just across the road from the cinema.'

'And you left the Fox and Hounds when? Approximately?'

Holbrook shrugged. 'I don't know. Quarter to eight or so, I suppose. Trev said we'd better be going, so we left. Anyway, I don't see the point of all these questions about where I was, unless –' his eyes narrowed as they met those of Tregalles – 'unless,' he said softly, 'you think that *I* had something to do with Laura's death. Is that what all these questions are about? Well, let me tell you, *Sergeant*, I loved my wife, and I had *nothing* to do with her death, so you can get that idea out of your mind right now. Apart from anything else, I was miles away at the time, sitting in a cinema with a witness by my side, so the sooner you stop wasting my time and start looking for the real killers, the better!'

'Three quarters of a mile, actually,' Tregalles said equably, 'and while this may seem like a waste of time to you now, it is important that we establish where everyone was when the crime was being committed.

Important,' he continued quickly as Holbrook opened his mouth to speak, 'because if or when this case comes to trial, the defence will be doing everything in their power to convince a jury that the murder could have been committed by someone else, usually someone very close to the victim. So, if you will just bear with me for just a few more minutes . . .? Now,' he continued without waiting for a reply, 'according to our information, the film ended at approximately ten past ten that night. Did you come straight home?'

It was hard to tell by the way he continued to look at Tregalles, whether Holbrook was convinced or not by the sergeant's explanation, but he answered the question. 'Yes,' he said, 'we came straight home.'

Tregalles nodded encouragingly. 'And when you first entered the house, there was no indication that anything was amiss. Is that right, sir?'

'Yes — at least at first.'

'So, while Mr Ballantyne went into the front room you went straight upstairs to check on your wife?'

Holbrook took a deep breath. 'Yes,' he said tightly.

'And, according to what we were told the other night, when Mr Ballantyne realized that something was wrong, he came out of the front room, saw you on the stairs, went up himself, then came back down again to call the police. A matter of three or four minutes, perhaps? Would that be about right, sir?'

'This may come as a surprise to you, Sergeant,' Holbrook said, his words laced with sarcasm, 'but I wasn't paying a lot of attention to what time it was. I had a little more on my mind.'

'I do appreciate that,' Tregalles told him, 'but you see, I do want to make sure that I haven't missed something here, because the times don't seem to add up. I'm sure there's a perfectly logical explanation, but I can't see it here. Perhaps you can explain it, sir?'

'Explain what, exactly?' Holbrook snapped.

Tregalles frowned and scratched his head. 'It's just that the film ended about ten past ten, and . . . where was the car parked, by the way?'

'Where we usually leave it,' Holbrook said irritably, 'in the car park beside the Fox and Hounds, but I fail to see—'

'Any problems getting out?' Tregalles interrupted. 'Any delays?'

Holbrook closed his eyes. His body language said plainly that he was having difficulty keeping his temper. 'We came out,' he said through gritted teeth, 'we walked across the road, got in the car and drove home. Is that specific enough for you, Sergeant?'

'Which means you would have been home about, oh, let's say no later than twenty-five past ten, assuming you didn't stop anywhere along the way. You didn't, did you, sir?'

'No, we did not stop along the way,' Holbrook said, enunciating each word carefully as if speaking to a backward child. 'And,' he added with emphasis, 'I've had more than enough of these questions. I assume I am free to leave?' He began to rise, but Tregalles waved him back.

'In a moment, *if* you don't mind, sir,' he said. 'Just want to clear up one small point. You see, according to what you've told me, you got home about twenty-five past ten and went straight upstairs. Both you and Mr Ballantyne agree that you weren't in the house more than a few minutes before Mr Ballantyne called us. But our records show that his call came in at 10.58, which leaves a gap of some twenty-five to thirty minutes unaccounted for between the time you got home and the time Mr Ballantyne called us. Is there something I'm missing here, Mr Holbrook?'

'Oh, for God's sake, man!' Holbrook flared. 'My wife was *killed* that night. Not just killed, but beaten to death by some madman, and you sit there asking me about what time it was when I did this or that? I have tried to be cooperative, but this is ridiculous! So we didn't get the times exactly right. So what? Do you think you'd be checking your watch to make sure you got the times right if it was *your* wife who'd been killed?'

Holbrook stood up. 'I think it's about time you got your priorities right,' he said scathingly, 'and you can do what you like with your damned statement, because I'm finished here.'

Seven

It was late in the afternoon before Dr Starkie telephoned Paget to give him a summary of the results of the autopsy on Mrs Holbrook.

'It's pretty straightforward,' Starkie told him. 'The woman died of repeated blows to the head. Six in all, as near as I can tell, and there is nothing to indicate that she put up a fight. In fact, I doubt if she was even awake. If, as we are told, she took sleeping pills along with paracetamol, some of which we found on the floor, if you remember, chances are she was asleep when the first blow was struck.

'The weapon was some sort of flat metal bar approximately three to three-and-a-half centimetres wide, and roughly half a centimetre thick, and I found traces of rust embedded in the wounds. Could be almost any old piece of scrap metal, but whatever it was, it was used with considerable force. The entire front of the skull was crushed, but then, I don't have to tell you, do I? You saw what it had done to her face.'

Paget remembered all too vividly the damage done to Mrs Holbrook's face: nose split; jaw broken; teeth smashed; left eye driven into its socket, and hair matted and tangled in the bloody wounds. It had been a vicious attack, and all the more incomprehensible if the woman had been asleep at the time.

'Sounds like the same metal bar they've been using on the back doors and the furniture they smash,' he told Starkie.

More and more this looked like the work of a psychopath, and psychopaths didn't need a logical reason for what they did, whether it was smashing things or killing people, and they could be very clever and unpredictable. Witness, for example, the way they had vandalized the other five houses without leaving so much as a clue – with the exception of some dog hairs and a few fibres.

'Any second thoughts about the time of death?' he asked.

'No. I'm leaving the one-hour spread as it is for the record, but as I said before, you won't be far wrong if you assume she was killed around nine o'clock, give or take fifteen minutes.'

'Good. That helps,' Paget told him. 'Now, Tregalles tells me that Laura Holbrook's wedding and engagement rings may have been pulled from her finger, and he said he'd passed that information along to you. Any luck with that, Reg?'

'There were slight abrasions on the knuckle,' Starkie said, 'but she could have pulled them off herself for all I know.'

Paget wasn't surprised, and he wasn't sure that it mattered very much. The point was, two valuable rings were missing, and there was a chance that the killer or killers would try to dispose of them, and that might just be the break they were looking for.

'Anything else I should know about?' he asked.

'Not unless something comes back from the lab. Otherwise it looks straightforward enough. No surprises as far as I can see.'

'Good. And thanks, Reg. Appreciate the call.'

Paget was pleasantly surprised to see Grace's car in the driveway when he got home at ten minutes to six that evening. With the way things had been going these past few months, between staff shortages and heavy workloads in both areas, they were lucky if either of them got home before six thirty or seven most evenings. Luckier still if they arrived more or less at the same time. So he was even more surprised when he opened the front door to be greeted by the aroma of beef roasting in the oven.

Grace appeared at the kitchen door, apron on, oven mitts on her hands.

'Thank goodness!' she said with feeling. 'I half expected you to phone at the last minute to say you would be late. Roast beef and Yorkshire pudding all right, is it?'

He shrugged out of his coat, and made a face. 'I was rather hoping for a green salad,' he said, 'but I suppose I could manage a bit of beef if that's all you have.'

'I can dump it in the dustbin,' she warned, 'so be careful what you say.'

He gathered her to him. 'Seems a shame to waste it since you've been to all that trouble,' he said, and kissed her. 'You must have come home early to do all this. What's the occasion?'

'I just felt like it,' Grace told him, 'and the work I have to do can be done just as well at home as in the office.'

'Oh, Grace, surely you don't have to—' he began, but she put a finger to his lips.

'It has to do with the Holbrook case,' she said, 'and I want to go over my findings with you and see if we come to the same conclusion. But let's not go into that now. Dinner is almost ready, so let's enjoy it.'

'But . . .'

'Roast potatoes, peas, Brussels sprouts, Yorkshire pudding and gravy? Enough meat on the joint to give you roast beef sandwiches for the next three days at least? One more word and I'll burn the lot!'

He sighed heavily and raised his hands in mock surrender. 'You're a hard woman, Grace,' he said, 'but then, I suppose I shall have to give in as always. Good cooks are so hard to find these days.'

'And you're so easily bribed,' she said. 'Now, get on upstairs and have your wash. Dinner is in fifteen minutes.'

After the table had been cleared, and the dishwasher loaded, Grace opened her briefcase, took out six folders, and set them out on the table.

'One for each burglary,' she told Paget as they sat down side by side at the table. 'They include itemized lists of the things that were stolen or vandalized at each location, and I believe that what I'm about to show you may be what Charlie was talking about when he sent me out to the Holbrook house.'

Grace opened the first folder and took out a single sheet of A4 paper. 'The first house to be hit was in Dunbar Road,' she said. 'I don't know what they expected to find there, because it's a poor district to start with, so all they came away with were a few coins they found in a drawer, and some bits and pieces of cheap jewellery left by the man's wife when she left him – worth maybe ten quid for the lot, if they were lucky, and some food. They smashed the glass in a cabinet, which would have cost something like ninety to a hundred pounds to repair, but it wasn't worth that much to start with, so it was a write-off, as was the small radio they smashed. They also damaged a couple of drawers, possibly in a fit of temper when they failed to find anything of value in them. Cost of repairs or replacement, if they had had them done, would amount to something like two, possibly three hundred pounds. I've left out the cost of repairs to the door because that was common to every burglary.

'Now, look at the one in Abbey Road. Better neighbourhood and they came away with approximately forty pounds – the owner couldn't be sure of the exact amount, but there was more damage. A TV set, fortunately an older one; a mirror, a clock and several telephones were all destroyed. Estimated cost of replacement approximately eight hundred and forty pounds. The owners are still arguing with their insurance company about the TV, but that figure isn't far off.'

Grace opened the third folder. 'Westfield Lane. Similar neighbourhood. A few pounds taken – the owner couldn't be sure how much, but said it wouldn't have been more than ten or fifteen at the most – but nothing else was taken, even though there were a number of valuable items worth taking in full view. But the damage there came to well over twelve hundred pounds, and then they stopped to have a meal of sorts. It's almost as if they are trying to tell us that they know they can take their time, and they have no fear of being caught.

'Number four,' Grace continued. 'View Street. No money taken at all, but the damage was even more severe. They lashed out at everything as they went through the place, and I think Tregalles is right: the damage had become their prime objective. They've developed a taste for it. And once again they not only stopped to have a meal, they had a fry-up, a sit-down meal that would take time to prepare and eat. Once again, it looks to me as if they are thumbing their noses at us.

'Then there was Holywell Street. According to the owners, they never leave money in the house, which may or may not account for the amount of damage they did there. You've seen it, Neil; they simply went mad. This time all they ate was half an apple pie, but just to make sure we got the message, they stopped long enough to make custard to go with it.

'You see the pattern, Neil? The amount of damage has been escalating with each burglary. It goes up every time, except –' Grace paused for effect – 'except in this latest case.'

She handed the last sheet to Paget. 'Take a look. Very little in the way of cash. Mr Holbrook says his wife didn't carry much in her handbag, but two very valuable rings are missing, her wedding and engagement rings, worth – and I verified this with the insurance company – just over twenty thousand pounds! There was other jewellery there to be taken, not much, but collectively it would have brought in a couple of thousand pounds, but it wasn't touched. More significantly, it is the only place where jewellery of any value was taken.'

'Which might suggest that there wasn't anything of value in the other houses, and the thieves knew what was worth pinching and what wasn't,' Paget said.

'That's one explanation,' Grace agreed, 'but let me go on. I went round with the insurance adjuster this morning, and I asked him to give me his assessment of the damage, and his estimate of the cost of repair or replacement. Just the damage, not property loss such as the money taken from Mrs Holbrook's handbag, or the rings. Take a guess at what he said.'

Paget shook his head. 'I haven't the foggiest,' he told her. 'How much?'

'Six hundred and twenty pounds! Even the picture they slashed was only a print worth about thirty pounds. Doesn't that strike you as strange?'

'Possibly,' Paget said thoughtfully, 'but on the other hand it might be because they decided to get out of the house as fast as they could after discovering and killing Mrs Holbrook.'

Grace shook her head. 'I don't think so,' she said, 'because the damage they did was in almost every room in the house. Which suggests that they were there for some time before becoming aware that someone else was in the house. I say "suggests", because again there are a couple of possibilities.'

Grace brushed the hair away from her eyes as she marshalled her thoughts. 'Look,' she continued earnestly, 'at first glance, it appears to be the work of the same thieves. The contents of Mrs Holbrook's handbag were emptied on the floor, and a small amount of money was missing. They didn't take her credit cards, nor did they in the other cases, which is strange, considering that they can be worth far more than cash.

'But then we come to the vandalism. And this is where I have trouble, because when I took a good hard look at the damage in the Holbrook house, it struck me as being very, very selective, and I think that may be what Charlie was getting at when he sent me over there. Admittedly, they made quite a mess; stuff is strewn about all over the place, but there wasn't anything of real value that was damaged. As I said, it appeared to me that someone was being very selective in what they broke, and six hundred pounds would be nothing to someone like Holbrook.'

'What about——?'

'The rings?' Grace finished for him, and shook her head. 'I don't know,' she admitted. 'Opportunism, perhaps? Too valuable to pass up? But that would suggest that they know enough about jewellery to realize their worth, and somehow I doubt that, because they demonstrated no such knowledge in the earlier burglaries.

'And let's not forget,' she continued before Paget could respond, 'this is the only time they didn't stop to take food or make a meal.'

Paget nodded slowly. 'We did wonder about that,' he said, 'but decided that even they wouldn't have the stomach to stay around for the usual meal after killing Laura Holbrook, so they got out as fast as they could. Which, as I said earlier, could also account for the lack of damage in this case. But you're suggesting it could mean that someone may have used the same MO as a cover to murder Mrs Holbrook. Right?'

Grace gave a non-committal shrug. 'All I'm saying is that it is a possibility,' she said. 'But if that should turn out to be the case, then the question is: who knew that Mrs Holbrook would be alone in the house at that particular time? I spoke to Tregalles this afternoon, and he told me that it was only a short time before they were due to leave that Mrs Holbrook said she had a migraine, and decided to go to bed. So, no one, other than Holbrook and the Ballantynes, knew she'd be alone in the house.' Grace gathered the folders together. 'But you're the detective, my love,' she said with a grin. 'You work it out.'

'All right, let's assume for the moment that you're right,' said Paget. 'Holbrook and Ballantyne were together the whole evening, assuming their stories check out. I understand there's a bit of a discrepancy in their statements about the times, but unless they are both lying they have alibis. If they *are* lying, then both would be equally involved, and I find that hard to believe.'

'Unless Holbrook hired someone else to do the killing while he was well away from the house and could count on Ballantyne and others for an alibi,' Grace suggested.

'Possible,' Paget admitted, 'but it's not very likely, is it? That is unless he has criminal connections we don't know about. Besides, he'd be laying himself open to blackmail. Either way, we need a motive.'

'As I said, you're the detective, darling. I just offer suggestions based on my findings.'

As always, Paget had toyed with other possible explanations for the killing of Laura Holbrook, if only because it had become second nature never to accept without question what appeared to be obvious at first glance. But Grace had put some meat on the bones – not a lot, but enough to give him something to think about, and past experience had taught him not to treat her ideas lightly.

'There was one other person who knew she would be alone in the house,' Grace said slowly, 'and that was Mrs Holbrook herself. What if the migraine was simply an excuse to stay behind that night? She could have arranged for someone to come round while her husband was out of the house. She knew approximately how long he would be gone.'

'Someone? Such as?'

'I've no idea. A friend, a lover, a blackmailer? It's just a thought, that's all. There may be nothing to it, but it *is* another possibility.' Grace leaned forward to emphasize her next words. 'Seriously, Neil, I am troubled by the fact that so little damage was done to things in the house in this case. As I said, a lot of stuff was strewn about on the floor, but it looked to me more like someone had tried to make it *look* like the others, but didn't want to spend too much time doing it. But what I find most troubling of all is the theft of the rings. I don't think they were taken because they were valuable – the thieves or vandals or whatever you want to call them, have always been more interested in trashing the place than they are in valuables. Yes, they've taken cash and one or two trinkets, but they've ignored cameras, laptops, credit cards and other things easy to carry, preferring to smash them instead. To me, taking the rings was something personal, especially if Laura Holbrook was wearing them when she died, and I think she was. Simon Holbrook says she rarely took them off. It simply doesn't fit with the other burglaries at all.'

Grace was right about that, at least, but there could be another explanation for that. 'Let's assume,' he said, 'that of the two people who have been trashing houses, one is the leader or instigator. He likes to smash things, and the longer it goes on, the more he enjoys doing it. But the other one, the follower, he's a bit more timid, so let's put these two in the Holbrook house.

'Now, let's assume that the leader goes upstairs leaving the second man or boy, whatever, to go to work downstairs. The second man pulls out a few drawers and knocks the odd thing over, but his heart isn't really in it; maybe he's getting tired of the game. Meanwhile, the leader has found Mrs Holbrook in the bedroom, and decides to smash her as well. The ultimate thrill for someone who loves to smash things.

'But, once it's done, he may have thought it best to get out of there, so he comes downstairs, collects his mate, and out they go.'

Grace nodded. 'It's possible,' she said, 'but it doesn't explain the rings, so I like my idea better.'

'I'll keep both of them in mind,' he promised, glancing at the time, 'but that's enough shop talk for tonight. I think I'd like to watch a bit of television for a change. What about you?'

Grace grinned. 'I thought so,' she said. 'I've been keeping an eye on the clock, but your secret's safe with me. I wouldn't want anyone to find out that you've learned everything you know by watching David Jason in reruns of *A Touch of Frost*. That would *really* spoil your image in the office, wouldn't it? Just don't get any bright ideas about talking back to Alcott the way Frost talks back to Superintendent Mullett.'

Eight

The local papers were full of it, and the rhetoric was escalating. This morning's editorial had started off by demanding to know what the police were doing to protect the citizens of Broadminster from the 'marauding band of thugs' invading local homes. It said that people were afraid to leave their homes for fear of it being vandalized, and since a woman had been murdered in her own bed, anyone living alone or left alone in the house, was at risk.

Scaremongering, plain and simple. Probably no more than two people were involved in the recent burglaries, Paget thought as he drove in to work, but now they were being portrayed as a marauding band of thugs! The pot was being stirred, and no doubt there would be a stream of angry letters to follow, to say nothing of the pressure that would be coming from New Street.

Headlines and editorials like that sold newspapers, but there was an unsettling kernel of truth in the tirade. People *were* concerned, and they had every right to be, which made it all the more maddening and frustrating to think that he couldn't do a damned thing about it until the villains made a mistake. And that could mean waiting for them to strike again.

The incident room was quiet as might be expected on a Saturday morning, but Len Ormside was there when Paget arrived, and Tregalles came in a few minutes later. Little, if anything, it appeared, had changed since the night before.

'Don't we have *anything* worth following up?' he asked Ormside after reviewing the meagre information on file. 'Whoever these people are, they're not invisible; someone must see them come and go.'

The grizzled sergeant shook his head. 'We've talked to everyone in Pembroke Avenue and the surrounding area,' Ormside told him. 'We've put out an appeal asking anyone who was walking or driving anywhere in the vicinity to come forward, and we've interviewed those who have – including the usual number of glory-seekers who were nowhere near the place. About all we have so far are sightings by people walking their dogs of other people walking *their* dogs; a jogger in the next street over, wearing a dark tracksuit with a hood, who could be either male or female, and a man who reported seeing a young couple with a suitcase at the top end of Pembroke Avenue about nine thirty that night. He thought it a bit odd because it wasn't a very pleasant night, and they just seemed to be hanging about, as he put it. The only description he could give us was that the girl was wearing a white plastic mac, had long hair and was "*really* built". As for the man, he *thinks* he was tall, so you can tell what he was looking at.

'The way I see it,' the sergeant continued, 'until these two villains make a mistake or try to flog those rings, I think there's a good chance they'll get away with it, because they've come up with an MO that works. It's completely dark in the evening by half past six or quarter to seven, so they have most of the evening to work with when they break into a house. And they know ahead of time which houses are going to be empty – I think that's obvious by the amount of time they spend inside – they *know* they won't be interrupted. I'm no psychologist, but I think this business of taking time to sit down to a meal is simply their way of telling us how clever they think they are.'

'Except they got it wrong in this case, didn't they?' Tregalles said.

'Only because of a last-minute decision by Mrs Holbrook to stay home,' Ormside pointed out. 'So where do they get their information from? How do they know exactly when the house will be empty, and why, after going to the trouble of breaking in and leaving unseen, aren't they stealing more?'

'I've been asking myself those very same questions,' Paget told him, 'but perhaps it doesn't make sense because our basic assumptions are wrong. SOCO has a theory that Mrs Holbrook was killed deliberately, and the vandalism was done to make us *think* she was killed by the people we've been looking for. They say the damage in the Holbrook house looks far worse than it actually is, and that is backed up by the insurance adjuster's estimate. In fact, since the first burglary in Dunbar Road, the damage has escalated steadily, and yet the cost of replacement or repair in the Holbrook house, excluding Dunbar Road, is the lowest of the lot.'

Paget sat down facing the two men, and summarized the case that Grace had made the night before. 'And the more I think about it, the more I'm inclined to think she may have a point,' he concluded.

'So that's what she was up to, yesterday,' Tregalles said. 'I did wonder. But if she is right, we need a motive. Like they say in France, *Chercher la beneficiary* – and I'll lay odds it'll turn out to be Simon Holbrook.'

'Which reminds me,' Ormside said. 'I have some background information on the Holbrooks and their company.' He rummaged into his pending tray, and brought out a memo containing pencilled notes.

He scanned it to refresh his memory. 'Simon Holbrook is forty-one. His wife is – or was – thirty-eight. The company is Holbrook Micro-Engineering Laboratories, and it's doing extremely well. They specialize in miniaturizing equipment used primarily, but not exclusively, in surgical and dental procedures, using laser technology. They also do contract work for the government. They've only been in business for six or seven years, but what started out more or less as a local business has expanded to the point where they are now selling overseas.

'Apparently, Simon Holbrook is something of a genius. He used to work for that Swiss firm, Drexler-Davies, but decided to strike out on his own a few years ago. He was born and raised here, which is why he decided to return to Broadminster to set up his business. That and to take advantage of some tax incentives the town was prepared to offer. But, according to my source, while Holbrook could turn out the product, he had trouble with the marketing and sales side of the business, so he was really struggling to stay afloat for the first few years.

'In fact, I'm told he was on the verge of bankruptcy when Laura Southern joined the firm – that was her name then – a couple of years ago. Bought into it, actually, and she's the one who's credited with getting it on its feet.'

'Must have had money,' Tregalles observed. 'And a fair bit of it if she was willing to chance it on a company that's about to go broke.'

'Inherited from her late husband,' Ormside said. 'Millions, according to my informant at the bank. He died eight years ago. Fell and hit his head on the ice while he was skating and died right there. But she has a pretty solid business background herself, so I think she knew what she was doing. University, London School of Economics, and something like seven years working for a forensic auditing firm in London before leaving for this job. Originally hired as a consultant, she bought into the company, in effect bailing them out, because they were sinking fast before she came along. And then she topped it off by marrying the boss and becoming an equal partner.'

'When did she and Holbrook get married?'

'About six months ago.'

'Could be a motive for murder if he gets her share of the firm and her money,' Tregalles suggested.

'It's possible,' Ormside agreed, 'but he didn't commit it if Starkie has his TOD right, and Holbrook's story checks out.'

Paget shook his head impatiently. 'We're wasting time,' he said as he reached for his coat, motioning for Tregalles to do the same. 'We can sit here all day and theorize, but we don't know anywhere near enough about the people involved, so let's go and find out what they have to say for themselves.'

Number 15 Pembroke Avenue was a solid-looking two-storey house set back from the road as were its neighbours. Large bay windows looked out over a patchy lawn bordered by shrubs, to the bare-limbed trees lining the street.

'Must be worth a bit the way prices are these days,' Tregalles observed as he pulled into the driveway that led to a detached garage at the rear of the house. The house wasn't nearly as big or as expensive as the houses bordering the river valley two streets away, but it was still worth at least twice the price of the sergeant's own modest home.

Paget led the way to the door and rang the bell.

A slim, petite, smartly dressed woman, opened the door within seconds. It was clear she was about to go out, a point emphasized by the car keys in her hand. 'Yes?' she said, looking faintly puzzled.

'Mrs Ballantyne?'

'That's right,' she said cautiously. 'And you are . . .?'

'Detective Chief Inspector Paget, and Detective Sergeant Tregalles,' Paget said as they held up their warrant cards for her inspection.

Moira Ballantyne took in a deep breath and said, 'Oh!' She looked anxiously at her watch. 'I'm sorry, but I was just on my way out . . .'

'Actually, it's Mr Holbrook we would like to see,' Paget explained. 'Is he here?'

'No. He left this morning. Went back home. He just lives up the street – well, of course you know that, don't you. He said he wanted to get things sorted out and start tidying up the house, and Susan – Susan Chase, Laura's sister – said she would meet him there to give him a hand.'

'I see,' said Paget slowly, and was about to thank her and leave, when he paused. 'I know you said you have to go out,' he said apologetically, 'but I wonder if you could spare us a few minutes before you go? There are one or two questions we need to ask you, and I'd appreciate it if we could do that now.'

Moira Ballantyne glanced at her watch again. 'I'd like to help,' she said, 'but I really can't think of any way I can. Trevor is the one who was there the other night. I was here all evening, so I don't know anything about it other than what he told me.'

'I realize that,' said Paget, 'but the questions I have in mind have more to do with your own relationship with Mrs Holbrook, since I gather the two of you were close friends.'

'I really should . . .' she began hesitantly, only to be cut off gently by Paget.

'And as I was about to say, Mrs Ballantyne, it would save you the inconvenience of having to come down to Charter Lane later on.'

Moira glanced around as if seeking help, then gave a sigh of resignation. 'I *had* intended to do some shopping before my appointment with my client,' she said somewhat ungraciously, 'but I suppose I could do it on my way home. You'd better come through.' She stepped back to allow them to pass before closing the door.

'Meeting a client on a Saturday? Do you mind if I ask what sort of business you're in?' Paget asked as they made their way down the hall.

'Trevor and I design security systems for businesses and private homes,' she said. 'We have our own company, but we work closely with some of the major security companies. Trevor is the clever one; he does most of the actual programme design, while I do the on-site inspections, layout, and customer requirements, then he designs the system based on the information I give him. And, yes, I do sometimes have meetings on a Saturday.'

'Yours must be demanding and exacting work,' Paget observed.

'It is,' Moira agreed as she ushered them through French doors into a large front room. 'A mistake by either one of us could prove costly to us and to our client.'

It was a comfortable-looking room, inviting, with its chintz-covered chairs and delicate lace curtains. The feminine touch was very much in evidence, thought Paget as he took a seat facing his reluctant hostess, and one that complimented the woman herself, because Moira Ballantyne was a very feminine woman.

Feminine or not, she seemed to have regained her composure as she said briskly, 'Now then, Chief Inspector, how can I help you?'

'As I said earlier, I gather that you and Laura Holbrook were close friends,' he began, but paused when Moira shook her head.

'We were friends in the sense that we spent time together and got on well enough,' she said carefully, 'but I can't say we were close. Mind you, I've only know her for a relatively short time. Trevor knew her long before I did. They were at school together, but Laura left Broadminster something like twenty years ago, so she was almost as much of a stranger to him as she was to me when she came back for her mother's funeral about three years ago.'

'Even so,' Paget persisted, 'from what your husband told us, you did see each other quite regularly, and I imagine you would have visited one another from time to time, living as close as you do?'

But Moira was shaking her head again. 'We play badminton together on a regular basis – or we *did*,' she amended quickly – 'and this past winter we started attending such things as plays and films together, but that was about it. Even though we're only a few houses apart, we've never spent time visiting back and forth the way some people do, if you know what I mean. But why are you asking me all these questions? What has it got to do with – with what happened the other night? I don't see the point of this at all. I mean some maniac broke into the house and killed her, and I for one would feel a lot happier, Chief Inspector, if you were out there looking for him instead of sitting here asking me a lot of questions about my relationship with Laura.'

'Unfortunately, Mrs Ballantyne, while we may *think* we know what happened, we do have to make sure that every other possibility is explored.' Paget told her. 'Tell me, when was the last time you were in the Holbrook house?'

Moira frowned in concentration 'It must be a couple of weeks ago,' she said. 'Yes, it was. We'd been to see the local production of *Noises Off*, and we went in for a drink afterwards.'

'And when did you last see Mrs Holbrook?'

Moira looked down at her hands. 'Last Tuesday,' she said quietly. 'At the club. Our regular nights are Mondays and Thursdays, but Laura was away in London or somewhere on business Monday, so we played on Tuesday instead.'

'And how was she? Did she say anything to you that suggested she might like to get out of going to see that particular film on Wednesday?'

Moira hesitated before saying, 'No, but I know she wasn't all that keen on going because it wasn't her kind of film, but she didn't say anything.' Her frown deepened. 'Are you suggesting that she *didn't* have a migraine, but used that as an excuse to beg off?'

'As I said, Mrs Ballantyne, we have to explore every possibility, and the fact that you chose not to go as well made me wonder if the two of you had decided on a mild deception to avoid going.'

Moira shook her head. 'I'll admit that I used it as an excuse, myself; it's not my kind of movie either, but there was no collusion, if that's what you're getting at.'

Paget nodded understandingly and sat back in his seat, a signal for Tregalles to take over.

'You mentioned playing badminton together, Mrs Ballantyne,' he said. 'You must enjoy the game if you play twice a week. The four of you play doubles, do you?'

'We used to when I was playing,' she said with a rueful smile, 'but now I'm the odd man out. It used to be Trevor and me against Simon and Susan, Laura's sister, but that changed when I broke my wrist a couple of years ago, and Susan brought Laura along to take my place. Since then it's been Trevor and Susan against Simon and Laura.'

'You still don't play after all this time?'

'I do, but I'm not in their league any more,' Moira told him. She raised both hands to display a right wrist that was clearly offset compared to its mate. 'They had to fuse some of the bones,' she explained, 'and the wrist just doesn't work as well as it used to. I go along with them, and I play singles with the juniors, in fact I teach a little, but the flexibility is gone, and I doubt if I will ever get it back.'

'Pity.' Tregalles made a note, then looked up again. 'Two years ago,' he said. 'Would that be when you first met Laura Holbrook?'

'That's right. It was when Susan and Laura's mother died. Susan was having some difficulty settling the estate, so Laura stayed on after the funeral to help sort things out. I had just broken my wrist, so Susan persuaded her sister to come along and play in my place – which was a big mistake.'

'Why do you say that?'

Moira shrugged guiltily as she waved a dismissive hand. 'I'm sorry,' she said, 'I shouldn't have said that. It has nothing to do with what's happened now.' Tregalles continued to look at her, one eyebrow raised in a silent question, clearly waiting for her to go on. A flicker of annoyance crossed her face. 'It's just that everyone expected to see Susan and Simon tie the knot one day,' she explained, 'but once Laura appeared on the scene, it was game over for Susan. Laura became Simon's partner, and Susan took my place as Trevor's partner.'

Tregalles made a face. 'Don't imagine Susan Chase would be very happy about that,' he said.

But Moira shook her head. 'I'm sure it must have been a blow,' she said, 'but Susan is the sort of person who takes everything in her stride. She really is a lovely person. Everyone likes Susan.'

'Still . . .' Tregalles began, but stopped when Paget rose to his feet. 'I think we've kept you quite long enough, Mrs Ballantyne,' he said. 'You've been most helpful, and we do appreciate your patience. I hope we haven't disrupted your morning too much?'

Moira didn't reply as she followed them to the door.

'There is just one more thing,' Paget said. 'Our people found a great many fingerprints at the crime scene, and the more we can eliminate, the better. So, since you say you and your husband have been inside the house recently, I'd like you to come down to Charter Lane in the next day or two, and we'll take your prints. It's just a formality, and they will be destroyed later. Your husband did the same for us the other day. I'm sure he must have mentioned it.'

'Yes. Yes, he did,' said Moira faintly.

'Good. Perhaps first thing Monday, if that's convenient? I'll have someone ring to arrange a time. It only takes a few minutes.'

Moira smiled mechanically as she closed the door, then leaned against it for support. Her legs were shaking, and several minutes passed before she felt confident enough to walk back to the room and sink into a chair.

'Oh, God!' she breathed as she sat down. Had he noticed? she wondered. He *must* have noticed. She'd felt the blood literally drain from her face when he'd mentioned fingerprints, and yet he hadn't said anything. But then, he wouldn't, would he if he suspected . . .

Or if he knew!

'Oh, God!' she whispered again, burying her face in her hands.

Nine

The front door of Simon Holbrook's house was open, and the sound of a vacuum cleaner could be heard. Paget knocked, but when it became clear that no one could hear it, he led the way inside.

The woman using the vacuum cleaner didn't see them at first, her attention focused as it was on what she was doing. Dressed for the task, she wore a faded T-shirt, jeans, scuffed and torn at the knees, moccasins that looked as if they were about to fall apart, and a light silk scarf holding her hair in place. If they hadn't been told in advance that Simon Holbrook's sister-in-law was in the house, they might have mistaken her for the cleaning lady.

Clearly startled by the appearance of the two men as they moved into her line of sight, she pulled back and shut the vacuum off. Paget held up his warrant card and introduced himself and Tregalles. 'Sorry if we startled you,' he apologized. 'We did knock, but . . .' He nodded in the direction of the now silent machine. 'We're looking for Mr Holbrook; is he here?'

The woman nodded. 'You must be the detectives who came here after Laura –' she drew a deep breath – 'after Laura was killed,' she said. She had a pleasant voice, low and slightly husky. 'I'm Susan Chase, Laura's sister. I came over to help Simon clear up the mess.' She raised anxious eyes to meet his own. 'I suppose it's too early to hope you've brought good news?'

They were nice eyes, grey-green, set wide in an oval face beneath a mop of dark hair. Paget had the feeling that he had seen that face before, but it was the earrings that clinched it: golden circlets, rings within rings that almost brushed her shoulders. He *knew* he'd seen those before, and yet he still couldn't place her.

'I'm afraid it is,' said Paget. 'Unfortunately, these things take time . . .' He paused, his curiosity getting the better of him. 'Tell me, Miss Chase, have we met before?'

Susan Chase smiled. 'Several times, Chief Inspector,' she told him, 'although I didn't know you were a policeman until now. I own the flower shop in the market square. Does two dozen roses ring a bell?'

'Of course! The Basket of Flowers. I'm sorry, Miss Chase,' he apologized. 'It's just that seeing you here like this – I didn't make the connection.'

'Dressed like this, I'm not surprised,' Susan said wryly, 'but there's no need to apologize; it's happened before. But you didn't come here to see me, did you? I'll take you to Simon.'

They found Simon Holbrook rubbing down walls and furniture with a damp cloth. 'Don't know who left the most mess,' he complained when he saw them, 'the bastards who killed my wife or your forensic people. Seems like they blew dust over everything in the house, and it's the very devil to get off. I should sue for damages.'

'It's unfortunate,' Paget agreed, 'but necessary, I'm afraid.'

'They don't seem to think it's necessary to stop and clean up, though, do they?' Holbrook set a chair back in place, then turned to face them. 'And by the look on your faces, I don't suppose you're here to tell me you've caught the bastards, are you? Laura would be alive today if you'd been doing your job.'

'I'm sure they're doing their best, Simon,' Susan said soothingly. 'I don't imagine it's easy.'

Holbrook gave a non-committal grunt as he turned his attention to Tregalles. 'As for you, Sergeant,' he said harshly, 'I thought I'd answered all *your* questions yesterday.'

'Most of them, yes, sir,' Tregalles agreed, 'and we appreciate your cooperation, but we're now pursuing another line of enquiry.'

Holbrook frowned as he turned to Paget. 'I don't understand,' he said. 'Another line of enquiry? What's he talking about?'

'There is evidence to suggest that the person who killed your wife did so deliberately,' said Paget, 'then tried to make it *look* as if it was done by the vandals who have been breaking into houses. If that turns out to be true, it opens up an entirely new line of investigation.'

'But that's preposterous!' Holbrook spluttered. 'Who would want to kill Laura? Of *course* it was done by the same people. They came in here to steal and wreck the place, and panicked when they found someone in the house.'

'I can assure you we would not be pursuing this line of investigation if we didn't think it relevant,' Paget said firmly. 'I'm not prepared to go into any details as yet, but what I can tell you is that there are elements of this crime that do not fit the pattern of the previous burglaries, and it would help us a great deal if we have your cooperation. I need to know as much as you can tell me about your wife, her background, who might benefit by her death, and if she had any enemies. I need to know if she has been involved in any arguments, received any threats, either at work or outside.'

Holbrook stared at him. '*Enemies?*' he repeated. '*Laura?* You can't be serious. We're talking about my wife, for God's sake! And what the hell are you implying when you say you want to know who benefits by her death? Are you suggesting that *I* had something to do with my own wife's murder?'

'Unfortunately, Mr Holbrook, it's a question that must be asked in such cases,' Paget told him. 'We are looking for a motive, and that is always a possibility.'

Holbrook opened his mouth to protest again, but Susan reached out to put a restraining hand on his arm before he could speak. 'Don't, Simon,' she said quickly. 'There's no point in getting upset. We all want to know who killed Laura, and if the chief inspector believes this may help, then let's do what we can to help him.'

Angrily, Holbrook shook her hand off. 'But that's what they're *really* saying, isn't it?' he snorted. 'In their eyes, if I benefit by her death, then I must have killed her. Never mind that I was somewhere else at the time. That's the way they think, Sue.'

'No one's accusing you, Simon,' she said quickly.

'Not much, they aren't!' he said heatedly, then rounded on Paget. 'And for what it's worth, I inherit everything Laura had, including her share of the business, and you can make what you like of that! But I did *not* kill my wife; so go ahead and ask your questions if you think it will do any good.'

Susan squeezed Holbrook's arm. 'Let's go through to the kitchen, where we can all sit down and talk about this calmly,' she said soothingly. 'It's the only room in the house that's really clean,' she explained. 'I'll put the kettle on.'

Paget was silent as they drove back to Charter Lane. It had been hard at first, getting Holbrook to calm down and talk rationally about his wife, and Paget suspected that it would have been a lot harder if Susan Chase hadn't been there. But he had talked more freely and seemed more comfortable talking about his company.

He confirmed much of what Ormside had told them earlier. He acknowledged that the fledgling company he had begun with such high hopes had not done well in the beginning. 'I was naïve,' he confessed. 'Developing products to meet specific needs wasn't a problem; it's what I've been doing for years, but what I failed to take into account was the importance of the sales and marketing side of things. If I do say so myself, I have a certain reputation in the field of miniaturization, and I suppose I thought that would be good enough, and buyers would come knocking on my door. Oh, a few with whom I'd had dealings when I was with Drexler-Davies did come, and we managed to stay afloat, but we were losing ground and on the point of going under when Laura came along. If she hadn't come to the rescue, I might have had to consider going back to work for Drexler-Davies – they certainly kept after me to go back, but I would only have done that as a last resort.'

He'd stopped there, but Paget had prompted him to go on, asking for details. What was Laura's background? Where had she come from? And what had she done to turn the company around in such a short space of time? He'd put the question to Holbrook, but it was Susan who had told them how Laura had become involved in the first place.

She confirmed what Moira Ballantyne had told them earlier. Laura, she said, had come down from London to attend their mother's funeral two-and-a-half years ago, intending to go back the day after the funeral. But when she saw the state of their mother's finances, she'd stayed on to help straighten things out.

'Dad's been in a nursing home for years, Alzheimer's,' Susan explained, 'so he couldn't help, but it was relatively easy for Laura because of her job as a forensic accountant. She'd been involved in auditing the books of some of London's biggest companies, so sorting out mum's finances was no problem for her, whereas it was nothing but a headache to me.'

She said it was while Laura was staying with her that Moira Ballantyne broke her wrist, and Susan persuaded her sister to take Moira's place in their badminton foursome. 'I forget how it came about, but something was said about Simon's cash-flow problems. Laura became interested, and the next thing I knew, Laura said she was staying on to see if she could help Simon out.'

'She understood exactly what our problems were,' Holbrook broke in, 'and she didn't mince words. She said we needed to do three things in order to survive, and the first thing I had to do was get back in the lab where I belonged and lock the door. She was pretty blunt about it, too. "You're a scientist, an innovator, and a good one," she told me, "but you have absolutely none of the skills required to run a business, so get back to your bench and let someone who knows what they're doing take over." I must say it rankled a bit at first, but I knew she was right.

'She said she'd been looking for an opportunity to get out of her present job and start a business of her own, but after looking at what we were trying to do here, she felt confident that, properly run, the firm had potential for growth and expansion, and she would like to be part of it. She said she'd be prepared to put up enough cash to pay off our debts and carry us through the next couple of years – Michael Southern, her late husband, was a financier in the City, and he left her very well off when he died – but only if I would agree to certain conditions.

'She was prepared to buy into the firm in return for a twenty-five per cent slice of the pie, but she insisted on being given a free hand to run the administrative and marketing side of the business. In effect, she was asking me to turn over the running of *my* company to her, and I must admit that it took a leap of faith on my part. But I didn't have a choice, so we agreed on a one-year trial period, at which time we would assess the situation.'

Holbrook leaned back in his chair. 'Best decision I ever made,' he said, 'because from that day on we never looked back. Laura went through the company from top to bottom, and one of the first things she did was move us out of our old cramped quarters into the building we're in now. But best of all, she had contacts everywhere, some through her previous job, and some through the social circles in which she and Michael had moved, and orders began to roll in. Laura was . . .'

He stopped speaking in mid-sentence, and the faraway look in his eyes faded.

'What *is* the point of all this?' he demanded. 'Because as far as I'm concerned, it isn't getting us anywhere. None of this has anything to do with finding Laura's killer.'

'I realize it must look that way to you, but it does help,' Paget told him, 'because if we are right, and this burglary was staged to cover the killing of your wife, we need to know as much as possible about your wife, her background, her work, her friends and so on. And speaking of her work, I suspect there must have been quite an upheaval when she first joined your company. How did that go down with your employees?'

Holbrook made a face. 'I'll admit it wasn't easy, those first few months,' he said, 'but people adapt; they realized that change had to come if their jobs were to be saved.'

'Even so, sometimes people resent change, even when the objective is to save their jobs. And some can harbour grievances for a long time. Did anyone lose their job?'

'No. Besides, that's all in the past, so you're wasting your time going down that road, Chief Insp—' He broke off as the muffled sound of 'Alexander's Ragtime Band' interrupted what he was about to say.

'BlackBerry,' he said tersely. 'Turn the damned thing off, Sue. It's in the jacket behind you. I'll get it later.'

Dutifully, Susan reached into the pocket of his jacket and switched it off.

'As I was saying,' Holbrook continued, 'if that is where this so-called evidence of yours is leading, it's a non-starter. It may sound like a cliché, but I regard the people who work for me more like part of my family rather than employees.'

'What about more recently? Has there been any trouble at work? Any disgruntled employees, who . . .' Paget stopped abruptly as he caught the look on Susan's face. 'Yes, Miss Chase?' he said. 'You've thought of something?'

Susan opened her mouth to speak, then closed it and shook her head. 'It was nothing,' she said in a low voice. 'Sorry – it was just . . .' She looked helplessly at Holbrook and fell silent.

'If you know anything at all,' Paget persisted, 'please don't hold back. It could be important.'

Holbrook was frowning, clearly puzzled. '*Do* you know something, Sue?' he said.

Susan looked from one to the other, and it was clear she felt trapped. 'I'm sorry, Simon,' she said unhappily, 'but it's just that Laura told me Tim had confronted her in the car park again, and that's the second time it's happened. She said she thought he'd been drinking . . . I'm sorry, Simon, but it just popped into my head, and since the chief inspector did ask . . .'

'Hardly what he meant, though, is it?' he said dismissively. 'That was just Tim blowing off steam, so let's not waste any more of the chief inspector's time on it.'

'On the contrary,' said Paget, 'I don't regard it as a waste of time, and I prefer to make up my own mind about things like that, Mr Holbrook, so I would like to know more about the person Miss Chase mentioned.'

'But it's so pointless,' Holbrook insisted. 'Tim Bryce is my nephew, and I'll admit that he and Laura didn't get along, but to suggest that he could even be considered as a suspect is absurd. In fact, if Tim had a grudge against anyone, it should have been me.'

'Which makes it even more important that I understand the situation,' Paget told him.

'Oh, very well, then,' he said, making no attempt to conceal his irritation. 'Tim used to work for me – for us, for the firm. Laura felt it was a mistake to bring him into the company, but I insisted. Turns out that she was right and I was wrong. Tim seemed to think that being my nephew gave him special privileges, and his behaviour among the staff was disruptive. I talked to him and kept hoping he would straighten out, but when things didn't improve, I had to agree with Laura that nephew or not, he had to go.'

'When was that?'

'Three weeks ago last Friday. And before you start jumping to conclusions, I'll admit that Tim did not take it well, but he is not by nature a violent person. As for the encounter with Laura in the car park the other day, he was simply trying to persuade her to give him his old job back. As Susan said, he'd probably had a couple of drinks, but I'm sure that's all there was to it.'

But Susan Chase was shaking her head. She'd been growing more and more agitated as she listened to Holbrook, and she could hold back no longer. 'But that is *not* the way it was at all, Simon,' she said emphatically, then softened her tone to add, 'That may be what Laura told you, because she knew how you felt about Tim, but that is not what she told me. I'm sorry, Simon, I know you think of Tim as if he were your own son, but he is not the golden-haired boy you would like him to be. He threatened Laura. She still sounded shaky when she told me about it later that evening.'

'Well, she certainly didn't tell me—' Holbrook began heatedly, only to be cut off by Paget.

'What, exactly, did she tell you, Miss Chase?'

Susan glanced first at Holbrook, then back to Paget. 'Laura said she'd just left work last Friday when Tim was suddenly there in front of her, blocking her way to her car. She said he'd been drinking – she could smell it on him, and he was extremely abusive.'

'You said he threatened her?'

'Yes, he did. I'm sorry, Simon,' she said firmly as Holbrook appeared about to protest, 'but it has to be said. Laura said Tim swore at her; called her names, and ranted on about how she had never liked him, and blamed her for turning his uncle against him, and said she would regret the day she sacked him, because he wasn't going to let her get away with it.'

'Did he say what he intended to do?'

'Laura said he looked at her car and said, "Nice car. Bet it cost a bomb. Pity if it went up like one. You might want to have someone check it before you get in." Then he laughed and staggered off.'

Holbrook stared at Susan, his face suddenly drained of colour. 'Did she *really* say that, Sue?' he asked hoarsely. 'Honestly? Is that why she stopped using her car? She told me it had been acting up, and she was leaving it at home until the garage could come and pick it up.'

'I know,' Susan said quietly. 'Laura told me she was going to do that. She said she thought twice before getting into the car after Tim left, but decided to take a chance because she didn't think Tim would have told her if he had done something to the car already. She said she didn't think Tim would have the guts to actually follow through on his threat, but she thought it best not to give him the opportunity in case she was wrong. That's why she started taking a taxi to work. Laura likes to start work very early in the morning,' she explained to Paget, 'which is why she normally uses her own car rather than go in with Simon.'

'Has your nephew ever threatened you, Mr Holbrook?' Paget asked.

Simon Holbrook shook his head. 'No – no, Tim would never . . . We've had a few words, yes, but . . .' Words failed him. He looked completely shaken.

Tregalles, who had been quietly making notes, spoke up for the first time. 'You've been referring to your nephew as a boy, Mr Holbrook, a youngster, but he can't be all that young if he was working for you. How old is he?'

'You might well ask, Sergeant,' Susan said swiftly before Holbrook had a chance to answer. 'I know Simon still thinks of Tim as a boy, but he'll be twenty-seven next month.'

'That's quite enough, thank you, Susan,' Holbrook said coldly. His voice was steady, and he appeared to have regained his composure as he looked at Paget. 'I'm not saying that Susan is wrong about what happened, but I'm quite sure that they were idle threats, especially if he'd had a few drinks. Look,' he went on earnestly, 'Tim is my late sister Catherine's boy. She and her husband died while on holiday in the

Philippines twelve years ago. Drowned when an overloaded ferry sank.
Tim came to live with Helen and me when he was fourteen. Helen was
my first wife, but we were divorced a year after Tim came to live with
us, so it was just the two of us after she left until Tim went off to university, and I became very fond of him. I'm not disputing that he may have
made threats, but it would all be bluster, letting off steam. I mean it's
only natural that he'd be angry about losing his job, but he'll get over
it. He'll get another job. And he's married, now. He has responsibili-
ties. I'm sure it was just the drink talking the other night.' He looked
to Susan as if hoping for her support, but she was looking elsewhere –
deliberately, Paget thought.

'For a man who's just lost his wife, I don't think Holbrook will have to
look far for another one,' Tregalles observed as they got out of the car
in Charter Lane. 'In fact, it looked to me as if she's already moved in
– or is planning to. Not that I'd say no if she wanted to move in with
me. I like her.'

  'If she is planning to move in,' said Paget, 'I don't think she did her
case much good by the way she was talking about his nephew. And if
Mrs Ballantyne is to be believed, Susan Chase was passed over once
before when Holbrook married her sister, but I agree, I think you're
right about her wanting to be the second – no, the *third* Mrs Holbrook.'

Ten

Like so many of the older, once proud three-storeyed houses at the bottom end of Bridge Street, Hereford House had been made over into flats. The names of the tenants appeared beside the front door at the top of the steps, but there was an arrow pointing downward to the basement flat below street level next to the names of Bryce/Craig. The two detectives retraced their steps and made their way down to what had once been the servants' entrance and rang the bell.

A young woman answered the door. Slim, pale, fair hair tied back in a ponytail, and wearing a flowered housecoat, she held a baby high on her shoulder. The baby was crying. The woman took her hand off the door and patted the child's back soothingly. 'He's not here if it's Tim you're after,' she said before Paget could say anything, 'and I don't know when he'll be back. He's gone to see about a job.' She began to close the door.

Paget put out his hand to stop the door from closing. 'And you are . . .?' he asked.

'Sally Craig.' The young woman made another attempt to close the door, but Paget held it firmly while he introduced himself and Tregalles. 'Sorry to trouble you,' he told her perfunctorily, 'but even if Mr Bryce isn't here, we would still like a word with you. May we come in? We won't take up much of your time.'

'He's in the middle of his feed,' she said, indicating the baby, but when Paget failed to respond and didn't move, she stepped back with an air of resignation and allowed them to enter. The baby's cries grew louder. 'He doesn't like to be interrupted when he's feeding,' she said accusingly as she led the way into a small sitting room, sparse on furniture but cluttered nevertheless. A playpen full of woolly toys took up much of the space in the middle of the room; baby clothes were draped over a clothes horse in front of the electric fire, and a jumbled pile of sheets and underclothes filled one of the chairs. The ironing board, with iron still plugged in, sat in a narrow space behind the open door.

'You can sit down if you like,' she told them offhandedly as she took her own seat in a chair beside the fire, then opened the top of her housecoat, and settled the baby to one of her breasts. Tregalles took it upon himself to clear the sofa of cushions, toys, paperback books, bits of clothing and a jumble of brightly coloured wools and knitting needles.

'Just put the stuff on the floor,' Sally told him when she saw him hesitate. 'It's clean.'

He did so, and the two men sat down facing her. The room was warm, too warm for Paget's liking. And humid. Steam rose from the clothes drying by the fire and, if Paget's nose was anything to go by, there was a nappy that desperately needed changing.

But Sally Craig seemed not to notice. She drew the broad lapel of her housecoat discreetly over her breast, then looked expectantly from one to the other. 'So what is it . . .?' she began, only to wince and draw in her breath. 'He's teething,' she explained as she pulled the baby's mouth away from her breast. 'Just watch it, you!' she scolded, then smiled as the baby started to fuss and his little fingers clutched at her breast. She pulled him to her and he began to feed again.

She looked up. The unexpected smile had transformed her face; she was a pretty girl – and she *was* just a girl, thought Paget, barely out of her teens by the look of her. She looked tired, but there was a hint of apprehension in her eyes as well.

'I take it someone told you we were coming?' Paget said. 'Would that be Mr Holbrook?'

'That's right,' she said with a defiant tilt of the chin, 'and he told me why. But what I don't understand is what you want with Tim? He's got nothing to do with what happened over there the other night when those robbers broke in, so why do you want to talk to him?'

Paget explained as he had done with Holbrook, but Sally Craig was shaking her head long before he had finished. 'You're wrong!' she said emphatically, 'and if you think you're going to pin the murder of that bitch of a wife of his on Tim, you've got another think coming! Tim had nothing to do with it – not that he didn't have good reason after the way she treated him. He worked all hours for that company, but did he get any thanks for it? No, he did not! He didn't even get paid for it. I told him he should claim for all those extra hours he put in, but he won't, though God knows we could use the money.'

Her eyes glistened, and defiant as she tried to sound, it was clear she was having trouble holding back the tears. 'It's a good thing I've still got my job, although what with babysitters and the price of every-thing going up in the shops, I don't know how much longer we can keep going if Tim doesn't find work soon.'

'You work full-time?' asked Paget. She nodded. 'At Gosford's Shoes in Russell Street. It's not been easy, and having someone like you come round to accuse Tim of something he didn't do doesn't make life any easier, either.'

'We're not here to accuse Tim of anything,' Paget told her. 'But considering that Tim is alleged to have accosted Mrs Holbrook on more than one occasion, and threatened her on at least one of those occa-sions, we will be asking him to tell us where he was on the night she was killed. But perhaps you can tell us that Ms Craig. Last Wednesday evening?'

The question appeared to touch a nerve. 'What I *can* tell you,' Sally said heatedly, 'is that he wouldn't be anywhere near his uncle's house, not after the way he's been treated by him. Tim was out jogging. He goes out two or three nights a week because of the stress he's under from losing his job, but he does a regular circuit, and I know that's not the way he goes.'

'Can you remember what time he left and what time he returned? Approximately?'

Sally looked off into the distance. 'Wednesday,' she said slowly. 'He went out a bit after seven, same as usual, and came back around ten. I think the news had just started when he came in. Billy was fussing a lot, and didn't settle down till well after nine, so, yes, it would be about ten when Tim came in.'

'That's a long time to be jogging,' Tregalles observed. He was a swimmer, himself, but he'd done a bit of jogging in his time, although not recently – as Audrey was fond of reminding him. 'Is he in training for something? A marathon, perhaps?'

'No, it's just that he likes to keep in shape, and as I said, it relieves the stress.'

'And you say he goes out two or three nights a week?'

'Pretty much every other night, yes.'

'And he's gone for something like three hours each time? That must be a bit hard on you, what with your job and the baby,' Tregalles said sympathetically.

Sally blinked rapidly and looked away, then hoisted the child to her shoulder and began to rub his back. 'I don't mind as long as it helps him,' she said. Her voice was muffled as she nuzzled the baby. 'At least it's better than when he was spending all of his time at work, till midnight sometimes. Not that they appreciated all the extra time he put in.'

'Does he go with anyone?' Paget asked. 'When he's jogging, I mean.'

Sally shook her head. 'Tim likes to run alone. Says he can think more clearly out there on his own.'

'So no one can actually confirm where he was that night?'

Sally Craig bristled at the implication. 'I don't see why anyone should have to,' she said tightly, 'but he has a regular circuit, and it doesn't go anywhere near Pembroke Avenue, if that's what you're getting at. Anyway, I don't know why you're so dead keen on picking on Tim. What about the others over there at the lab? Have you asked any of them where they were? There are a good many there who won't be sorry she's gone.'

Sally frowned, and softened her tone as she said, 'Not that I'm suggesting for a minute that she deserved to die in such a horrible manner, but she certainly had enemies. Tim will tell you. I mean, look what happened to Peggy Goodwin for a start.'

'Peggy Goodwin?' Paget echoed. The name was unfamiliar to him. 'What happened to her?'

Sally grimaced as she eased the baby away from her breast and began to pat his back. 'Pushed aside, wasn't she?' she said. 'After all she'd done for Simon, keeping things running up front while he tinkered away in the back room with his toys. And then Miss Knowitall comes barging in to take over, and Peggy Goodwin is out in the cold.'

She flicked a strand of hair away from her eyes. 'Funny the way things turned out, because Tim said Laura had some good ideas at first, and she did get them out of that dingy hole they used to work in. And she did bring in the customers, but Tim says they were mainly people she'd dealt with in her old job, so it wasn't as if she had to exert herself, because the things that he and the others on the team were inventing would almost sell themselves once the customers got to see them.'

Tregalles stirred in his seat. 'I thought it was Mr Holbrook who was the inventor,' he said, but Sally shook her head. 'That's what everybody thinks. He's even been written up in *Hi-Tech News,* and magazines like that, and Tim says he *was* good once, but he's past it now. Tim says technology is changing and moving on so fast these days, that people like Simon are being left behind, and it's really the younger people like Tim and the others who have the skills and the knowledge to keep up with things. I hate to say this about Tim's uncle, because he has been good to Tim in the past, but he's been riding on his reputation and other people's coat-tails for years, now. Oh, they still use his name and his reputation, but Tim says he's been more or less shoved into the background since Laura took over, and she's running the firm now. See, that's why she was so dead set against Tim,' Sally continued earnestly. 'It was because he could see what she was up to. He tried to warn his uncle, but he wouldn't listen, because he was so besotted with her and wouldn't have anything said against her.'

The baby burped loudly, spraying a mouthful of warm milk across his mother's shoulder. A sickly, cloying smell filled the room. 'Good boy, Billy,' she said as she wiped the baby's mouth and settled him to her breast again.

But it was too much for Paget. He looked at his watch, then rose to his feet and said, 'I think that will be all for now, Ms Craig, and thank you for your time. No, please, don't get up,' he said quickly as Sally started to get to her feet. 'We can see ourselves out.'

'Got to anyway,' she said. 'Billy needs changing.'

And not before time, thought Paget as he moved toward the door. 'But we still need to talk to Mr Bryce,' he said. 'Do you have any idea when he might be home, or where we might find him?'

'No idea. Honestly,' she said with a vigorous shake of the head. 'I really don't know. Tim went out early and said he didn't know when he'd be back. It's my day off today, and I had hoped to see something of him myself, but with him out looking for a job every day, I hardly see anything of him at all. Not that I'm complaining, because I know it's hard on him as well. As he says, with the economy in a downturn, it's not easy finding another job even with all his qualifications. Tell you the truth,' she ended, cuddling the baby to her, 'I think we've seen more of the babysitter lately than we have of Tim. She comes in while I'm at work.'

Paget took out his card and offered it to her. 'Ask him to ring me at this number when he does come back,' he said.

'Put it on the mantle,' she told him. 'I'll tell Tim when he comes in, but it will be up to him whether he calls or not.'

Once outside, Paget took a deep breath and exhaled thankfully. 'Pong getting to you in there, was it, boss?' Tregalles asked guilelessly as they made their way to the car. 'Granted it was a bit thick, but the kid was carrying a full load when we arrived, and we didn't give her much choice. She could either feed him or change him, and he was hungry.

'Couldn't help feeing sorry for her, though,' he continued as they got in the car. 'She seems like a nice kid, but it sounds to me as if this Tim Bryce has her pretty well brainwashed into his way of thinking. What she was telling us about him and the company certainly didn't fit with what we were told earlier today.

'And I'd like to hear him explain this jogging lark several nights a week. I mean *three hours* or more in the kind of weather we've been having? I don't buy it.'

'I'm not sure she does, either,' Paget said as he started the car. He rolled down the window and took several more deep breaths. The cloying odour was fading, but not fast enough for his liking. 'I think she *wants* to believe him, but I think she's having a hard time convincing herself. And you're right; it should be interesting to hear what Bryce himself has to say about that.'

Eleven

Sergeant Ormside was there ahead of him as usual when Paget and Tregalles arrived at the same time. Seated at his desk, shirtsleeves rolled up, he held a steaming mug of coffee in both hands.

'Waste of time looking at them,' he said dolefully when Paget went straight to the whiteboards to see if anything new had been added since he'd looked at them the day before.

He and Grace had spent Sunday morning at home. Grace, who had been thinking about it throughout the winter, had finally taken the plunge and signed up for a beginner's art class, so she had shut herself away to read the pre-course instructions and experiment with the paints she'd been told to buy.

Paget had spent most of the morning washing the two cars and cleaning out the garage, a job he'd been putting off for months on one pretext or another, and he was only too happy to stop when Grace suggested a run into Broadminster for lunch. 'I have some shopping to do afterwards,' she told him, 'and some of the shops have their summer stock in already.'

'Ah. Then you won't want me along, will you?' he said, 'so perhaps you could drop me at the office and pick me up later? It's appraisal time again, and I'm barely halfway through the reviews of Ormside's people, and they have to go up to Alcott next week. So give me a couple of hours at least.'

Ormside had good people, so Paget didn't find it hard to endorse the sergeant's recommendations. The sergeant was of the old school, and was inclined to mark a little hard, but he was fair, and those who had worked for him for any length of time knew that and accepted it. Paget worked quickly, and was almost through when he opened the file on DC Molly Forsythe. He scanned the appraisal. Nothing unexpected there – except for the handwritten memo attached to it. Paget read it carefully, then glanced at the calendar. Not a problem, he decided; there were still a few days left. He set the folder aside, but he was still thinking

about what the note said when Grace rang to say she was on her way
to pick him up.

Grace arrived just after four, and the last thing he'd done before
leaving was to check the notes on the whiteboards. There'd been nothing
new then, and as Ormside had said, there was nothing new this
morning.

'What about Bryce?' he asked sharply. 'Any word from him?'

Ormside shook his head. He was about to say more, but was cut off
by the ringing of his phone. He picked it up, then held up his hand to
gain their attention and mouthed, 'Forensic.'

They waited while the sergeant scribbled notes on a memo pad, then
paused 'You're *quite* sure about that?' he asked, pen poised above the
pad. He listened for a moment longer, then said, 'Right,' and made
another note. 'Fax it to me right away, and thanks.'

'Interesting,' he said as he put the phone down. 'They've examined
the wood taken from the broken door jamb on Holbrook's house, and
they say the pry bar that was used could be the same instrument used
in previous burglaries, but they couldn't swear to it in court. Too much
splintering of the wood to get a good impression.'

Tregalles snorted. 'So what's so interesting about that?' Tregalles asked
scornfully. 'I could have told them *that* much myself.'

'The interesting bit,' Ormside said, 'is that they found traces of blood
– Mrs Holbrook's blood – and hair embedded in the splintered wood
on the door jamb. Which means . . .'

'That the door was pried open *after* Laura Holbrook was killed,'
said Paget. 'And *that* tells us that Laura Holbrook was the target,
and the killer simply tried to make it look as though there had been
a burglary. We know she had one enemy in Holbrook's nephew,' he
continued, 'and from what we've been told and what we've seen for
ourselves, Susan Chase can't be ruled out as a suspect. But there
may be other reasons for wanting Laura Holbrook out of the way,
so, Len, I want someone at the house to go through all her personal
records, including anything on her computer that might give us a
clue, and I want the same thing done at her office. We'll need
warrants, so I'll square that with Mr Alcott before I leave. And I
want you, Tregalles, to find Tim Bryce and bring him in for questioning. Meanwhile, I think it's time for another chat with Simon
Holbrook, and I think I'll take Forsythe with me if that's all right
with you, Len?'

A hint of a smile touched Ormside's craggy face as he met Paget's gaze. 'Quite all right,' he said. 'I'm sure she'll be pleased to get away from her desk for a change.'

'Good. I have to go upstairs first, so have her meet me in the car park in twenty minutes.'

An interior decorator's van stood in the driveway of number 9 Pembroke Avenue. The front door of the house was open, and a workman in paint-spattered overalls sat at the bottom of the stairs drinking tea from a plastic mug.

'He's gone,' he said when Paget identified himself and asked if Simon Holbrook was inside. 'Said he couldn't stand the smell of paint, so he went off to work. Mind you, I don't think that was the only reason, not that I blame him after what happened up there.' He jerked a thumb over his shoulder, indicating the stairs. 'I think he just wanted an excuse to get out of the house. He wouldn't even go in the bedroom to show us what he wanted when we came to see about the job the other day; just told us to do it over in the same colour as it was before.'

The man set the mug aside and lit a cigarette. 'Pity about the carpet, though. I mean all it needed was a good scrubbing in that corner where the woman died, but he had the whole thing taken out. Lovely stuff it was, too, but out it came. He said he told them to burn it, but I bet they don't. Cost of carpet these days, and a big piece like that? Not on your life. They'll clean it if they can or cut that bit off and sell the rest on the quiet and pocket the money.'

The man drained his mug and put the top on his Thermos. 'Got the time?' he asked.

'Twenty past ten,' Molly told him. The man looked surprised. 'I'd better get started then, hadn't I?' he said as he shoved the Thermos and mug into a paper bag. 'Here's me chatting away to a couple of coppers when I should be getting on with it. Be my dinner time soon. Mr Holbrook said he wanted it all done by tomorrow, but I told him there was no way, not if he wants two coats, even if it is quick dry. Come to that, I wouldn't be surprised if it needs three to cover that bloodstain in the corner where she was killed. I told him he should put paper on, but he wouldn't have it.'

He wetted his fingers and pinched the end of his cigarette, then popped the butt back in the packet. 'Can't afford to waste them these days, can you?' he said. 'Not at the price they are. Anyway, nice meeting you. The wife will be that chuffed when I tell her I met the bloke in charge of the murder.'

Molly paused beside the van as they made their way back to the car. 'Just making sure I remember the name of the firm *not* to have in if I ever need one,' she told Paget as she slid behind the wheel. She snapped on her seat belt. 'Where to now, sir? The industrial park?'

'Right. Six hundred and something Cavendish Way. I forget the exact number, but it shouldn't be too hard to find.'

The front third of the single-storey brick building housing Holbrook Micro-Engineering Laboratories was given over to offices and reception area, while the other two thirds housed the research and production facility. The reception area was open and spacious. The receptionist's desk and matching credenza occupied the area facing the door, but apart from several comfortable-looking deep leather armchairs, the area was remarkably free of clutter. A deep-burgundy hard-twist carpet covered the floor, and a series of pictures featuring some of the Holbrook product lines were on display around the walls.

A very young, very thin, long-legged girl stood beside the desk arranging papers. She was dressed – if one could call it that, thought Paget – in a tight-fitting tank top, with about six inches of bare midriff between it and a very short skirt, bare legs and platform shoes. Both ears were studded with clusters of seed pearls, and Paget couldn't help wondering how she could manage a telephone.

Somewhat incongruously, she wore a black armband on one of her bare arms. She would be quite pretty with a bit more meat on her bones, he thought, and he was surprised that a businessman like Holbrook would put a young girl dressed like that out front to greet the public.

The girl moved behind the desk as they approached and smiled brightly as she said, 'May I help you?'

The smile vanished, replaced by a worried frown when Paget told her who they were and asked to see Mr Holbrook. 'He's in a staff meeting,' she told him breathlessly, 'but he said he wouldn't be very long, so if you would like to wait . . .?' A long thin arm waved in the general direction of the armchairs.

The girl waited until they were seated before sitting down herself. She began fiddling with papers, but it was clear that her mind was not on her work. Paget watched her through lowered lids. The girl was bursting to say something and was doing her best to hold back.

She failed.

'Do you mind if I ask you something, sir?' she asked in a small voice. 'I don't mean to pry, but it's come as such a shock to all of us, Mrs Holbrook being killed like that, and I wondered if there was any news yet? I mean about who did it?'

Paget glanced at the nameplate on the desk. 'I'm afraid not, Miss West,' he said, 'but we are making progress.'

'Oh, well, that's good, then, isn't it?' she said brightly. 'But I'm not Mrs West. I'm Miranda. Mrs West is away. Took ill last Friday and they had to send for the ambulance. Gallstones,' she confided in a whisper. 'That's what someone who saw her yesterday said it was. That's why I'm here this morning. I usually work in the back, but someone has to look after the phones when they're all at a meeting, so being as I'm the junior, I'm it. Not that I mind. It makes a nice—'

Miranda cut short what she was about to say when a door behind her opened and a smartly dressed woman appeared. She, too, wore a black armband. Her manner was brisk but pleasant as she said, 'Good morning,' before turning to Miranda to raise an enquiring eyebrow.

'They're from the police, Miss Goodwin,' the girl said hastily. She picked up a piece of paper and studied it. 'Detective Chief Inspector Paget and Detective Constable Forsythe. They're waiting to see Mr Holbrook.'

'Peggy Goodwin,' the woman said, coming forward to introduce herself. 'I'm Mr Holbrook's personal assistant.' She was tall and slim. Her handshake was firm but brief, and there was a vibrant energy about her that suggested she kept herself in trim. She had short, fair hair, and deep blue eyes, and while Paget would have stopped short of calling Peggy Goodwin beautiful, he did say she was a very attractive woman when describing her to Grace that evening.

'If you would like to come with me, I can take you to his office now,' she said. 'But first, we'll need to sign you in and give you a couple of Visitor badges. Security,' she explained. 'No one is allowed to wander around unaccompanied in here. Not even policemen,' she added with a smile as she clipped the badge on Paget's lapel. She had a nice smile, and the perfume or cologne she wore had a delicate tantalizing fragrance.

She held the door open for them, but paused to speak to Miranda before following herself.

'Ring Mr Holbrook and tell him we are on our way,' she said quietly. 'And, Miranda, whatever happened to that lovely cardigan you had on earlier today? The long one. I think you should wear it, my dear.'

Twelve

'How long have you been in this building?' Paget asked as he and Molly followed Peggy Goodwin down the corridor.

'A little over a year,' the woman told him. 'And I must say it's a vast improvement over our first quarters down by the river. That was little more than a shed, but at least it gave us our start.'

'So you've been with Holbrook Micro-Engineering from the beginning, then?'

'That's right. I was Mr Holbrook's secretary when we both worked for the Drexler-Davies Corporation. When he left to set up his own business, he asked me to come with him, and I've never regretted it.' She laughed softly as she added, 'Although there have been days when I had doubts about my sanity.'

They came to an office door with the name 'Simon Holbrook' in gold on the frosted glass, but as Peggy Goodwin raised her hand to knock, Paget stopped her to ask, 'Where is your office, Miss Goodwin?'

'That's mine,' she said, pointing to an open door down the hall.

'I know you must be busy, but I wonder if you could spare us a few minutes after we've spoken to Mr Holbrook? We would like to get as much background information as we can, and since you must have worked closely with Mrs Holbrook, we'd appreciate your input.'

Peggy Goodwin looked surprised. 'I'm not sure I understand,' she said, clearly mystified by the request. 'Why——?'

'We won't take up any more of your time than necessary,' Paget said firmly, ignoring the obvious question in her eyes.

The woman looked at him for a long moment, then shrugged and said, 'Very well, then, Chief Inspector, if you think it will help.' She gave two sharp raps on the door before opening it and ushering them inside.

If he hadn't known that Simon Holbrook was head of the company, Paget would never have guessed it from the look of his office. It was a big room with a window overlooking the street; the walls were painted a pleasant, restful green, and a good quality carpet covered the floor, but the place looked more like a storeroom than the office of the head of a successful company.

A drafting table covered with drawings and blueprints took up almost a quarter of the space; a six-foot high set of shelves stuffed with books and loose-leaf binders lined one wall, while more books were piled on the floor beside the desk. The desk itself was covered with papers, and the man in the rumpled shirt with sleeves pushed back was pawing through them as if searching for something. Clearly it was the office of an inventor rather than a CEO.

'Detective Chief Inspector Paget and—' Peggy began, only to be cut off by Holbrook.

'Yes, Peg, I do know who they are.' He rose and came out from behind his desk. 'At least I know the chief inspector,' he said, turning an appraising eye on Molly.

'Detective Constable Forsythe,' said Paget formally.

'Please, sit down,' he said, addressing Molly rather than her superior. He flipped an errant lock of hair away from his eyes with a practised gesture, and waved her to a chair close to his desk. Molly smiled her thanks and took out her notebook. Behind them the door closed softly as Peggy Goodwin left the room.

Holbrook returned to his own seat, and almost reluctantly, turned his attention toward Paget. 'Didn't expect to see you here so soon,' he said ungraciously. 'I don't want to appear rude, but I have a long day ahead of me, so I hope this won't take long.'

'I'll try to be brief, then,' Paget said, 'so I'll come straight to the point. We now have evidence confirming our suspicions that your wife's death was no accident, so we will be concentrating our efforts on talking to the people who were closest to your wife, both at work and outside. In addition, we'll be looking at everything Mrs Holbrook had in the way of records at home and here at work.'

Holbrook's eyes narrowed. 'Evidence?' he said sharply. 'What sort of evidence?'

'I'm afraid I'm not at liberty to share that information at the moment,' Paget told him, 'but I can tell you that there was no burglary at your house last Wednesday evening; your wife was the intended target, and whoever killed her tried to throw us off by making it appear to be the work of vandals. When we spoke before, you dismissed the idea that your wife had any enemies, but clearly that's not true, so we need to know as much as possible about events leading up to the time of her death.'

Holbrook continued to stare at Paget. He appeared to be shaken by the news. Colour had receded from his face, and his head began to move from side to side in a gesture of denial. 'I find that *very* hard to believe,' he said when he found his voice. He coughed to clear his throat. 'Very hard indeed. Are you *quite* certain of your facts?'

'Quite certain,' Paget assured him.

Holbrook drew a deep breath. 'Assuming that is the case,' he said heavily, 'I suppose I have no choice about letting you search our home, but I don't know what you expect to find here in the office.' His voice gathered strength as he went on. 'Much of that information is highly confidential, and I don't want someone from outside poking through the files for no good reason.'

'The fact that your wife was murdered is reason enough,' said Paget, 'so we have to cover every possibility. There could be emails, memos, correspondence that may or may not be work-related, and possibly a personal diary in there. Our people are professionals who have done this sort of thing many times, so I can assure you that your business will not be compromised.'

Holbrook glowered. 'I'll need to see a warrant before anyone touches anything,' he warned.

'You will,' Paget assured him.

'Is that it, then? Is that what you came to tell me?'

'I would like to confirm some of the things you told me last Saturday, particularly about your nephew,' Paget said.

A hard look came into Holbrook's eyes. 'I heard you had been to the house looking for Tim,' he said coldly, 'but you're wasting your time. Tim couldn't do a thing like that. I know him. I suppose in your eyes the very fact that he and Laura had a row the other day makes him a suspect, but I'm telling you it's ludicrous to think that he would go so far as to *kill* Laura. As I told you, if Tim was going to kill anyone, it is much more likely it would be me.'

'Perhaps not,' said Paget. 'If it had been you rather than your wife who died, she would have been the beneficiary, and by all accounts that would have left Mr Bryce out in the cold. But now that your wife is gone, I suspect that your nephew might become a beneficiary if something should happen to you, especially if you manage to patch up your differences.'

'That,' Holbrook snapped, 'is not only absurd, it is pure speculation on your part. And for your information, while it's true that the business assets would have gone to Laura, Tim would have been well provided for, and he has always known that.'

'Still, since you did side with your wife when he was sacked, he might not have been so confident that he would remain a beneficiary. However,' Paget continued before Holbrook could interject, 'as you say, it is speculation, but it is something we have to take into consideration. Tell me, did your nephew work much overtime while he was employed here? Evenings or weekends?'

Holbrook snorted. 'Tim? Overtime?' he said. 'Where did you get that idea? Of course he didn't work overtime. It pains me to say this, but the reason we had to let him go was because he seemed to think he could come and go as he pleased; he had the idea that just turning up for work was sufficient reason for him to be paid. Wherever did you get the idea that he worked overtime?'

Paget countered the question with another of his own. 'How deeply was he involved in the research and development side of your projects?'

Holbrook's eyebrows shot up. 'Look,' he said, 'I don't know where you're getting this from, but Tim was never involved in that side of the business. No doubt he thought he should be, but he was a programmer. The stuff he was working on was administrative, office management procedures, internal stuff, developing new forms and formats to meet our changing needs. With her background as a forensic accountant, Laura insisted on having records of absolutely everything, and as I think I told you the other day, Tim worked for Laura – well, strictly speaking, Peggy was his immediate boss, but it was Laura who had the final say. The trouble was, he took too many liberties and she couldn't rely on him. I thought I'd made that plain the other day.'

'You did, sir,' Paget agreed, 'but we received a rather different view of things when we spoke to Ms Craig on Saturday.'

'Sally? Ah!' Holbrook nodded slowly as he sat back in his chair. 'So that's it, is it? I should have guessed. I don't know what she's been telling you,' he said, 'but I wouldn't be too surprised to find that she thinks Tim was pretty well in here. As I said, I only met the girl once, but I got the impression then that she thought Tim had a pretty important job here, and I saw no point in disillusioning her if it made her happy to think that.'

'If you've only met your nephew's partner once, does that mean that you and Tim haven't been getting along for some time?'

Holbrook didn't answer immediately, distracted momentarily as Molly Forsythe shifted in her seat and recrossed her legs before settling down again with her notebook in her lap. His eyes lingered there for a moment, then moved on as he became aware that she was watching him. He smiled, and with the faintest of shrugs, swung back to face Paget.

'Look, Chief Inspector,' he said with an air of taking Paget into his confidence, 'I'll be honest with you. Tim and I haven't really had much to say to each other since he came out of university where he barely scraped through. He's had several jobs since then, but either left or was let go for one reason or another. As for his liaison with Sally Craig, I was led to believe that they were married, but if they were I certainly wasn't invited to the wedding, so I doubt it. Nor have I ever been invited to their home. But as I told you the other day, he is still my nephew, so when he asked me for a job I felt I should at least give him a chance, and you know how that turned out. I'll admit the boy has faults, but he is not a killer.

'So, if that's all, Chief Inspector,' he said brusquely, 'I really must get on.'

Paget remained seated. 'Just one more thing before we go,' he said. 'In your statement you said that you and Mr Ballantyne stopped for a drink at the Fox and Hounds before going across the street to see the film last Wednesday evening. You also mentioned that the landlord there is a friend of yours. Did you see him that evening? Speak to him, perhaps? I'm sure you understand that we have to check out everyone's statement, so it will simplify matters if he can confirm that you were there that night.'

The colour that had been absent returned swiftly to Holbrook's face. 'Oh, for God's sake!' he groaned. 'I've had enough of this. You have my statement, and you have Trevor's statement about where we were. Isn't that enough?'

'All I'm looking for is confirmation, Mr Holbrook. It's standard procedure, and it's a simple question: did you speak to your friend that evening?'

Holbrook eyed Paget for a long moment then shook his head. 'No,' he said at last, 'I did not speak to Bill that evening, as it happens. They were busy; there was a crowd around the bar, and we were only in there for a short time before the show. Besides, it was Trevor's turn to buy the drinks, so he's the one who went to the bar while I found a table, and we only had one drink, so you can make what you like out of that!'

'Thank you, Mr Holbrook,' Paget said as he got to his feet. 'That is all I wanted to know. There's no need to see us out, because we have arranged to talk to Miss Goodwin before we leave.'

Holbrook scowled. 'Peggy? Why do you want to talk to her?'

'For the same reason we've been talking to you and Miss Chase,' Paget told him. 'And we will keep you informed of any progress,' he concluded.

Holbrook nodded absently, his eyes on Molly as she smoothed her skirt carefully and stood up. 'You've been very quiet, Miss Forsythe,' he said lightly. 'Don't you have any questions?'

'Detective Constable, actually,' Molly corrected, matching his bantering tone, 'and I do have a question, if you don't mind?'

'Not at all,' Holbrook said expansively. His whole attitude underwent a subtle change as he came out from behind his desk to stand close to Molly. 'What's your question?'

'You said you'd heard that the police had been to Mr Bryce's house, and I wondered who told you that since you don't appear to be on regular speaking terms with your nephew or with Sally Craig?'

'Sally rang me,' he said. 'She was afraid that Tim might be arrested, and she wanted me to intervene.'

'In what way?'

'That wasn't exactly clear,' Holbrook said with a wry smile, 'but there was another reason for her call, which was to ask me – actually, to *plead* with me – to take Tim back.' In a seemingly natural gesture of courtesy, he took Molly by the elbow as he steered her toward the door. 'Unfortunately, I had to tell her I couldn't do that, which, as you might expect, did not go over well, so I very much doubt if I shall be hearing from her again.'

Thirteen

'First impressions, Constable?' Paget asked quietly as they walked the short distance to Peggy Goodwin's office.

'I didn't get any sense of grief,' she told him. 'Of course, I could be wrong; perhaps he's just very good at hiding his true feelings.'

'Not when it comes to women,' Paget said drily. 'But I suspect you deduced that for yourself.'

Peggy Goodwin met them at the office door. Clearly Holbrook had alerted her as soon as they left his office. She ushered them inside, saw them settled in their seats, then sat down to face them across her desk. Molly took out her notebook and opened it to a new page.

Peggy Goodwin's office was smaller than the one Paget and Molly had just left, but the difference was like night and day. Everything was arranged neatly and in its proper place, and apart from a solid stack of papers in both the in and out trays, and a telephone on her desk, the surface was not just clean – it was polished.

'Now,' said Peggy briskly, 'perhaps you will be good enough to tell me what this is all about, Chief Inspector. I really don't understand what I can do for you, unless, of course, it has something to do with the company.'

'Then I'll explain,' said Paget, and went on to tell her much the same as he had told Simon Holbrook, concluding with, 'So we believe that Laura Holbrook was the intended victim all along.'

The expression on Peggy Goodwin's face turned to one of concern as she absorbed the news. 'Oh, my God,' she breathed softly as Paget fell silent. 'The fact that Laura was killed was hard enough to take, but this must be devastating for poor Simon.' Her brows drew together in a puzzled frown. 'Are you *quite* sure of your . . .?' She cut herself off with an impatient wave of the hand. 'But I suppose you must be, or you wouldn't be telling me this, would you? But to be honest, Chief Inspector, I'm finding it very hard to take this in.'

Simon Holbrook seemed to attract, and be attracted to, good-looking women, thought Paget as he watched Peggy Goodwin's reaction. The late Laura Holbrook had been something of a beauty herself, according to the pictures he'd seen of her. Her sister, Susan Chase, was also very attractive, as was the other female member of the badminton team, Moira Ballantyne.

And now Peggy Goodwin. It was hard to judge her age, because there was a fullness to her features that made her look younger than she probably was. Middle thirties, perhaps?

'From what Mr Holbrook told me,' Peggy continued, 'I didn't think there was any doubt that Laura was killed by someone who broke into the house, so this comes as a complete shock. And quite frankly, I don't see how you think I can help you.'

'With background, mainly,' Paget told her. 'Now, according to the information I have, this company was on the verge of bankruptcy when Mrs Holbrook, or perhaps I should say, Mrs Southern, came in, and it was due largely to her efforts, together with a substantial investment of capital, that turned it around and made it what it is today. Would that be a fair statement, Miss Goodwin?'

'I suppose it is,' she said.

It was a grudging admission at best, thought Paget, and perhaps a glimpse into the relationship between the two women.

'We were struggling, and we were in financial trouble. We had the products and we had the expertise – Simon's work is well known throughout the industry – but once we left Drexler-Davies and struck out on our own, it became a classic example of Catch 22. Buyers were reluctant to put their business our way until they were satisfied that we were going to survive as a separate company, but we couldn't survive without their business. Our research and development costs, as well as general overheads, were escalating, but we had very little coming in. Lots of people expressed interest in what we were doing, and they were impressed with some of the pioneering work Simon has done, but they weren't buying. We needed money to stay afloat, and we needed someone with marketing and sales experience, and Laura had both.'

'But at what cost, I wonder?' Paget said. 'There must have been quite an upheaval; quite a change in direction. In effect, a total stranger was coming in to tell you how to run your company. That must have been very hard to take.'

'It was,' Peggy agreed candidly. 'We were like a family here, and there was a great deal of resentment at Laura coming in off the street, as it were, and taking over. But, like it or not, we had to face the fact that it was better than losing our jobs, and that's all in the past now.'

'What about you, personally, Miss Goodwin? I understand that you had been working very closely with Mr Holbrook until then, so how did you feel about this upheaval?'

The corners of Peggy Goodwin's mouth turned down. 'How do you think I felt, Chief Inspector?' she asked softly. 'Ask anyone around here and they will tell you how I felt. To be truthful, I was mad as hell! Which was why I handed in my resignation.'

'But you're still here. What changed your mind?'

Peggy shrugged. 'Simon talked me round, and now I'm glad he did, because it turned out to be the shot in the arm we needed. Business picked up; there was enough money available to hire more staff, and it was a real boost to morale when we moved from our old quarters into this building, and for the first time in years I was no longer working sixteen hours a day.'

'Even so, it must have been very hard to go from being in charge to taking orders from a newcomer,' said Paget sympathetically.

Peggy smiled wryly. 'Oohhhh, yes,' she said with feeling. 'And what was *really* hard to accept was that, because I had been the one running the administrative side of the business, it fell to me to bring Laura up to speed. Simon took on the task of teaching her what she needed to know about his side of the business, but as for the rest of it, that was left up to me, and you're quite right, I wasn't very happy about having to do that. But, to give him his due, Simon recognized how difficult it had made things for me, so he took some of the sting out of it by raising my salary. That didn't sit well with Laura, who said the firm couldn't afford it, but Simon held firm on that one, and even Laura had to admit she needed me.'

'And all this took place two-and-a-half to three years ago?'

'That's right.'

'What about the rest of the staff? How did it affect them?'

'People grumbled, of course, because Laura completely changed a lot of the things we'd been doing for years, but that's always the response to change in the workplace, and it didn't last long.'

'How would you summarize your own relationship with Mrs Holbrook in recent times?' Paget asked.

Peggy smiled. 'Businesslike,' Peggy said crisply. 'We respected each other, but that was it. You have to understand, Laura kept everyone at arm's length; everything was business with her, and to give her her due, she was good at her job, but as for friends . . .?' She shook her head. 'She knew a lot of people, but I'm not sure she had any real friends.'

'Can you tell me where you were last Wednesday evening, Miss Goodwin?'

'Wednesday? The night Laura was . . .? You're serious, aren't you?' Peggy drew a long breath and looked off into the distance. 'I was at home that night,' she said. 'At least most of the time. I did go out briefly about eight, I think it was. There's a corner shop that stays open until nine, and I went down there to pick up one or two things for the morning. Bran flakes, orange juice, things like that. I don't know if Mr Lee will remember me or not, but you can ask him. He knows who I am, because I've been going in there for years.'

'And where do you live?'

'I have a flat in Caledonia Street.'

'Would there be anyone else who could verify that you were there that evening?'

A flicker of irritation crossed Peggy's pleasant features. 'I'm afraid not,' she said. 'I live alone.'

'What about phone calls?' Paget asked. 'Did you make or receive any that night?'

'I didn't make any, but I did receive one from Simon. He phoned to tell me that Laura had one of her migraines and wouldn't be in next morning. He said she had a meeting with a client next morning, and he asked me to call first thing and let the client know she wouldn't be able to make it.'

'Do you remember what time that was?' asked Paget.

'Seven – seven-thirty, perhaps. I don't remember exactly, but it was around that time.'

'Did he happen to say where he was calling from?'

'Not exactly. He said that he and Trevor Ballantyne, a friend of his, were on their way to see a film. He's a bit of a film buff,' she confided, 'especially sci-fi stuff.'

'Why would he call you then?' asked Paget. 'Couldn't he have told you that in the morning?'

'He could,' Peggy agreed, 'but Simon is like that. If he happens to think of something that needs to be done, he just picks up the phone and calls.'

'We'll try not to keep you too much longer,' Paget told her as he saw her glance surreptitiously at her watch, 'but I would like to know what will happen here now that Mrs Holbrook is gone? And what this will do to your own position?'

'It will be difficult, as I'm sure you can imagine,' she said. 'In fact, I can see myself working those sixteen-hour days again for some time to come. Laura was our prime interface with clients, so we're going to have to find someone to take her place, and that will not be easy. I only hope we don't start losing ground again.'

'Just one more thing then, before we leave,' said Paget. 'What can you tell me about the dismissal of Mr Holbrook's nephew, Tim Bryce? He worked for you, I believe?'

'That's right — at least he was supposed to, but he was a problem from day one. Simon wanted him in the firm, but Laura didn't. She had met Tim several times before he came to work here, and she was not impressed with him at all. I've known Tim for several years myself, and in this case I agreed with Laura. I couldn't see him fitting in here, but Simon insisted, and he is the boss.

'But Tim took advantage of their relationship. He could twist Simon around his little finger. There's no denying that Tim can be a charmer when he wants something, but to put it bluntly, he's a slacker, and there is no room here for slackers.

'We tried to make it work for Simon's sake. Laura and I did our best to sort him out, but we were wasting our time. Tim was warned numerous times about his unexplained absences, sloppiness in his work, and his general attitude, but nothing changed. Tim thought he was fire-proof. He thought all he had to do was run to his uncle and Laura would be overruled, so when Laura had me dock him three days' pay, Tim went mad. He went charging into her office and they really had a set-to. I could hear it all in here — Laura's office is the one between mine and Simon's — and when she told Tim he was finished here, he really lost it. He said something to the effect that she might be Simon's wife, but she would soon find out which one of them would be leaving, then went storming off to find Simon.'

Peggy looked at each of them in turn as if to make sure she had their attention. 'But even Simon can be pushed only so far,' she said with something like satisfaction, 'and Tim must have got the shock of his life when Simon told him he agreed with Laura, and held firm.'

A deep-throated rumbling sound and a sudden rush of cold air from overhead made them all look up. Peggy rolled her chair away from her desk, and tissues appeared in her hand as if by magic. She sneezed three times in rapid succession; her eyes watered and she sneezed again. She held her breath, then gradually relaxed and dabbed cautiously at her nose.

'Sorry about that,' she apologized as she took another tissue from her sleeve and wiped her eyes. 'Allergies,' she added by way of explanation, pointing to a vent in the ceiling. 'Our air-conditioner is being overhauled, and they keep turning it on and off. The trouble is, they've had to take the filters out, and this being March, all the moulds and pollens are in the air.'

She dabbed at her nose again. 'The work was supposed to have been done six weeks ago,' she continued, clearly annoyed, 'but you know what some of these people are like in this town. It's just one more thing that we *don't* need right now.' Peggy rolled her chair back to her desk and dropped the tissues into a waste-paper basket, then took a couple more from a box in a drawer and tucked them in her sleeve.

'And we're not making things any better, are we?' Paget said as he got to his feet. 'But we do appreciate your help, Miss Goodwin.'

'Just one question, Chief Inspector,' Peggy said as she came out from behind her desk. 'Is Tim a suspect? I mean seriously?'

'We have to consider every possibility,' Paget said ambiguously. 'Why do you ask?'

'It's just that – well, I can't deny that he and Laura didn't get on, but I didn't mean to suggest that things had gone *that* far. Honestly, I can't see Tim as a murderer, so I hope you will bear that in mind.'

Peggy followed Paget and Molly into the corridor, shepherding them along as if to make sure they didn't stray on their way out. 'Tell me,' Paget said as they went along, 'if someone is working overtime or comes in after hours, is there a record of that?'

'Absolutely,' said Peggy. 'We have tight security here. Everyone must sign in and out, and everything is recorded on security cameras.'

'So no one has their own key, for example?'

'Certainly not.'

'Did Timothy Bryce work overtime?'

'Tim?' Peggy turned to look at Paget to see if he were joking. 'We couldn't get him to do a decent day's work when he was here, let alone overtime. That's why he was sacked.'

'So we wouldn't find a record of him coming in after hours, then?'

Peggy all but snorted with derision. 'You certainly would not,' she said. 'I check those records myself, and I would have been astonished

– and suspicious – if I'd seen Tim's name on there. Whatever made you think that Tim worked overtime?'

'Just something someone said,' Paget said vaguely. 'And thank you once again. There's no need to take up any more of your time; we can find our own way out.'

But Peggy Goodwin stayed with them, and made sure she retrieved their Visitor tags when they reached the reception area, where Paget paused to ask one more question. 'You mentioned the security system. Is it the system designed and installed by the Ballantynes?'

'That's right. Why do you ask?'

'Just curious, that's all,' Paget told her.

'Well, Constable?' said Paget as they left the building and made their way to the car. 'Any thoughts?'

'Quite a few,' Molly told him. 'But it may take some time for me to sort them out.'

'Any more thoughts about Holbrook himself? My own impression was that he took quite a fancy to you.'

'It was a bit obvious, wasn't it, sir? I've been thinking about that, and I don't think he can help it. I think he's one of those men who react automatically whenever a woman appears on the scene. He certainly fancies himself, but then, he is quite an attractive man. I think he *expects* women to be attracted to him, because he has that little-boy-lost air about him that appeals to some of them even if he is almost past his sell-by date.'

'But not your type, I take it?' Paget said as he unlocked the door of the car.

'Oh, I don't know,' Molly said thoughtfully as she settled into the passenger's seat and buckled up. 'It would depend.'

'Oh?' Paget turned to look at her. 'On what, Constable?'

'Circumstances,' Molly said evasively. 'It's a bit hard to explain, you not being a woman. What did you think of Miss Goodwin?'

Paget wasn't quite sure whether Molly Forsythe was pulling his leg or not, and perhaps wisely decided not to pursue the matter until he felt more sure of his ground. 'I can't make up my mind about her,' he said. 'She strikes me as a very intelligent woman, probably very dedicated and loyal to Simon Holbrook. What do you think?"

'I think you're right there, sir,' she said. 'They've been together a long time so I wouldn't be at all surprised if there is or has been, shall we say, a close personal relationship between them. In fact, I don't think

Simon Holbrook could work with someone as attractive as Peggy Goodwin without trying it on. On the one hand he did *marry* Laura, but on the other hand I doubt if that would stop him from playing away from home if he got the chance.'

Returning to Charter Lane, Paget and Molly were about to enter the building when they met Tregalles on his way out. 'Just on my way to lunch at the Crown,' he said with a nod in the direction of the pub across the road. 'They've got salmon steaks on today, and Audrey keeps on at me to eat more fish, so I thought I'd give it a try. Like to come? They've got other things as well. Steak and mushroom pie, scampi, and there's always a ploughman's. And you could fill me in on how you got on with Holbrook while we're there.'

Paget looked at his watch. He was hungry, and it would be nice to have a change from the bag-lunch that awaited him in his office. 'Why not?' he said. 'It's been a while since I had salmon.'

'My lunch is in the fridge,' said Molly diplomatically, 'so I'd better get inside before someone nicks it if they think it might be better than theirs. You can't trust anyone these days. Will you be needing me again this afternoon, sir?'

Paget shook his head. 'Not this afternoon,' he told her, 'but I would like those notes transcribed, with a copy for Sergeant Ormside and Sergeant Tregalles.'

'Right, sir. I should have them done by three, if that's all right?'

'Very good,' Paget said, 'and thank you for your comments on the interviews this morning,' he added with a smile.

'Hope you found them useful, sir,' Molly said. She didn't actually grin, but there was a sparkle to her eyes as she ran up the steps and entered the building.

Tregalles, who had been following the exchange closely, said, 'Good morning, was it, boss?'

'Productive, I think,' said Paget cautiously. 'At least we gained an insight into the sort of person Laura Holbrook was as well as Simon Holbrook himself.' He fell into step with Tregalles as they made their way across the road. 'How about you, Tregalles?'

'I was beginning to wonder if Bryce had done a runner,' the sergeant said, 'and I wasn't expecting much when I got hold of his mobile number and left a message for him. But he rang me back within half an hour. Said he was in Telford looking for a job. He said he hadn't come in or called us because he'd had this job interview set up since last week, and didn't want to miss it, but promised to come in tomorrow.'

'You're sure he was in Telford?'

'Oh, yes,' Tregalles said. 'He was there all right. I had him go to the Victoria Road cop shop and ring me from there.'

The conversation lapsed while they stood in the short line-up waiting to place their orders, but once seated at a table with their drinks in front of them, Tregalles couldn't contain his curiosity any longer. 'Molly helpful this morning, was she?' he asked tentatively.

Paget nodded. 'Oh, yes, very helpful in fact,' Paget told him as he picked up his drink. 'Ah! Good! Here comes our lunch.'

Molly Forsythe delivered the transcript of her notes a few minutes before three that afternoon. Fourteen pages, printer perfect. But then, that was one of the advantages of having Molly taking notes; she took them down verbatim in shorthand.

Paget took the time to read them through, pausing every now and then to think about the answers he'd received. He was puzzled by Simon Holbrook's attitude. Apart from that first night immediately following the discovery of Laura Holbrook's body, Holbrook had shown almost no signs of grief. Anger, yes, annoyance, irritation, impatience, yes, but not grief. True, people reacted to tragedy in different ways, but Holbrook's behaviour still seemed odd to Paget. Forsythe had commented on it as well.

He picked up his copies of the rest of the statements and thumbed through them. Moira Ballantyne hadn't been in yet, he noted, but it triggered another thought. He picked up the phone and called Tregalles's number.

'Got another job for you,' he said when the sergeant answered. 'Have you ever played badminton?'

Fourteen

'Timothy Bryce will be in at ten this morning,' Tregalles said as he sat down in Paget's office. 'I'm assuming you want to talk to the man yourself?'

'I do, indeed,' said Paget. 'So, how did you get on last night?'

Tregalles looked pleased with himself as he opened his notebook. He had spent much of the previous evening talking to members of the badminton club, and some of their comments had been most enlightening.

'I never thought of badminton as much of a sport before,' he said with a grin, 'but after watching them play last night I think there might be something to it. All those women leaping about in their frilly little skirts. Mind you, there are some who shouldn't be wearing . . .'

He caught the look in Paget's eye and decided he'd better come to the point.

'I talked to Bernard Fiske. He's the chairperson of the club. He was quite cagey at first, but he became quite chatty over a beer – that's another thing about the club, they have a bar. For one thing, Simon Holbrook has quite a reputation as a womanizer, which didn't surprise me, although Fiske said he seemed to have settled down – at least for a time – following his marriage last year to Laura. When I asked him what he meant by "at least for a time", he said there'd been quite a bit of bickering between them in recent months, and he had wondered how long the marriage would hold up.

'But Fiske said it didn't stop them from coming. The four of them continued to play together, and Moira was usually there as well, but he said you could tell there was an undercurrent there.'

Tregalles flipped a page in his notebook. 'So I stuck around for a while and spoke to some of the players,' he said. 'Most of them were pretty cagey; some wouldn't talk to me at all, but there was one woman who was more than willing to talk: a Mrs Jordan, a widow in her mid-forties or thereabouts, and not bad-looking either. She said that she'd heard Laura Holbrook and Moira Ballantyne "exchange words", as she put it, the night before Laura Holbrook was murdered.'

'Did she say what it was about?' asked Paget.

'She *thought* Mrs Holbrook was warning Moira off, telling her to stay away from her husband, but when I tried to pin her down – figuratively speaking, of course, boss – she said she couldn't hear properly because they were in the changing room and people were opening and closing the doors on the metal lockers, which made it difficult to hear.'

'Not that she wasn't trying, of course,' Paget observed drily. 'Any chance that she's making the whole thing up to gain attention?'

'I think there might have been a bit of jealousy there,' Tregalles conceded, 'so I'd be inclined to treat what she told me with a certain amount of caution, but I don't think she was making it up.' A sly smile crept across his face. 'But she did make a point of telling me twice that she was a widow, and it was really hard to get used to living without a man about the house.'

Paget raised an eyebrow. 'Did she, now?' he said. 'Did she say anything else of interest? About the case, I mean,' he emphasized.

Tregalles nodded. 'Yes, she did. She claims that Simon Holbrook and Moira Ballantyne had something going a year or so ago, and that was after Laura had come on the scene and things were going hot and heavy between her and Holbrook. She said it didn't last long, but everyone in the club knew about it, except Laura and Moira's husband, Trevor. She said she and some of her friends were surprised that he'd taken up with Moira, because they had always thought that if Holbrook did settle down, it would be with Susan Chase. But then Laura came along and all bets were off.'

'It's a wonder this woman has any time left to play badminton, what with listening to all the gossip,' Paget observed. 'Still, if it weren't for people like her, we would never learn half the things we do. Anything else?'

Tregalles shook his head as he folded his notebook and slipped it into his pocket.

Paget eyed the sergeant thoughtfully. 'You know,' he said, 'if this Mrs Jordan is right, and everyone in the club knew what was going on between Moira Ballantyne and Holbrook, I'm willing to bet money that Trevor Ballantyne and Laura knew as well. And the question that comes to mind, is: why didn't they say or do anything about it? Or did they behind the scenes?'

'Don't know,' Tregalles admitted, 'but I don't see how it would have a bearing on what happened to Laura Holbrook. I could see Trevor killing Holbrook or Moira if he thought the affair had started up again, but he would have no reason to kill Laura.'

'True,' said Paget thoughtfully, 'but *Moira* Ballantyne might.'

If Paget had been asked to form an image of Timothy Bryce in his mind, based on what he'd been told, it wouldn't have come within a country mile of the man now facing him across the table.

With his mop of tousled hair, wide-set eyes and overly generous mouth, Bryce looked younger than his almost twenty-seven years, and whether deliberate or not, the illusion was strengthened by the clothes he wore. The faded jeans, denim jacket with metal fasteners, soft leather boots, and even the diamond stud in the lobe of his left ear reminded Paget of the university campuses where such attire had been almost mandatory a few years ago for students and the younger members of the staff.

Bryce was a tall lad . . . Paget mentally stopped himself. He was doing the very same thing he had questioned in others, and suddenly realized why everyone seemed to refer to Bryce as if he were a boy. He *looked* like a boy, tall, thin and gangly, all knees and elbows as he sat slumped in the chair, and there was an air of bewildered innocence, almost shyness, in the way he looked from one to the other of the two men. He didn't look anything like his uncle, but there was a marked similarity in the way they presented themselves to the world, and Paget found himself wondering if it had something to do with the genes or if it was something he'd learned from his uncle.

Timothy Bryce had big hands; strong hands. They were at rest now, clasped together loosely on the table in front of him. Could they be the hands that had held the metal bar used to smash Laura Holbrook's face to a bloody pulp?

With the recorder in motion and the formalities disposed with, Tregalles settled himself at the end of the table rather like an umpire on the centre line as Paget said, 'Now, Mr Bryce, I'd like you to tell me in your own words about what took place between you and Mrs Holbrook a week ago last Friday, when you accosted her in the car park. We've heard a couple of versions, but I would like to hear what you have to say about it.'

Bryce shifted nervously in his seat, and the lines around his mouth tightened. 'To tell you the truth,' he said sheepishly, 'I'm a bit ashamed about that,' he said. 'I'd been out all day looking for a job, and I wasn't having any luck. I didn't want to go back home to Sally and say I'd failed again, so I stopped in to have a couple of drinks. Unfortunately, I didn't stop at a couple, and suddenly it seemed like a good idea to tell Laura exactly what I thought of her.'

He shrugged helplessly. 'So that's what I did,' he concluded. 'I know it's a bit late to say I'm sorry—'

'I might believe you if that was the only time,' Paget broke in, 'but it wasn't, was it? We're told you went berserk when you were docked pay; that you had a screaming match with Laura Holbrook in her office, and you confronted and threatened her on at least one other occasion since then. Late? Yes, I'd say it's a bit late, Mr Bryce.'

'That's not true,' Bryce said heatedly. 'I'll admit I was upset when she sacked me for no reason, and I have tried to talk to her since then, but she wouldn't listen to anything I had to say. And I never actually threatened her.'

'She told others that you did. She said you suggested that it would be a shame if her car went up like a bomb. You don't call that a threat?'

'Well, she would say that, wouldn't she?' Bryce countered. 'But the truth is she wanted to be rid of me from the start. It had nothing to do with my work.'

'What did it have to do with, then? Why do *you* think you were let go?'

Bryce shrugged. 'I think it's pretty obvious,' he said. 'She didn't want me around to see what she was up to. She set out to drive a wedge between me and my uncle from the very beginning, and she succeeded. Laura didn't want me working for the firm at all, and she tried very hard to keep me out when Simon insisted on hiring me. He managed to overrule her on that, but she made sure that I was given nothing but Mickey Mouse jobs that a first year programmer could do with one hand behind his back. It was insulting, and when I objected, she went running to Simon to say I wasn't up to the job. I'll admit I left the office a few times when I was supposed to be there, but I couldn't just sit around twiddling my thumbs because I had nothing else to do until she came up with some other menial task. She used that and a few other things to stick the knife in whenever she got the chance until she finally won Simon over.'

'And what, in your opinion, was Mrs Holbrook "up to", as you put it?' asked Paget.

'She was after the firm. She wanted control. The woman was a control freak; ask anyone who works there. She simply walked in and took over, and Simon let her. She bought her way in at a time when he was on the ropes financially. I grant you she was instrumental in turning the firm around, but it was only because it was a means to an end. She wanted it all. Simon couldn't see it, but that was what she was after. That's why she married him. She didn't love Simon, but he was besotted with her and let her walk all over him.'

'But you saw through all that,' said Paget.

'Yes, I did, and I tried to warn my uncle, but he wouldn't listen.'

'In fact he backed up his wife's decision when she sacked you, so you decided to take matters into your own hands. Isn't that right?'

Bryce shook his head wearily. 'Look,' he said, 'I've been straight with you. I admit I had every reason to hate Laura, but I had nothing to do with her death. Sally didn't want me to come here today; she said you'd already made up your minds that I killed Laura. But I chose to come in and answer your questions as honestly as I can, because I am innocent.'

Paget sat back in his chair and folded his arms, and it was Tregalles who put the next question. 'Sally Craig tells us you were out last Wednesday evening. Where were you around nine o'clock that night?'

'Yes, she told me,' he said. 'I was out jogging. I find it relieves the stress. I usually do between six and eight miles; sometimes more, sometimes less. Depends on the weather and where the mood takes me.'

'And where did the mood take you that night?'

'I have a couple of regular circuits,' said Bryce. 'On that particular night, I went down the road to King George Way, across the bridge and out along Velacourt, along the old towpath where the canal used to be before they filled it in – you know, where it runs beside the main road for about a mile – then came out at the bottom of Strathe Hill, across the fields from Woodbourne Road, over the footbridge to Barnfield, then home.'

'We have a report of someone jogging not far from your uncle's house around nine that night,' Tregalles said. 'Are you quite sure you didn't go south down Lower Bridge Street or along Riverview Road, or possibly into Pembroke Avenue?'

'Quite sure.'

'What were you wearing?'

'A tracksuit.'

'Colour?'

Bryce looked puzzled, but he answered readily enough. 'Dark blue with flashes on it to make it visible in the dark.'

'So you left the house around seven. How long were you out?'

'A couple of hours, give or take.'

'Which would bring you home at around nine? Is that what you're saying, Mr Bryce?'

'That's right.'

'Was the television on when you went in?'

Bryce looked puzzled, but he nodded. 'I think so. It usually is.'

'What was on?'

'Oh, for God's sake! How should I know? I had a shower as soon as I came in. I didn't hang about watching TV.'

'Sally Craig tells us she was watching the ten o'clock news when you came in.'

Bryce shook his head vigorously. 'No, that can't be right; she's got it wrong,' he insisted. 'It must have been the nine o'clock.'

'All right,' Paget said, taking over from his sergeant, 'give us something that proves you right. Was anyone with you while you say you were jogging?'

'No,' said Bryce irritably. 'I don't like company when I'm jogging. I like to go at my own pace.'

'Did you meet anyone along the way? Anyone who could verify where you were at a given time?'

Bryce grimaced. 'Not really,' he said. 'I mean I passed a lot of people, but whether they would remember me or not, I have no idea.'

'Did you stop anywhere? As I recall, there are a couple of pubs along that route, and the supermarket on Barnfield stays open late.'

Bryce shook his head. 'Sorry, Chief Inspector, I'd like to be of more help, but that's all I can tell you.'

Paget's expression expressed his disbelief, but he said, 'All right, let's assume for a moment that you are telling the truth. Sally Craig told us that, prior to your dismissal, you spent a lot of time at work after regular hours. Overtime for which you haven't been paid. Is that correct?'

Bryce waved his hands and shrugged in a self-deprecating way. 'It goes with the job,' he said modestly. 'You know how it is, Chief Inspector? You can't always be governed by the clock when there are problems to be solved.'

'And were there a lot of problems that needed to be solved in your — what was it you called them? — Mickey Mouse jobs, Mr Bryce?'

A flush came to Bryce's face. 'It's quieter there at night,' he said. 'And no one was there to disturb me.'

Paget's voice hardened as he leaned forward across the table. 'I have better things to do with my time than listen to a pack of lies from you, Mr Bryce,' he said scathingly, 'so the sooner you get it through your head that this isn't some sort of game, the better. Now, where were you on the nights you told your partner you were at work?'

Colour rose in Bryce's neck. 'I don't know what . . .' he began, but Paget brushed the words aside.

'You've been lying through your teeth, haven't you, Mr Bryce? You've been telling your partner a pack of lies about where you go. And now you're trying to do the same with us. You've never worked an hour of overtime for your uncle's firm in your life, so where did you go on those nights, Mr Bryce? And what's your excuse since you lost your job? Out looking for a job, is it? That's what Sally Craig seems to believe. Or does she? I wonder. So where do you go, Mr Bryce?'

'That,' said Bryce sullenly, 'is none of your business. It has nothing to do with what you're after. Nothing to do with Laura or who killed her.'

'In that case, there's no harm in telling us, is there? And what about this obsession with jogging? How do you expect us to believe you were where you say you were if we know you've been lying to us about working overtime?'

'But I do jog. I really do,' Bryce said earnestly.

Tregalles shook his head. 'Since when does it take a dedicated jogger like you three hours to cover six to eight miles?' he asked scornfully. 'I could do better than that on my hands and knees. Perhaps we should get Ms Craig down here,' he suggested, looking at Paget. 'I'm sure she would be interested in the explanation.'

'No!' Timothy Bryce closed his eyes and drew a deep breath. 'Look,' he said, 'if I tell you where I was when I told Sally I was working, do I have your word that you will not tell her?'

Paget shook his head. 'We are not interested in what goes on in your private life *if* it has nothing to do with the matter at hand, but we do not make promises. And if we have reason to believe that you are lying to us, we will talk to anyone and everyone who may be able to help us. Do I make myself clear?'

Bryce slumped back in his chair. He looked up at the ceiling, and blew out his cheeks. 'She'll kill me,' he groaned. 'I mean it! She'll bloody kill me.'

'Your partner?' asked Paget.

Bryce grimaced as he shook his head. 'She would as well, if she ever finds out,' he muttered more to himself than to Paget. 'No, I mean – do I have to give you a name? I mean I'm not going to lie about it, but if you could just sort of . . .' Timothy Bryce sighed as he saw the look on the chief inspector's face, and took a deep breath. 'Her name is Lenore, Lenore Lattimer. Her husband works for the company. He's a security guard. Bill Lattimer. He's older than she is. He works evening shift most of the time. That's when I see her.'

'Her husband works as a security guard at the same place you do – or did?'

Bryce nodded. 'That's right. I suppose you'll have to talk to her?'

'Yes, we will have to talk to her,' Tregalles told him flatly. 'Address, please.' He sat there with pen poised over his notebook.

'Nineteen Grandview Gardens. Could you wait till the evening before you talk to her?' he asked hopefully. 'And let me phone her first just to let her know – I mean I would like to warn her. It will come as a bit of a shock if two policemen walk in and start asking about, well, you know.'

'No phone call,' said Paget firmly. He eyed Bryce narrowly for several seconds before asking, 'Does this have anything to do with why you were sacked?'

Bryce looked horrified. 'Good God, no!' he breathed. 'Jesus! If my uncle ever hears about this he'll go up the wall, even though the randy old sod's been doing the same sort of thing himself for at least as long as I've been close to him, and probably a lot longer than that. I've never seen anyone like him for pulling birds. But Bill Lattimer is a friend of his, so he'd *really* let me have it if he found out I was bonking Lattimer's wife.'

'Let me understand this,' said Tregalles heavily. 'You are out there every other night, screwing this man's wife while he's at work? You're unemployed; your partner is supporting you *and* looking after a baby, yet you go out night after night and leave her stuck at home worrying herself silly about how she's going to manage?'

Timothy Bryce seemed to shrink before the sergeant's malevolent glare. 'I didn't mean it to turn out like that,' he said sulkily. 'It just sort of happened. Lenore was lonely, left all by herself night after night,' he protested. 'He's pushing fifty, and she's only thirty three or four, and she needed . . .'

'A toy boy?' Tregalles broke in. 'Oh, yes, very understandable,' he said derisively as he wrote something in his book. 'At least Sally has the baby to keep her company. Yours, is he?'

'Of course he's mine. And I *have* been out looking for a job. I have been trying.'

'Have you now? Very commendable, I'm sure. How long have you known this Lenore?'

'We met at the Christmas party. We danced together and she came on to me. We'd both had a bit to drink, and we ended up in one of the offices. You know how it is, Sergeant? I mean it happens, doesn't it?'

'Obviously. Now, let's get back to Wednesday, the fourth of March. Are you saying that this Lenore Lattimer will verify that you were with her that evening?'

Bryce looked startled. 'Wednesday, *the fourth?*' he repeated, hoarsely. 'I thought . . .' He tilted his head back, covered his face with his hands and said, 'Oohh shit!'

Tregalles exchanged glances with Paget. 'Mr Bryce, I am asking you if Lenore Lattimer will confirm that you were . . .' He stopped. Bryce, face still covered with his hands, was shaking his head violently. 'Mr Bryce?'

Slowly, Bryce lowered his hands. 'I made a mistake,' he said in a voice so low that Paget asked him to repeat it. 'I made a mistake,' he said more clearly. 'In the date. I was confused; I thought we were talking about . . .' He lifted his hands in a helpless fashion and let them drop as he shook his head and said, 'Oh, never mind; it doesn't matter now.'

'Are you saying you were *not* with Mrs Lattimer that night?' Tregalles prompted.

Bryce nodded slowly.

'But you were out of the house?'

'Yes.'

'Jogging?' Tregalles asked sceptically.

'Yes. Well, not exactly.'

'Which is it, Mr Bryce? Yes or not exactly? I'm waiting for an explanation and I haven't got all day. Do you have a dog?'

'A *dog?*' Bryce stared at the sergeant as if he couldn't believe what he was hearing.

'That's what I said. Do you or don't you have a dog? It's a simple enough question.'

'No – well, yes, we did until last week, but it's not our dog. It belongs to Sally's parents. Sally agreed to look after it while they were away.

We don't have it now. But I don't understand this. What the hell has a dog got to do with anything?'

'It could have everything to do with whether you will be charged or not,' Tregalles said as he turned to Paget. 'I'd say we are back where we started, sir. Mr Bryce was out jogging – or not, as the case may be – and we have a report of a jogger in the next street to Pembroke Avenue about the time of the murder. Dark tracksuit – could very well have been Mr Bryce, don't you think, sir? I think that warrants a search of the house for a start.'

'And three hours unaccounted for,' said Paget. 'So, in the face of the evidence, and since you can't account for your movements that night, I'm afraid we're going to have to hold you on suspicion of—'

'Jesus Christ, man, you can't be serious?' Bryce burst out. 'I've been telling you the truth! I made a mistake, that's all. About the date. Look,' he said desperately, 'what If I *do* have an alibi? Can we at least keep all this from coming out?' His voice dropped to an urgent whisper. 'I don't want Sally to know. I love her, I really do. It's just . . .'

Paget eyed him stonily. 'If you have something to say, Mr Bryce, then say it,' he said, 'and stop wasting our time. And you had better get it right the first time, because if you don't, there is every chance that you will go down for the murder of Laura Holbrook.'

Although the tape was still running, Tregalles opened his notebook again. 'All right, Bryce,' he sighed as if already weary of the subject, 'this is your last chance. Where were you between the hours of seven and ten in the evening on the night Mrs Holbrook was killed? And don't mess me about this time.'

Timothy Bryce's eyes flicked from one to the other but both faces were impassive. 'Look,' he said again, 'it's not really the way it looks. Honestly. I was with a girl I know. We were at uni together; we shared digs there for a while, and now she's living here in town. Her name is Hilde DeGraff. She works in the municipal offices, and she has a flat two streets over from where I live. It was a spur of the moment thing. I started out to go jogging that night, but when I realized I was passing her door, I thought I'd just drop in to see how she was doing, and we stayed chatting for most of the evening. I didn't tell Sally because I didn't think she would understand.'

'I wonder why?' Tregalles muttered, shaking his head. 'Let's have it, then – the address of this Hilde DeGraff.'

Fifteen

Paget had just settled to the task of finishing off his daily progress report when Ormside called from downstairs to report that Bryce's prints had been taken. 'We don't have enough hard evidence to apply for a search warrant,' he said, 'but I made a deal with him. He's agreed to turn over the tracksuit and anything else he was wearing last Wednesday night, as long as we don't mention where he was to Sally Craig. We'll also be looking for dog hair, and anything else that Forensic might find interesting. As for the DeGraff woman, she's at work today, so I thought it might be best to wait till after work to talk to her.'

'Agreed,' said Paget, 'but make sure that Bryce understands that he'll be in serious trouble if he attempts to talk to her before we've had a chance to talk to her ourselves. And have Forsythe do that. DeGraff might be a little more forthcoming to another woman. Anything else?'

'Couple of things,' Ormside said. 'Just received a fax saying that Mrs Holbrook's body can be released for burial.'

'Better let Mr Holbrook know, then,' Paget told him. 'And find out when the interment will take place and let me know. What's the other thing?'

'It seems that Mrs Ballantyne forgot to mention a couple of things when you spoke to her on Saturday. The prints we took from her yesterday – once she eventually turned up – match some they found in the Holbrook house. They were on the banister, on the bedside lamp, the telephone, and the bedroom window sill. Could be the break we're looking for, especially since we now know that something may have been going on between her and Holbrook.'

The information was sobering. It was hard to imagine the diminutive Moira Ballantyne beating another woman to death, but stranger things had happened. 'Have Tregalles bring her in,' he said. 'Better send a policewoman with him just in case Mrs Ballantyne doesn't want to talk to us and he has to arrest her. And let me know when she arrives. I'd like to talk to her myself.'

*　　*　　*

Moira Ballantyne was trying hard to look composed as she watched Tregalles set up the tape recorder, but she couldn't conceal her apprehension completely.

She was a small woman, fine-boned and dainty. Her blonde hair was cropped and combed straight back with just the hint of a wave in the boyish cut. But there was nothing boyish about the perfect oval of her face, unblemished skin, full lips, and hazel eyes. Nor could the straight-cut two-piece suit in a heather tweed, and snow-white blouse with just a touch of lace at the neck, conceal the trim figure and slender legs. And, despite the weather, fashionable, open-toed shoes completed the ensemble, adding inches to her height.

She was an attractive woman, and whether or not it was true that she and Holbrook were having an affair, or had had one in the past, Paget could see how gossip at the club might link the two together.

Tregalles set the recorder in motion and entered the time, date, location, and those present, including the name of the policewoman who sat just inside the door.

Paget began by thanking Moira for coming in – not that she'd had much choice in the matter – to help them clear up one or two things that seemed to be, as he put it, 'at variance' with what she had told them a few days ago. Their eyes met across the table, and Paget sensed a flicker of fear before Moira looked away.

'It's the fingerprints, isn't it?' she said before he had a chance to ask a question. She shook her head sadly. 'I knew I should have told you the truth the other day, but I was afraid you wouldn't believe me if I did. I didn't have anything to do with Laura's death; you have to believe me about that, and I was hoping . . .' She spread her hands and shook her head again.

'Hoping we wouldn't find your prints at the scene?' Paget finished for her. 'But you were there, in the room, weren't you, Mrs Ballantyne?'

She nodded. 'It was the light in the window, you see,' she said in a low voice. 'That's what made me decide to go in. I had no idea . . .'

'Let's begin at the beginning,' Paget suggested. 'You told us the other day that you were at home all evening on March fourth, the evening Mrs Holbrook was murdered. I take it you are now saying that was not true?'

Moira nodded. 'I went out to post—'

'Please answer yes or no for the tape, Mrs Ballantyne,' Tregalles broke in.

'Oh! Oh, yes, of course. Yes. I mean I did go out that night to post a letter to my mother. The letterbox is at the top of the street. I didn't notice a light in Laura's bedroom window on the way up there, but I did on the way back, and that surprised me, because she hates any sort of light when she has a migraine. So I went in.'

'What time was this?'

'Quarter past nine, nine thirty, something like that. I don't remember exactly.'

'You say you went in. How did you get in? Was the door unlocked?'

'No. I have a key. I keep it on my key ring because I look after the plants and things when they're both away.'

'So you went in. Tell us what you did then.'

'I went up the stairs. I didn't call out or anything just in case she was asleep. I thought perhaps her migraine had cleared up and she'd turned the light on, then fallen asleep again.'

'You went into the bedroom,' Paget prompted. 'What did you see?'

Moira chewed on her lip and drew a deep breath before answering. 'At first, I thought she had fallen out of bed. I really did. The sheets were pulled half off the bed, and although I couldn't see the lamp itself, I could see the light shining from the floor, so I thought – I don't know what I thought, really, except that something had happened to Laura. I think I called out. I went around the end of the bed, and that's when I saw the blood . . .' The words died in Moira's throat. She swallowed hard and took a deep, shuddering breath, then sat back and looked at Paget and shook her head.

'How was she lying?' he asked quietly. 'Was she lying on her back, her side . . .?'

Moira looked up at the ceiling and took another long breath before she answered. 'Sort of on her side but face down,' she said. 'The lamp was on the floor beside her. It was tipped over on its side, but still on. I tried to turn her over, but the lamp was in the way, so I picked it up and set it on the little table beside the bed. It's funny, Laura wasn't very big, but she seemed to be so heavy. Down on my knees like that I couldn't seem to get a good grip on her, and – this probably sounds silly now – I didn't want to hurt her. Then, quite suddenly, she rolled over and I saw her face.'

Moira's face was pale, her breathing shallow. Paget poured a glass of water and handed it to her. She sipped it slowly at first, then deeply, gulping the liquid down until she'd almost emptied the glass.

Paget gave her a minute to recover before asking what she had done next.

Moira looked down at her hands. 'I didn't know what to do. I was in shock. I'd never seen anything so brutal in my life before. I knew it was no good calling a doctor or an ambulance. There was no doubt whatsoever that Laura was dead, and the only thing I could think about was getting away from there, because it suddenly occurred to me that whoever had killed her might still be in the house.'

'Did you hear or see anything that would suggest someone was still in the house?'

'No, but I imagined all sorts of things, and as I said, I just wanted to get away from there.'

'Tell me again why you decided to go *into* the house in the first place.'

A small frown drew the delicate eyebrows together as if puzzled by a question she thought she had already answered. 'As I believe I said, Chief Inspector, I saw the light on, and I wondered about it. It crossed my mind that Laura might have used the migraine as an excuse to get out of going to see a film she wasn't keen on, and was there on her own, so I thought I would just pop in.'

Paget glanced across at Tregalles. The sergeant took his cue and said, 'For a friendly chat, that sort of thing, was it, Mrs Ballantyne?'

She frowned. 'I suppose you could say that,' she said. 'I had nothing specific in mind.'

'And you saw nothing to suggest that someone had broken into the house? Nothing suspicious? There was no other reason for you to go into the house?'

'No.' Moira shot a puzzled look at Paget as if seeking an explanation for the sergeant's questions. 'I don't understand what you're getting at,' she said, turning back to Tregalles.

'It just seems odd to me that you would go into the house and go up to Mrs Holbrook's bedroom for no other reason that to have a bit of a chat, when you say yourself she might well have been asleep. Are you sure there wasn't another reason, Mrs Ballantyne?'

'I really don't know what you expect me to say,' she said softly. 'It's the sort of thing one does on a whim, I suppose. I hadn't *meant* to go into the house when I went out to post the letter. It was just the fact that the light was on that prompted me to go in. We were friends, and—'

'Were you really?'

'I beg your pardon?'

'I mean,' said Tregalles softly, '*were* you still friends after Mrs Holbrook accused you of having an affair with her husband the day before she was killed?'

The colour drained from Moira's face, leaving two bright spots on her cheeks, but she remained silent.

'We need an answer, Mrs Ballantyne,' said Paget. 'What was your relationship with Mrs Holbrook at that point?'

Moira closed her eyes and drew a deep breath. She exhaled slowly. 'All right,' she said tightly, 'since you seem to have been prying into our affairs . . .' She stopped, perhaps realizing that she could have chosen a better word. 'Laura more or less accused me of having an affair with Simon,' she continued, 'but it wasn't true. If Simon was having it off with someone – and I can't say I would be all that surprised if he was – it wasn't with me. And that is why I went into the house; I wanted to clear that up once and for all.'

'And yet there must have been some reason for Mrs Holbrook to believe that you were having an affair with her husband,' said Paget. 'Why do you think that was?'

Moira compressed her lips and shook her head. 'I don't know,' she said, 'but I do know she was wrong!'

'You said you wouldn't be surprised if Mr Holbrook was having an affair with someone. Why is that, Mrs Ballantyne? Does he have a history of such behaviour?'

Moira drew a deep, steadying breath. 'Look,' she said, 'I don't *know* anything for certain, but I don't think it's any secret that Simon does have that sort of reputation, and things have been a bit strained between him and Laura recently. But Laura was wrong to think that I was involved.'

'Strained?' said Paget. 'I don't recall you mentioning that when we spoke to you last week. Would you like to explain that, Mrs Ballantyne?'

Moira sighed. 'It's been that way for the past few months,' she said wearily. 'I didn't want to say anything to you before because it's really none of my business, but there was some sort of friction between them.'

'How *did* you get along with Laura Holbrook?' Paget asked. 'That is before she accused you of having an affair with Simon? You and your husband seem to have enjoyed the company of the Holbrooks; you did a number of things together, and yet I have the impression that your feelings toward Laura in particular were ambivalent to say the least. Is that true?'

Moira eased back in her chair and thought about that for a moment. 'I don't know how to answer that,' she said slowly. 'It's hard to explain.

You see, it was almost as if Laura had two personalities. She could be charming and gracious, and one of the nicest people you would ever wish to meet, and you couldn't help but like her. But there was another side to her, a harder side. When it came to business she was like a machine. She knew exactly what she wanted, and she made sure she got it, which is why the company is doing so well today. Simon was thrilled with the results, at least at first, because it allowed him to get on with what he likes to do best. He could spend his time in the lab and not have to worry about the marketing end of things, and the day-to-day running of the office, so he was pretty happy. But it's been clear for some time, now, that things were getting a bit strained between them. In fact there were times when it was rather uncomfortable being around them when they were sniping at each other.'

'About what, exactly?'

'Anything and everything, although I think it was mainly to do with the business. Simon didn't like the way Laura was taking over. Trevor said Simon told him he felt as if it was slipping away from him and he was losing control. He said Laura had even gone so far as to counter-mand decisions he'd made, and he was getting fed up with it.'

'And yet Mr Holbrook himself talked about his wife and what she had done for the company in glowing terms,' said Paget, 'and Peggy Goodwin indicated that Mrs Holbrook's death would be a serious blow to the business.'

'Oh, I don't think there can be any doubt about that. Laura saved that business from going under. She poured a lot of her own money into the firm, moved them into new premises, but even that wouldn't have been enough without her contacts and expertise, so she is going to be missed. But as I said, the woman was like a machine when it came to business. She was spending more and more time away from home, drumming up new business, and that was all she talked about when she was here, and I know Simon was unhappy about that.'

'Would you say he was looking for a way to end the partnership?'

'Yes, I think he . . .' Moira stopped abruptly as she realized the impli-cation. 'But *not* in the way you're suggesting,' she said quickly.

'In what way, then?'

Moira shrugged helplessly. 'I don't know. I only meant to say that I think he was getting a bit frustrated, that's all.'

'Did Mrs Holbrook ever say anything to you that would indicate there were problems between her and her husband?'

'Not really. Well, there was once, about a month ago, when we were having coffee together at the club. She seemed to be a bit wound up, and she'd been pretty short with Simon during the game, so I asked her if anything was wrong. She said something to the effect that she wished Simon would stick to what he did best and leave the running of the business to her. She said she couldn't understand what his problem was; he had only to look at the bottom line to see how well they had done under her guidance. The trouble was, I don't think she could see what she was doing to Simon's pride,' she concluded.

'Did you try to point that out to her?'

'Good Lord, no! Laura wouldn't have listened anyway, especially if she thought I was taking Simon's side.'

'But you did have some sympathy for Simon?'

'Well, yes, but . . .'

'Because I understand the two of you were very close at one time,' said Paget, 'so perhaps Laura had good reason to think that the two of you had resumed your earlier relationship.'

The Cupid's bow of Moira's mouth disappeared into a thin, hard line. 'You have been busy, haven't you?' she said icily. 'And I resent the implication. I'll admit we did have a brief, a *very* brief fling – you couldn't even call it an affair – before Simon and Laura were married, but it was a mistake and one I deeply regret. Simon . . .' She shook her head as if lost for words. 'Simon is one of those people you can't help liking. He's attractive, he can be fun to be with, and women like him, but there's no depth to him, no commitment to anything but his work. Laura may well have been right in believing that Simon was having an affair, but as I said before, it wasn't with me. I made a mistake once, but I love my husband, and I wouldn't want to do anything to destroy the relationship we have. That's it. End of story!'

'Not quite,' Paget said. 'You said that once you realized that Mrs Holbrook was dead, your only thought was to get away from the house. All right, fair enough, I can understand that, but why didn't you call the police as soon as you got home?'

Moira didn't answer at once. Instead, she looked down at her hands, spreading her fingers as if trying to decide whether her nails needed retouching. 'I was afraid,' she said at last. 'I thought if no one knew I'd been in the house, I could stay out of it. I had blood on my hands, on my coat.' She shrugged. 'As I said, I was scared. I know it sounds weak, but I didn't want to be involved.'

'Because you might be suspected of killing her,' said Paget bluntly.

'No!' It was more a cry of anguish than negation, then: 'Well, yes, I suppose that was part of it. I knew that people had overheard her accuse me of having an affair with Simon; I'd gone in to try to have it out with her, and I knew people would probably think the worst.'

'And why shouldn't they, Mrs Ballantyne? You admit that the two of you had quarrelled; you *say* there was nothing going on between you and Simon Holbrook, but we only have your word for that. You were involved in an earlier relationship, whatever you choose to call it, and you've as good as told us that Simon Holbrook was unhappy with his wife.

'Looking at it from our point of view, let's assume, for the moment, that you had never really given up on having Simon Holbrook for yourself, and when it became obvious that he was becoming dissatisfied with his marriage, you saw your chance. But Laura caught on, so you had to do something if you wished to get Simon back.

'So when you learned that Laura Holbrook would not only be alone that night, but would be half drugged, sleeping off a migraine, you saw your chance. You begged off going to see the film yourself, then you went along to the house, used your key to get in, and went upstairs to Mrs Holbrook's room. You killed her, then went downstairs, pulled out drawers and tossed a few things around to make it look as if the place had been vandalized. You then pried open the back door to make it look like a burglary, and went home and waited for someone else to find the body. Tell me, what did you do with the weapon?'

Moira was shaking her head. She looked dazed. 'I don't know anything about a weapon,' she said desperately when she found her voice. 'I can only tell you what happened. I don't know how you could think that I could do such a thing to anyone.' She compressed her lips and closed her eyes tightly to hold back the tears. 'I've told you the truth, I swear,' she whispered. 'Are you going to arrest me?'

Paget sat back in his seat. It was tempting. Moira's prints were all over the murder scene; she admitted to being there at or about the time Laura Holbrook was killed; admitted she had blood on her clothes, and they only had her word for it that she and Simon weren't having an affair.

Which could mean that she and Simon Holbrook had hatched the plot between them, and had used Moira's husband, Trevor, to give Simon an alibi.

It was very tempting – but it wasn't enough.

'No,' he said, 'but we will be searching your house and the surrounding area, and we will need the clothing you were wearing that night for forensic examination.' He looked at his watch and nodded to Tregalles. 'This interview is terminated at 15.23,' he said. 'However,' he continued as Moira rose somewhat shakily to her feet, 'I'm afraid we are going to have to keep you here until we have arranged for our people to begin the search. Do you have a mobile phone with you, Mrs Ballantyne?'

'Why, yes, I have it here. I was about to phone Trevor, though God only knows what I'm going to say to him.' Moira opened her handbag, but Paget held out his hand as she took out the phone.

'Sorry,' he told her, 'but I'll take charge of that. It will be given back to you as soon as you get home.'

Moira wasn't asleep. She was trying to pretend she was, but he could tell. She was lying too still, too rigid – as he was himself. She'd always twitted him about the way he could fall asleep almost as soon as his head touched the pillow, but she didn't know how often he'd lain awake, pretending to be asleep. The illuminated hands of the bedside clock stood at twenty minutes to two, and Trevor Ballantyne had been going over and over in his head the events of the past few days ever since coming to bed at eleven.

The police had picked Moira up and brought her back in an unmarked car. Trevor had offered to come with her, but she'd said no, she'd be fine on her own. But she'd looked anything but fine when she returned, accompanied by two plain-clothes officers. A second car arrived moments later, and he'd been handed a search warrant when he opened the door.

There were four of them – three men and a woman. They'd spent more than three hours in the house and garden. They'd examined every piece of clothing, including everything in the hamper waiting to be washed, and they taken away her coat, her shoes, even the underclothes she said she was wearing that night, and he'd felt so damned helpless, because there was nothing he or anyone else could do to stop them.

Moira had rushed to the door and locked it the moment they'd gone, then stood there with her back to it as if barring the way should they decide to return.

'It's all right,' he'd said soothingly. 'Everything is going to be all right, Moira. Believe me.'

But she'd shaken her head. 'They'll be back,' she'd whispered.

'They don't believe me, Trevor. They think I did it. They think I killed Laura. They're going to arrest me. They . . . Oh, God! What am I going to do?'

She'd pulled away from him when he'd tried to comfort her, and they'd said little to each other throughout the rest of the evening. He'd called their solicitor; explained the situation to him, only to be told there was nothing to be done unless or until Moira was actually arrested and charged.

Now, staring into the darkness, he couldn't help wondering. The police weren't in the habit of arresting people without good reason, and Moira had admitted to being in the house about the time Laura was killed; they had her fingerprints, and there was that bloodstain on her coat. So why *hadn't* she called the police? And why hadn't she told him that night if she had nothing to hide?

He'd heard about what had happened at the club. One member in particular had made sure that he knew his wife was being accused of having an affair with Simon, but he'd dismissed it as malicious gossip. But now . . .?

Was there some truth to it? Had it started up again? He'd never told Moira that he knew of her affair with Simon. He'd agonized about it; waited for her to say something . . . Waited in vain.

He hadn't spoken of it himself, not to Moira, not to anyone. He'd convinced himself that she was too ashamed of what she'd done to speak of it, and perhaps that was punishment enough. He'd pushed it to the back of his mind. But it was there, always there, a shadow of suspicion, lurking in darkness like some silent creature, dormant now, but waiting, waiting for a chance to raise it's ugly head.

And now it had.

The sudden, sharp sound as he sucked in his breath caught him by surprise. Too late he buried his face in the pillow to stifle the sound. He felt Moira stiffen beside him; held his breath, waiting as he stared blindly into the darkness, waiting and wondering how long it would be before the police discovered that the statement *he* had made was false.

Sixteen

The search of the Ballantyne house had turned up nothing more than the bloodstained coat and a long-sleeved blouse with stains on the cuffs that Moira herself had produced for them. Neither had a search of the garden, as well as the gardens between the two houses, produced anything in the way of a weapon.

Even so, both Ormside and Tregalles felt there was enough evidence, both physical and circumstantial, to arrest Moira Ballantyne. As did Superintendent Alcott. He wanted Moira brought in and charged.

'Good God, man, what more do you want?' he demanded when Paget demurred. 'Next to an outright confession, you have all you need. She admits to being there at or about the time Starkie says the Holbrook woman was killed; she admits she had a key to the house; she admits that Mrs Holbrook had accused her of having an affair with Simon Holbrook, and she admits that she had an affair with him at the same time that he was involved with Laura whatever-her-name-was-then. And I wouldn't be too surprised to find that the two of them planned it together.

'You have motive, means – we may not have found the weapon, but it will probably turn up if you look hard enough – and opportunity,' he continued, 'and you don't get a better package than that! So what are you waiting for?'

'I can't help but agree,' said Paget, 'but if Moira Ballantyne did kill Laura Holbrook, she made a hell of a hash of it. This woman and her husband design security systems; she is the one who does on-site inspections; she has to take in every detail in order to design an effective system, because they wouldn't be in business long if they didn't get it right. It's an exacting job, and I can't see her planning all this and leaving fingerprints all over the crime scene, and not getting rid of the bloodstained coat and blouse if she was the killer. She's a lot cleverer than that, in my estimation.'

'Even clever people panic and make mistakes,' Alcott countered.

'I don't think Moira Ballantyne is the type to panic easily,' Paget said. 'If she wanted to kill someone, I think she would put her skills to work and make damned sure that she didn't leave any evidence behind. Besides, let's look at her so-called motive. Unless we can demonstrate unequivocally that she and Holbrook are having, not just an affair, but a strong relationship, I think the motive is weak. Even assuming she did commit the crime, what did she hope to gain? Simon Holbrook? What about her husband? There is nothing to indicate that they don't get along. They live very comfortably in a nice house in a good neighbourhood, and they have a successful business. I had Ormside check that out, and they're doing very well. I can see her having a brief fling with Holbrook; as she herself said he's an attractive man, but I can't see her *killing* to get him. She has more to lose than she has to gain. It just doesn't make sense to me, whereas what she told us is consistent with the evidence, and Henderson agrees.'

He knew the minute he'd said it that he shouldn't have mentioned Henderson. Alcott's eyes narrowed, and the muscles around the superintendent's jaw tightened as he said, 'You're telling me that you've already spoken to the CPS about this?' He remained silent for a long moment, then rose from his chair and said, 'Shut the door.'

Paget pushed the door shut. He knew what was coming, so he wasn't surprised when Alcott opened the window, took out a cigarette and lit it. The superintendent had been struggling for a long time to curb his addiction, but to no avail, and every now and then he simply had to have a cigarette, regardless of the no smoking rules. He sucked the smoke deep into his lungs, then leaned back and blew it out again in a long thin stream toward the ceiling before returning to his seat.

Clearly, this was one of those times.

'So,' he said, 'you discussed this personally with Henderson, did you, Chief Inspector? Correct me if I'm wrong,' he continued ominously, 'but I was under the impression that presenting a case to the Crown Prosecution Service was *my* prerogative, or has that changed?'

'There was never any suggestion that I was presenting an actual case to them,' said Paget, choosing his words carefully. 'What I was trying to do was put the case against Moira Ballantyne into perspective in my own mind, and I wanted to find out how the evidence would look from the standpoint of someone trying to convince a jury. So I had an off-the-record chat with Henderson and gave him a hypothetical case. His opinion was that a much better case could be made against the burglary artists who had demonstrated a growing taste for violence, despite the evidence of the blood on the door jamb, and we would be well advised to dig deeper before we tried to hang this murder on a particular suspect.'

Alcott snorted derisively. 'That's a load of bollocks, and you know it,' he snapped. 'Henderson would know exactly who you were talking about.'

'But he does have the ability to make a distinction between what he is *told* and whatever he might *think*, and treat it as a hypothetical case. And as I said, sir, it was off the record.'

Alcott dismissed the explanation with a wave of the hand. 'You know damned well what I'm getting at,' he said irritably. 'No doubt you presented the case with your own spin on it in order to get the answer you wanted, and Henderson obliged. Which means he's not likely to change his mind if I present him with the case against Moira Ballantyne for prosecution.'

The superintendent drew deeply on his cigarette. 'I believe you knew *exactly* what you were doing when you spoke to Henderson,' he went on, 'and I'm warning you, Paget. One of these days you're going to push me too far, and I won't stand for it. If you want to talk to the chief prosecutor about *anything* in future, you talk to me first, understand?'

'Understood, sir.'

'Good! Now, get back out there and bring me something that *will* stand up in court! And make sure you close the door behind you.'

'We're losing it,' said Ormside flatly. 'It's been a week, now, and we've still got sod all!'

'I still think Simon Holbrook and Moira Ballantyne were in it together,' Tregalles said stubbornly. Paget, Ormside, Tregalles and Molly were in one of the interview rooms, where they had been going over every-thing again from the very first burglary to the cold-blooded murder of Laura Holbrook without coming up with anything new.

Tregalles elaborated. 'Holbrook goes off to the cinema, using good old Trevor Ballantyne to give himself an alibi, while Moira nips along and does the deed, then uses the bar on the back door and turns the place over to make it look as if it was done by our burglars. Simon gets what he wants, and presumably she gets what she wants.'

'I'll admit it could have happened that way,' Paget conceded, 'but I still think that if they went to that much trouble to plan the killing, why did Moira make such a hash of it? Prints all over the place, and keeping a coat and blouse covered with Laura's blood? I simply do not believe that she would be that clumsy or that stupid.'

'On the other hand,' Tregalles persisted, 'she could have been great on the planning, but went to pieces once she saw the results of what she'd done. We know she had an affair with Holbrook a year or so ago; maybe it never stopped – and she told us herself that the Holbrook marriage was a bit rocky. Anyway, if she didn't do it, who did? Bryce had motive, but I haven't seen any evidence that puts him at the house.'

'But I don't think we should rule him out,' said Molly, 'because his alibi for the night of the murder doesn't hold up. As I said in my report, Hilde DeGraff says he arrived at her place around seven, but it wasn't just a drop-in for a chat, because he brought wine – as he does quite regularly – and they spent much of their time together in bed. But she says she doesn't know what time he left because she fell asleep. She says wine always makes her sleepy, and Bryce knew that, so he may have counted on it. She claims she didn't wake up until just before midnight, and Tim Bryce was gone by then. I tried to pin her down about when she fell asleep, but she said it could have been anywhere from eight o'clock on. She told me they drank wine when Tim first arrived, then they went to bed and made love, and she fell asleep shortly after that.

'Her story was straightforward enough, and she certainly didn't go out of her way to protect him. In fact she as much as told me that her only interest in Tim Bryce was because he was good in bed, and I didn't detect any depth of feeling for him at all. And someone was seen jogging not far from the Holbrook house around the time of the murder.'

Tregalles grunted. 'I suppose we could have him in and have another go at him,' he said, 'but my impression of Bryce is that he's a light-weight. I don't see him as a cold-blooded killer.'

'I agree,' said Paget, 'and it would be his word against DeGraff's. He couldn't prove that he stayed there until ten, and she couldn't swear that he didn't, so let's leave him alone for the time being.'

'So where does that leave us?' Ormside said. 'Virtually everything in Laura Holbrook's files at work and at home were work-related. There was almost nothing in the way of private correspondence; nothing of a personal nature, nor could they find anything that could be considered threatening. Same thing on her computer and her BlackBerry, nothing out of the ordinary. Forsythe and DC Carter talked to most of the staff out there, as you suggested, but they didn't learn anything we didn't know before.'

Paget looked enquiringly at Molly, who shook her head. 'They more or less confirmed everything that Peggy Goodwin told us,' she said. 'On the one hand they were grateful to Laura for saving their jobs, but they didn't like her. Cold and stand-offish were words we heard several times, but we didn't get the feeling that anyone had a major grievance – with the exception of Holbrook's nephew, of course, and they were happy to see him go – at least the men were, but I'm not so sure about some of the girls.'

'Anyone in particular?' Paget asked.

Molly smiled. 'No, but the feeling was most prevalent among the younger girls.'

'So where does that leave us?' Tregalles asked.

'With either a psycho or someone who *really* hated Laura Holbrook,' said Molly quietly.

All eyes turned to her. Paget gave an encouraging nod and said, 'Go on.'

'Well,' she said hesitantly, 'I wasn't at the scene, and I didn't see the body, but I have studied the pictures and read the results of the autopsy, and it seems to me that whoever killed Laura Holbrook went right over the top doing it. I mean just look at the damage to her face. She was struck repeatedly, vicious blows after she was dead, which suggests to me that there was a lot of rage and pent up feelings behind those blows.'

'You have someone in mind, do you, Molly?' Tregalles asked quietly.

'I don't have a name, if that's what you mean,' she said. 'Simon Holbrook seems to attract a lot of women, and we haven't explored that angle to any extent as yet, but it could be someone who has been harbouring a grudge for a long time. Peggy Goodwin was more or less elbowed aside when Laura came in, and she admits she wasn't happy about that.'

'But if it was a case of jealousy,' said Paget, 'why now? Why didn't she do it long before this? And using your criteria, we do have another suspect. You haven't met Susan Chase, but according to what we've been told, everyone thought that she would be the one to settle down with Simon, but then her sister Laura came along and cut her out. But did Susan get upset about it? Apparently not. In fact, we're told that she took it all in her stride and remained friends with everyone. But as Tregalles and I saw last Saturday, she was right there with Holbrook helping clean up the house, and the two of them looked pretty cosy together. And she was the one who pointed the finger Tim Bryce's way as a possible suspect.

'And there's something else. Laura believed her husband was having an affair with someone, and she thought that Moira was the other woman. But what if she was right about him having an affair, but wrong about who the woman was? Holbrook has a reputation for playing the field in the past, so why should he change just because he's married? It may be that he had started to look round again, and there, ready and waiting in the wings, is Susan.'

'But the same argument applies to her,' Tregalles objected. 'That all took place a year or so back. Why would she wait till now?'

'No idea,' said Paget. 'Opportunity, perhaps? But I agree with Forsythe: whoever killed Laura Holbrook, really hated her, and I think we should make every effort to make sure that everyone was where they say they were last Wednesday evening, and I do mean everyone.'

'And find out if the Chase woman has a dog,' Ormside put in. All eyes turned to him as he continued. 'See, I've been thinking about that,' he said, 'and something's not right about those dog hairs. It doesn't make sense, because what I don't understand is how the killer knew about the dog hair in the earlier burglaries? We've never made that information public.'

'It would make sense if it was the same person in both cases,' Molly said quietly. 'I mean we've been working on the assumption that the person who killed Laura Holbrook copied the MO used in the previous burglaries. But what if the killer is the same person responsible for all the other burglaries, and he or she or *they* set out to lay a false trail? Except in the Holbrook case they had a key, so they could enter the house without alerting Laura. And they did the back door and the rest of the damage after they killed her.'

'They'd be taking a hell of a risk,' Tregalles said doubtfully. 'All those burglaries just to set the scene, so to speak.'

'Not if they knew for certain when the occupants would be away and for how long.'

'Even so, Molly, you must admit it's a bit of a stretch. We know there were two people involved in the other burglaries, so are you saying there were two people involved in Laura Holbrook's murder?'

'Not necessarily,' Molly said. 'One of them could have done it while the other made sure that he or she had an alibi for that time.'

'If you're right,' said Ormside, 'then I come back to Simon Holbrook and Moira Ballantyne. They did the burglaries together, but she did the killing while her husband gave her lover an alibi.'

'And botched it completely,' Paget said. 'Sorry, Len, but I still don't buy it. Besides, the same could be said about Simon and Susan Chase or some other combination we haven't even thought of. But I'll say one thing: it's a theory worth pursuing, because we've got little else to go on. And the first thing we need to do is find out where all our suspects were on the nights the houses were broken into.'

Seventeen

Paget listened carefully, asked a couple of questions, then looked at the grandfather clock in the hall and gave a sigh of resignation. Another evening gone, he thought, and couldn't help thinking that it was just this sort of thing that led to the break-up of so many marriages among members of the police service. The thought chilled him, but there wasn't much he could do about that now.

'I'm on my way,' he told the custody sergeant, 'and make sure you keep them separated. Better get Tregalles in as well.' He hung up the phone and turned to face Grace. 'Looks as if we may have a break,' he told her. 'That was Broughton, the custody sergeant, on the phone. Two young people were caught breaking into a house in Hatch Lane. The homeowners returned unexpectedly, tackled the two of them and held them until the police arrived. Looks like the same MO as all the others, so I'd better get going.'

Grace looked at the clock. 'It's twenty to nine,' she said. 'Couldn't it wait till morning?'

'It could, but I'd prefer to talk to them before they have a chance to get over the shock of being nicked. Sorry, love, but I have to go, so don't wait up. And make sure you lock up after me. You never know who's about these days.'

Tregalles was already there when Paget arrived, and they sat down together with the custody sergeant to review the information provided by the arresting officers.

The burglary, Broughton told them, was reported by a woman named Denise Grey of The Willows in Hatch Lane. She said that she and her husband, Evan, had caught the two youngsters ransacking the house, and were holding them. A patrol car was dispatched immediately, and a seventeen-year-old male, and a sixteen-year-old female were taken into custody.

The back door of The Willows had been forced and, although the thieves couldn't have been inside the house more than a few minutes, drawers had been pulled out, and the contents thrown on the floor.

The tool used to gain access was identified as a leaf spring taken from a car or truck, with one end filed down to make it easier to insert between door and jamb, while the other end was taped to give it a better grip. Mr Grey told the arresting officers that the girl had tried to use it as a weapon on him when he apprehended her, and showed them a bruise on his upper right arm as evidence. He also showed them bruises on his shins where he alleged the girl had kicked him before he could subdue her.

He explained that he was a marshal arts instructor, and his wife was a fitness trainer. They were on their way to the recreation centre, where they were both teaching classes, when he realized he'd left a set of instructions behind, and they'd returned to the house. His wife remained in the car while he entered the house to find two teenagers ransacking the place. They tried to make a run for it, but he caught the girl, and shouted to his wife, who tackled the boy as he tried to jump the hedge at the front of the house. The boy made no attempt to fight, and he'd accompanied Mrs Grey into the house and remained there passively while she telephoned the police.

'Just kids?' Paget said to the custody sergeant. 'I suppose I shouldn't be surprised by their ages, but I am. What do we know about them?'

'The boy is seventeen, the girl is sixteen going on thirty,' Broughton told him. 'Terry Coleman and Chloe Tyler. We have nothing on the boy, but the girl has quite a record. Prostitution, possession, dealing, and a couple of assaults to her credit. She's a hard case, and she's not volunteering anything, but the boy's a different story. They were both cautioned at the time they were apprehended. She's not talking, but he certainly is. He claims this is the first time he's done anything like this, and he blames it all on the girl. And he may be right. Like I said, she's a hard case, living rough in one of those old buildings on King George Way – the ones the local authority keeps saying are to be torn down but never seem to get around to. I knew you'd want it secured for search, so I took the liberty of dispatching one of your blokes with one of ours to turn it over. We should be hearing back from them soon.

'Coleman says the girl talked him into it,' the sergeant continued. 'He said she needed the money for drugs, and the bloke who used to do houses with her is away. He says she promised him sex if he'd do it.'

'Looks like he can forget that,' observed Tregalles drily.

'I've kept them separate as you asked,' Broughton continued. 'I don't think you'll have any trouble with Coleman – he's scared shitless about what his parents will say when they find out, so he's more than willing to tell us anything we want to know, but I doubt if you'll make much headway with the girl.'

'Have the parents been notified?' asked Paget.

'Nobody home at the Coleman house. We're told by the boy that his parents are in Switzerland on holiday. As for Chloe Tyler, she left home when she was fourteen. She's from Sheffield originally. She's got form there and in Leeds and Newcastle. There's no record of a father, and according to this –' Broughton tapped the face of the monitor in front of him – 'her mum's been on the game most of her life, and she's moved around a lot as well. Last known address was in West Brom, but she disappeared not long after Chloe left home. If the girl knows where her mum is, she's not saying, and I get the impression she's not interested anyway.'

'You said Coleman mentioned someone who has worked with her before on other burglaries?' said Paget.

'That's right. Someone who goes by the name of Josh. The boy describes Josh as "a bit of a weirdo", and he gave us a description. Tall, thin, maybe twenty-five or so, pale eyes, nose is always running because he snorts coke. Talks like a schoolteacher. He says Chloe told him that Josh had gone off to visit some traveller friends who are camped over Cleobury Mortimer way.'

'Shouldn't be too hard to track down, then,' Tregalles observed. 'I can get someone started on that now.'

'Right,' said Paget, 'then let's hear what else Terry Coleman has to say while he's still in a talkative mood. We're going to need a duty solicitor by the sound of it.'

'Carmichael,' Broughton said. 'He's waiting for you.'

'Good. At least we know where we are with him,' said Paget as he pushed his chair back. 'As for the girl, I think we'll leave her until we've heard what Mr Coleman has to say for himself.'

Terry Coleman was a skinny, spotty-faced kid who barely looked his age. A shock of lank, unruly hair kept falling forward over his face, and he was forever pushing it out of his eyes. The interview room wasn't particularly warm, but he was sweating profusely, and he looked as if he might burst into tears at any moment.

The procedure was explained to him, and he was reminded once again that he was still under caution. 'Do you mind if I call you Terry?' Paget asked pleasantly.

The boy licked his lips several times and said, 'Yeah – I mean no, I don't mind.'

'Good. Now, I'd like you to tell me in your own words exactly what you were doing in the home of Mr and Mrs Grey of The Willows in Hatch Lane earlier this evening, and how you came to be there in the first place.'

As far as the burglary was concerned, despite cautionary advice from the duty solicitor, Lionel Carmichael, the boy could hardly wait to tell his side of things, and his story was pretty much a repeat of what he had told the arresting officers. 'I was just supposed to be the lookout, that's all,' he ended, 'but once we were inside Chloe said we might as well give the place a good going over, and it would be best if we both did it. She said we'd have plenty of time because they wouldn't be back for hours. But we hadn't been there five minutes when they came back, so we never had a chance to steal anything. Not that I wanted to in the first place,' he added hastily.

'Let's go back a bit, then, Terry. Tell me when and how you met Chloe Tyler.'

'I met her a few weeks ago at a friend's house. His parents were away for the weekend, and he invited a few of us over, but word got round somehow, and a bunch of kids we'd never seen before crashed the party. Chloe came in with them.

'I danced with her a couple of times, and when we left she cadged a ride home. That's when I found out she was living in a squat down on King George Way.'

'Cadged a ride, Terry?' Tregalles said sharply. 'How old are you, Terry?'

'Seventeen.'

'Who's car were you driving, Terry?'

Colour rose in the boy's face. 'My dad's,' he mumbled.

'You have a license and your dad's permission, do you?'

Terry wilted beneath the sergeant's gaze and shook his head. 'Not-not really,' he admitted. 'But you see—'

'Never mind the excuses,' Tregalles said roughly. 'We'll talk about that later. Let's get back to your giving this girl a ride. Trying to impress her, were you?'

Terry Coleman shrugged and looked down at his hands. 'I thought she liked me,' he said. 'I went down to the squat a few times, but then I realized she had something going with this bloke, Josh. It was like he had some sort of hold over her; she'd do whatever he said. But he was out of it half the time, and when that happened, Chloe and I would take off somewhere. She's had a rough life, and I felt really sorry for her.'

'You say it was Chloe who suggested the burglary. When was that, Terry?'

'Yesterday. She said she needed money, and she knew of this house in Hatch Lane where the people would be out all evening. She said it would be easy; she said she and Josh had done houses before.'

'Did she say where or when?'

'Mostly other towns, I think. I don't think they've been here all that long. The way she talks about other places, I think she and Josh have moved around quite a bit. But things have been sort of rough for her since Josh went off to see some friends, and she was getting a bit desperate. Trouble was, she said she didn't like going in alone, and she asked me to go with her.

'I knew I shouldn't do it,' he said bitterly, 'but she kept on at me about putting a bit of excitement into my life; she said she'd find someone else if I was afraid to do it, but if I would just go along with her this once, I wouldn't be sorry.'

'What did you think she meant by that?' asked Paget.

'That she'd sleep with me,' the boy said sheepishly. Then, more spirit-edly, 'See, she never had before, although we'd come close, and I thought if I could just prove to her that I wasn't afraid, she'd . . .' He shrugged the thought away.

'All right. Now, tell me about the burglary itself. Were you watching the house?'

Terry nodded. 'We watched from the car. There's a sort of curve halfway down Hatch Lane, and we sat back there waiting for them to leave, and when they did, we waited a few minutes, then went in the back.'

'This was your dad's car, was it?'

'No. It was hers. Well, she said she'd borrowed it from a friend.'

'*Borrowed* it, Terry? Surely you didn't believe that? Who would loan a car to a sixteen-year-old girl living in a squat?'

'Sixte——? No, you're wrong. She's eighteen! She told me.'

'And you believed her? Come on, now, Terry, I thought you were going to tell me the truth. Chloe Tyler is sixteen, and she has a long record with us. Did you tell the constables who arrested you about the car?'

'No, I never even thought about it and they never asked.'

'So it should still be there?'

'I suppose so,' the boy said miserably, 'but if it was stolen, I didn't have anything to do with it. Honest!'

'Make? Colour? Style? Registration?'

'Ford Focus. Dark blue. Not very old. That's all I can tell you. Honest,' he said again, 'if it was stolen, I didn't know about it. You have to believe me.'

Paget caught Tregalles's eye. 'Better have someone bring it in,' he said. 'Sergeant Tregalles is leaving the room at . . .' Paget checked his watch and entered the time.

'Now, then, Terry, let's get back to the burglary itself. Who used the bar on the back door?'

'Chloe. She had it open in a couple of seconds. It made a hell of a noise, all that splintering wood, and I was sure the neighbours would have heard, but next thing I knew Chloe grabbed my arm and pulled me inside.'

'She used the metal bar? The leaf spring?'

'That's right.'

'Did that belong to you or to her?'

'It was hers. She brought it with her. She said she got it out of an old car down at the junk yard at the bottom of Fox Lane.'

'Who pulled out the drawers?'

'I started to, because she told me to look in them for money while she looked around to see if the woman had left a purse or wallet there. But Chloe told me I was doing it all wrong, and pulled them all the way out and dumped everything on the floor. She said it was quicker that way.'

'And did you find any money?'

The boy shook his head. 'It was about then that this bloke came in. He must have come in quietly, because all of a sudden he was there in the room and he had hold of Chloe, and she was screaming at him.'

'So what did you do?'

The colour deepened in the boy's face. 'I took off,' he said so quietly that Paget had to ask him to repeat it for the tape. 'Well there was no point in hanging around, was there?' he said, trying to justify his actions.

'I mean this bloke had Chloe and there was nothing I could do about it, was there?'

'And you ran straight into the arms of Mrs Grey.'

'I got caught up in the hedge, and she got this sort of hammer-lock on me. I couldn't move.'

'What happened then?'

'We went back into the house and she rang the police.'

'How did she manage that while still holding onto you?'

'She wasn't. She told me to sit in a chair and stay there, so I did.'

'What was Chloe doing while this was going on?'

'Spitting and screaming, mostly, but she wasn't getting anywhere. He was a big bloke.'

Tregalles came back into the room, and Paget announced his re-entry for the benefit of the tape. 'They're on their way,' Tregalles said, referring to the car in Hatch Lane. 'And we have a car that matches the description reported stolen from a car park earlier this evening.'

'Right. In that case, I think we've almost finished here for the time being,' said Paget. 'Just one more thing, Terry, before we wrap it up. You told us that your parents are on holiday in Switzerland. Is that true?'

The boy eyed him suspiciously as he nodded.

'Yes or no, please, Terry. The tape doesn't record nods.'

Coleman swallowed noisily. 'Yes,' he said hoarsely.

'And I'm sure they left a number where they could be reached in case of an emergency. Right?'

Coleman looked as if he wished he could sink through the floor. 'Do you really *have* to?' he pleaded. 'Dad will kill me.'

'We won't let him do that,' Paget told him, 'but we do have to notify him, so let's have it, Terry. Where is he and how can we get hold of him?'

Chloe Tyler was a stocky girl, well-developed for her age. She wore a faded blue anorak over a tight-fitting black jumper and short skirt. Her legs were bare, but her feet were clad in scuffed black trainers with most of the tread worn off. Paget wouldn't have described her as a pretty girl, but with long black hair, dark, satin-like skin, and even darker, predatory eyes, there was an aura of sexuality about the girl, and he could well imagine how someone as young and naive as Terry Coleman would be attracted to her like a moth to an open flame.

As Broughton had said, Chloe had been in trouble with the police often enough to be familiar with the routine, and she hotly denied almost everything Terry Coleman had told them. She said it was his idea to enter the house, and she was scared of what he might do to her if she didn't go along with him. As for the leaf-spring, she claimed she'd never seen it before Terry took it out from under his coat to use on the back door.

How was it, then, Paget asked, that she had had it in her hands and hit Grey with it when he was trying to detain her?

'Terry dropped it when he ran, didn't he?' she said blandly. 'Snivelling little coward. Forced me into going with him then ran like a bloody rabbit as soon as there was trouble. I picked it up when I saw this big bloke coming at me. It was self-defence. I thought he was going to kill me.'

'Speaking of killing,' Paget said, 'is that the weapon you used on Mrs Holbrook? The one you killed her with?'

'Killed?' Even Chloe appeared to be shaken by that. 'I don't know what you're talking about.' She turned to Carmichael. 'What's he on about?' she demanded. 'Is this a wind-up or what?'

'He is very serious,' the solicitor told her. 'The police are investigating the death of a woman who was killed during the course of a burglary.'

Chloe gaped at him. 'And you're just sitting there like a bloody great dummy while they fit me up for it? You're supposed to be working for me, remember, and I had nothing to do with anybody being killed, so tell him. Go on, do your job and bloody tell him!'

'I take it, then, that you've changed your mind,' Carmichael said. 'Are you prepared to talk to me now?'

'Well, I'm not going to bloody sit here and let them fit me up for murder,' the girl declared, 'so, yeah – but I don't want them listening.'

Carmichael looked at Paget. 'I'd like a few of minutes alone with Miss Tyler before we continue,' he said, then nodded in the direction of the WPC who was seated just inside the door. 'The WPC can stay, of course.' Having the WPC remain was as much for his own protection as it was a safeguard for the girl. Some females weren't above accusing their assigned solicitors of sexual harassment if they thought it might gain sympathy when they appeared in court.

The recorder was turned off, and Paget and Tregalles withdrew until some ten minutes later when Carmichael came to the door to say they were ready to continue. Back in the room with the recorder turned on, Carmichael said he would like to make a statement for the record.

'Miss Tyler categorically denies any knowledge whatsoever of the killing of Mrs Holbrook,' he said. 'She denies ever having entered the house in Pembroke Avenue, and claims to know nothing of that crime. In fact, she has an alibi for the evening of March fourth. She claims that—'

'I don't *claim* anything,' the girl broke in angrily. 'I was *there* at the hospital getting sewn up.' She pulled up her sleeve to reveal a six-inch long gash, and marks still red where stitches had been. 'See? You ask them at the hospital. They'll tell you. Sat there half the bloody night bleeding all over the floor before they got round to me. Had the stitches out yesterday.'

'I see,' said Paget. 'That looks like a knife wound to me. How did that happen?'

The girl shrugged. 'Don't remember,' she said, meeting his eyes defiantly.

'Was anyone else injured at the same time? Were there any witnesses to what happened?'

'Like I said, I don't remember.'

Paget turned to Tregalles. 'Check with the hospital and see if they can verify that Miss Tyler was there last Wednesday evening. They should have a record of the time she was booked in. Meanwhile,' he continued as Tregalles left the room, 'regardless of where you were last Wednesday, Chloe, let's talk about the rest of the burglaries, beginning with the one in Dunbar Road.'

Eighteen

Almost everything they found in Chloe's squat in the basement of a boarded-up warehouse on King George Way, together with the clothes she was wearing at the time of her arrest, was turned over to Forensic for examination.

The girl had steadfastly denied taking part in any of the burglaries, and yet Paget had found her responses revealing as he went through each location. While she denied knowing anything about the burglary on Dunbar Road, she did so in an almost offhanded way, a programmed response by someone well-versed in the judicial system: deny every-thing in the hope that the police wouldn't find enough evidence to make the charges stick. But when Paget moved on to the one in Abbey Road and the rest, Chloe became quite agitated and vehement in her denials.

'I don't even know where some of those streets are, so don't think you're going to pin those jobs on me! And I don't know anything about any murder, either.'

Despite her record, Paget was inclined to believe her. He'd checked the list of stolen items against those found among the girl's possessions in the squat, and while much of the stuff had probably been stolen at one time or another, the only items that matched his list were the brooches and pendants taken from the house in Dunbar Road. Not a single item listed as missing from the rest of the homes could be found. And the hospital records confirmed Chloe's story about having the deep cut on her arm attended to on the night Laura Holbrook was killed.

To say that Paget was surprised when Joshua Davenport was brought in would be an understatement. Terry Coleman had described the man reasonably well, but the image conjured up in Paget's mind was quite different from that of the man who sat across the table from him now.

Davenport had form, petty stuff, most of it drug-related in one way or another. Four convictions for possession, two acquittals, one convic-tion for theft, and one for being drunk and disorderly in a public place.

'Hardly the record you'd expect of a twenty-eight-year-old Cambridge man, who has a PhD after his name,' Ormside observed as he handed the sheet to Paget. 'Still, takes all sorts, I suppose. Seems like he was coming off an all-night session with some friends when we picked him up, though God knows how someone like him has friends among the Gypsies. He's not what you might call fit, but the doc says we can question him.'

Davenport was tall and thin to the point of emaciation. His cheeks were sunken, his eyes pale and watery. He looked as if he had a cold, his nose was red, and he dabbed at it as unobtrusively as possible from time to time with a wad of tissues concealed in his hand. But his hair was neatly combed, and most surprising to Paget was the fact that Davenport was wearing a suit, white shirt and tie. The suit was old and threadbare, and the sleeves of the jacket were too short for his long arms, but the material was clearly of excellent quality. The shirt was yellowing with age, and the tie was fraying at the ends, but the overall impression was of someone who was doing his best to maintain a semblance of dignity despite being down on his luck.

He sat upright in the chair, feet tucked beneath it, perhaps trying to hide the fact that he was wearing worn and ragged trainers rather than shoes. He watched calmly, waiting until Ormside, sitting in for Tregalles, had the recorder up and running before he said, 'May I say something for the record before we begin?'

'Of course, bearing in mind that you are still under caution,' Paget told him.

Davenport nodded perfunctorily. 'As I'm sure you know, having read my file, I am well acquainted with the procedure, so there is no need to waste time on that. Also, I do not wish to have a solicitor present. It's been my experience that most of them are neither interested in someone like me, nor are they particularly competent, and I find I spend less time in confinement when I plead guilty and throw myself on the mercy of the court, than I do if they try to defend me. So, if it's all right with you, can we cut to the chase, as they say?'

He paused to eye Paget speculatively before continuing. 'I take it you have been talking to Chloe, since she is the only one who knew where I would be. Tell me, did she do another job?'

'I can tell you that Miss Tyler and another young person are helping us with our enquiries into certain matters,' Paget said neutrally.

'Another young person?' Davenport looked pained. 'It must be young

Coleman,' he said with an air of resignation, then closed his eyes and shook his head sorrowfully. 'Oh, Chloe,' he said softly as if speaking to the girl herself, 'will you never learn?'

Paget had the feeling that control of the interview was beginning to slip away from him. Davenport would take over if he didn't step in now.

'You mentioned pleading guilty,' he said a little more sharply than he'd intended. 'Is that what you wish to do in this case?'

'Ah! Now that rather depends on what you intend to charge me with, doesn't it, Chief Inspector? I mean, all Chloe and I were doing really was looking for a bit of spare change. I'll admit there was some peripheral damage, but—'

'*Peripheral* damage? Oh, no, Mr Davenport, I'm afraid it's far more serious than that. You and Miss Tyler are looking at some very serious charges: five burglaries, theft, criminal damage and murder.'

'Murder?' Davenport's voice rose sharply, the bantering tone suddenly gone. 'You can't be serious? And *five* burglaries? That's utterly ridiculous! I may be guilty of a bit of pilfering, and possibly – I say *possibly* – what you call burglary, but only out of necessity when I have no other means of support. But I have never hurt anyone in my life, so let's get this misunderstanding cleared up now.'

'There is no misunderstanding,' Paget told him, 'so I suggest you stop trying to treat this as if it's some sort of schoolboy prank. These are serious charges, and I think you would be wise to reconsider your position regarding whether or not you wish to have a solicitor present.

'Oh, yes, and Forensic will need your clothes – all of them.'

'Strange sort of bloke,' Ormside mused, referring to Josh Davenport when he and Paget were reviewing the transcripts at the end of the day. 'But then if he's one of that lot from Cambridge, what can you expect? And he really doesn't like solicitors, does he? Not even after you warned him several times that he could be facing serious charges. Good job *that's* on the tape.'

In Davenport's opinion, solicitors went out of their way to make relatively simple matters more complicated than they really were, and the result rarely had anything to do with justice, so he wanted no part of them. He stuck to the story regarding the burglaries. He admitted to breaking into the house on Dunbar Road with Chloe, but only, he claimed, because they were hungry and desperate. He said they had left Broadminster two days later for Chester, which was exactly what Chloe

Tyler had told them. He and Chloe had gone to stay with a friend of his from his Cambridge days, now doing postgraduate work at the university there. Normally, Davenport told them, he would not have imposed on his friend's good nature, but he needed a place to stay until he felt well enough to try for another job, and had asked his friend if he could bring Chloe with him because she had been good to him while he was ill, and they were both flat broke.

The day staff had gone and the incident room was quiet except for the burbling gasps of Ormside's coffee pot.

'I can't see those two committing a murder,' Ormside said as he closed the file. 'They're not even very good at thieving, and young Coleman certainly isn't cut out for it.'

Davenport had told them that when he became ill and lost his job at the car wash on Prince Street, it was Chloe who had looked after him as best she could, so when she said she was going to break into a house to look for cash, and he couldn't dissuade her, he felt the least he could do was go with her to make sure she wasn't caught.

When asked how the house was chosen, he said Chloe had had her eye on it for some time, because she knew that the man who owned it worked the evening shift at one of the clubs.

Ormside had spoken to the proprietor of the car wash on Prince Street, and he confirmed that Josh had worked there until just before Christmas, but when he failed to come in to work two days running, someone else was hired to take his place. 'Don't know what happened to him,' he admitted when Ormside asked, 'but then, that's not my problem, is it? Not when I've got a business to run.'

There had been no hesitation when Davenport was asked to give the name and address of his friend in Chester, and the man had confirmed Davenport's story when Ormside contacted him by phone. 'Shame about old Josh,' he'd said. 'Nice chap; brilliant in many ways, but just can't hack it in the real world. Turns up here every so often. Give him a bed, feed him up, but then I'll wake up one morning to find him gone.'

When Davenport was asked who did the damage in the Dunbar Road burglary, he said it was Chloe who did that. 'She was so frustrated when she couldn't find any money that she just lashed out with that bar of hers. Which,' he continued, 'was another reason I decided to take her with me to Chester. I thought she might do something daft if I left her in that state.'

Paget swirled the remains of his coffee in the bottom of the mug as he said, 'Which means, if we accept as fact that Josh and Chloe only did the one burglary, then it looks as if Forsythe is right, and the rest of the burglaries were staged as a lead-up to the killing of Laura Holbrook. But two people working together? If that is the case, then it seems at least likely that one of them had to be Holbrook himself. Especially if there is any truth to the suggestion that he was unhappy about the way Laura had taken over. But who is the other one? Susan Chase? She was certainly in there straight away. Moira Ballantyne is another possibility, as is Tim Bryce – he had something to gain by getting rid of her. Peggy Goodwin had good reason to hate Laura, but why wait a couple of years before killing her? But one thing we do know – provided Trevor Ballantyne isn't lying through his teeth, and I can't think of a reason why he would do that – Holbrook himself couldn't have killed Laura; his partner has to be the one who did that. I know, I know,' he said as he saw the look Ormside gave him, 'your money is still on Moira, but I think I'm leaning more and more toward Susan Chase. She's just too good to be true.

'But that's for another day,' he said, glancing guiltily at the clock. Tonight was to be Grace's first painting lesson, and he didn't want to be late getting home.

'Just one thing before you go,' Ormside said. 'Laura Holbrook's funeral is at eleven o'clock tomorrow morning at St Margaret's, which would make it roughly eleven forty-five at the cemetery for the interment, according to the chap I spoke to. You planning on going?'

'To the cemetery, yes,' said Paget as he shrugged into his coat. 'After all, you never know who will turn up at funerals, do you?'

Nineteen

The cemetery was on the side of a hill. It wasn't a steep slope, but the long grass was wet and slippery underfoot, the results of a shower during the night, and some of the ladies in their open-toed and high-heeled shoes didn't look too happy as they followed the casket to the graveside.

There was quite a large gathering around the grave. Simon Holbrook and his late wife's sister, Susan Chase, stood next to the vicar, and slightly behind them and to one side stood Trevor and Moira Ballantyne. Beside them were several people who seemed to be more or less on their own, possibly friends or distant relatives. Tim Bryce was there as well. He had placed himself at a respectful distance from his uncle, but in such a way that Simon Holbrook was bound to see him there.

At the bottom end of the open grave, facing the vicar, was another small group, some of whom Tregalles was able to identify as members of the badminton club, headed by Bernard Fiske, while on the side opposite Holbrook, completing the circle, were what must have been almost the entire staff of Holbrook Micro Engineering Laboratories, led by Peggy Goodwin.

But there was one man who stood a little apart from the rest as if not quite sure which group, if any, he should join. Fiftyish, perhaps, grey hair, slim, very well-dressed. He stood with head bowed, hands resting on the handle of the furled umbrella in front of him.

The two detectives stayed well back from the graveside. They were there only to observe.

The interment service was brief, and the casket was being lowered when Tregalles spoke. 'Take a look at sister Susie,' he muttered. 'See how she's holding on to Holbrook's arm? Doesn't look to me as if he's grieving all that much, either.'

Tregalles might well be right in his assessment of the situation, but Paget couldn't help thinking back to his own tragic loss, when he should have been there at the graveside to say his last goodbye to Jill. But he hadn't been there; hadn't even known the funeral was taking place. Oh, there were pictures, and friends had done their best to tell him every-thing. His old boss and close friend, Bob McKenzie, had even had the ceremony and the interment videotaped, but it wasn't the same. He had no actual *memories*! Nothing. The weeks immediately following Jill's death had been taken from his life as neatly as if they had been surgically removed. Gone, never to be recaptured, and he felt cheated as he watched the casket containing Laura Holbrook's body disappear into the ground.

His thoughts were interrupted by a nudge from Tregalles. 'Take a look at Mrs Ballantyne,' the sergeant said softly.

Paget scanned the faces around the graveside. Almost everyone's eyes were cast down as the vicar read the closing prayer, but Moira Ballantyne's eyes were fixed on Holbrook and Susan Chase. It was a speculative look, and there was something about the set of her jaw, the slightly narrowed eyes, and the way her head was tilted that suggested she was trying very hard to work something out.

The service ended with the lowering of the casket while Holbrook and Susan Chase each came forward to drop a single rose as it dis-appeared from view. The vicar closed his book and stepped away.

One by one, people began to leave, some pausing to say a few words to Simon and Susan, while others simply drifted away to their cars lined up on the road below. The man they'd observed standing apart from the others waited until the very last to approach Holbrook. Simon said something to Susan Chase, who moved away and began to walk slowly down the hill by herself. The detectives were too far away to hear any words, but it seemed to Paget that there was a certain stiffness between the two men. The man stepped back, said something, then turned and walked rapidly away. Holbrook followed more slowly to join Susan, who stood waiting at the bottom of the hill.

The grey-haired man was in his car and pulling out by the time the two detectives reached the road, and more from habit than for any other reason, Paget took out his notebook and jotted down the numbers on the fast receding plate.

'Just curious,' he said by way of explanation, 'but let's find out who he is anyway.'

'Probably a solicitor by the look of him,' Tregalles said as he copied the numbers in his own book, 'but it shouldn't take long to find out since he's driving a brand new Mercedes.'

*   *   *

'Fiona wants you to ring her,' Ormside told Paget when he and Tregalles returned to Charter Lane. 'The super's gone home with some sort of bilious attack — probably the flu by the sound of it, so he won't be able to attend a meeting with Mr Brock this afternoon, and he'd like you to stand in for him. Fiona says she has the information you'll need if you would like to study it beforehand.'

Paget eyed the sergeant stonily. An afternoon in a meeting with Chief Superintendent Brock was not his idea of how to end the week. 'Did she say when, where and what it is all about?' he asked.

Ormside wrinkled his nose in a way that told Paget he wasn't going to like the answer. 'Clear-up rates and the lack of,' the sergeant said. 'Two o'clock in Mr Brock's office.'

Paget was about to leave when he caught sight of the calendar on Ormside's desk. Friday the thirteenth! He might have known.

Saturday afternoon, March 14

'Just going to pop down the road to Milverton's,' Peggy Goodwin told her mother as she slipped a coat over her shoulders. 'Won't be long. Anything you need?'

'Don't think so, love. Oh, yes there is, come to think of it,' her mother said. 'Bring back a lasagne for supper. Arthur likes that, and you'll be staying, will you?'

Peggy paused at the door. She had a lot of work waiting for her at home, and she wasn't keen on the deep-dish frozen lasagne her mother was so fond of, but she knew her mother would be disappointed if she said no. 'Yes, I'll be staying,' she said, 'but I shall have to leave soon after. I have a lot to do at home.'

It was the same every Saturday. Business in the gift shop always tapered off by mid-afternoon, and that was when Peggy did her shopping for the week. Milverton's wasn't the best place in town to shop, but it was handy, and Tesco's was half a mile away, parking would be at a premium, and the store would be packed. Peggy went through the same mental exercise almost every week, and she always ended up at Milverton's.

With her mind on other things, Peggy barely noticed the short, plump, middle-aged woman coming toward her until they were only a few feet apart, and even then it took her a moment to realize that she knew the woman. 'Billie?' she said, stopping dead in her tracks. 'Billie Strickland? Is that really you?'

'Peggy!' The woman beamed 'Well I'll be damned! Fancy running into you on the street like this.' The smiled faded into a guilty grimace as she glanced around. 'You won't tell anyone you saw me, though, will you? I mean John would be furious if he knew, but I just had to come to check out the lie of the land, so to speak. Do you live around here?'

'My mother has the gift shop,' Peggy told her with a nod over her shoulder. 'But what are you doing here, Billie? And why mustn't John know?'

Billie Strickland leaned closer to Peggy. 'As if you didn't know,' she said in a hoarse whisper, then drew back and winked. 'But the boys must have their little secrets and play their little games, mustn't they? Still,' she sighed, 'I suppose it's necessary in this sort of business. John says the deal is as good as done, but it's all hush-hush until it's finalized. But then, you'd know more about that than I do, wouldn't you, being in the thick of things, so to speak?'

Peggy had no idea what Billie Strickland was talking about, but her curiosity was piqued, and she wanted to know more. 'Look,' she said, taking Billie's arm, 'there's a lovely little tea room at the end of the street. Why don't we go down there and have a cup of tea and a scone – or a butter tart?' Billie could never resist the pastries.

The woman closed her eyes and heaved a gentle sigh. 'You're like an angel from heaven,' she breathed. 'My feet are killing me and I could murder a cup of tea. Please, lead on, and it's my treat.'

'Sorry I took so long, Mum,' said Peggy breathlessly as she entered the shop and set two bags of groceries on the floor behind the counter, 'but I bumped into an old friend I haven't seen in years, and she insisted that I go and have a cup of tea with her down at Mabel's, and the time just slipped by.'

'That's all right, love,' her mother said. 'I've only had one customer since you left, and it will soon be time to shut the shop in any case. You did say you'd stay for supper, didn't you, Peg?'

'I did, but I shall have to eat and run, I'm afraid.' She glanced at the time. 'In fact, if it's all right with you, I'll put the oven on now and get started on the vegetables. Is Arthur still out the back in the workshop?'

Her mother nodded. 'Better give him a shout and tell him supper will be early so he can come in and wash up,' she said.

Peggy took the packaged lasagne from one of the bags and went down the passage to the kitchen. Only part of her mind was on what she was doing; the rest of it was still back there in the tea shop, listening to Billie Strickland talk about her husband, John.

'He wanted me to come with him, of course, and I said I'd think about it, but having seen the place for myself, I've made up my mind. There is no way I could come here to live, even if it is only for six months to a year. Not that I have anything against Broadminster, *per se*,' she added hastily. 'It's a charming town in its own way, but you must admit it isn't Birmingham or even Solihull, now is it, Peggy? I mean where are the shops? The theatres? The restaurants?'

That would be a sticking point with Billie, Peggy thought. Cutting Billie off from the amenities of the big city would be like depriving her of air.

'No,' Billie continued determinedly, 'John will have to commute and come home on the weekends. Henry has assured him that everything will be ready for the move back to Solihull by the end of the year, so it's not as if we will have to put up with it for long. In fact we might all be together again for Christmas.'

Peggy had sipped her tea to give herself time to think. At least a dozen questions were hammering away inside her head, all looking for answers, but how could she put them without revealing that this was all news to her?

She set her cup aside. 'I'm afraid we don't hear much down here about what is going on back at the old firm,' she said, choosing her words carefully. 'What, exactly, is John's title, now?' Her recollection of John Strickland was of a rather plodding junior manager, but from the way Billie was talking, it sounded as if he had finally started up the corporate ladder.

'Special Projects Manager,' Billie told her with a touch of smugness. 'There were three others in the running, but they chose John, and Henry as good as told him that he could be in line for VP in two or three years if everything goes smoothly with this move. So, perhaps it's a good thing I bumped into you this afternoon, because I want John to succeed down here, and I know I can count on you to do everything you can to help him. He will be bringing in his own office staff, of course, but I'm sure that you and he will be working very closely together.'

Billie popped the last piece of butter tart into her mouth and sighed contentedly. 'I feel so much better now after talking to you,' she said. 'But please don't tell John I was here.'

Peggy's mind had been so busy trying to absorb what she was hearing that she barely acknowledged the implied question before asking, 'Just when does all this take place – John's actual move down here, I mean,' she added hastily as she saw Billie's pencilled browns begin to draw together in a questioning frown.

'Oh, sometime next month is what he told me. I don't know the exact date.'

Sometime next month! Peggy tried to get the words out of her head, but they were still there an hour later when she left her mother's house. Not for home as she had told her mother, but to the office. But John as a future VP? No way. But then, that was the way Henry Beaumont worked.

Twenty

Paget arrived at work some twenty minutes late. It had rained hard all the way in from Ashton Prior to Charter Lane; an accident at the top of Strathe Hill had slowed traffic to a crawl, and the traffic lights were out at the bottom of the hill. Not the way he'd hoped to start the day after spending the previous one standing in for Alcott, still off with the flu, at yet another of Chief Superintendent Brock's interminable meetings. He'd heaved a mental sigh of relief when the meeting concluded at three o'clock – still time to do a little work – but Brock had asked him to stay behind to discuss the case.

Discussion was hardly the word. Brock had been hell-bent on setting up a special task force to take over the investigation, and it had taken Paget the best part of an hour to try to dissuade him. He'd finally succeeded, but he knew that Brock wouldn't let the matter rest for long if he couldn't be shown results.

'Morning, boss,' Tregalles greeted him when Paget entered the incident room. He looked remarkably cheerful, considering as Paget could see at a glance, there was nothing new on the whiteboards. Even Ormside looked slightly less dour than usual as he acknowledged Paget's entrance with a nod.

'All right, Tregalles,' he said, 'what's happened?'

The sergeant grinned broadly. 'Must be your birthday, boss,' he said. 'Got a present for you.' The grin faded. Clearly Paget was in no mood for games. 'Trevor Ballantyne,' he said soberly. 'He's in room number 1. Came in first thing this morning to say he wanted to make a correction to his statement about the night of the murder, but he wouldn't say any more until you got here. Could be the break we've been looking for.'

'Sounds promising,' said Paget cautiously, 'so let's see what he has to say.' He started for the door, then paused in mid-stride. 'Where's Forsythe?' he asked Ormside as he scanned the room.

'Next door picking up faxes,' the sergeant told him.

'Send her along as soon as she gets back,' Paget told him. 'I'd like her to hear what Ballantyne has to say as well.'

Tregalles didn't say anything as he followed Paget out, but he couldn't help wondering why the boss had been taking so much interest in Molly Forsythe lately. Not that she wasn't worth taking an interest in, he thought. Good-looking woman like that, and smart. And clearly she'd caught Paget's eye. Could that be the reason for . . .? He gave his head a mental shake. No, couldn't be, he told himself. Not Paget, not with someone like Grace Lovett living with him. On the other hand, you could never tell when something like that might happen. Tregalles had seen it before – office romances springing up between the most unlikely people working closely together. And even DCIs were human.

Trevor Ballantyne looked as if he hadn't slept for days. He was neatly dressed and clean-shaven, but his face was grey, and there were dark hollows under his eyes.

Paget and Tregalles faced him across the table, while Molly Forsythe sat near the door. 'Now, then, Mr Ballantyne,' said Paget, 'exactly what is it you wish to tell us?'

Ballantyne ran his tongue across his lips to moisten them. 'I know I should have told you before,' he began hesitantly, 'and I'm sorry, but I didn't see any harm in it at the time. But with Moira under suspicion, and the way things look, I decided I had to speak up and set the record straight so to speak. I don't know who killed Laura, but I do know who had the opportunity, and perhaps a motive, and in a way I was part of it – although I didn't know it at the time, of course,' he added hastily.

'A name . . .?' Paget prompted.

Ballantyne drew a deep breath. 'Simon,' he said. 'I'm not saying he did it,' he went on quickly, 'but he wasn't where he said he was, and with the way things were with the marriage, it could have been him. But I do know that Moira had nothing to do with it.'

'You're saying you lied when you told us Simon was with you that evening? Is that correct, Mr Ballantyne?'

He nodded. 'And I'm sorry. I know it's a crime to mislead the police but, as I said, I couldn't believe it at first, but it's the only thing that makes sense.'

Ballantyne went on to tell them that he had picked up Simon Holbrook shortly before seven o'clock as he'd originally stated, but they had only gone a short distance before Simon said he was sorry, but Susan Chase had telephoned just before he left the house to ask if he could help her with a problem she had with the shop's security system. It wasn't working properly, and she was nervous about leaving it overnight, so Simon said he'd come over and see what he could do. But he'd made it clear that he didn't want Laura to know, because she might get the wrong idea, so he'd asked Trevor to say that they'd been together all evening if the subject should ever come up.

'I dropped him off at the shop,' Ballantyne explained, 'and picked him up on my way back. I was going to drop him off then go on home, but he invited me in for a nightcap – a sort of thank you for going along with him, I thought at the time – so I went in.

'Because it was all fiction, of course,' he continued. 'We both knew it; I mean I knew that he and Susan had been seeing each other on the quiet for months, but I didn't see any real harm in it. Simon hadn't said anything, at least not in so many words, but you could see that things were beginning to go pear-shaped with their marriage, so I wasn't exactly surprised when Simon asked me to drop him off.'

He paused, frowning as if something was puzzling him. 'Except he seemed to be more on edge than usual that night,' he said slowly. 'Mind you, he's a funny chap at the best of times, up one minute, down the next. It's tension. When it's really bad it makes him ill, and I knew he was worried about the situation at home, so I left it. You wouldn't think it to look at him, but he suffers from depression, and he only gets more upset if you try to talk to him about it.'

Paget said, 'What did you mean when you said you knew he was worried about the situation at home? What situation, exactly?'

'Just the way things had changed,' said Ballantyne. 'Less than a year ago he couldn't stop talking about how wonderful Laura was, and how she had saved the company, and how bright the future was. And he was right; the woman is brilliant – or was, of course, but I haven't heard him utter one good word about her in recent months. Not one!'

'So what brought about the change?' asked Paget.

'Laura's attitude, mostly. The business was all she thought about; she couldn't talk about anything else, and she was constantly putting Simon down. Like he told me himself a couple of weeks ago. He said, "She isn't interested in me at all. All she ever wanted was the company. I mean without me and my ideas there wouldn't be any –"' Ballantyne glanced at Molly, and decided to leave out the actual words that Holbrook had used, and said instead – '"friggin company". He said she was overruling him at work, putting him down in front of others, and it was just as bad at home.'

Ballantyne shook his head sadly. 'We've noticed the change in them ourselves,' he continued. 'Moira and I have talked about it. Simon's been trying to put a brave face on it, but we've noticed it at the club. Just the odd word now and again, but Laura could really put the knife in when she wanted to, and she was so good at it that you hardly knew she'd done it until you thought about it later.'

'What did you mean when you said it was just as bad at home?' Paget asked. 'Did Mr Holbrook elaborate?'

'Sex,' said Ballantyne, lowering his voice. 'He told me that he and Laura hadn't had sex in months, and *that* must have been the last straw for poor old Simon. I felt sorry for him, I really did, which was why I was willing to go along with him that night when he gave me that cock-and-bull story about Susan's security system. Funny, though, when you think about it, isn't it? I mean him and Susan after he left her for Laura. Mind you, it was Laura who did the running, but Simon was as much to blame, so I'm still amazed that Susan would have anything to do with either of them. But she took it all in her stride the way she does with everything else.' He frowned. 'If it were anyone else but Susan, I'd be tempted to think she could be doing it for revenge – taking Simon back from her sister, if you know what I mean.'

'You and Simon Holbrook must go back a few years,' Tregalles said. 'How long have you known each other?'

'On and off ever since our schooldays,' he said. 'Not that we ever chummed around together or anything like that. He was a couple of years ahead of me, and that's a lot when you're kids. And then, of course, we went our separate ways: university, jobs that took us in different directions, and it was only when Simon came back to Broadminster to set up his business here that we came into contact again. Even then we didn't really get together until we met through the badminton club.'

'Your wife mentioned that you also knew the Chase sisters during those early years,' said Paget.

'Right, I did. At school. In fact Laura and I were in the same form for a while. Susan was a year ahead of her sister to start with, but Laura went into an accelerated programme, which meant that she and Susan ended up in the sixth form at the same time. And it didn't matter what Susan did, Laura always had to do the same or go one better. The two girls were as different as chalk and cheese. Laura was always looking for a challenge; she always had to be best; top of the class, but Susan wasn't like that at all. She was a good student, mark you; always well up there near the top, but she wasn't interested in competing with her sister, and I think that used to annoy Laura more than anything – that Susan didn't respond when she was challenged, I mean.'

'Lovely girl, Susan,' Ballantyne continued wistfully. 'She really didn't deserve to have a sister like Laura always nipping at her heels. She would have made someone a wonderful wife, but it wasn't to be. She never married. Not that she didn't have the chance.' The way he said it made Paget wonder if Ballantyne had had hopes in that direction himself back then.

'Funny,' Ballantyne continued, frowning, 'I haven't thought of it for years, but the only time I ever saw Susan get really upset, was because of something Laura did to her. Laura treated it as a huge joke, but it was anything but a joke to Susan. She put on a brave face, but I'm sure she could have killed her . . .'

Ballantyne stopped abruptly. 'Sorry,' he said. 'Just a figure of speech. Didn't mean to run on like that. It's just that I hadn't thought about some of those things in years.'

'What exactly was it that Laura did?' Tregalles asked.

Ballantyne looked uncomfortable. 'It's all in the past,' he said. 'Doesn't mean anything now. I'm afraid I got off track.'

'Nevertheless, we would like to hear it,' said Paget, taking the lead again.

'It was just a figure of speech,' Ballantyne said. 'I didn't mean . . .' He looked from one to the other as if expecting a response, but when no one spoke, he sat back in his chair and shrugged in a way that said he thought it was a waste of time.

'Susan would have been about eighteen at the time,' he said. 'She was going with a chap a couple of years older than she was, and things were beginning to get pretty serious when Laura moved in on him and took him away from her. Laura dumped him later, but the damage was done. As I said, she treated it as a big joke at the time, but it wasn't a joke to Susan. And then, along comes Laura again some seventeen or eighteen years later, and damned if she doesn't do it again with Simon.'

Ballantyne saw the look that passed between the two detectives. 'Look,' he said earnestly, 'if it had been anyone else but Susan, maybe they would have reacted differently, maybe even violently, but not Susan. She's not like that. In fact I've never met anyone who didn't like Susan.'

'Except Laura,' Paget observed drily. 'But let's get back to the night Laura was killed. Did you see Simon actually go into the shop?'

Ballantyne shook his head. 'No. I dropped him off and drove away.'

'And now you are suggesting that, instead of going in, he made his way back to the house, killed his wife, then returned in time for you to pick him up again outside the shop. Is that right, Mr Ballantyne?'

Ballantyne squirmed in his seat. 'I said it's possible, that's all,' he protested. 'I don't know that's what happened, but *somebody* killed Laura, didn't they? I didn't think of it at the time, of course. It was such a shock finding Laura the way we did, that it didn't occur to me to connect the two things.'

'Any ideas about how he would get from the shop to the house and back again?'

Ballantyne shrugged. 'He could have walked; it's less than a mile. Or he could have used Susan's car. I suppose it's possible that he and Susan were in it together, but I really can't see Susan being involved. But Simon would hardly take a taxi, would he?'

'There is another possibility,' Paget said. 'And that is that Mr Holbrook had arranged to be picked up by *your* wife, and the two of them went back to the house, where it was she who killed Laura Holbrook. They were *her* fingerprints we found all over the crime scene, and *her* clothes that were stained with Laura Holbrook's blood. Doesn't that seem a more likely explanation, Mr Ballantyne?'

'No! No, that's not true,' Ballantyne protested. 'Moira explained all that. Laura was dead when she got there. Moira tried to help her until she realized Laura was dead. Besides, it's Susan Simon is having the affair with, and that's where I took him that night.'

'Even if that's true,' Tregalles said, 'it doesn't rule out the possibility that Simon Holbrook was having an affair with someone else at the same time. He does have that sort of reputation, doesn't he, sir? And it has been suggested to us that Simon Holbrook and your wife have enjoyed a close relationship in the past. Perhaps that relationship still exists.'

The grey pallor in Trevor Ballantyne's face gave way to a rush of colour. 'That's not true,' he whispered. 'Not true at all!'

'Not true that they are having an affair now?' Tregalles asked, 'or not true that they had an affair in the past?'

Trevor Ballantyne closed his eyes and breathed deeply, trying desperately to remain calm. 'Not true that they are having an affair now,' he said, opening his eyes and enunciating each word carefully. 'As for what might or might not have been in the past, it remains in the past as far as I'm concerned, because it isn't relevant.'

'Unfortunately, since this is a murder enquiry, we can't afford to dismiss it quite so lightly,' Paget told him. 'As I'm sure you are aware, we look primarily for motive and opportunity, and your wife had both.'

'But that was over long ago!' Ballantyne insisted. 'Besides, you couldn't even call it an affair. We were going through a bad patch. Moira and Simon were working all hours together getting the security system sorted out, and it just happened. There was nothing to it; it was over in a week.'

'How do you know that, Mr Ballantyne? Did your wife tell you that?'

'She didn't have to. I just knew, that's all. Everything's been fine between us ever since.'

'So how did that make you feel about Simon Holbrook?' Tregalles asked. 'Knowing that he was having it off with your wife. I mean didn't that upset you?'

'Of course it upset me,' Ballantyne snapped, 'but that doesn't mean that Moira and I couldn't work through it.'

'You've talked about it, then, have you, sir? With your wife, I mean?'

Trevor Ballantyne's eyes narrowed. 'No,' he said tersely. 'In my estimation, there are times when it is better not to talk about things like that, and let things work out for themselves.'

Tregalles looked puzzled. 'And yet you remained friends with Simon Holbrook,' he said. 'I don't understand how you could do that.'

Ballantyne shook his head impatiently. 'I wouldn't say we're friends, exactly,' he said. 'It was more of a business relationship. We do have similar interests; we've helped each other out with technical problems from time to time, and there's the badminton, of course, but we're hardly bosom pals.'

'Still, it must have made you somewhat uncomfortable at times when the four of you were out together,' Tregalles said. 'I mean, if I knew my wife had had an affair with a friend of mine, no matter how brief, I think I'd be watching the two of them like a hawk whenever they were together.'

'As I said,' Ballantyne said stiffly, 'I knew it was over; I knew Moira regretted it, so it was done with as far as I was concerned.'

'But it must rankle,' Tregalles persisted. 'Is that why you came in today? To point the finger in Simon Holbrook's direction? To suggest that he and Susan Chase were in this together? To divert suspicion away from your wife?'

'No!' Ballantyne burst out. 'That is *not* why I came. I came here this morning to try to set things right, and tell you what really happened that night. I mean, why would Simon have me drop him outside Susan's if he and Moira . . .?' The words dried in his mouth. He clamped his lips together and squeezed his eyes shut as he sank back in his seat. 'You're wrong,' he whispered. 'You have to believe me. I swear, there is nothing going on between Moira and Simon. Nothing!'

Tregalles and Paget exchanged glances. 'Let's hope you're right, then, Mr Ballantyne,' Paget said. 'But I'm afraid that we will be the ones who have the final say on that.'

Trevor Ballantyne's hand shook when he signed the statement, and his face looked even greyer than it had when he'd first sat down. He put the pen down and slumped back in his seat. 'So, what happens now?' he asked nervously 'Do I have to stay here? Am I to be charged?'

'Not for the moment,' Paget said as he picked up the statement. 'You're free to go, but you may be charged later. Meanwhile, you are required to let us know if you or your wife plan to leave the area, and I suggest that both of you avoid contact with Mr Holbrook, at least until we've had a chance to talk to him. Constable Forsythe will see you to your car.'

'I don't believe that anyone can be *that* tolerant,' said Tregalles when Ballantyne had gone. 'Especially when Laura really stuck it to her sister twice. Susan Chase may be one of the nicest people in the world, but even she must have her breaking point.' He sounded sad; he'd taken quite a liking to Susan Chase.

'And she was there in the house almost within hours of her sister's death, helping Simon,' Paget reminded him. 'On the other hand, it's still possible that it was Moira, not Susan, who killed Laura.'

'Coming round to that view, then, are you?' Tregalles asked hopefully.

Paget smiled. 'Let's just say I'm keeping my options open,' he said.

Twenty-One

'Oh, for God's sake, Peg, I thought I had made myself clear when I said I didn't want any interruptions,' Simon Holbrook snapped as Peggy ushered Paget and Molly into his office. 'I'm sorry, Chief Inspector,' he continued, not sounding sorry at all, 'but I really don't have the time to talk to you today, so come back some other time. Peggy will arrange it. We're doing bench tests on a new device, and it's important that I be there, so if you'll excuse me . . .?' He picked up a batch of papers and began to come out from behind his desk.

'Unfortunately, it's even more important that we talk to you now,' said Paget firmly. He moved into Holbrook's path, not blocking him exactly, but enough to make the man stop. 'We would prefer to do that here, but we can do it at the station if necessary. It's your choice, Mr Holbrook.'

Holbrook stepped back a pace, eyes narrowed as he studied Paget's impassive features. Suddenly he laughed, a short, staccato sound that sounded forced. 'For a moment there, I almost thought you meant that,' he said nervously, 'but I really must insist—'

'And so must I, Mr Holbrook,' said Paget brusquely, 'so I suggest that we stop wasting each other's time and get on with it.'

'You can't . . .' Holbrook began defiantly, then stopped. 'Oh, very well, then,' he said peevishly, 'if it's *that* important to you, I suppose I can spare a few minutes.' He stepped around Paget to thrust the sheaf of papers into Peggy's hands with such force that she almost dropped them. 'Take those down to the lab and tell Stan I'll be down in ten minutes,' he said roughly. 'Ten minutes,' he repeated for Paget's benefit as he returned to his seat behind the desk and sat down.

Peggy Goodwin's face betrayed nothing, but her body language more than made her feelings clear. She turned to leave, but Molly stopped her. 'Your hand, Miss Goodwin,' she said. 'It's bleeding. Do be careful or you'll get blood on your clothes.' She glanced around. 'Can I get you something to put on it?'

Peggy examined her hand. Blood oozed from her little finger. 'It's just a paper cut,' she said, juggling the papers in her hand to dab it with a tissue. 'Thanks all the same, but I have a dressing in my office.'

'Now, what's this all about, Chief Inspector?' Holbrook said crossly as the door closed behind her.

Paget took his time opening his coat and settling himself in the chair, then glanced across at Molly as if to make sure she was ready to take notes. 'It's about why you lied to us about where you were the night your wife was killed,' he said abruptly. 'I'd like an explanation.'

Simon Holbrook's face turned red. 'I told you, I was at the cinema with Trevor . . .' he began heatedly, then stopped when he saw the look on Paget's face. Whatever he had been about to say died in his throat, and Paget could almost see him shifting gears inside his head.

Holbrook coughed and cleared his throat to start again. 'I see,' he said quietly. 'Trevor? Am I right? Been talking to you, has he? I was afraid he might. What did he tell you?'

Paget smiled. 'That's not the way it works, as I'm sure you know,' he said, 'so please don't waste any more of my time. I'm giving you the opportunity to explain why you lied, and where you were between the hours of seven o'clock and ten thirty the night your wife was killed.'

Holbrook looked up at the ceiling, blew out his cheeks and said, 'Honestly, the only reason I didn't tell you the truth was because I didn't want you to get the wrong idea. The truth is I had Trevor drop me off at Susan's – I'm sure he told you. Her security system wasn't working properly, and since I was the one who'd recommended it to her in the first place, she asked me to take a look at it.'

'She phoned you at home?'

'That's right.'

'Did you tell your wife where you were going?'

'She was in bed by that time,' Holbrook said evasively, 'and I didn't want to disturb her.'

'And because she might not understand, either?'

Holbrook grimaced. 'That's true,' he said. 'Laura was . . . well, to be honest, she was inclined to be jealous. Not that she had any reason to be, but it was sometimes simpler to, well, leave her out of the loop, as you might say.'

'And this was one of those times,' said Paget. 'Tell me, when, exactly, did Miss Chase make this phone call?'

'Just before Trevor picked me up. What with all these burglaries of late, and since there is access through the shop to her living quarters above, she was a bit nervous about leaving the problem till the morning, so I agreed to go, because—'

'That will be quite enough!' Paget broke in angrily. 'Can you not get it through your head, Mr Holbrook, that you are a suspect in the murder of your wife? And the more you lie to me, the more convinced I am that you're guilty. Now, you have one last chance to tell me the truth about where you were that night and what you did, or we will continue this conversation in Charter Lane. Do you understand?'

Holbrook turned pale. He raised his hands in front of him as if he thought Paget was about to attack him physically. 'All right, all right,' he said sullenly as he sank back in his chair. 'But you can't *really* think that I killed Laura,' he said shakily. 'She was my wife, for Christ's sake!'

'With whom you were less than happy,' Paget countered swiftly. 'A wife who had taken over the running of your firm, and a wife who was overruling you at work and making life miserable at home. A divorce would have ruined you and destroyed the company you'd built up from scratch, but if your wife died, you'd be in clover. You have lied to me about where you were, and you have signed a statement that is false. How many more reasons do you think I need to arrest you, Mr Holbrook?'

Simon Holbrook, mouth half open, stared at Paget. 'Look,' he said weakly, 'I swear I had nothing to do with Laura's death. I was with Susan; she'll back me up. Trevor will tell you; he dropped me off there and picked me up from there later. Honest to God, that's the truth.'

Paget remained silent, waiting, his expression grim.

'It is the truth,' Holbrook pressed on. 'I'll admit I lied about what I told Trevor. You're right, there was no phone call, but I had to tell him something so he wouldn't be suspicious, so I made up the story about the security system.'

'Then tell me why, after setting off to see a film with Mr Ballantyne, you suddenly felt the need to see Susan Chase? Why not cancel your night and simply go there?'

Simon looked at him for a long moment before he spoke, and Paget felt almost certain that he was about to lie once more. 'I needed cover,' he said with an air of candour. 'I couldn't let Laura know that I was going to see her sister, because she would think the worst. You're quite right, things weren't going well at work or at home. I had to talk to someone, someone who would understand, and perhaps help me get things back on track with Laura. The tug-of-war that was going on at work I could understand – at least in a way. Laura could run rings around me when it came to business decisions, and there were times when I felt I was losing control of my own business because she was making all the decisions. I didn't like the feeling, but I couldn't argue with the fact that what she was doing was good for the business. But what I couldn't understand was why, when we'd hit it off so well in the beginning, that Laura had gone off me. Believe me, Chief Inspector, I loved my wife. I just wanted things to be the way they were at first. But Susan is her sister, and sometimes Laura would confide in her, so I thought . . .' Holbrook raised his hands and let them drop. 'I just thought she might have said something to Susan. I'd been thinking about it all day, and when Trevor picked me up that night, I just knew I had to find out, so I asked him to drop me at Susan's. That's the truth.'

Scepticism lingered on Paget's face. 'And what did you learn from Miss Chase?' he asked.

Holbrook sucked in a long breath. 'Nothing,' he said as he let it out again. 'Susan said Laura hadn't said anything to her.'

'Hardly surprising, though, was it?' Paget said. 'As I understand it, the two sisters were hardly on the friendliest of terms, so why would Laura confide in Susan?'

Holbrook flushed. 'I suppose that came from Trevor as well,' he said, 'but it's not true. I'll admit they've had their differences but they did talk.'

'All right, we'll leave that for the moment,' Paget said, 'but I'd like to know what you did with the rest of the time you were together.'

The colour in Holbrook's face deepened. 'I don't understand,' he said stiffly. 'What are you implying?'

'I'm not implying anything,' Paget told him. 'I'm asking a simple question. You say Susan could tell you nothing; that Laura had not talked to her, so what did you do for the next three hours? Did you leave the premises at all? Go out for a meal? Did you go back to your house and kill your wife before returning to be picked up by Ballantyne?'

'We talked,' Holbrook said defiantly. 'Susan made tea and we just sat around and talked. We've known each other for a long time, and it was rather pleasant to be able to have a relaxing evening for a change. And I did not kill my wife.' He rose to his feet. 'So, if you've quite finished, I have work to do, and I'm running very late.'

'And we thank you for your time,' Paget said as he, too, stood up. 'However, busy or not, you are required to present yourself at Charter Lane within the next forty-eight hours to give us a revised statement.

And I should warn you that it is an offence to waste police time, and you could be charged, so you may wish to advise your solicitor.'

The word 'solicitor' reminded Paget of a question he'd meant to ask Holbrook earlier. 'Tell me,' he said. 'Who was that gentleman who spoke to you at the cemetery on Friday? Well dressed, driving a Mercedes?'

The question, at least as far as Paget was concerned, was prompted by little more than idle curiosity, but the effect on Holbrook was strange. He stared at Paget blankly, mouth half open before finding his voice. 'Henry Beaumont,' he said. 'Henry is the Research and Development VP in the Drexler-Davies Corporation, UK Division. I used to work for him before going out on my own. He came to the funeral as a representative of the company to offer their condolences, that's all. Why do you want to know?'

'Just curious, that's all,' Paget told him, truthfully, but Holbrook's reaction was something to think about.

Peggy Goodwin was either watching for them or Holbrook had called her on the intercom, because she came out of her office to escort them out of the building. Paget had the feeling that she would love to know what had gone on in Holbrook's office, but she said nothing as she removed their Visitor's badges and saw them out of the door.

'Well, Forsythe, you were very quiet in there,' said Paget when they reached the car. 'What did you make of it?'

'I thought you were doing very well on your own, sir,' Molly said boldly, but smiled to make sure he understood she meant no offence. 'But seriously, I don't think he's telling the whole truth. I have trouble visualizing the two of them just sitting there *talking* for three-and-a-half hours. I don't think it's in Mr Holbrook's nature to sit that long with a woman without making some sort of move on her. And from what Sergeant Tregalles told me about the way she acted at the house and at the funeral, all we *really* know is that there are three-and-a-half hours unaccounted for by both of them.'

Simon Holbrook sat slumped in his chair behind his desk when Peggy Goodwin entered his office and closed the door behind her. His brow was furrowed as if he was trying to work something out and several seconds passed before he looked up to acknowledge her presence.

'What is it, Simon?' she asked anxiously. 'What did they want? You look worried.'

He held her gaze for a moment longer, but Peggy had the feeling that he wasn't seeing her at all. 'They think I did it, Peg,' he said abruptly. 'I'm sure Paget's convinced that I killed Laura.'

'That's ridiculous! I mean how could you? You were with Trevor all evening. Surely they don't think that he would lie for you over something as serious as that?'

Holbrook looked away. 'I know,' he said, 'but still . . .'

Peggy's eyes narrowed. 'I know you, Simon,' she said softly, 'and there's something you're not telling me, isn't there? You didn't lie to them about that, did you? I mean about Trevor? You *were* with him the whole time, weren't you?'

'Of course,' he said quickly, 'but— '

'Then I don't see what you have to worry about.'

'It's the motive,' Holbrook said. 'They keep coming back to the fact that Laura and I weren't getting along, and that I had the most to gain by . . . by killing her.'

Peggy made a face. 'Unfortunately, that's true,' she said gently, 'and they'd be even more suspicious if they'd heard the things you've said to me about her, but honestly, Simon, I don't see why you should worry, so why not go down to the lab and get on with the tests and forget about it.'

Holbrook came out from behind his desk, but as he made for the door, Peggy put a hand on his arm. 'There *is* something else, though, isn't there?' she said shrewdly. 'There's something you're not telling me What is it, Simon? What are you *really* scared of?'

'Nothing,' he said brusquely, shaking off her hand. 'I have to go. I'm late as it is.'

'But Simon—'

'For Christ's sake, leave it, Peg!' he snarled. 'It's none of your business anyway.' He brushed past her and opened the door, then stopped. 'Sorry,' he said without turning. 'Didn't mean to bite your head off, but I've answered more than enough questions for one day, so just leave it for now. I don't want to discuss it any more. All right?'

'I understand,' she said. 'I know it's been hard on you. It's just that . . .' She stopped speaking. Simon Holbrook was already walking away.

Twenty-Two

Wednesday, March 18

The Basket of Flowers was an attractive little shop in the middle of a row of small shops and boutiques on one side of the market square. The buildings themselves were some of the oldest in Broadminster, and many of them had gone through a number of transformations over the centuries. But the town fathers, at least in recent years, with an eye to the summer tourist trade, had imposed severe restrictions on anything that might detract from the old-world ambience and atmosphere of the square. But it seemed to Molly that there was something different about the shop, and she asked Susan Chase about it.

'It's the bay window,' Susan told her with a smile. 'We had it done when we extended the shop by three feet just before Christmas last year. The plans went before the Planning Commission two years ago, but they spent more than a year hemming and hawing about it before they finally agreed to let me do it. Still, it wasn't a complete waste of time, because I realized there were other things I could have done at the same time. It allowed me to rearrange the counters, which meant the lighting had to be moved as well, and the floor had to be done – you know how one thing leads to another – and with the shop next door being broken into around the same time, it seemed prudent to add some basic security, and on and on it went. But it's all done now, and I think it was worth it.'

'It really makes a difference,' Molly agreed. 'And I think . . .' She caught Paget's eye and grimaced guiltily.

Susan caught the look and turned her attention to Paget. 'But I take it you aren't here to admire the shop or order flowers today, Chief Inspector. Simon phoned me last night to say you might be coming.'

'I rather thought he might,' said Paget. He glanced toward the back of the shop where two young women were preparing bouquets. 'Is there somewhere we can talk more privately?'

'Of course. I live above the shop, so we can go upstairs. Can I offer you a cup of tea?'

'That would be very nice, thank you,' said Molly quickly before Paget had a chance to reply.

'Good. I'll just let the girls know.'

The flat was long and narrow like the shop below. Molly expected it to be gloomy, but was pleasantly surprised to find the long living room bathed in the light – and warmth – of the late-morning sun coming in through a large window overlooking the street.

'Do make yourselves comfortable while I pop the kettle on,' Susan said. 'I'll let Brandy out and you can get acquainted while I make tea. Don't worry, she's very good with strangers, and she's doing well in obedience class. We go once a week, and we both enjoy it. Just don't let her up on the furniture. She'll try it if she thinks she can get away with it.'

She opened the door to the kitchen, and out came a young Shetland sheepdog, all legs and wagging tail. She paused, standing with her head on one side as if trying to decide whether to approach Molly or not. Molly leaned forward and put her hand down close to the floor and said, 'Come on, Brandy, there's a good dog.'

The young Sheltie trotted forward, now curious to see what might be in Molly's hand. She sniffed delicately, then lay down and rolled over to let Molly stroke her tummy.

'Aren't you a little beauty, then?' Molly murmured as she glanced across at Paget. She could almost read his thoughts. Dog hair! She drew the dog closer and ruffled her fur.

'I see she's made a friend,' said Susan when she returned carrying a tray. She set it down on a low table in front of them. 'Milk? Sugar?' she asked, teapot poised. 'Do have a biscuit,' she urged once their cups were filled.

'Now,' she said, her voice taking on a serious note, 'I'm told you want to know if I can verify that Simon was here the night Laura died, and I can. He was here from roughly seven o'clock to something like ten thirty. I know he gave you that story about coming to fix the security system, but he only said that because it's what he told Trevor. He didn't mean to mislead you. It's just that he didn't want you or others to get the wrong impression about our relationship. The truth is he came here because he couldn't understand what was happening to his marriage, and he wanted to find out if Laura had said anything to me about it.'

Molly leaned forward to stroke the dog behind the ears, but her attention was on Susan Chase. She was a very attractive woman, strong features, dark hair, and those long, finely-braided golden earrings suited her perfectly. Molly would love to be able to wear earrings like that, but with her rounder face and shorter hair she knew they would never look right on her, no matter how exquisitely made.

'So how would you describe your relationship with Simon Holbrook?' Paget was saying.

'We're friends – good friends, and have been for many years.'

An almost imperceptible nod from Paget gave Molly permission to pick up on what Susan had said earlier. 'You said that Mr Holbrook wanted to ask if your sister had confided in you,' she said. 'Were you and Laura very close?'

'I think I would have to say only sometimes to that,' Susan said. 'Laura was a rather secretive person, and yet there were times when she would suddenly take you into her confidence. But those occasions were decided by her, and they didn't occur very often. You could ask all the questions you liked, but if she didn't think she owed you an answer, you wouldn't get one.'

'Were you able to help in this case?'

Susan shook her head. 'No. Laura hadn't said anything to me, although I knew she was unhappy about something.'

'How?'

Susan smiled. 'I could always tell,' she said. 'Even when we were children, I could tell when something wasn't going Laura's way – or the way Laura *thought* it should go – because she would become very short with everyone, very irritable, but you rarely knew the reason. She never shared her thoughts, so you never knew if it was something you had done or if it was something that had nothing to do with you at all. But no matter what the problem was, she would never ask anyone for advice or help. She had to solve every problem herself.'

'Can you recall when you first noticed it in this case?'

'Two, possibly three months ago, perhaps.'

'And how was Mr Holbrook taking all this?'

Susan hesitated, lips compressed, her delicate eyebrows drawn together in a deep frown as if trying to decide how much, if anything to tell. 'Not well,' she said at last.

'And . . .?' Molly prompted.

Still Susan hesitated. 'I know Laura's gone,' she said, 'but I still feel as if I'm talking behind her back. But the fact of the matter is, Simon thought his marriage was falling apart. He thought Laura was seeing another man.'

'He told you this?'

Susan nodded. 'As I said, he wanted to know if Laura had said anything to me. She hadn't, of course, and I told him I didn't think he was right, but he was like a dog with a bone. We'd spoken about it only a few days before Laura died, but he said when he got in the car with Trevor the other night, he kept wondering if I had heard anything since, so he told Trevor to drop him off here. He said he wouldn't have enjoyed the film anyway in that state of mind.'

Paget spoke up. 'And yet we are told that Laura became quite vehement when she accused Moira Ballantyne of having an affair with her husband. Surely she wouldn't do that if she were having an affair herself?'

'She would if she thought someone was trying to take something away from her when she considered it to be hers in the first place,' Susan said sharply, then grimaced guiltily. 'Sorry,' she said contritely. 'I didn't mean it to come out quite the way it sounded, especially now she's gone, but Laura could be very possessive.'

'Is it possible that she was right, though?' Molly asked. 'I mean Mr Holbrook is a very attractive man, and . . .' She shrugged suggestively and let the rest of the unspoken words hang there in mid-air. 'And if not Moira Ballantyne,' she continued, 'someone else, perhaps?'

'Certainly not!' said Susan forcefully. 'Simon loved Laura. It was he who was afraid that she might be having an affair with someone else. Oh, no, you're wrong. Why else would he have come to me that night if it wasn't to ask if I knew if Laura was having an affair?'

'Why, indeed?' said Paget quietly. 'But let me ask you something else. I'm told it was believed by some that you would be the one to marry Simon Holbrook, but all that changed when your sister appeared on the scene. Is that true?'

The muscles of Susan Chase's jaw stiffened visibly as she stared into her cup. 'I suppose it might have looked that way to some,' she said stiffly.

'Were you ever engaged to be married?'

Susan shook her head, but she wouldn't look at Paget.

'But you did have that expectation?'

'Whether I did or not, Chief Inspector, I really don't see it as relevant to your investigation, and with all due respect, I don't think it is any of your business.'

'On the other hand, looking at it from our point of view, it could be relevant if, for example, you resented the fact that your sister walked in and took away the man you hoped to marry? I think most people would resent it under those circumstances – especially if it had happened before.'

Susan raised her head; her dark eyes flinty as they met Paget's own. 'Trevor!' she breathed. 'That's where this came from, isn't it? I thought he'd changed, but apparently not. But I wonder if he mentioned *his* little fling with Laura back then, and the way she led him on, then dumped him. She did that with a lot of boys; everyone was fair game as far as she was concerned, because they all wanted the same thing. Unfortunately, Blair, the boy I was going with, was no different, so Laura really did me a favour. Not that he had any better luck than the others, because, as Laura put it so succinctly herself, the first man to get into her knickers was going to have to be rich enough to pay for it. And I must say she made good on that promise when she married Michael Southern.

'But for your information, Chief Inspector, I am not "most people", and I don't know why you think you have the right to pry into my private life. Yes, there was a time when I thought that Simon would ask me to marry him, and yes, I was hurt when he chose Laura, but when I saw how happy the two of them were together, I knew it would have never worked for us. I got over it and moved on, and we've all remained friends. As to what happened to the marriage since then, I have no idea. I was just as surprised as Simon when it started to fall apart.'

'Thank you,' said Paget, 'but for *your* information, Miss Chase, we don't ask these questions to embarrass you; we ask them because we have to look at anyone and everyone who may have had a motive for killing your sister.'

'I'm sure you do, but I can't say it makes me feel any better, knowing that you are looking at me as a suspect in the murder of my own sister.' She looked pointedly at her watch. 'And it's time I got back to the shop,' she said. 'So, unless you have any more questions . . .?'

'Just one or two more,' said Paget blandly. 'Did you or Mr Holbrook leave here at any time during the evening in question?'

The question seemed to catch Susan by surprise. Her expression didn't change, but there was a flicker of something in her eyes that was hard to read, and for just a moment she seemed uncertain about how to answer.

She shook her head, then frowned. 'Apart from going down to make sure I'd locked the car, no, we didn't go out.'

'Do you remember what time that was?' Paget asked.

'Seven fifteen, seven thirty. I know it wasn't long after Simon arrived. But why are you asking?'

Paget ignored the question. 'Did anyone phone that evening? Either for you or for Mr Holbrook?'

'No, and I fail to see the point of all these questions,' Susan flared. 'Simon came here to talk. He stayed here until Trevor came to pick him up, and I was with him all the time, and all your questions aren't going to change that, so I'm sorry, but I have no more time for this.'

'In that case, thank you, Miss Chase,' Paget said as he stood up. 'And thank you for the tea. But I must ask you to come down to Charter Lane sometime tomorrow to give us your statement for the record. We can see ourselves out.'

'Just give me a minute, if you don't mind, sir,' said Molly as they got into the car. 'Brandy is a lovely dog, but she left quite a few hairs on my clothes.' She took an evidence bag from her pocket and tweezers from her handbag. 'I think Forensic might like to take a look at them,' she said as she began picking hairs off one by one.

'I don't understand it,' Tregalles said later that evening. 'I mean I should have been the one to follow up with Holbrook after we interviewed Ballantyne, but he took Molly instead. Said he wanted a woman's perspective on Holbrook and Susan Chase.'

'So what's wrong with that?' Audrey asked. 'Molly's a good copper – you've said so yourself, so it's probably a good idea to get a woman's point of view, especially with someone like this Holbrook chap, the way you say he is with women.'

'There's got to be something else behind it, though,' Tregalles said stubbornly. 'I mean I've always gone with Paget; we're a team, and he's never done anything like this before. Do you think he fancies Molly? I mean she is a good-looking gal, she's ambitious, and . . .'

'And you are talking nonsense!' Audrey scoffed. 'You said yourself you've never seen the man so happy as he's been since Grace Lovett went to live with him. Fancies Molly, indeed! You should be ashamed of yourself!'

'It can happen,' Tregalles said defensively. 'It's happened more than once that I know of, and Molly is a good-looking—'

'So you keep saying,' Audrey said tartly. 'Seems to me that you've been keeping a pretty close eye on her as well. Bit of wishful thinking, is it, love? Reaching that age, are we?'

Tregalles grinned. ''Course not,' he said. 'And you're probably right. It's just that it's a bit strange, that's all, and they seem to get on so well together . . .'

Susan Chase put the phone down as soon as she heard the answering machine cut in. She'd left a message earlier; so there was no point in leaving another one. Almost nine o'clock. Surely Simon wasn't still at work?

She rang his office number. The phone was answered by a security man who told her that Mr Holbrook had left shortly after six o'clock. 'But Miss Goodwin is still here if you would like to talk to her,' he'd said, and put her through to Peggy before she could stop him.

She'd met Peggy a number of times, but she didn't know her well. Simon used to mention her in passing from time to time, but she'd heard very little of Peggy Goodwin since Laura had joined the firm.

'Peggy?' she said, 'it's Susan Chase. Sorry for disturbing you, but the man who answered put me through before I could stop him. But what on earth are you doing there at this hour?'

'No rest for the wicked,' Peggy said, 'but so much needs to be done now that . . . now Laura's no longer here, and there doesn't seem to be enough hours in the day to do it. What can I do for you?'

Despite what she'd just been told by security, she said on impulse, 'Is Simon there by any chance?'

'No. He left some time ago. He's had a stressful day. Is there anything I can do for you?'

'No. Thanks anyway.' *Careful now, remember who you're talking to*, a small voice whispered inside her head. 'It was just something that occurred to me about Laura's estate, but it's not important. It will keep till morning. Sorry to have troubled you, Peggy.'

'No trouble at all,' Peggy assured her. The tone of her voice changed to one of concern. 'But how are you coping, Susan? I know how hard this has been on Simon, but it must have been just as hard on you.'

'It is,' Susan said. 'I can still hardly believe it happened the way it did. Work helps, of course, and business has been surprisingly brisk for the time of year. How has business been at your mother's shop? And how is she? I'm afraid I haven't been in for ages.'

'Not too well, I'm afraid,' Peggy told her. 'It's the arthritis in her hands, mainly, but she has an electric wheelchair, now, so that helps a lot, and she manages to stay cheerful with it. But business has been quite good. I know I'm kept busy on the weekends there. Now, sorry, Susan, but I must go if I'm ever to get to bed tonight.'

'Of course. I shouldn't be holding you up like this. Say hello to your mum when you see her. And speaking of bed, I think I might have an early night myself.'

Susan put the phone down and looked at the clock. Ten past nine. What did Simon think he was playing at? He'd had all evening to call her, and she'd had the phone switched to the shop while she was down there, so she couldn't have missed it if he had called.

The suspicion that was never far from her thoughts pushed its way forward. She tried to ignore it; tried to tell herself that all that was in the past. It had to be. She'd waited so long. He wouldn't dare . . . She closed her eyes. God! If Simon was up to his old tricks again, she'd kill him!

Susan's mind went into overdrive. Peggy Goodwin? Not very likely, since the woman was still at work. But there was Moira, sweet little butter-wouldn't-melt-in-her-mouth Moira, who lived so conveniently just down the street from Simon, and Susan knew for a fact that Trevor Ballantyne would be out of town sometime this week, because Moira had mentioned it the other night. Attending an electronics fair in Wolverhampton, she'd said, and she'd sounded pleased at the prospect of having time to herself for a change. 'Working and living together twenty-four hours a day can be a bit much, sometimes,' she'd confided, 'so I'm looking forward to being able to do what I like, when I like.'

Simon had been there when Moira had said that, and he'd made some remark at the time. It had seemed innocent enough, but was it? Had Moira been telling him quite openly in front of others, that she would be available?

Or was there someone else she'd never heard of?

Susan shivered. She looked at the clock again, and decided to give him fifteen minutes more to return her call before making a move herself.

Simon Holbrook sat slumped in the big leather recliner chair facing the blank screen of the television set in the corner. He had often talked disparagingly of the mind-numbing pap masquerading as entertainment these days, but even it had failed to numb his mind this evening, and he'd turned it off. The neck of the bottle rattled against the glass as he poured himself another drink. Straight whisky, unusual for him, but then, everything had been different since Laura died, and he needed something to dull the senses.

And Paget had him in his sights, he was sure of it. Prime suspect – wasn't that what they called it? Why else would Paget keep coming back to him? Simon sipped his drink and laid his head back against the cool leather. He'd really made a balls up of his alibi. He should have known better than to rely on Trevor to back him up. But then, he hadn't expected things to turn out quite like this. And that call from Trevor this afternoon to say that he was sorry, but he'd had to do it for Moira's sake, was the last straw.

'Honestly, Simon, I don't *really* think you did it, and I'm sure the police will get it right, so I don't think there's any real harm done. It probably was the same lot who've been breaking into houses all over town.'

Bollocks! Stupid little shit!

But he should have erased those emails before the police started poking about, because he had the uneasy feeling that they could come back to haunt him. Not that there was anything in them relating to Laura's death, but the police might wonder about the timing.

He rubbed his face with his hands. *No need to worry, Simon. The hell there wasn't!*

He leaned his head back, closed his eyes and opened his mouth, trying desperately to control his breathing. The last thing he needed now was for another panic attack like the one he'd suffered earlier in the day. Thank God he'd been in his office and there was no one there to see it, but next time . . . He found the pulse in his wrist and started counting.

Twenty-two. Times four. Eighty-eight. A bit high, but not all that bad, he told himself as he took his fingers off his wrist. His breathing steadied. Simon sat up and poured himself another drink.

He thought suddenly of Moira. What the hell had she been up to that night? She was the talk of the street after the police brought her home and all but torn the Ballantyne's house apart. Trevor had finally admitted that Moira had been in the house the night Laura was killed, but he wouldn't say why, and Simon had been afraid to ask Paget about it in case the chief inspector misconstrued his interest.

Paget again. A cold shiver ran down Simon's spine. Damn the man for prying into things that didn't concern him. And that question about Henry Beaumont. Was it simply an innocent enquiry, or was it Paget's way of telling him that he knew more than he was letting on? It was a question that had continued to trouble Simon for the rest of the day, clouding his thinking to the point where he'd had to tell Stan to carry on the tests without him.

And then there was Peggy. He couldn't fob her off much longer; she knew something was up. He emptied the glass and reached for the bottle.

'Oh, Simon, Simon darling, what on earth do you think you're doing? Sitting here in the dark drowning your sorrows? You know you can't take that stuff. You're going to have a fearful headache in the morning.'

He blinked his eyes. Susan? He thought at first he must be dreaming, then he smelt her perfume as she came up behind him and put her arms around his neck. He struggled to get up, but Susan held him back and bent to kiss the top of his head.

'I let myself in,' she said unnecessarily. 'I thought you might need company tonight. Hard day, was it my love?'

He grasped her hand. 'Paget knows about Beaumont,' he whispered. 'Did he say anything to you?'

'Not a word,' Susan assured him. 'You worry too much, Simon. He doesn't know anything, so don't let him get to you. He's fishing, that's all. Now, stop worrying and relax. Everything is going to be all right, so let's get you upstairs to bed.'

Twenty-Three

It was trying to rain, and the reflection of the ornamental street lights glistened on the wet pavement when Susan let herself out of the house just after five o'clock in the morning. She could have parked within yards of Simon's house last night – there were still a few spaces open this morning – but she didn't want anyone to recognize her car, so she had left it some distance away in Tavistock Road and come the rest of the way on foot.

She turned the corner into Tavistock Road, then paused beneath a street light to open her handbag to search for keys. At first, she thought the owner of the car beside her had left the windows open by mistake, but then she saw the glint of broken glass in the gutter. Her heart sank as she looked ahead and saw her fears confirmed. Her own car, together with several others, had received the same treatment.

Susan could feel the rage boiling up inside her as she approached her car and peered through the broken window. Gingerly, she opened the door. More glass fell out, but there didn't seem to be any other damage. The radio/disk player was still there; even the box of disks that the police were always telling you to hide had been ignored. She gritted her teeth. Just a mindless bunch of yobs roaming the streets late at night with nothing better to do than smash windows for the hell of it. Bastards! It was time the police did something about these roving gangs. Hanging by their thumbs would be too good for them.

Susan glanced up and down the street. There wasn't a soul in sight. She closed the door and went around the other side and got in. 'Bloody yobs!' she breathed disgustedly as she took out her mobile phone, preparing to phone the police, then paused. They were bound to ask questions about why she had left the car there overnight. Name and address, then: *Why were you parked so far away from home? Visiting? Visiting whom? May we have the address? What time was it when you left the car? What time did you return?*

Susan put the phone back in her handbag and started the car. The last thing she needed was to draw attention to herself and Simon, so best forget it and simply have the window repaired. She started the engine, glanced in the side-view mirror and pulled away from the kerb.

Good! She was clear. Let one of the other poor devils report the damage. Let them talk to the police.

'Are you quite sure that Mr Holbrook didn't leave a message, Janice?' Peggy Goodwin asked the receptionist for the second time that morning. 'You know what he's like. Stick a note up somewhere with Sellotape and expect someone to find it. I've looked but I can't find one, and no one down at the lab has heard from him, although they did say he didn't seem himself yesterday.'

Lips compressed, Peggy looked at her watch again. 'He *promised* he'd be in early this morning,' she said, 'and just look at the time! Quarter past nine and not a sign of him, and he knows we have a lot to do before the meeting at the bank this afternoon. I've called his house, I've left a message, I've tried his mobile phone, which, as usual, he hasn't switched on, and I've even emailed him, and still no reply.'

Janice West shook her head. 'I've looked around, but I can't see any note, and there's nothing in the overnight log. I have tried to call Mr Holbrook several times myself, but there's no answer.' She lowered her voice, although there was no one else in the room. 'Perhaps he was up late last night and slept in this morning,' she suggested. 'He has been under a lot of stress lately, what with one thing and another. He was quite short with me yesterday, and that's not like him. It could be happening again.'

Peggy eyed Janice thoughtfully. 'You mean depression,' she said. It wasn't a question. 'I had hoped we were past that,' she said, 'but you could be right, and if you are . . .'

'He could be hung-over if he's started drinking again,' Janice finished for her.

Peggy drew in her breath as she looked at the time again. 'Well, hung-over or not,' she said, 'I need him here, so someone had better go to the house to see if he's there, and I'm afraid that has to be you, Janice. If he has been drinking, I don't want anyone else to see him in that state, so I'll have Miranda look after the desk while you're gone. If he is there and still in bed, he probably won't want to come down to open the door, but don't give up. Keep pounding on it until he answers. Then get him down here as fast as you can.'

* * *

Simon Holbrook's car was in the driveway, but Janice found a vacant space a couple of doors down. She parked the car and walked back. She'd been to the house only once since Simon and Laura were married. A Christmas party arranged by Laura for their friends and a few carefully chosen members of the staff. Finger food and wine, catered, of course, but Janice hadn't felt comfortable there. She'd made her excuses and left as soon as she could without causing offence.

She mounted the shallow steps and rang the bell. No answer. She leaned on the bell and kept the pressure on for a good half minute. Still no sign of life. She grasped the doorknob and turned it. She hadn't expected it to yield, but it did and the door opened to her touch.

She gave it a push and looked down the empty hall.

'Mr Holbrook?'

No answer. Janice stepped inside, calling out as she moved down the hall, poking her head inside each room as she went. No sign of Holbrook, but then she hardly expected him to be pottering about downstairs, because he would have answered her calls by now.

Janice didn't like the thought of going upstairs, but she couldn't put it off any longer. She called out loudly as she mounted the stairs; paused on the landing to call again.

Nothing. The door to the front bedroom was open. She peeked inside and found it empty and smelling of fresh paint. Of course! This would be the bedroom where Laura . . .

Janice turned away and knocked on the door of the second bedroom before pushing it open. The bedclothes had been thrown back and lay in a heap in the middle of the bed, partly obscuring the pyjama-clad form of Simon Holbrook, who lay facing away from her on the far side of the bed.

'Mr Holbrook?'

Suddenly, Janice was angry. This was the man who was supposed to be in charge; a man she'd looked up to before Laura Southern had virtually taken over the company, yet here he was, drunk as a lord and oblivious to the world.

She raised her voice, unable to disguise her anger as she shouted, 'Mr Holbrook! It's Janice from work. You have to get up. Please, Mr Holbrook . . .'

She didn't really want to go any further into the room; it didn't seem right to go marching round the large bed to shake the man in his pyjamas,

even if he was in a drunken stupor. But she'd come this far and she had
to do something. Gingerly, she leaned over the bed and touched his
shoulder. 'Mr Holbrook!' she called loudly. ' Please wake up.'

No response. Angrily, she put one knee on the edge of the bed and
reached for the man's shoulder. 'Mr Holbrook!' she called sharply, and
shook him hard. 'Please wake . . . Oh, my God!' she breathed as
Holbrook rolled onto his back. His eyes were wide open and he was
covered in blood.

And the black-handled knife buried to the hilt in his stomach like a
crude exclamation mark only served to confirm what Janice already
knew.

Paget counted five stab wounds on the body, although there could be
more concealed by the pools of crusted blood. Whoever had done this
must have hated the man as much as they had hated Laura – different
weapons but the same result – assuming, of course, that both had been
killed by the same person. The possibility that there could be *two* killers
out there was something he didn't even want to think about.

'Looks pretty straightforward to me,' said Starkie as he stripped off
his gloves. 'Don't quote me until I have the results of the autopsy, but
I think it would be safe to say he's been dead for at least four hours
and no more than six.' He looked at his watch. 'Let's say somewhere
between four and six this morning. Depends to some degree on what
sort of activity he was engaged in immediately prior to his death. The
blood on the floor suggests that he was standing beside the bed when
he was first attacked, and he probably put up some resistance before
falling back on the bed as his assailant continued to stab him. As you
can see by the way the blood is spread all over the sheets, he must have
struggled, but he would be dying by that time.

'If he was standing beside the bed when the first blow was struck,'
he continued, 'then was struck again and again before being manhandled
into his present position, the killer would probably have some of that
blood on himself. It would certainly be on his shoes; you can see where
blood was tracked across the carpet.' He indicated a number of dark
patches that had been marked off by the quick-thinking constable who
was first on the scene. 'Interesting that they stop there at the foot of
the bed; there doesn't seem to be anything beyond that point.'

Paget stepped gingerly around the stains on the carpet to the end of
the bed. 'I think that he – or she – sat down on the end of the bed in

order to change before leaving the room,' he said, pointing to a smear of blood on the bottom of the duvet. 'Very deliberate, I'd say.'

'Probably a "she",' said Starkie. Paget looked at him. The doctor rarely ventured into the realm of speculation on something as specific as the sex of a killer. But he might well be right this time. Someone had been in bed with Holbrook; someone who had left a few tell-tale strands of dark hair on the pillow.

Starkie pulled back the bedclothes. 'Semen stains,' he pointed out. 'We'll need these sheets. However, I've got better things to do than stand here solving your case for you. I think it would be safe to assume that he died from his wounds, but I'll let you know if I find anything to the contrary.'

Tregalles entered the room. 'No sign of a forced entry,' he told Paget. 'The back door is locked and the key is on a ledge beside the door, but the spring-loaded lock on the front door was set on the latch, so it didn't lock when the killer went out.'

He moved closer to the bed. 'Nasty,' he said with a grimace. He put his face close to one of the pillows and wrinkled his nose. 'Don't know if that's perfume or hair spray,' he said, 'but it looks like he was sleeping with someone with dark hair. Susan Chase, maybe? You think she killed him?'

'Certainly looks that way. We'll need to talk to her.'

Tregalles nodded slowly. 'Not just a crime of passion, though, is it?' he said. 'I mean that knife isn't exactly the sort you'd normally take to bed with you. But if she did, why wait till morning to kill him? Unless she wanted a sort of farewell ride-to-hounds before she did it. Unless, of course, it was the other way round, and it was her way of telling him she didn't think much of his performance in bed. So she nips downstairs, gets the knife, then comes back up and stabs him. Either way it doesn't sound quite right.'

'As you say, it is odd,' said Paget thoughtfully, 'although I'm not sure I would have expressed it in *quite* the same way, but in either case it suggests premeditation.'

Tregalles sighed. 'Want me to bring her in for questioning?' he asked. He didn't sound as if he was looking forward to the task.

'Lets talk to the people downstairs, first.' Paget nodded to the man from SOCO who had been waiting patiently by the door for them to leave the room so he could get on with his job.

In the kitchen, Janice West sat at one side of the table, nursing the remains of a mug of tea, while Peggy Goodwin sat across from her, elbows on the table, her tea apparently untouched as she stared into space. At the far end of the table, Molly stood up as Paget and Tregalles entered.

Paget said, 'Are you all right, Mrs West? Would you like to see a doctor?'

Janice shook her head. 'I'll admit it was quite a shock,' she said, 'but I'm all right now if you want to ask me some questions.'

Paget turned his attention to Peggy Goodwin, explaining that he needed to talk to each of them separately, and he would be talking to Janice West first. 'So, if you don't mind,' he concluded, 'I'd like you to go with DC Forsythe until we're finished here. It's a matter of procedure, and I shan't be long.'

Peggy looked at him blankly for a moment, then rose without a word and allowed herself to be led from the room by Molly. Paget pulled up a chair facing Janice West, while Tregalles took up his position at the end of the table and took out his notebook.

'Let's begin with what prompted you to come to the house in the first place,' said Paget. 'I believe you said something earlier about Mr Holbrook being late for a meeting?'

Janice shook her head. 'He had promised to come in early so that he and Peggy could prepare for a meeting with the bank this afternoon,' she said. 'But when he hadn't come in by nine, and we couldn't reach him by phone, we wondered if he might be ill, so Peggy sent me to see if he was all right.'

'Now, I believe you told the first man on the scene after you called the police that the front door was open when you arrived. Is that correct?'

'No, not open, but it was unlocked. I rang several times, and when no one answered I gave the doorknob a twist, like you do, you know, never expecting it to open, but it did. It surprised me at the time, and it worried me a bit, because it seemed to me that he must be home if the door was unlocked, and yet he hadn't answered the bell or my call.'

Paget said, 'I know you told us this before, but please bear with me, because I want to be absolutely sure I have it right. You said that Mr Holbrook was lying on his side, partly covered with his back to you, and he looked as if he were asleep when you first saw him. Is that right?'

'Yes.'

'But the constable who was first on the scene said Mr Holbrook was lying on his back and *wasn't* covered when he first saw him. Did you move him?'

Janice grimaced guiltily. 'I didn't mean to,' she said. 'But when he didn't answer, I leaned across the bed to shake him by the shoulder. That's when he sort of flopped over on his back and the bedclothes fell away and I could see . . .'

She stopped and took several deep breaths. 'I could see that he was dead,' she ended.

'Did you see any sign of anyone else having been in the room?'

Janice looked down at her hands. 'I think there might have been,' she said softly. 'It's a big bed and the other pillow looked as if someone's head had been on it. I don't *know*, mind you, but since you ask, that's the way it looked to me.'

'I see. Anything else?'

'No.'

'Did you touch anything in the room?'

'No. At least I don't think I did.'

'What about in the rest of the house?'

Janice thought. 'The front door, some of the door handles downstairs, and the banister, but I think that's all.'

'You called us on your mobile phone?'

'That's right. When I saw the way things were, I didn't want to touch anything, not even the phone, so I used my own.'

Apparently television did have some educational value after all, thought Paget. 'You didn't call an ambulance?'

'Not much point, was there? It wasn't just the wounds and the blood. His eyes were open and he was stone cold to the touch.' Janice shivered at the memory.

'And you waited outside on the step until the first car arrived?'

'That's right.'

Paget got to his feet. 'Thank you very much, Mrs West,' he said. 'I must say you kept a very cool head under the circumstances, and I appreciate it. We will arrange for you to make a formal statement in the next day or two, but in the meantime I can arrange to have someone take you home.'

'Thank you, but there's no need,' she told him. 'Besides, there's no one at home so I'll be going back to work. I'm sure there will be lots to be done, and Peggy's going to need help with it all.'

Twenty-Four

There was a stillness about the way Peggy Goodwin sat stiffly in her chair, hands folded neatly on the table in front of her. She held her head up high – unnaturally high, Paget thought – as if steeling herself for the questions she knew must come.

'I realize how distressing this must be for you,' he said quietly, 'and my questions can wait if you don't feel up to—'

'No.' Peggy closed her eyes and shook her head. 'No,' she said again. 'It's all right. I'll be fine, thank you.' Her mouth twisted into a wry caricature of a grin. 'But I'd give anything for a cigarette right now.'

'I'm afraid I can't help you there,' said Paget, 'but I can ask—'

But Peggy was shaking her head. 'No, no,' she said wearily, 'I didn't *really* mean that. I gave them up years ago. It's just . . . Oh, God, I don't know. I can't seem to get it through my head that Simon is dead. And in such a horrible way.'

'You've seen the body?'

Peggy shook her head. 'Janice told me in rather more detail than I wanted to hear. She said . . .' Peggy seemed to lose her train of thought, and her eyes drifted off as if she were seeing something far beyond the room. 'I shouldn't have sent her,' she said softly. 'I should have come myself.'

'Why did you send her?'

Peggy brought her attention back to Paget with some effort. 'To be honest, I was afraid that Simon might be suffering from a hangover, and I knew I could trust Janice to keep whatever state she found him in to herself. I would have come myself, but there was so much to do, and with Simon not there, I was trying frantically to get all of our financial statements in order for his meeting with the bankers this afternoon. Simon wanted everything to go as smoothly as possible, and most of all we wanted to assure them that Laura's passing would not affect the future of the business.'

Peggy's brows drew together in a deepening frown, forcing herself to concentrate on what she was saying. 'You see, the banks preferred to deal with Laura; they talked the same language and they understood one another, so they wanted some assurance from us that they would have someone equally competent and knowledgeable to deal with in the future.'

'But now . . .?'

'God knows,' she said wearily. 'I don't even know if we have a future.'

'Difficult for everyone,' Paget agreed, 'but especially for you, I'm sure.' He paused for a moment. 'You said you thought Mr Holbrook might be suffering from a hangover this morning. Would you say he was prone to that sort of thing?'

'No. Simon didn't drink much at all. In fact about the only time he drank spirits was when he became depressed. I don't know if you were aware of it, but he suffered from bouts of depression, and sometimes he would try to get rid of it by drinking. And he has been under a lot of pressure as you know.'

The muscles around Peggy's mouth tightened as she fixed her eyes on Paget. 'And to be brutally frank, Chief Inspector, the pressure *you* were putting on him wasn't helping. In fact, he was in something of a state when you left yesterday, because he was convinced that you believed he had killed his wife.'

Paget refused to rise to the bait. 'Do you have any idea who might have killed him?'

'No. He was such a sweet man . . .' Words failed her as she buried her face in her hands. 'I can only think it must be the same person who killed Laura,' she mumbled through stifled sobs.

'And the motive?' Paget prompted.

Peggy wiped tears from her eyes and blew her nose. 'God knows,' she said in a small voice. 'I mean Laura wasn't particularly well liked, but even so, I can't think of anyone who hated her enough to want to *kill* her – unless it was Tim Bryce, of course – but I doubt if he would have the nerve. But Simon . . .? I just don't know.'

'Interesting that you should mention Bryce,' Paget observed, 'because from what I've been told, he could be the main beneficiary now that both Mr and Mrs Holbrook are dead.'

Peggy Goodwin stared at him blankly for a couple of seconds while the words sank in. 'Oh, my God!' she breathed. 'If you're right, and the firm does belong to Tim, then we're all in trouble, because that would be disastrous!'

Peggy Goodwin had gone, and Tregalles was still finishing his notes when Charlie Dobbs appeared in the doorway. 'Thought you might like to know that we found prints and bloodstains on the inside of the wardrobe door,' he said. 'And more blood on one of the taps in the bathroom. Looks like she washed the blood off her hands in there. They're dismantling the taps for Forensic to look at, and they're taking the trap underneath the basin to see if anything is caught in it. The bloodied prints are smeared, but those adjacent to the blood look like they belong to Holbrook and Chase. We'll need Forensic to confirm, of course, but I don't think there's much doubt.

'And there's something else as well. We found a strip of plastic and a label from a plastic bag mixed up in the bedclothes. Come on upstairs and take a look. I've got my own ideas about them but I'd like to see what you make of it.'

The hands of the town hall clock stood at twenty minutes to one as Paget, accompanied by Molly Forsythe, pulled up outside the flower shop and went in.

Susan Chase was with a customer. She glanced up with what started out as a welcoming smile, but her expression changed to a questioning frown when she saw who it was. One of the girls came forward from the back of the shop, then hesitated when she recognized them. 'Can I help you?' she asked tentatively, 'or did you wish to see Miss Chase?'

'We'll wait for Miss Chase, thank you,' Paget told her. The girl retreated to the rear of the shop, where she engaged the other girl in a whispered conversation.

The customer, a short, plump woman with what sounded like an asthmatic condition, was ordering a wreath, but she was having trouble making up her mind about the size of the arrangement.

'It's so hard to choose,' she said. 'It's not as if I knew her really *well*, you understand,' she told Susan. 'I mean we weren't what you might call close, so I wouldn't want the family to think I was putting myself forward, so to speak, but on the other hand one doesn't want to appear to be too . . . how much did you say the lilies were?'

'The arrangements are there on the price list,' Susan reminded her, indicating the sheet of paper the woman held in her hand.

'Well, yes, but . . . It's not as if it's going to be around for long, though, is it? And as I say, I didn't really know her all that well.'

'Perhaps a spray?' Susan suggested. 'Something small but tasteful. And they are less expensive. As you can see, we have several on display.'

'Really?' The woman showed renewed interest. 'How much are they?'

There followed a lengthy discussion about size and composition of the spray, until, finally, the choice was made. Throughout it all, Susan remained outwardly calm and courteous, but it seemed to Paget that she was becoming more and more distracted by their presence as time went on.

Susan ushered the woman to the door and closed it with a sigh of relief. She stood there for a moment with her back to them, head bowed as if gathering strength before turning around. '*More* questions, Chief Inspector?' she asked wearily. 'I had hoped we were finished with all that.'

'I'm afraid not, Miss Chase. Can you tell me where you were between the hours of four and six o'clock this morning?'

Colour flooded into Susan's face. Her eyes narrowed and her lips tightened. 'Now *that*,' she said angrily, 'is none of your business. And I'm getting more than a little tired of your prying into my private life, and I don't see why I should have to account—'

'Please answer the question, Miss Chase. Believe me, I'm really not interested in your private life, but I do have a good reason for asking in this case, and I would like an answer.'

Her eyes flashed angrily. 'A good reason, Chief Inspector?' she said. 'And what would that be?'

Instead of answering the question, Paget posed one of his own. 'Would I be right if I said I believe you spent the night with Mr Holbrook?'

'So, what if I did?' she shot back. 'It's still none of your business, and I don't see why I should have to explain myself to you.'

'What time did you leave Mr Holbrook's house?'

Susan gritted her teeth in exasperation. 'I don't believe this,' she muttered, 'but if you *must* know, I left around five o'clock, give or take a few minutes. Sorry I can't tell you to the exact second,' she added sarcastically, 'but I didn't know at the time it would be of interest to the police. Now, I hope you're satisfied, Chief Inspector Paget, because I do not intend to answer any more of your questions.' She turned to go.

'Just one more question, Miss Chase,' said Paget softly as she walked away. 'Was Mr Holbrook alive when you left him?'

'He was sleeping peacefully if you . . .' She whirled to face him, hands to her mouth as if afraid of voicing the question she was about to ask. 'What do you mean, was he *alive*?' she whispered. 'Has something . . .?'

'Mr Holbrook is dead,' said Paget. 'Murdered, and since it appears that you were the last person to see him alive, I must ask you to come with us to the station to answer further questions.'

'Simon's *dead*?' Susan's mouth fell open. 'No! It can't be. Oh, please God, no!' Her eyes grew wide, and Molly, who was watching closely, thought the blend of astonishment and shock was very well done. Very well done indeed! Unless, of course, it happened to be genuine, but that seemed unlikely, considering the evidence.

Susan closed her eyes tightly, fists clenched. 'No, no, you're wrong,' she insisted in a strangled voice. 'You have to be. He was all right when I . . . I don't believe . . .'

She stopped speaking when she saw the expression on Paget's face. Her breath caught in her throat. Suddenly, her legs buckled and she dropped heavily to her knees. Both Paget and Molly reacted swiftly, but they only just managed to catch her in time to prevent her head from hitting the floor.

For the second time in two weeks, police were knocking on doors, searching gardens, and asking everyone they met in and around Pembroke Avenue if they had seen or heard anything unusual between the hours of four and six o'clock that morning. And since a number of people had already gone off to work, it meant there would be call-backs after business hours. But those assigned to that task were the lucky ones, because the members of a second team were spending their day searching dustbins and public rubbish bins as well as the odd skip still to be found behind some of the local shops and small businesses in the area, and Ormside was not happy about it.

'We're stretched to the limit as it is,' he complained when Tregalles phoned in. 'I haven't got anyone left in here. I've had to borrow Sylvia from Control just to answer phones. So tell me, Tregalles, if we've got the weapon, why are we going through dustbins? As far as I'm concerned, it's a bloody great waste of time.'

'Don't tell me,' Tregalles said, 'tell the boss, but I doubt if you'll shift him. He and Charlie seem to think that whoever killed Holbrook changed clothes before they left the house, then took them away with them. He didn't find anything like that at Chase's flat or in her car, so he's got everybody searching the area around here, because he thinks the killer would want to be rid of them as soon as possible rather than chance being caught with them.

'And that's not all,' Tregalles continued. 'He's done it to me again.

He wants me to find out where Tim Bryce was at five this morning, and have him come in to identify his uncle, while he goes off with Molly to bring the Chase woman in for questioning. I tell you, Len, something's going on between those two.'

'Well I'm more concerned about what he's thinking than I am about that,' Ormside growled. 'He's had the killer handed to him on a bloody plate, so what else does he want in the way of evidence?'

'You tell me,' Tregalles said glumly. 'Anyway, I'd better go and see if I can find Bryce. According to Peggy Goodwin, he could be her new boss, and I don't think she's too thrilled about that prospect.'

'Susan Chase will be in hospital for another day or two at least,' Paget told Ormside. It was late-afternoon, and he had just returned from the hospital. 'She admitted spending the night with Holbrook before she fainted, but claims that he was alive and well when she left there around five o'clock this morning, which just happens to be the estimated time of death, according to Starkie. But the thing that puzzles me is, if she did kill him, why would she go home and carry on as if nothing had happened, when she must have known that all the evidence would point to her? Tregalles thinks she could have been so shocked by what she'd done that her mind shut it out and she went into denial, but I have trouble with that. When we arrived at her shop, she was going about her business in the normal way. There was no sign of stress; no sign of fear. If anything, her reaction was one of annoyance, which would be normal if she is innocent.

'Unfortunately, we can't question her just yet, because she fractured one kneecap and damaged the other when she went down, and her doctor says she is suffering from shock. We've closed the shop and the girls have been sent home until we've had a chance to make a thorough search of it and the flat upstairs. Funny thing about her car; two of the windows were broken, and it must have happened recently because there was still a lot of glass in the car. But there were no bloodstains, at least none that we could see with the naked eye, and nothing in the boot, but Forensic has it now, so we'll see what they come up with.'

Paget turned to the whiteboards where a uniformed constable was ticking off the homes visited in the area, and gardens searched, adding notes when they seemed appropriate.

There weren't many notes.

'So,' said Ormside heavily, 'did Susan Chase kill him or not? It seems

straightforward enough to me, but I get the feeling that you're not satisfied. So what's the problem?'

'Perhaps there is no problem,' Paget said, 'but I can't help remembering the way Susan Chase collapsed when I told her Holbrook was
dead. Until that moment, everything she did and said was normal, but
the minute I told her Holbrook was dead, she began to stammer; her
face turned white and she collapsed, and I just don't see how she could
fake that.'

'Forsythe was there. What does she think?'

'She said she thought it was a great piece of acting at first, but now
she's not quite so sure.'

Twenty-Five

Friday, March 20

'I'm told you have news for me, Len,' said Paget as he approached the sergeant's desk next morning. He glanced at the boards where two people were adding notes. 'Care to fill me in?'

'Looks like you were right after all,' Ormside conceded as he joined Paget in front of the boards. 'I told the men to pack it in at eight o'clock last night if they hadn't found anything by then, but one of them happened to mention that it was collection day today, so I told them to carry on. Good job, too, because it was shortly after eight they found a black bag in a skip behind the corner shop in Caxton Road. It contained trainers, gloves, shoes, tracksuit, all with bloodstains on them, and a plastic hat – the sort of thing women wear in the shower.'

'So the killer came prepared,' Paget murmured as he continued to eye the boards. 'Where are they now?'

'Forensic has them. I knew you'd want the results as soon as possible, although I suspect it will be next week before we get them.'

'In that case,' Paget said, 'since Mr Alcott is away, I'd better have a word with them myself and try to speed things up. Anything else?'

'Yes, there is,' Ormside said, sounding unusually pleased with himself. 'I'm waiting for confirmation, but Forensic tells me that they've found a match between some of the dog hair taken from Westfield Lane, Holywell Street jobs and Laura Holbrook's bedroom, to Susan Chase's dog, Brandy, so I don't think there can be any doubt now. I think Holbrook and Chase have been in it together from the beginning, but I don't know which one actually killed Laura, or if they did it together, but both were in Chase's flat, so both could have picked up hair from the dog. As for the dog hairs still unidentified, Chase could have picked them up from the obedience classes she attended, and it shouldn't be hard to track those dogs down.'

'That certainly does put another nail in the coffin,' Paget agreed, 'but assuming the reason for killing Laura – at least for Simon – was to regain control of the company, and Chase was willing to help him because she wanted him for herself, why kill Simon?'

'Perhaps she thought he was beginning to crack?'

'Possibly,' Paget said doubtfully. 'But if he was, he showed no sign of it to us. Anyway, first things first. We need to get another sample of hair from Brandy, because the hair we submitted to Forensic wasn't obtained legally. That won't be a problem now we have the search warrant, so make sure they get the samples over to Forensic right away. Anything else before I go?'

'Charlie said they found an impression of a bicycle tyre in soft earth by the back door, but there's nothing to indicate that either of the Holbrooks owned a bike. It may not amount to anything – there's no indication as to when the impression was made – but he said they'll check it out just in case.'

'Right,' said Paget, his thoughts already moving on. 'I'm going over to the hospital to find out how Chase is getting on. I doubt if she will be in a fit condition to be questioned, but I'd like to impress on her doctor how important it is that we talk to her.'

Susan's doctor's name was Barraclough. Paget had seen him around the hospital, but knew very little about him, except the nurses spoke well of him. He was an older man, tall, spare, fiftyish, and soft-spoken.

'As far as Miss Chase's physical condition is concerned, her injuries are by no means life-threatening,' he said in answer to Paget's question. 'Her left knee is bruised and swollen, and no doubt somewhat painful, but nothing appears to be broken. She does have a displaced fracture of the patella in her right knee, and that will require surgery. As far as we can tell, not too much damage has been done to the extensor mechanism – that is the bones, muscles and tendons which act to extend the knee – but again there is a lot of swelling, which makes it hard to tell until we can get a better look at it.

'As I said, her physical injuries are not serious, but she is suffering from delayed shock and uncontrollable bouts of weeping, so I wouldn't want her subjected to undue pressure. In short, Chief Inspector, I don't think she is in a fit state to be questioned at this time, and I suggest that you wait until after she's had the operation on her knee. At least that will be one less thing to worry about, and I think there's a good chance she will be sufficiently recovered by then.'

'And when will that be, Doctor?'

'Ah, now there, I'm afraid, we do have a bit of a problem,' Barraclough said. 'Ordinarily, Miss Chase would have been scheduled for surgery today, but one of our surgeons broke his arm while skiing in Austria last weekend, so we've had to rearrange his schedule. And to make matters worse, our Mr Featherstone is attending a conference in Helsinki, so we cannot possibly schedule Miss Chase's surgery until first thing Monday morning.'

'Would I be right in assuming they also ski in Helsinki?'

The doctor smiled. 'Cross-country, I'm told,' he said.

'Safer,' said Paget, 'so let's hope Mr Featherstone doesn't break any bones. What sort of recovery time are we looking at, Doctor?'

Barraclough shrugged. 'Assuming there are no complications with the knee surgery, and her mental health improves, I see no reason why she shouldn't be discharged the same day. Believe me, Chief Inspector, we don't keep anyone in longer than necessary these days. Miss Chase will be on crutches, of course, but the swelling on her other knee should be down by then, so she should be mobile. At the very worst she might need a wheelchair for a day or two, but I doubt it.'

The doctor paused. 'Is Miss Chase in serious trouble?' he asked hesitantly.

'I'm afraid she may be, Doctor,' Paget said. 'Very serious trouble indeed.'

'Sad,' Barraclough said with a shake of his head. 'She seems to be such a nice person. It's hard to believe . . .' He shook his head again and fell silent as they made their way to Susan Chase's room.

On Paget's return to Charter Lane, Ormside handed him several sheets of paper stapled together. 'Something one of Charlie's men picked up from Holbrook's BlackBerry,' the sergeant told him. 'It's a series of emails between Holbrook and this bloke Beaumont from Drexler-Davies, and I think you'll find them interesting. It looks as if they were working out some sort of deal whereby Holbrook's company would become part of Drexler-Davies. Take a look at the dates. It could be a coincidence, but the first one is dated two days before the Abbey Road burglary, which, if we discount the Dunbar job done by Chloe and her boyfriend, was the first of the series leading up to the killing of Mrs Holbrook.'

Paget scanned the papers briefly. 'Interesting,' he observed, 'especially as Simon Holbrook told us that the last thing he wanted to do was go back to work for Drexler-Davies. I'll take these with me, but it looks as if I'd better give this chap Beaumont a call and find out exactly what's been going on between them.'

Later, as Paget was preparing to leave for the day, Ormside called from downstairs to tell him that he had the results of the autopsy on Simon Holbrook. 'No surprises,' he said. 'Holbrook died as a result of multiple stab wounds. Nine altogether, although three of them were superficial. Only one of them actually punctured the heart, but the others did so much damage to his other organs that he would have bled to death within minutes if the heart hadn't been penetrated.

'Dr Starkie places time of death at between four thirty and five thirty, but for all practical purposes he says we won't go far wrong if we assume he died within a few minutes either side of five o'clock.'

Paget thanked him and was about to hang up when Ormside said, 'Any luck with the emails, sir?'

'Not yet,' Paget told him. 'I'm told that Beaumont is attending a meeting at head office in Switzerland, and he won't be back till Monday. His secretary assures me that he will have Beaumont return my call as soon he gets back, so we'll see what he has to say then. Give it a rest for now, Len, and we'll pick it up again on Monday.'

Twenty-Six

Molly Forsythe could hardly believe her luck when a shaft of sunlight crept over her face and woke her. Sunshine *and* a day off? Incredible! She lay there, eyes closed, revelling in the warmth, reluctant to get out of bed, yet wanting to be up to make the most of the day. She opened one eye and squinted at the clock. Ten minutes to seven. Good! She'd allow herself twenty more minutes.

She lay there planning her day. Nothing very exciting. She should really do a proper shop at the new supermarket on the edge of town – it had been there something like four years now, but almost everyone still referred to it as the 'new' supermarket. For the past couple of weeks she'd been stopping on her way home to pick up a few necessary items, and she'd fallen into the habit of picking up frozen dinners, because she didn't want to be bothered with a lot of preparation, cooking and washing up after a long day. The trouble was, it was beginning to show when she stepped on the scales, and that was not good.

Molly slipped out of bed and went into the shower. So, shopping first before the mob got there, and then the remainder of the morning would be spent preparing and freezing single servings of something more nourishing and less fattening than pizza, quiche Lorraine, and sometimes fish and chips. She wasn't a vegetarian, but she didn't eat much meat. Given the time, she generally opted for stir-fries, adding a few bits of chicken or shrimp, and sometimes cheese, but she also liked soups, so she would make a pot of that as well if she had time.

Time – there it was again, and if she didn't get a move on she would find herself wasting another ten minutes looking for an empty space in the car park. Oh, yes, and she mustn't forget to pick up a gift and a card for her god-daughter, Melissa, who would be five in two weeks' time. Molly grimaced guiltily as she stepped out of the shower. Melissa and her mother, Jane Thomas, didn't live far away – just over the border in Herefordshire, in fact – and yet Molly hadn't seen either of them in months; there simply never seemed to be enough time. Jane, Molly's best friend since their schooldays, was a single mother who worked full time, so she had little time to spare, while Molly's job . . .

Molly shook her head. Excuses, excuses, she admonished herself, but it *was* hard to find the time, and it was going to be even harder in the future, but she should really make an effort to be at Melissa's birthday party and spend some time with Jane.

Later that morning, with most of her shopping done, Molly drove into the centre of town to the Carriage House Gift Shop, the one owned by Peggy Goodwin's mother, to look for a special card for Melissa. Mrs Johnson always had a good selection, and perhaps there would be something there for Jane as well. A sort of peace offering to make up for staying away so long.

The bell over the door jangled as she entered the shop. A young girl behind the counter was attending to a customer, while Mrs Johnson, in her wheelchair, was arranging cards on one of the revolving stands. She moved with difficulty, and it seemed to Molly that the woman was even heavier than she'd been when Molly had last been in the shop, a result, no doubt, of a lack of exercise and a penchant for the chocolates so readily available to her.

'Hello, love. Haven't seen you for a long time, have we?' she greeted Molly. 'What can we do for you, today?' Her breathing was heavier than Molly remembered. 'Lovely out there, isn't it? It's so nice to see that sun coming in through the window. I thought my poor old tulips weren't going to come to anything this year, but perhaps this will persuade them to get a move on.'

'I'm looking for a birthday card for a five-year-old girl,' Molly told her. 'Something special.'

'Top right on the far rack,' the woman said. 'I think you'll find something suitable up there.'

Molly spent some ten minutes reading all the cards, while half listening to another customer telling Mrs Johnson all about her latest grandchild. 'We're going up to Chester on the weekend for the christening,' she said. 'They're calling her Penelope Asquith Martin, which neither Fred or I like very much, but Asquith was my daughter-in-law's maiden name, so what can you do? Mind you,' she sighed, 'I warned Roger – he's my son – that with initials like that I just know she's bound to be called Pam at school, so you can forget Penelope.'

Molly settled on a very pretty card featuring a kitten tangled in a skein of wool, peeking out guiltily from beneath a chair. She looked at the various boxes of chocolates, but decided to give that idea of a gift for Jane a little more thought.

The woman who was going up to Chester on the weekend left the shop, and Mrs Johnson turned her attention to Molly as she approached the counter. 'You're that policewoman, aren't you?' she said. 'The one who's been talking to our Peggy?'

Molly nodded. 'Yes, I am,' she said cautiously. It was hard to tell by the woman's tone what might be coming next. But whatever Mrs Johnson was about to say was cut off when a young dog pushed its way through a partly open door at the back of the shop.

'Come to see who I'm talking to, have you?' said Mrs Johnson as the dog trotted to her side. She reached down to fondle the dog's ears.

Molly stared. 'Brandy?' she said. 'What on earth are you doing here? I thought you were with one of the girls from the shop.'

Mrs Johnson chuckled. 'Oh, you know Brandy, do you?' she said. 'But then, of course you would, wouldn't you? But you're wrong; this isn't Brandy; this is Gypsy, Brandy's sister. Identical twins, they are. It's easy to make a mistake.'

Molly, still staring, couldn't believe it. 'You are joking, aren't you, Mrs Johnson? This *is* Susan Chase's dog, isn't it? I saw her at the shop only yesterday.'

'Go over there and call her, then,' the woman said. 'See if she comes to you.'

Molly moved a few feet away and squatted down. 'Come on, then, Brandy,' she coaxed. 'You know me.'

The dog eyed her curiously but remained where she was.

'Gypsy.' Mrs Johnson patted her lap. 'Come on, then, girl,' she called. The dog turned immediately and put her paws on Mrs Johnson's lap.

'Well, I'll be . . .' said Molly as she stood up again. 'I could have sworn that was Brandy. She's beautiful, whoever she is, and I'm especially fond of Shelties.'

'You like dogs, then, do you?' Mrs Johnson asked.

'I do, and I'd love to have one, but with my job it wouldn't be fair. I never know when I'll be home or for how long.'

Mrs Johnson swung her chair around. 'Come out back with me, then,' she said as she made for the door, 'and you can see the two dogs together. I was going to make myself a cup of tea, so why don't you stop and have one with me?'

Molly hesitated, but her curiosity had been aroused by the appearance of the dog, which she still had trouble believing was not Susan's dog, Brandy. 'I can't stop long,' she said, but Mrs Johnson was already at the door, leaving Molly little choice but to follow.

'Close the door,' Mrs Johnson said sharply as Molly was surrounded by dogs. 'Gypsy's the only one allowed in the shop, and the others will soon settle down once they've had a good sniff of you. The Golden Lab is Rory; he belongs to a friend of mine who's in hospital. Misty, the cairn, has been here for a couple of weeks, but she goes home tomorrow, and I know I shall miss her. The springer is called Robbie. His master's work takes him up to Aberdeen from time to time, so Robbie stays with me. Then there's poor old Sam.' She pointed to a large black dog of indeterminate breed stretched out in a patch of sunlight. 'He's twelve, and he has rheumatism, so he loves the warmth. Poor old thing. I've had him since he was eight weeks old.

'Ah, yes, and there's my little Brandy,' she said as the twin of Gypsy trotted into the room and paused, tail wagging gently. 'Aren't they like two peas in a pod? Michelle – that's Michelle Marshall, the one who looks after the shop whenever Susan's away – says the police even took samples of poor Brandy's coat while they were searching Susan's flat, though why they would want to do that, I don't know.'

It was strange, thought Molly. Mrs Johnson knew that Molly was a policewoman, yet she didn't seem to connect her directly with what had happened to Susan Chase.

'Call her,' the woman urged Molly. 'See if she remembers you.'

Molly bent and called to the dog. The Sheltie hesitated only for a moment before trotting forward to sniff at Molly's outstretched hand. 'It's amazing,' she said as she looked from Brandy to Gypsy and back again. 'How *do* you tell them apart?'

The older woman's face creased in a secretive smile. 'Ah, well,' she said, 'they were from one of my litters, weren't they, my dear? You get to know their little ways. But you can tell if you look at their ears. Gypsy's ears are tipped more than Brandy's, and the left one is tipped a little bit more than the right. As a matter of fact, we were worried that Brandy's ears weren't going to tip at all, but they did in the end, but not quite as much as Gypsy's.'

Molly frowned. 'Why do you say you were worried about her ears? Would that mean there was something wrong with them?'

'Oh, no, at least not physically, but judges don't like prick-eared Shelties, and both of these dogs have potential in the ring.'

Mrs Johnson's voice was soft as she went on. 'I've always loved dogs,' she explained, 'so I take them in for friends while they're away. I make sure they all eat the same things they eat at home, and Peggy grooms them on the weekends while she's here; puts that old tracksuit of hers on and gets right down on the floor with them; checks their teeth and cuts their nails if they need it, and plays with them. She calls it her unwinding time. Gypsy and Sam are mine, of course, but the others are used to coming here, and they have the run of the house like they do at home, so it's better than going into kennels.' She leaned down to rub the cairn behind the ears. 'Isn't it, Misty, love,' she said as if talking to a child.

The living quarters behind the shop were surprisingly spacious, although the living room itself was cluttered with boxes stacked on boxes, most of which were unopened. 'New stock,' Mrs Johnson explained. 'Peggy usually takes care of it when she comes over, but she's not here today. Come on through.' She continued on down a short hall to a bright, sunlit kitchen. A large window looked out on a very long and narrow garden, bordered on both sides by a brick wall that must have been at least seven feet high.

'Fortunately, the garden faces south and gets the sun, what little we've seen of it lately,' Mrs Johnson continued, 'and it's a good thing, too, otherwise those walls would make it hard to grow anything back there, and I like my garden. Not that I can do much in it now I'm stuck in this thing –' she banged the arm of the wheelchair – 'but I can still get out there and tell Arthur what to do. Arthur's my husband, and he doesn't mind. At least I can tend to the pots, so I'm not completely useless.'

'I'd say you do extremely well, what with the shop and everything,' Molly said. 'But tell me, is that what I think it is at the end of the garden?'

Mrs Johnson laughed. 'You mean the van? Once seen never forgotten,' she chuckled. 'Yes, that's Arthur's van all right. That yellow is hard to miss, isn't it? I thought he was crazy when he said he was going to have it painted egg-yolk yellow, but he was right. It makes people look, and they remember the name 'Garage on Wheels'. In fact it's gone over so well he can't keep up. He'd like to put a second van on the road, but he can't find a mechanic he can trust to take it on.'

Mrs Johnson swung her chair around. 'Pop the kettle on,' she said to Molly. 'It's over there by the stove. The water's in; just plug it in.

There's McVities HobNobs on the counter, or there's Bourbon Creams and Cadbury's Chocolate Fingers. The plates and mugs are in that cupboard, and the milk is in the fridge. Take what you like, but I'll have the fingers; I love my chocolate. Then sit yourself down; the kettle won't take long to boil.'

Molly couldn't escape the feeling that she should have left the shop when she had the chance, because she thought she knew what was coming. But she could hardly walk out now, so she took her seat at the table, and hoped the kettle would boil quickly.

Her instincts were right, because no sooner had she sat down than Mrs Johnson started in with: 'I couldn't believe it when Michelle from Susan's shop came round with Brandy the other evening, and told us that Susan had been arrested for killing Simon. I don't know Susan all that well, in fact the first time I met her was when she bought Brandy from me, but she seemed very nice. It's hard to believe that someone you think you know could do a thing like that, isn't it? But Michelle said she reckons the two of them have been having it off on the quiet for a long time, even before her sister was killed, and that *did* surprise me, I can tell you. Don't think it surprised our Peg, though, when I told her, not after what she said when she came back from Mrs Holbrook's funeral last week.'

'Oh? What was that, then?' asked Molly. She felt guilty about asking the question of this nice grey-haired lady who had asked her to share a cup of tea, but on the other hand they did have a murder to solve.

'Oh, I knew *something* was wrong the minute Peg walked in that Friday,' Mrs Johnson said sadly. 'Peg looked like death herself, she was that pale, and she kept saying, "I couldn't believe it, Mum. You should have seen her. Susan. There she was, bold as brass, hanging on to his arm as if she owned him. Right there beside the grave, and Laura barely cold!"'

The Golden Lab sidled up to Mrs Johnson and laid his head in her lap. 'Soft old thing,' she said as she fondled his ears.

She looked off into the distance as if reliving the scene in her mind. 'Like I said, I was surprised to hear it was Susan Simon had taken up with, but I wasn't surprised about him. Not a bit! I've been telling Peg for years she was wasting her time working all hours and looking after him the way she did, because he was never going to change. But would she listen? Oh, no. What does her old mum know about things like that, eh? And now he's gone, so it doesn't much matter any more, does it?'

The kettle was boiling. Molly rose to make the tea. In her mind's eye, she saw Peggy sitting there in Simon Holbrook's house, white-faced and visibly shaken as she answered Paget's questions in a monotone. 'So, how is she taking it?' she asked quietly.

'A lot harder than she's letting on,' Mrs Johnson said forcefully. 'But then our Peg's always been like that. Keeps her feelings to herself. I wish she would let go; have a good cry and get it out of her system instead of holding it in. But, no, all business she was when she rang me. Said there would be a lot to do now that Simon was gone, and she would have to look after things until everything was sorted out. That's why she isn't here today.'

She shook her head in a bewildered fashion. 'I can't make heads or tails of it,' she said, 'because if what Michelle said *is* true, and the two of them were, well, you know, why would Susan want to kill Simon?' She shot a glance at Molly. 'Are you quite sure she did it?'

'I'm sorry, Mrs Johnson, but I really can't discuss the case. It's . . .'

Mrs Johnson plucked a biscuit from the packet and dipped it in her tea. 'Took to him right from the start,' she continued as if Molly hadn't spoken. 'From the time she first went to work for him at Drexler-Davies. Talked about him all the time, she did, but I warned her. I told her it's never a good idea to take up with your boss. Leads to trouble every time, I told her. Not that it did any good. Peg's not the sort to listen if she's got her mind set on something, and she certainly had her mind set on him.

'Funny, though,' she continued, eyes focused on a distant memory that only she could see, 'I would never have known how far it had gone if it hadn't been for young Valerie telling me about having to move out so he could come to the flat whenever he felt like it.'

Molly hesitated. On a personal level, she felt guilty about allowing Peggy's mother to run on about her daughter, who was one of a number of possible suspects in a murder investigation, but as a detective, she couldn't afford not to take advantage of the opportunity to gather valuable information. 'Valerie . . .?' she said hesitantly as if the name were vaguely familiar to her. 'What was her last name? Did she work for Drexler-Davies as well?'

'Oh, no, dear. She worked in one of the big hotels in Birmingham, but she and Peg had been best friends ever since school. That's why they went in together in the flat. Wade, that was her name. Mind you she's probably married by now and has half-a-dozen kids. Nice girl, she was, and I felt ever so sorry when she told me she was leaving. Said she felt as if she was in the way, so she thought it would be best if she moved out. Pity, because they never got back together again after that, and I always liked her.'

Molly said, 'It sounds as if Valerie was your friend as well as Peggy's. Have you seen her recently?'

'No. The girls used to come down here together, but Val never did come on her own after she moved out.' Mrs Johnson sighed and clucked her tongue. 'I didn't like the idea of them carrying on like that, but then I thought maybe he'd do the right thing by her and there'd be wedding bells one day and everything would be all right, but it wasn't to be. I don't know what happened, but nothing came of it, and yet they seemed to get on so well together at work.'

Mrs Johnson shook her head sadly. 'After all the years she's worked for that man, and the things she's done for him – she even put all her savings into the business to help him get started – and yet somehow it never went anywhere. She knew what he was like; she knew he was seeing other women, but she'd never say a word against him, not even when he went off and married Laura. "It won't last, Mum," she says. "You'll see. He only married her for the sake of the firm. He'll come back to me. He always does."'

Mrs Johnson lowered her voice as if afraid of being overheard. 'I know it's an awful thing to say, but to tell you the truth I think Peg was pleased when Laura was – well, when she died. She even said it was like the old days around the office again, when it was just him and her planning and talking for hours about what they should do next to make a go of the firm. I really think she thought she was in with a chance at last, so it came as quite a shock to see Susan hanging on his arm at the funeral, and then to have Michelle tell us he'd been seeing her all along.'

Molly had intended to go straight home and get started on preparing her meals for the week, but as Mrs Johnson continued to talk, she couldn't help wondering about the two dogs, Brandy and Gypsy. Was it possible that Forensic had made a mistake, and the hair they'd tested had actually come from Gypsy?

Probably not, she told herself as she left the shop. If anything, DNA was even more reliable than fingerprints, and all the evidence still pointed to Susan as Simon Holbrook's killer. Still, it wouldn't hurt to run it past Sergeant Ormside, if he happened to be in the office, and Charter Lane was only a short distance away.

But Ormside, too, had decided to take some well-deserved time off, and the incident room was deserted. According to the log, two detective constables were out taking statements from Holbrook's neighbours in Pembroke Street; the Scenes of Crime team were in the last stages of their examination of the house and immediate surroundings, and Susan Chase was in hospital and wouldn't be going anywhere for a while.

If Sergeant Ormside had been there, she would have stayed to write up her notes and talk to him about what she had just learned. But she could write up her notes just as well at home; in fact, she was beginning to wonder why she had come in at all when the sun was shining outside and she had the weekend off. Was it because this was where her life was centred now? Whatever she'd wanted to talk over with Ormside could certainly have waited until Monday, so why *had* she come?

Molly got back in her car and sat there, fingers drumming on the steering wheel as she thought about that. She had no social life. That had come to a full stop when Craig had walked out three years ago, unable to understand why she would not give up her career while he continued on with his. Not that she hadn't had offers since then, some of them from quite nice blokes, but they were usually coppers, and she didn't want to go through that experience again.

She would have to think about that, she told herself as she started the car and headed for home. The sun was still shining, and the air was warmer than it had been for a long time, but somehow the prospect of spending the rest of the day on her own had lost its appeal.

Twenty-Seven

Ormside and Molly were talking earnestly when Paget walked in, and one glance at the whiteboards told him that something had been added since he'd last looked at them. 'Looks as if someone has been busy,' he remarked as he read the notes. 'What's all this about dogs and Peggy Goodwin?'

'Dogs and Peggy Goodwin?' Tregalles echoed the chief inspector's words as he came through the door carrying a mug of steaming coffee. 'Sounds interesting.'

'I think Forsythe had best tell you herself,' the sergeant said. 'Go ahead, Molly.'

With only the occasional glance at the notes she had written up on Saturday, Molly related the conversation she'd had with Mrs Johnson almost verbatim, ending with: 'So I stopped in at the animal clinic on Chapel Road on my way home, and I spoke to a veterinarian there who said he couldn't be absolutely certain, but he felt that it would be possible for two dogs from the same litter to have the same DNA. They would have to be identical twins, which he says is rare, but, as with humans, it does happen occasionally.

'Which made me wonder if it was possible that we have the wrong dog,' she concluded. 'It would also explain the presence of the other dog hairs found at the scene of the burglaries, and if Peggy *was* in love with Holbrook, as her mother said, isn't it possible that he played on that to get her to help him rid himself of Laura, while secretly carrying on with Susan? In fact, perhaps he and Susan planned this together? She had every reason to hate her sister. But when Peggy realized how she'd been used, she turned on Simon and killed him at a time when she knew Susan would be blamed.'

'What about the burglaries leading up to the killing of Laura?' Tregalles asked. 'Who did those? Somehow I can't see Simon vandalizing houses.'

'I can see Peggy doing it though,' Molly said, 'and I think I know how she might have chosen the houses for each burglary.'

Suddenly, she had the full attention of all three men, and she almost wished she hadn't spoken. Two sergeants and a DCI all waiting for her to speak? 'It . . . it's only a theory,' she said hesitantly. 'I mean I could be completely wrong, but—'

'Go on then, Molly,' Ormside said quietly. 'Theory or not, let's hear it.'

'Well, I was thinking about it last night, and I remembered a conversation I overheard in Mrs Johnson's shop. A woman was buying a card to take to the christening of her granddaughter, and she mentioned that she and her husband were going up to Chester next weekend. Later, I remembered that Peggy usually works in the shop on Saturdays, so she must hear similar stories from people who are buying cards or chocolates to take as gifts when they are going away. All she would have to do is encourage them to talk and she would know when the house would be empty. We could ask the people whose houses were broken into if they were in the gift shop on a Saturday before they left, and if they talked about where they were going. If it *was* Peggy who was doing the burglaries, it would explain the different types of dog hair in the houses, because her mother told me that Peggy helps with the grooming of the dogs when she comes round on Saturdays. We would have to check which dogs were in her mother's care and when, of course, but that shouldn't be too hard.'

The three men exchanged glances. It was Ormside who broke the silence. 'It would explain how the houses were selected,' he said. 'But do you really think Goodwin's got the sort of nerve it would take to break into someone's house and do all that damage?'

'I really don't know,' said Molly, 'although I think she is a very determined woman. But I have to admit, all the rest of the evidence does point to Susan Chase, who could be just as determined.'

'So it's a case of take your pick,' Tregalles said.

'It is,' said Paget, 'so the sooner we start sorting it out the better. I think Forsythe's theory is worth following up,' he told Ormside, 'so I want someone to start digging into Goodwin's background. Build a profile on her; find out who her friends are, and what they have to say about her. And if this Valerie Wade is still around, let's see what she has to say about her old school friend. However, we can't ignore the fact that all the evidence still points to Susan Chase when it comes to the killing of Simon. Have they found anything in the flat or shop?'

Ormside shifted uncomfortably as he said, 'Yes, well, I was coming to that, sir. We didn't get the warrant till late in the day on Friday, and what with one thing and another, they didn't get started until this morning. But they are there now,' he hastened to add.

Paget eyed Ormside narrowly. 'What, exactly, do you mean by "one thing and another", Len?'

'Seems that Mr Brock phoned Charlie Friday afternoon to say he didn't see the need for people working the weekend at double time, when the work could be done just as well on Monday.'

'And no one thought to let me know?' Paget said.

Ormside said, 'I didn't know myself until this morning, and Charlie probably thought you knew already. Oh, yes, one more thing before I forget. The super's back today and he wants to see you in his office to bring him up to date.'

'Right,' said Paget. 'I'll go up when we've finished here. Anything else?'

'We'll need a warrant to search Peggy Goodwin's flat,' Ormside said, 'and one for her mother's place as well. And we'll need hair samples from the dogs.'

'Except, apart from Mrs Johnson's own dogs, Gypsy and Sam, the dogs she's looking after now probably aren't the ones she had there over the time period of the burglaries,' Molly pointed out. 'So we'll need to get a list of every dog Mrs Johnson has taken in over the last few months.'

But Paget was shaking his head. 'Too early for that,' he said flatly. 'We don't have enough hard evidence to apply for a warrant. Let's find out first if any of the burglary victims did visit the gift shop when Peggy was there, and if they mentioned going away. But I want it done discreetly, because some of these people may have known Peggy and her mother for a long time, and I don't want word of our enquiries to get back to either of them. So let's be careful about how we ask the question. And since this is your idea, Forsythe, I think you should be the one to follow it up – that is unless Sergeant Ormside has other plans for you.'

Ormside shook his head, and Molly picked up her handbag and slung it over her shoulder. 'In that case, I'd better make a start,' she said.

'Before you go, it might be a good idea to check the statements of the people whose homes were vandalized in case they did mention the card shop,' Ormside said. 'Save yourself some time.'

Molly patted her handbag. 'I did when I first came in this morning,' she told him. 'None of them mentioned the shop, so if there's nothing else, I'll be on my way.'

The grizzled sergeant looked thoughtful as he followed Molly with his eyes as she left the room. 'I think you should be very nice to that young woman,' he said softly to Tregalles as Paget moved away to study the boards once more.

'Why?' Tregalles asked suspiciously. 'What do you know that I don't?'

Ormside shrugged. 'Just a thought,' he said. 'I won't be around to see it, but if she goes on the way she's going, you could be working for her one of these days.'

The flashing light on the phone told Paget that it was the direct line from Control. 'A Mr Beaumont is asking for you, sir,' said a female voice when he picked it up. 'He says he is returning your call. Shall I put him through, sir?'

'Please,' said Paget, and a moment later exchanged introductions with Henry Beaumont.

'I assume this has something to do with the unfortunate death of Simon Holbrook,' Beaumont said, coming straight to the point. 'How can I help?'

'I have here copies of a series of emails taken from Simon Holbrook's BlackBerry, and I would appreciate it if you could enlarge on what they seem to be telling me. Would I be right in assuming that you were negotiating some sort of amalgamation between Drexler-Davies and Holbrook Micro-Engineering?'

There was a lengthy silence from the other end before Beaumont said, 'I'm afraid that is confidential information, Chief Inspector, and I'm not at liberty to discuss it with—'

'Perhaps I didn't make myself clear, Mr Beaumont,' Paget interjected. 'I was hoping to deal with this particular matter in an informal way rather than put you to the trouble of travelling here to answer questions and making a formal statement. And since Mr Holbrook is dead, I assumed that confidentiality would no longer be an issue. Would tomorrow be convenient?'

Once again there was a long pause before Beaumont responded. 'I must apologize, Chief Inspector,' he said smoothly, 'but sometimes we become overcautious in this business of ours, and we tend to treat everything as confidential. But as you say, that may no longer be a consideration in this case. What, exactly, would you like to know?'

* * *

'Henry Beaumont has been trying to persuade Simon Holbrook to come back to work for them ever since he left Drexler-Davies, but Holbrook has always refused, insisting that he wanted to be in control of his own company. But suddenly all that changed, and it was he who approached Beaumont early to mid January saying he was prepared to consider a deal.'

Paget was in Alcott's office, briefing him on the latest developments in the Holbrook case.

'They had several secret meetings, and it was all but wrapped up, according to Beaumont,' Paget continued. 'In effect, Holbrook Micro-Engineering was to become a subsidiary of Drexler-Davies, and the reason Holbrook gave for the sudden about-face – *he said* – was because Laura was leaving the company. He told Beaumont that he knew it would be extremely difficult to find someone with the same strengths and credibility in the marketplace that she had, and said he had neither the time nor the energy to go through all that again. He said all he wanted was to be left alone to get on with his own research without having to bother about all the things that a company like Drexler-Davies could do for him in finding markets and dealing with clients. But he still wanted some autonomy, which was why he proposed bringing his company in as a subsidiary, a separate entity, over which he would have some control at least. That way, he said, they would both benefit. Drexler-Davies would have a valuable addition to their Research and Development division, and he and his people could get on with what they did best, knowing that their products would be marketed aggressively.'

Alcott frowned. 'Holbrook actually said that his wife would be *leaving* the firm?' he said. 'And he first proposed this in January?'

'Right. Just a few days before the first burglary that we are attributing to him or to someone doing it on his behalf.'

'How is it that we are only hearing about this deal now? Surely there must have been some buzz among the staff?'

'Beaumont says that Holbrook wanted it kept completely secret until the deal was done. As it is, Beaumont has already assigned a new manager to come down here and take over. I asked him if that would affect any of the present staff, and he said the new manager would be bringing in a transition team, and some of the present staff could be culled during the "rationalization", as he put it.'

'Which is business-speak for redundancies, I take it?' Alcott said.

'Something like that,' Paget agreed.

'So what would happen to Goodwin if the deal had gone through?'

'I asked Beaumont that, and he said they might be able to use her during the transition, and there would probably be a place for her in the new organization, but it would be nothing like the position she holds now.'

'So, chances are Holbrook would not have told her what he was doing. But do you think she knew?'

'I'm sure she didn't – at least not when I first spoke to her. She was working flat out trying to keep the place together and find someone to take the place of Laura, and she was very protective of Holbrook. I think she sees the company as partly hers, and I think she would have found the prospect of abandoning the idea of remaining an independent company devastating. But if it was she rather than Susan Chase who killed Laura for him, then found out later what he intended to do with the company, it could be a powerful motive for killing him, especially if she also learned that he'd been sleeping with Susan Chase all along.'

'Could she have found out more recently?'

'It's certainly possible. Holbrook carried the BlackBerry in his jacket pocket rather than on his belt, and Goodwin was always in and out of his office, so yes, it is quite possible.'

Alcott pursed his lips as he thought about that. 'So what's going to happen to this deal with Beaumont now that Holbrook's dead?' he asked.

'It died with him,' Paget said. 'In fact, Beaumont told me he thought it a bit suspicious when Laura was killed, but he couldn't bring himself to believe that Simon was involved. He said he spoke to Holbrook about it at the funeral, and Holbrook assured him that it was nothing more than a tragic and unfortunate coincidence. Now, of course, he is no longer interested in Holbrook Micro-Engineering as a company, because its main asset was Holbrook himself and the reputation he had for invention and innovation. But he's not above picking off some of the top technicians, in fact he's already spoken to some of them about coming to work for Drexler-Davies and, as he put it, made them an offer they'll find hard to refuse under the circumstances.'

'Not a man to look a gift horse in the mouth, obviously,' Alcott observed. 'So, are you trying to tell me that you now think it was Goodwin who did the killings and she's setting up Chase to take the fall?'

'All I'm saying, sir, is that this raises some questions, and I'd like to find the answers, because there could be more than one motive for murder.'

'*Could* be,' Alcott said dismissively, 'but from what you've told me, the preponderance of evidence points to Chase. She even admits she was there at the time Starkie says Holbrook was killed, for God's sake! I know you seem to think it's all too pat, but there are times, Paget, when things are exactly as they seem, simple and straightforward, so let's not make them any more complicated than they really are.'

'A Dr Barraclough called while you were with Mr Alcott,' Ormside said when Paget returned from lunch. 'He said to tell you that the operation on Susan Chase's knee has been scheduled for four o'clock this afternoon, and barring complications, she will probably be discharged tomorrow morning. He said we should check with him in the morning for the actual time.'

'Did he say anything about her mental state?' Paget asked. 'Delayed shock?'

Ormside shook his head. 'No, never mentioned it.'

'Good,' said Paget. 'In that case, let's make sure that someone is there to bring her in. Anything else?'

'Ooohh, yes,' Ormside said in a way that suggested he'd been saving the good news. 'Forensic hasn't finished with Miss Chase's car yet, but they thought we might be interested in what they found tucked away in the bottom of the glove box, so they sent it over.' He took a sealed polythene bag from his desk drawer. He handed the bag to Paget. 'Laura Holbrook's rings,' he said. 'They were screwed up inside that wad of tissue in there. I've checked them against the pictures the insurance people gave us, and they're the ones all right, so I'm afraid that blows young Forsythe's theory right out of the water.'

Paget held the bag up to the light. Even inside the plastic bag the stones seemed to have a fire of their own.

'They also faxed us a list of what they've found so far,' Ormside continued. 'Dog hair all over the inside of the car, probably from Chase's own dog, but Forensic can check that out. No sign of anything that looks like the weapon that killed Mrs Holbrook, but lots of fibres that need to be checked against the ones found in some of the houses that were burgled.

'Lots of glass from the broken windows inside the car,' Ormside continued, 'but nothing to indicate why they were broken. No dents or scratches that might suggest an accident, so I suppose we'll just have to wait for Chase to tell us what happened.'

Paget handed the bag containing the rings back to Ormside. 'Make sure they are properly logged in,' he told the sergeant. 'The last thing we need is to lose the only tangible piece of evidence we have – especially something as valuable as these.'

'I spent most of the day working for you,' said Grace as she and Paget sat down to dinner that evening. 'Going through Susan Chase's flat and the shop,' she elaborated. 'I can't say I found anything particularly incriminating, although there was certainly evidence that Simon Holbrook has been spending quite a bit of time there. There were jackets, trousers and shirts on hangers in one of the closets; underwear and socks in one of the drawers; shoes, aftershave, toothpaste and other things of his in the bathroom, plus a few odds and ends in the laundry basket.'

'You're sure they all belonged to Holbrook?' he asked, only half facetiously.

'They match the clothing in his house, and the aftershave is the same. Even so, I sent hair from the comb and the shower to Forensic for verification. And the reason I think the affair has been going on for some time is because I found two ticket stubs from a play at the Birmingham Repertory Theatre dated January fourteenth in one of his pockets. Don McIntyre, one of our financial analysts, has been going through Simon and Laura Holbrook's papers – it was Don who found the email messages to Beaumont on Simon's BlackBerry the other day – so I asked him to check Holbrook's credit card statements for me. The February statement shows he stayed in a double room at the Crowne Plaza that night; he had a meal at Simpsons, presumably dinner for two by the size of the bill, breakfast in the hotel the following morning, and lunch on the way home on the Sunday in Tenbury Wells.

'I asked him to check Laura's business diary, and he told me she was away in London that weekend, so I'd say there's a good chance that Simon's companion in Birmingham was Susan Chase.'

'Could have been anyone,' Paget said, playing devil's advocate.

Grace grinned. 'I thought you might say that,' she said, 'and you're right, it could have been anyone. Except Susan is a bit of a pack-rat – at least when it comes to things with a romantic attachment – and she had the programme for that performance tucked away in a drawer along with other little mementos of their time together.'

'Good.' Paget nodded approvingly. 'That's exactly the sort of hard evidence we need to show their relationship,' he said. 'Anything else?'

'Nothing that ties her directly to the murder of either one of the Holbrooks. No bloodstained clothing; no weapon; nothing like that. She has some beautiful clothes, but I couldn't find anything made of a similar material to that mentioned in Forensics' report on the fibres found in the vandalized houses and in Laura Holbrook's bedroom. In fact there was nothing to suggest she ever wore anything like that. There were lots of shoes, twelve pairs to be exact, but none of them were trainers, and the girls in the shop said they had never seen her wear anything but stylish shoes, even when she took the dog for a walk.'

Grace set her knife and fork down and leaned forward, elbows on the table. 'Are you *quite* sure it was she who killed Simon?' she asked. 'I've never met the woman, but having gone through her things, and in talking to the girls in the shop downstairs, my impression of her is of a rather gentle person. She's certainly a romantic. She has stacks of Mills & Boon and Harlequin romances in her bedroom.'

'On the other hand,' he countered, 'it could be argued it's *because* she's a romantic, living in a dream world, that she was prepared to risk everything for her lover by getting rid of his wife so they could live happily ever after, as the fairy tales say,' said Paget. 'But when she realized that her lover was likely to cave in under questioning and blame her for everything, she killed him. It wouldn't be the first time that love has turned to hate.'

Grace looked doubtful. 'I'm not sure that would get you very far in court,' she said. 'But you haven't answered my question, Neil. Are *you* convinced she killed both of them?'

'I'm not sure I can answer the question,' he said. 'The evidence against her is pretty strong, but I must confess I have niggling doubts about some of it. However, with any luck at all we should be interviewing her tomorrow, so perhaps I'll have an answer for you then.'

Twenty-Eight

Tuesday, March 24

'Chase is to be discharged from hospital between ten and eleven this morning,' Ormside told Paget. 'The doctor says everything went well. Apparently it wasn't a particularly severe fracture, but she'll be on crutches for a while.' Ormside consulted a slip of paper. 'He said to tell you she'll be experiencing some pain later on in the day when the painkillers begin to wear off, and while there is no medical reason why she can't be questioned, she has been under considerable stress, and we should bear that in mind.'

Paget smiled. 'Did he, now?' he said. 'It sounds to me as if Susan Chase has made quite an impression on Dr Barraclough. Anything else?'

'Well, I don't know how much this means now, considering the evidence we have against Chase,' the sergeant said hesitantly, 'but Forsythe has spoken to all of the people whose homes were broken into, and every one of them visited the gift shop on a Saturday when Peggy Goodwin was there. Which means we have an explanation for how Goodwin would know when the houses would be empty, but we don't have the same for Chase. So which one do we go with?'

'That's what I hope to find out today,' Paget told him. 'But until I've talked to Chase, I'm keeping my options open.'

Susan Chase, looking paler than usual, appeared to be calm and composed as she faced Paget and Tregalles across the table. She sat sideways in her chair, her right leg stretched out in front of her to keep it well out of harm's way. A uniformed WPC had helped Susan to her seat, propped her crutches against the wall, then taken her own seat by the door. The recorder was activated, and names, date and time were entered by Tregalles.

'Before we begin,' Susan broke in quickly as Paget started to speak, 'I would like to say that I did *not* kill Simon, and I have no idea who did, but if I am to be charged, I will not talk to you without my solicitor present.' There was a slight tremor in her voice, but her eyes held those of Paget as she spoke.

'Whether or not you will be charged depends very much on you,' Paget told her. 'We do need to ask you some questions regarding the death of Simon and Laura Holbrook and, depending on your answers, you may be free to go or you may be charged and detained. And you are quite within your rights to have your solicitor present if you so choose.'

'I see.' Susan chewed on her lip as her eyes searched his face. 'Does that mean I can call my solicitor at any time?'

'Yes.'

Susan drew in a long breath and let it out again. 'Then let's get on with it,' she said tightly.

'First, for the record,' said Paget briskly, 'you have only just come out of hospital after having an operation on your knee, and your doctor there has declared you fit for questioning. But tell me, Miss Chase, are you in any pain or discomfort?'

Susan grimaced. 'Except for having to hobble around on crutches, no,' she said, 'but the sooner we're finished here, the better.'

'Duly noted,' Paget said. 'Now, tell me, when and where did you last see Simon Holbrook?'

Susan's eyes suddenly filled with tears. 'Thursday morning in his house,' she said huskily, 'and I told you that the other day.' She fumbled in her handbag for a tissue and dabbed at her eyes. 'And he was asleep when I left him.'

'What time was that?'

'I told you that as well. It would be about five o'clock.'

'Did you leave the door locked or unlocked?'

'Locked. It locks automatically. It's a spring lock.'

'And where did you go?'

'Straight home.'

'This was not the first time you had spent the night with Mr Holbrook, is it, Miss Chase? In fact I believe you have spent most nights together since the death of his wife – your sister. Is that correct?'

Her chin came up defiantly. 'Yes.'

'In fact you and Simon Holbrook were having an affair for some time *before* your sister was murdered. Isn't that correct, Miss Chase?'

Susan closed her eyes and shook her head. 'You don't understand,' she said. 'You make it sound so tawdry, but it wasn't like that. Simon was at his wits' end. Their marriage was falling to pieces, and Laura had literally taken over his business; the business he had built up over the years. His heart and soul were in that business, and he felt as if he were on the outside looking in. He came to me for . . . for help. We've been friends for many years, and he thought that since Laura was my sister, perhaps I could help him.'

'By sleeping with him?' Tregalles put in softly.

Colour flooded into Susan's cheeks. 'That – that just happened,' she said defensively. 'We didn't mean it to happen – it just did.'

'You say it just happened, but isn't it true that you have been in love with Simon Holbrook for many years? I think you hated your sister for taking him away from you, because it wasn't the first time she'd done that to you, was it, Miss Chase? I think that you saw an opportunity to get Simon back, and you persuaded him that the only solution to his troubles, at home and at work, was to get rid of your sister. Permanently. Is that not true, Miss Chase?'

'No, that is not true!' she flared. 'All right, I admit I was in love with Simon; I admit that I was hurt when he married Laura, but I knew how Laura worked, and I knew it wouldn't last. Laura could be very charming and persuasive when she wanted something, and she wanted Simon and the challenge of the business. But she soon tired of Simon, as I knew she would, because she saw him only as a means to an end. It was the business she wanted, but Simon was genuinely in love with her – or thought he was at the time – and he couldn't understand why Laura had changed so much. And to make things worse, while she was no longer interested in Simon as a husband, she was *very* much interested in his skills as an inventor and in the business.'

Susan sighed deeply. 'The problem was it was no longer *Simon's* business; it was *Laura's*. She held the reins and wouldn't let go, and that was when Simon came to me.'

'When was that, exactly?'

'Christmas – just after.' Susan frowned and looked away. 'Simon was desperately unhappy, and we used to talk long into the night when Laura was away on one of her overnight business trips. We didn't mean it to happen; it just did. We fell in love all over again.'

'But nothing could come of it while Simon was married to Laura,' Tregalles continued. 'If Simon tried to divorce her and she chose to fight him, it could mean the end of his company. But if she died, the business would revert to Simon; the money she had invested in the company, which I understand was considerable, would remain, and he would inherit whatever else she might have.' Tregalles leaned back in his chair and clasped his hands behind his head. 'I think that prospect would be very tempting to anyone, very tempting indeed,' he said. 'You say you talked long into the night when Laura was away. Was that when you came up with the plan to kill her?'

'No! That's utterly absurd.'

'Whose idea was it to break into houses in order to set a pattern of vandalism and escalating violence so that Laura's murder would look like a burglary gone wrong? Yours or Simon's?' Tregalles prodded. 'I suspect it was yours, and it was you who broke into those houses, because the hair we found in those houses came from your dog, Brandy.'

Susan stared at him. 'That's impossible!' she declared. 'I don't know what you are talking about. I had nothing to do with Laura's death, and neither did Simon. We were together at my flat the night Laura was killed.'

Paget stirred. 'Does the name Henry Beaumont mean anything to you?' he asked.

'I – I've heard Simon mention him,' said Susan cautiously.

'He is, as I believe you know very well, Miss Chase, Vice President in charge of Research and Development with Drexler-Davies' UK Division. Have you ever *met* Mr Beaumont?'

Susan tried to meet his eyes and failed. 'Once,' she said huskily.

'That would be the night he came to your flat; the night your sister was killed, would it not, Miss Chase?'

Susan cleared her throat. 'That's right. He came to see Simon.'

'To finalize the secret negotiations that were going on between Mr Holbrook and Mr Beaumont,' Paget said. 'Negotiations that would have meant that Holbrook Micro-Engineering Labs would no longer be independent, but would become part of the Drexler-Davies Corporation. That was the real reason Simon came to your flat that evening, wasn't it, Miss Chase?'

Susan's eyes flashed. 'If you know all this, why are you asking me?' she flared.

'Please answer the question.'

'Yes, that's why he was there. All right?'

'Who else knew about the negotiations?'

'No one,' she said sullenly. 'Simon didn't want anyone to know until everything was settled.'

'Especially his wife, to say nothing of the employees who would be losing their jobs.'

'Simon regretted that, but there was no other way.' Susan was having trouble keeping her voice steady. 'He said he couldn't face the thought of rebuilding the business again. Too much stress; too much time wasted. He said it was impossible to be creative in that sort of atmosphere. You have to understand, Chief Inspector, Simon was the best in his field; he had a unique talent and a reputation, but he couldn't get on with what he loved doing while trying to rebuild the business. It was just too much, so he went to Henry Beaumont and they worked out this arrangement where Holbrook Micro-Engineering Labs would become a separate division of Drexler-Davies. Simon would be in charge of that branch of technical research. He would be able to get on with what he did best without having to worry about interfacing with clients or any of what he called the front-end stuff.'

'So what would happen to someone who had been there since the beginning? Someone like Peggy Goodwin, for example? What would happen to her under this new arrangement?'

Frowning slightly, Susan gave Paget a quizzical look. 'Funny you should mention her specifically,' she said, 'because I think Simon was quite concerned about Peggy. He said she didn't really have much of a life of her own outside work, and because they have worked together since the beginning, she thought of herself as a partner rather than an employee. But as he said, even if she does call herself his PA, she is only a glorified secretary. A very good one, but a secretary just the same.'

Paget wondered how Peggy Goodwin would have reacted to that statement, had she heard it. 'Would the company have remained here in Broadminster if the deal had gone through?' he asked.

Susan looked down at her hands. 'For a while, yes,' she said, 'but Simon did say he expected there would be some sort of consolidation within a year, and we would probably be moving to Solihull, where we could leave all this behind and make a fresh start.'

'*We*, Miss Chase . . .?'

Susan raised her eyes to his. Tears glistened on her cheeks. 'We were to be married,' she whispered. 'Simon promised me. He *promised*. We could have been so . . .' Susan's hands fluttered in a helpless gesture before falling into her lap.

'Oh, I don't expect you to understand,' she went on as she saw the look of scepticism on their faces, 'but Simon never really loved Laura. He thought he did for a time, but it was nothing more than infatuation. Laura had that sort of power over men; she could draw them in; they

were fascinated by her. It was as if they were mesmerized, but it didn't
last because she soon lost interest once she had what she wanted. When
Simon came back to me, he said it was as if he were coming out of a
dream that had turned into a nightmare, and I was the only one he had
ever truly loved. He said that this time we would . . .' She stopped and
turned her eyes toward the ceiling, trying hard to hold back the tears.

'You were there, throughout this meeting, were you?' Tregalles asked.

Susan shook her head. 'No. I left them to it. Simon said he thought
Mr Beaumont would feel more comfortable if there wasn't a third party
there, so I took Brandy for a walk.'

'What time did you leave and how long were you gone?'

'Mr Beaumont arrived shortly after seven thirty, and I left a few
minutes later and came back around nine thirty or quarter to ten.'

Tregalles looked sceptical. 'You walked the dog for two hours?' he
said.

'No,' Susan said displaying exaggerated patience. 'I walked Brandy
for something like half an hour, then came back and sat in the car and
listened to the radio. I knew they had a lot to discuss, so I didn't want
to go back too soon.'

'Can anyone verify that? Did you see anyone you know on your walk?
Stop anywhere? Talk to anyone?'

'Apart from exchanging the odd "good evening" with other dog
walkers, no, I did not,' Susan said, allowing her irritation to show. 'Why
is that so important, Sergeant?'

Paget eased himself forward again. 'Tell me, Miss Chase,' he said,
'did Simon explain to you how he intended to acquire his wife's share
of the business, because, according to your own words, her reason for
marrying Simon was to get her hands on the business. So how did he
intend to persuade her to give that up without a fight?'

'I–I don't . . . We didn't discuss . . .' Susan began haltingly. 'Simon
said Drexler-Davies would be advancing him the money to buy her out,
and they would be making her an offer she couldn't refuse.'

'And you believed that?'

Once more the tell-tale colour began to rise in Susan's face. 'Yes,'
she said shakily. 'Laura was always looking for new challenges. I'm sure
Simon had it all worked out.'

But Paget was shaking his head. 'I don't think you *really* believed
that, did you, Miss Chase? You knew your sister better than anyone,
and you knew that she wouldn't stand for that. She had literally put

Holbrook Micro-Engineering Labs on the map; she wasn't about to give that up, which meant that whatever you were hoping for was nothing more than a pipe dream unless Laura could be taken out of the picture permanently.'

Paget sat back in his chair. 'Do you know what I think, Miss Chase?' he asked softly. 'I think you and Simon had it all worked out ahead of time. I think the two of you planned this months ago. I think you read about that burglary in Dunbar Road and decided to use it as a model, vandalizing houses, doing more and more damage each time to give us the impression that a couple of psychos were responsible, and it would look like their work when the Holbrook house was targeted and Laura was killed.

'I think,' he continued relentlessly, 'that while Simon was with Beaumont, you went to Simon's house, entered by the front door, using a key, then crept upstairs where you proceeded to beat your sister to death with a metal bar. You then pulled her wedding and engagement rings from her finger and took them with you. I'm not sure why you did that, but considering what she'd done to you over the years, perhaps it was simply a spur of the moment symbolic gesture on your part. Then you went downstairs and proceeded to make it look as if the place had been vandalized, pried open the back door to make it look as if entry had been forced, then left. And rather than carry the rings around with you, you wrapped them in the closest thing to hand and shoved them into the glove box of your car.'

Susan's face was ashen as she stared at him. 'I've never heard such a load of rubbish in all my life,' she gasped when she found her voice. 'I don't know what you are trying to do, but . . .'

She stopped abruptly as Paget produced the clear plastic bag containing Laura Holbrook's rings and placed it on the table in front of her. 'Then how do you account for the fact that Laura's rings were found in the glove box of your car?'

Susan stared at the rings. She opened her mouth to speak, but no sound came out. 'Do you deny that these are your sister's rings?' he prompted.

She looked dazed. 'No, they're Laura's rings,' she said in a strained voice, 'but I didn't put them there, and I didn't kill my sister. The real killer must have put them there . . .' Susan raised her hands and let them drop in a helpless gesture as she saw the look of scepticism on their faces.

'You had motive, means, and certainly opportunity,' Paget told her. 'In fact all of the evidence points straight to you. But let's leave that for the moment and go back to the killing of Simon Holbrook. The estimated time of death is roughly five o'clock on Thursday morning, which is when you say you left the house. We've taken fingerprints from the wardrobe and one of the taps on the bathroom. They have Simon Holbrook's blood all over them. I expect we'll find they're yours. The tests are due back any minute. There will be evidence—'

'No! That's not true!' Susan broke in harshly. 'It can't be. Simon was alive when I left him. He was sleeping, and I didn't even go into the bathroom for fear of making too much noise. So I took my clothes and tiptoed out of the room and dressed downstairs before leaving the house. So you're wrong; they couldn't be my prints.'

'Forensic will say they are,' Paget said.

'I don't care what Forensic or anyone else says,' Susan shot back. 'They are not my prints, and there was no blood in that room when I left.'

'Was there anyone else, besides Simon in the house when you left?' he asked. Then: 'Please answer for the tape, Miss Chase,' he said sharply as she shook her head.

Susan cleared her throat and said, 'No.'

'And you admit that you had spent the night with Simon Holbrook, sleeping together in the same bed. Is that right, Miss Chase?'

'Yes, but—'

'As you have been doing both before and after your sister's death. But Simon wasn't in love with you. In fact I seriously doubt if Simon Holbrook ever loved anyone other than himself. The plain and simple truth is he wanted to be rid of his wife, and he used you to do it for him.'

Paget leaned forward, hands on the table in front of him as he said, 'You told us earlier that your sister enjoyed the thrill of the chase, but from what we have learned during this investigation, Simon Holbrook was very much the same. He never did stay with one woman for long, did he? In fact he and Laura were two of a kind, but he wanted to move on and she didn't. In fact she would fight him tooth and nail for a share of the assets of the firm if he tried to divorce her, and he could see everything he'd worked for going down the drain if he tackled her head on. So he came to you looking for help to get rid of her.

'He used you, Miss Chase, promising to marry you once Laura was out of the way, but then things started to go wrong, didn't they? Once we realized that the burglaries had been staged, and told him so, he began to panic. I think he knew that sooner or later we would find the evidence that would convict him, and whether you care to admit it or not, you knew there was no depth to the man, and you were afraid he would try to save his own skin by putting all the blame on you. So you killed him. You got up out of his bed and stabbed him with one of his own kitchen knives. Isn't that the way it happened, Miss Chase?'

Susan's eyes met his own defiantly. 'No, that is *not* the way it happened!' she grated, jabbing a finger at the rings that lay between them. 'And I don't care where you say you found her rings, I had nothing to do with Laura's death. And Simon was alive when I left him.'

Paget was barely conscious of her words. He, too, was looking at the bag containing the rings, and somewhere in the back of his mind a memory stirred. He lifted his eyes to meet those of Susan Chase across the table, angry, frightened eyes, yet still defiant.

'Tell me how the windows of your car came to be broken?' he said.

Susan eyed him suspiciously. 'I don't see what you're getting at, and I don't see what that has to do with anything.'

'*Please*, just answer the question, Miss Chase. It's important.'

Susan shook her head as if to say she couldn't see the point of the question, but it was easier to answer than to argue. 'It was just mindless vandalism,' she said. 'Some drunken yobs with nothing better to do smashed my windows along with half-a-dozen others in Tavistock Road where I parked my car the other night.'

'The night Simon was killed? Was anything stolen?'

She shook her head. 'No, in fact it might have made more sense if there had been,' she said. 'It was sheer bloody-mindedness on their part.'

'Did you check the glove box to see if anything was missing?'

'No. Why should I? There was nothing in there to steal.' She sat back in her chair and folded her arms. 'And that *is* the last thing I intend to say to you, so if you're going to charge me, go right ahead, but I want to talk to my solicitor now!'

Paget shook his head as he got to his feet. 'Not for the moment,' he said, 'so you are free to go, Miss Chase. But please don't leave the immediate area without telling us.' He nodded to the WPC. 'Please make sure that Miss Chase gets home safely,' he said.

* * *

A short time later, when Paget entered the incident room, Ormside said, 'Tregalles tells me you let Susan Chase go without charging her.' The sergeant kept his voice neutral, but it was clear he, too would like to hear an explanation.

Paget smiled. 'Did he also tell you he thinks I've gone mad?'

'Not in so many words, no,' Ormside said diplomatically. 'But he said the evidence against her was pretty conclusive.'

If the sergeant was hoping for an explanation, he was disappointed. Instead, Paget took the bag containing Laura Holbrook's rings from his pocket. 'I want you to get this over to Forensic immediately, and tell them I want a complete analysis of the tissue the rings were wrapped in,' he said.

Ormside eyed him narrowly. 'You're thinking DNA?' he suggested.

'That would be nice, but I doubt if we'll be that lucky,' Paget said. 'I'm thinking smell.'

Twenty-Nine

'I'm not ruling Susan Chase out as prime suspect,' Paget insisted after bringing Alcott up to date, 'but the more I think about it the more I'm inclined to believe that she is being set up. In the case of the Simon Holbrook killing, it doesn't make sense for her to kill him, then simply walk away without so much as attempting to cover her tracks. And if she didn't care about being caught, then why would she change her clothes and shoes before leaving the bedroom, and go to the trouble of hiding them in a bin a couple of streets away? And I really can't see her leaving Laura Holbrook's rings in the glove compartment of her car. I think they were planted the night the window of her car was smashed.'

'Along with windows of half-a-dozen other cars,' Alcott pointed out.

'To make it look like random vandalism and hide the fact that only one car was being targeted,' Paget countered. 'And there are reports on file of vandalism in Tavistock Road that night.'

'And you think the rings were planted by Goodwin?' Alcott said.

'I think there is enough evidence to bring her in for questioning,' said Paget. 'Her mother told Forsythe that Peggy has been in love with Holbrook for years. She and Holbrook were partners in the new venture when they left Drexler-Davies – at least I suspect that she looked at it that way – so when Laura came along and not only took away the position she considered to be hers by right, but took Simon away from her as well, Goodwin had every reason to hate her.

'Women were fascinated by Holbrook; there was something about the man that made women believe him, even against their better judgement, and I think he not only enjoyed their attention, but he enjoyed manipulating them. Forsythe tracked down Valerie Wade, Goodwin's friend from their schooldays, and spoke to her on the telephone. Wade told her that the real reason she and Goodwin parted company was because Holbrook came round to the flat one day when Goodwin happened to be out and he tried it on with her. Wade said she tried to warn Goodwin about him, but Goodwin wouldn't listen. They had a row and Wade moved out.

'Peggy Goodwin would do anything for Holbrook, and I suspect that if he told her he wanted to be rid of Laura, and it was she he really loved, she would have bought it, because she wanted to believe it. In fact, I wouldn't be too surprised if it was she who came up with the idea of the burglaries after reading in the local paper about the damage done by Chloe Tyler and Davenport in the Dunbar Road burglary.'

'So you think she killed Holbrook when she realized that he'd been cheating on her all along with Susan Chase?'

Paget nodded. 'And if by chance she discovered that Simon was planning on turning the company over to Drexler-Davies, after she had worked so hard to make it his own, *and* that she was to be left out in the cold, yes, I think there is a very good chance than she killed him.'

'So what are you proposing?'

'I'll be bringing Goodwin in for questioning first thing tomorrow morning,' Paget told him. 'I don't expect a confession out of her, but you never know what might turn up during an interview.'

'Anything back from Forensics on the clothing recovered from the bin?'

'*Maybe* tomorrow, but they're swamped as usual, so I'm not holding my breath.'

'Oh, you are home, then, Peg,' said Mrs Johnson, sounding surprised when her daughter answered the phone. 'And about time, too. You can't go on working all hours like this, you know. Here it is almost eight o'clock and you just home from work? It's no good, you know. You'll make yourself ill.'

'I'm fine, Mum, really. It's just that there are so many things to do now that Simon's gone. Clients want to know where their projects stand; the staff want to know if they will have a job tomorrow, and with virtually everything in the hands of the lawyers, it's a mess. So, until things settle down, I'll be spending most of my waking hours at the office. In fact you only just caught me now, because I'll be going back to the office as soon as I've had something to eat.'

'Well, you don't sound fine to me,' her mother said. 'You sound dead tired, and I think you should stay home and put your feet up. The world won't come to an end if you do. Let someone else take over for a while.'

'There isn't anyone else who can do that,' Peggy told her. Irritation crept into her voice as she said, 'Was there anything in particular you called about, because I really do have to get back as soon—'

'I just wondered if you'd heard the news?' her mother broke in, 'but I'm sorry if I'm holding you up. Work must come first, and whatever I have to say will keep till later, when you're not so busy.'

'I'm sorry, Mum, I didn't mean to sound like that. I'm just tired, that's all. What news?'

'About Susan. She's home. She phoned me just now to tell me she's back home, and to ask about Brandy. She said she's had a horrible day. They took her straight from the hospital to the police station, where they questioned her for ever such a long time. She said she was sure she was going to spend the night in the cells, but suddenly they told her she was free to go.'

Mrs Johnson clucked her tongue. 'I *knew* the police must have made a mistake. I mean I can't see someone like her doing a dreadful thing like that, and I told that young policewoman as much on Saturday.'

'What policewoman?' her daughter asked sharply. 'What were the police doing there?'

'Oh, it wasn't like that, love. She's that nice one; the one who talked to you after Laura died. She came in for a card for her god-daughter, and we got to talking. She thought Gypsy was Brandy, and—'

'And she just happened to come into the shop for a card?' Peggy cut in.

'That's right, love, and she picked out the one I like. The one with the kitten under the chair. Remember?'

'Yes, yes, I remember. But what's this about Susan? You say the police let her go? Is she out on bail or what?'

'I don't think so, love. She said they just told her she could go. She had her knee done in the hospital, and she's all bandaged up, but she said the tablets the doctor gave her for the pain aren't working, and she's having trouble getting used to the crutches, so I didn't like to ask any more about it. I mean it's not the sort of thing you ask after someone's been questioned by the police, is it? And she sounded awfully tired, so I didn't like to ask her anything else. Anyway—'

'Look, Mum,' Peggy broke in, 'I'm sorry, but as I said, I have to get back to work, so I'll try to ring you tomorrow. All right?'

'You're going to wear yourself out at this rate,' her mother warned, 'but I suppose you know best.' Her tone belied the words. 'Just don't go working halfway into the night, or you'll be no good to anybody.'

The entrance to Susan Chase's flat was through a separate door next to the shop. The square was all but deserted, the shops were shut,

and while the old-fashioned street lights might look quaint and ornamental, they left a lot to be desired as far as illumination was
concerned.

Even so, Peggy Goodwin kept her hood up and her back to the square
as she pushed the button below the intercom and waited for Susan to
answer. No response. She placed her finger on the button and kept it
there. If Susan was on crutches she wouldn't have gone out. Perhaps
she'd fallen asleep, but if she had, Peggy was determined to keep her
finger on the button until Susan woke up and answered.

Nothing!

Peggy stepped back to the edge of the pavement to look up at the
big window above the shop. No light. Perhaps Susan was in bed – or
in the shop.

Peggy pressed her face against the glass door of the shop. The blind
was down, but there was a gap of an inch or so between the edge of
the blind and the frame of the door, and she could see a dim light at
the back of the shop. She cupped her hands around her eyes. The light
was coming from a partly open door at the rear of the shop.

Peggy rapped sharply on the glass and waited. She banged again,
harder, and this time Susan came to the office door to see what was
going on. Peggy could see her peering toward the door, but of course
the blind was in the way. Peggy bent low to the letter box in the door
and pushed open the flap.

'It's me, Peggy,' she called. 'I came round to see how you are.'

She stood up again and looked through the crack to see Susan start
forward. She was moving awkwardly, not used to the crutches yet.
Fluorescent lights flickered into life. Susan's face was pale and set, and
she was clearly in pain. She fumbled awkwardly with the lock, then
propped herself up on the crutches as she opened the door.

'I hope I didn't put you to too much trouble, coming round tonight
instead of tomorrow morning,' said Michelle Marshall as she took
Brandy's leash from Mrs Johnson. 'But I spoke to Susan a little while
ago, and she sounded so down that I thought I'd take Brandy back to
her tonight instead of waiting till the morning. And thanks again for
looking after her. I'd love to have Brandy myself, but they don't allow
dogs in the place I have now.'

'It's no trouble at all,' Mrs Johnson assured her. 'And Brandy's never
any trouble either. Good as gold, she is. And I'm sure Susan will be

glad to have her back. It's no fun being on your own when you're not feeling up to par.'

She reached out from her wheelchair to pat Brandy affectionately. 'I don't suppose Susan happened to say anything about what went on at the police station?' she ventured. 'I mean like how they treated her. You hear such awful stories these days; you don't know what to believe, do you?'

'She was very tired,' Michelle said diplomatically. 'And I don't suppose it's something she would want to talk about anyway.' She glanced at her watch. 'Quarter to nine!' she exclaimed as she began to edge away. 'I'd better get on, or Susan will have gone to bed by the time I get there. Thanks again, Mrs Johnson. Talk to you later.'

'It was good of you to come round,' Susan said as she closed and locked the door. One of the crutches caught on the mat, and she had to hop a couple of steps to prevent herself from falling. 'God! These wooden crutches are awkward,' she said through gritted teeth, 'but they were all they had at the hospital. I swear these things will have me over before I'm done with them. I tell you, Peggy, it's been a very rough day. The painkiller they gave me at the hospital was supposed to last all day, but it wore off not long after I left the police station. I didn't want to take another one too soon, so I put it off until a few minutes ago, and as soon as it begins to work I'm going straight upstairs to bed. But that won't be for a while yet, so come back to the office and sit down. Then, if you don't mind, perhaps you could help me tackle the stairs.'

The spiral metal staircase was something Susan had had installed at the back of the shop some years ago to allow her to come and go between the flat and the shop without having to go outside each time. Normally, she went up and down it with ease, but it had never been designed with crutches in mind.

With Susan leading the way to the office, Peggy followed, pausing momentarily to find the light switch to turn off the lights in the shop. Susan eased herself into her seat behind the desk and motioned Peggy to take the chair on the other side. 'Take your coat and gloves off,' she said, but Peggy shook her head. 'I won't stay long,' she began, when suddenly her eyes began to water and she was seized by a fit of sneezing. She fumbled for a tissue, but Susan was quicker, pulling from a drawer an open box of Kleenex. She pushed it across the desk and Peggy grabbed a handful.

'Sorry, it's the allergies,' she mumbled from behind the wad of tissues. 'They've been bad this year.'

'Oh, dear, it's the flowers, isn't it?' Susan said. 'It was good of you to come, but perhaps you shouldn't—'

'I'll be fine,' Peggy insisted as she wiped her eyes. 'Sorry about that, Susan. To tell you the truth I forgot about the flowers myself. Silly, isn't it? Coming to a flower shop and forgetting about the flowers.' She blew her nose, then looked round for somewhere to deposit the tissues. Susan picked up a wicker basket from beside the desk and held it out for Peggy to drop the tissues in.

'I really do appreciate your coming,' she said as she set the basket down, 'but a flower shop is hardly the best place for you, especially now, so I'll understand if you have to leave.'

But Peggy shook her head. 'As I was about to say before that interruption, I shan't stay long, but I wanted to make sure that you were all right after the way the police treated you. I couldn't believe it when I heard you'd been arrested last week. I mean how could the police possibly believe that you could have killed Simon?'

'I suppose they thought they had good reason,' Susan said with a rueful grimace. She hesitated for a moment before going on. 'I know this must sound awful, but Simon and I have been seeing each other for some months now, and I was with him until about five o'clock last Thursday morning. They knew that, and I never denied it, but they're saying that Simon was killed about the same time that I left the house, and they believe I did it. And to make matters worse, they claim they found Laura's rings in the glovebox of my car.'

Peggy's brows drew together in a frown. 'Laura's rings?' she echoed. 'Simon said that they were stolen when Laura was killed, but how did they get into your car? Unless . . .' Peggy put her hand to her mouth and her eyes opened wide. 'Oh, Susan, I'm so sorry,' she said contritely. 'I didn't mean . . . Oh, God, Susan, whatever must you think? I don't believe for a minute . . . But how *could* they get there?'

Susan rubbed her eyes. She was having trouble keeping them open. The tablets were beginning to work; at least they were making her sleepy, but they didn't seem to be doing much for her knee, which was throbbing painfully.

'I think someone must have put them there the other night,' she said, and went on to explain about finding the windows of her car smashed when she'd left it parked on the street. 'I thought it had been done by some idiot with nothing better to do, because the same thing had happened to other cars as well,' she explained. 'But thinking about it now, I believe those other windows were smashed to cover the real reason for breaking the window of my car, and I think that was when the rings were planted in the glovebox. I'm not sure, but I think that Chief Inspector Paget might be coming around to the same idea. It has to be something like that or I don't think he would have let me go.'

Susan drew a shaky breath. 'But to be honest, Peggy, I'm scared to death that they'll be waiting at the door tomorrow morning and the whole horrible nightmare will start all over again.'

Peggy frowned. 'But who would do such a thing? Try to frame you, I mean.'

Susan struggled to her feet. 'I really don't know,' she said, 'and right now I'm beyond caring.' She adjusted her crutches, then paused. 'You don't suppose it could have been Tim, do you? I mean he and Laura never did get on, and he's the only one I can think of who will benefit.'

'Well, best not to worry about it any more tonight,' said Peggy as she stood up. 'Let's get you upstairs to bed. Can you manage those iron stairs with those things?'

'It will be easier for me if I use a single crutch and the handrail,' Susan told her, 'so perhaps you could follow me up with the other one.'

She made her way to the bottom of the stairs and switched the stairwell light on before handing one of the crutches to Peggy. 'Thanks again, Peggy,' she said with feeling. 'It was good of you to come, and I shall feel much safer on these stairs with you behind me.'

Thirty

'Oh, not again! I think there is something very odd about these stairs,' Grace said. 'Particularly at this time of night when we're on our way up to bed. Do you think if I came down again the phone would stop ringing?'

'Sorry love, but I don't think it works that way,' said Paget as he picked up the phone.

Grace sat down on a step halfway up the stairs, elbows on her knees, chin cupped in her hands as she waited to find out if it was yet another call-out.

'Who found her?' she heard Paget ask sharply. 'The assistant? Yes, I know who you mean . . . When? . . . But she is still alive? . . . I'll call at the hospital first on my way in, but I want the shop and flat sealed off and someone posted there. And no one is to touch anything until I get there. Understood? And get hold of Tregalles and tell him to meet me at the shop in, oh, say forty-five minutes or so.'

'It's Susan Chase,' he told Grace as he hung up the phone. 'There's a spiral staircase between her flat and the shop, and it seems she tripped over her crutches and fell. Apparently she has a fractured skull. She was found by Michelle Marshall, one of the shop assistants, who had gone round there for some reason. But the prognosis is not good.'

He came part-way up the stairs and took Grace's hand. 'I'm sorry, darling,' he said, 'but I have to go. From what I'm told, it appears to be an accident, but considering her position as a suspect in the Holbrook murders, I want to make absolutely sure there's no more to it than that. Michelle Marshall is at the hospital, so I'll call in there on my way. I could be gone for some time, so don't wait up.'

Grace eyed him quizzically. 'Do you have any reason to believe it *wasn't* an accident?' she asked. 'I mean accidents do happen, and trying to use crutches on a spiral staircase is just asking for trouble.'

He shook his head. 'No reason,' he said, 'and it probably was an accident, but . . .'

'But you won't be happy until you've had a look yourself, I know,' Grace finished for him.

'That's about it,' Paget admitted. 'Anyway, I'd better be on my way. I'll make sure I lock up on my way out.'

Paget found Michelle Marshall alone in the lounge at the end of the hospital corridor. She sat slumped forward, elbows on her knees, staring blankly into space. She started to get to her feet when she heard him come in, but sank back in her chair when she saw who it was.

'Oh, it's you,' she said tonelessly. 'I thought it might be the doctor. Have you spoken to him?'

'No. But a nurse told me the doctors are still with Miss Chase, and it may be some time before they're free to talk to us.' He sat down facing her, noting as he did so that she wore a wedding band. 'Can you tell me what happened, and how you came to be at the shop, Mrs Marshall?' he asked.

Michelle lifted her head and Paget could see tears in her eyes, and she was older then he'd originally thought. Perhaps it was the clothes, or the fact that she had little or no make-up on. She'd always looked trim and smart in the shop, but tonight she wore faded blue jeans, a denim jacket, and trainers. Her hair was in disarray, and a woollen hat lay in her lap.

'Thank God I did go round,' Michelle said with feeling. 'And it was just on the spur of the moment because Susan sounded so low when I spoke to her on the phone, that I decided to take Brandy back tonight instead of tomorrow morning as I'd planned. So I picked Brandy up from Mrs Johnson's and took her round to the shop.'

'Do you remember what time it was when you got to the shop? Approximately.'

'About nine, I think. Susan said she was going to have an early night, once she'd finished checking tomorrow's orders, so I wanted to get there before she went to bed.'

'She was working?'

Michelle shrugged. 'It's the way she is. I know she trusts me to carry on while she's away, but she can't help wanting to know everything as soon as she gets back. She tried to talk to me about how things had gone over the weekend when she first got home, but I told her to get some rest and we'd talk about it tomorrow. But I knew she'd phone back. I knew she wouldn't be able to wait until tomorrow.'

'I see. So, you took the dog around to the shop. What happened when you got there?'

'I couldn't see any light in the window upstairs, but there was a light coming from the back of the shop, so I thought Susan must still be working. I should have known something was wrong, because Brandy was getting all excited, jumping up and scratching at the door, and she's never done that before. Anyway, I let myself in and that's when I saw her. She was lying there at the foot of the stairs. One of her crutches was broken and lying under her, and there was blood all through her hair . . .' The words caught in her throat and tears welled up in her eyes. 'I thought she was dead,' she ended faintly. Michelle took out a tissue to wipe away the tears and blow her nose hard.

Paget waited. 'I was going to try mouth-to-mouth,' Michelle continued. 'I took the CPR course years ago, but I'd never had to do it to anyone, but I didn't know what else to do. The trouble was Brandy kept getting in the way. She was all over Susan, whining and licking her face, and making an awful fuss, so it wasn't until I'd tied her up and got down on my knees that I realized Susan was breathing, so I called the ambulance instead.'

Michelle glanced at the open door of the lounge. 'I wish they'd come and tell us *something*,' she said. 'This waiting . . . '

'It is hard,' Paget agreed. Then: 'Tell me,' he said gently, 'why did you call the police?'

Michelle shook her head. 'I didn't. They were passing and saw the ambulance, so they came in to see what was happening. They said they'd just come from an attempted burglary at the top end of the street, so they stopped to see if the two things were related. It was only when they were about to leave that I thought to mention the back door. It was probably nothing, but Susan was always very careful about locking up, and I know that door was locked when we left the shop at six.

'Anyway, one of them got on the phone, and the next thing I knew he said they'd been told to stay there. He wanted me to stay as well, but I wasn't having that, not with Susan on her way to hospital, so I left.'

'Tell me about the back door. Are you saying it was unlocked?'

'It wasn't even fully closed,' Michelle said, 'and I *know* Susan wouldn't have left it open like that. Especially at night.'

'She was taking strong painkillers, which would tend to make her drowsy and a little bit out of it,' Paget pointed out. 'Perhaps—'

Michelle dismissed that idea with an emphatic shake of the head. 'Besides,' she countered, 'I thought it was my imagination when I first opened the shop door, but the more I think about it the more I'm almost certain that somebody was there.'

'Where, exactly?'

'Back there behind the stairs. It was . . . I don't know, more of a feeling, but I could almost swear something moved in the shadows as I came in. But I was so shocked to see Susan lying there on the floor that it didn't really register at the time. It was only while I was waiting for the ambulance to arrive, and I felt a draft, that I went to look and found the back door partly open.' Michelle shivered. 'It gave me a funny feeling, I can tell you.'

'Did you happen to look out in the lane behind the shop?'

'No way!' Michelle said with feeling. 'I just shut the door and locked it as quick as I could.'

A tall, bald-headed, bespectacled man in surgical blues appeared in the doorway. 'Mrs Marshall?' he asked, looking at Michelle. She nodded. 'My name is Mr Carradine,' he said. 'Are you a relative?'

'No. I work for Miss Chase, but I am—'

'And you, sir?' he asked, peering over the top of his glasses.

'Detective Chief Inspector Paget.'

'But not a relative?'

'No, but Mrs Marshall and I are very much concerned about Miss Chase's condition, so we would appreciate your prognosis.'

'Can either of you tell me if Miss Chase has any close relatives and where we might reach them?' Carradine persisted.

'Her only living relative is her father, who has Alzheimer's,' Michelle told him. 'He's in a home and hasn't recognized Susan for years.' Her voice rose. 'But why do you keep asking? Why can't you just tell us how she is? Is she dead?'

Carradine shook his head. 'No,' he said wearily, 'but her condition is extremely critical. She has a compound skull fracture, which means in this case that small fragments of bone have penetrated the brain, and they are lodged in a particularly sensitive area. It's far too early, and frankly, too dangerous to attempt to remove them until we can get the swelling down and relieve some of the pressure. Even then . . .' Carradine shrugged and spread his hands in an eloquent gesture that said more than words.

Paget frowned. 'She suffered *that* much damage from a fall on the stairs?' he said. 'They are metal stairs, but even so . . . Where is the head wound, exactly?'

Carradine pointed to a place on the right side of his own head, low down behind the ear. 'It's on the suture between the occipital and parietal bones,' he said. 'It's where the two bones meet; not the best place for it to be, I'm afraid.'

'I wonder . . .' Paget said with a thoughtful eye on Carradine. 'Have you shaved her head around the wound?' he asked.

The surgeon frowned at the question. 'Is this a police matter?' he asked.

Paget said, 'I honestly don't know yet, but I'd appreciate it very much if you would have someone take pictures of the fractured area in case it does become a police matter.'

'First thing tomorrow morning,' Carradine said crisply. 'You're in Charter Lane, are you?' Paget nodded and handed him his card. The surgeon glanced at it briefly, then turned his attention to Michelle. 'I'm sorry about your friend,' he said, 'but you can't do anything for her by staying here, so please go home and try not to worry. You can rest assured that we will be doing everything we can for her.'

'Did you come by car?' Paget asked Michelle as Carradine left the room.

'By ambulance,' Michelle told him. 'They weren't supposed to do it, but I badgered them so much that the ambulance men let me ride with them. I walked from Bishop's Gate to the shop to give Brandy a bit of a run before handing her over to Susan, because I knew she couldn't get out to walk her, so my car is parked in front of Johnson's gift shop.'

'In that case, I'll give you a lift,' Paget told her, 'but I'd like you to come back to the shop with me first, and show me exactly where you found Miss Chase.'

They were almost there before Paget thought to ask, 'What happened to Brandy? Where is she now?'

For the first time since they'd met that evening, the taut muscles around Michelle's mouth relaxed. 'Being spoiled, I expect,' she said. 'The last time I saw her, one of the policemen was feeding her a piece of his sandwich.'

Michelle opened the door with her key, and Tregalles and a uniformed constable came forward to meet them as they entered the shop. 'Didn't know exactly what you wanted,' the sergeant greeted him, 'because it looks as if Miss Chase simply tripped over her crutches coming down the stairs and fell and hit her head. But since you asked for the shop to be secured, I assumed you weren't satisfied with that explanation, so we just sat tight and didn't touch anything. How is Miss Chase, by the way?'

'Not good, I'm afraid,' Paget told him. 'We may know more in the morning, but right now she is in a critical condition. Fortunately, Mrs Marshall decided to bring the dog back this evening instead of waiting till tomorrow morning. Otherwise I'm not sure if Miss Chase would be alive now.' He glanced around the shop. And said, 'Where is the dog?'

'Behind the counter, sir. She was fussing that much, I had to tie her up,' the constable told him.

'Right. Let's leave her there for the time being,' Paget said. 'Now, Mrs Marshall, I'd like you to show me exactly how Miss Chase was lying when you first saw her.'

Michelle led the way to the bottom of the stairs. 'She was lying more or less on her back just there,' she said, pointing to a dark patch on the carpet. 'You can see where her head was, and her legs were over there. One of the crutches – that one,' she said, indicating the two pieces of a broken crutch lying some distance away, 'and the other one was more or less where it is now.'

'Did you move her?' Paget asked.

Michelle shook her head vigorously. 'I was afraid she might have broken her neck,' she said. 'I don't know much about first aid, but I do know you shouldn't move anyone if that's a possibility.'

Paget examined the iron steps. 'Looks like skin and blood on the fourth step up,' he told Tregalles. 'Let's make sure no one goes up or down these steps until SOCO's had a look at them.'

'You don't think it was an accident?' Tregalles ventured.

'I don't know yet,' Paget admitted, 'which is why I would like to make sure. Now, Mrs Marshall, do you know where Miss Chase was calling from when she rang you earlier this evening?'

'From the office. She was going through the orders for the week, and they're in there.'

'What time was that?'

'Quarter to eight, something like that. I can't tell you exactly.'

'Did she say if anybody was with her?'

'No, but I think she would have said if there was someone there, because we were on the phone for a good fifteen minutes.'

'So she was already downstairs at that time. Was the light on or off in the office when you came in?'

'Off. The only light on was this one on the stairs.'

Paget moved to the office and turned the light on. The desk was tidy, the filing cabinet was closed. 'Susan Chase wasn't coming down when she fell,' he said. 'She'd been working here and was going back up. Which makes me wonder how she managed to hit the *back* of her head rather than the front.'

'She could have tripped, spun round and fallen backward,' Tregalles suggested.

'The spiral's too tight,' said Paget, 'and *that* makes me wonder how she managed to end up on the floor the way she did.'

Thirty-One

'I stopped at the hospital to see how Susan Chase is,' said Paget as he took off his coat and joined Ormside, Tregalles and Molly in front of the white boards. 'She's still unconscious and by no means out of danger, so if this wasn't an accident, we could have another murder on our hands. Has SOCO been informed?'

'Should be on their way now,' Ormside told him. 'Tregalles filled me in last night, so I let Charlie know.'

Paget stifled a yawn. It had been half-past one when he'd dropped Michelle Marshall at her car, where she'd left it in front of the gift and chocolate shop in Bishop's Gate, and two o'clock before he climbed into bed, where Grace was still awake and anxious to hear what had happened.

'I told Mrs Marshall the shop will be closed until we're done with it, so she can sleep in this morning – which is more than I'll be doing,' he concluded as he buried his face in the pillow.

'You should,' Grace said softly. 'You know you won't go to sleep right away. You'll lie there thinking about everything that went on last night. You need something to take your mind off it; you need to relax.'

He felt the warmth of her as she snuggled up beside him; felt her slender fingers slide beneath his pyjama jacket to caress his skin; felt her breath against his ear . . .

He groaned. Resistance was pointless – not that he intended to try very hard. 'You are a witch and a temptress,' he said sternly, 'and you are asking for trouble.'

Her hair brushed his face. 'Yes, please,' she murmured as her lips came down on his.

That was the other reason for being late.

'Tom Maxwell in Forensics left a call for you last night,' Ormside said. 'He wants you to call him before nine this morning, because he'll be tied up in meetings for the rest of the day after that.'

'Did he say what it was about?'

'No.'

'Let's hope it's good news,' Paget muttered as he picked up the phone. 'We could certainly use some.'

'Was it?' Ormside asked cautiously when Paget put the phone down.

Paget nodded. 'I think we might be getting somewhere at last,' he said. 'First of all, they've identified a perfume on the tissue the rings were wrapped in. It's called Fetish.'

Molly looked up from the notes she was copying from the board and said, 'That's Peggy Goodwin's perfume.'

'Is it?' said Paget, smiling broadly. 'I wonder why that doesn't surprise me? And it makes sense of something else Tom Maxwell told me. He says the tissue also contains someone's DNA. Apparently someone used it to wipe their nose.'

Molly grimaced. 'Then used it to wrap the rings?' she said. 'That wasn't very nice.'

'Perhaps it was unavoidable,' said Paget. 'The last time I was in Tavistock Road, the spring flowers were in bloom, and there was fresh green on some of the trees. A deadly combination for someone who has allergies – someone like Peggy Goodwin. If Laura's rings were planted in Susan's car, and it was Peggy who planted them, she might well have had a fit of sneezing and had to use whatever came to hand.'

'Even so . . .' Molly said.

'On the other hand,' Tregalles suggested, 'perhaps she was making a statement, showing her contempt for Susan.'

'That's even worse,' Molly muttered, wrinkling her nose. 'You'd think she'd have—'

'Maxwell also told me,' Paget broke in, 'that the blood on the clothing found in the skip matches Holbrook's blood, the trainers have fibres stuck to them from the bedroom carpet where Holbrook was killed, and there were tiny particles of glass that match the glass from Susan Chase's car embedded in the soles and heels of the trainers.

'As well, they found a finger dressing with blood on it inside one of the rubber gloves. They'll be doing DNA tests on that and the wrapping around the rings.'

'Little finger, right hand,' Molly said. 'Remember, sir? Goodwin cut her little finger when Holbrook shoved those papers at her the other day.'

'I remember,' Paget told her, 'and I think this little lot is going to clinch the case against Peggy Goodwin. We'll need search warrants for all three locations: Goodwin's office, her flat, and her mother's place in Bishop's Gate,' Paget said.

A uniformed constable entered the room and made straight for Paget. 'Something for you, sir,' he said. 'Delivered by hand from the hospital.' He handed Paget a brown envelope.

Paget thanked the man and opened it. Six high-definition pictures, together with a folded note slid out on to the desk. The pictures were close-ups of a shaved area of Susan Chase's skull, and there was a note.

'Since Dr Starkie is more familiar with the sort of thing for which you may be looking,' Carradine had written, 'I asked for his opinion, and you will see his comment at the bottom of the page. Hope this proves to be of some value.' An indecipherable squiggle followed.

Starkie's note was short and to the point. 'Look familiar?' it said.

Starkie was right. The shape of the wound looked very much like those on Laura Holbrook's head. Paget turned to Ormside. 'I want someone assigned to the hospital immediately,' he said. 'If Susan Chase's injuries are the result of an attack rather than an accident, I want to make sure that no one tries to finish the job.'

'A woman from SOCO is in the office, sir,' the uniformed constable told Paget as he entered the Basket of Flowers. 'And a bit of all right she is, too, if you don't mind my saying so. Name of Lovett.'

'Really, Constable?' Paget said. 'I shall have to take a look for myself, then, shan't I?'

Paget went through to the back and stood in the open doorway to the office. Grace was on her hands and knees behind the desk, and she wasn't aware that he was there until he spoke. 'I'm told by the constable out front that the woman from SOCO is a bit of all right,' he said. 'I think you have an admirer there.'

Still on her knees, Grace popped her head up above the desk. 'I suppose I should be flattered,' she said, 'but I suspect that anything in a skirt would be a bit of all right to that man.'

'You're in a boiler suit.'

'You know what I mean.'

'I told him he didn't know the half of it, and you were—'

'Oh, Neil, you didn't!' Grace looked horrified as she started to get up, then shook her head when she saw the grin on his face. 'You had better not have if you value your life,' she warned.

'So what's Charlie's chief analyst doing here scrambling about on hands and knees?' he asked.

'Cliff was here taking pictures first thing this morning, but most of our people are over in Tenborough at the scene of a warehouse robbery that went wrong last night. So I'm it for the moment.'

'Find anything useful?'

'Hard to say what is and what isn't, but I'm bagging anything that looks promising. Are you looking for anything in particular?'

'Yes, I am. I'd like to know, if Susan Chase fell backwards and hit her head on that fourth step from the bottom of the stairs, how she managed to end up on the floor at the bottom? It would have made more sense to me if she'd been found part way up the stairs.'

'Perhaps she managed to push herself to her feet, then tumbled the rest of the way?'

Paget shook his head. 'I doubt that,' he said. 'It's a bad fracture and she's still unconscious.'

'Not necessarily,' Grace pointed out. 'There are documented cases of people who have carried on as if nothing had happened after severe blows to the head, only to collapse later.'

Paget squatted down to examine the iron steps. 'It's possible,' he agreed, 'but I saw the pictures of the wound this morning, and I don't think she fell against this step. I think her injury was caused by the same weapon that killed Laura Holbrook, and so does Starkie.'

'You think all this was staged?'

'I can't prove it, at least not yet, but I don't think it was an accident.'

Grace studied the marks on the carpet. 'According to what you told me last night, or should I say this morning, and the way it's drawn out here, one of the crutches was broken, and Susan was lying on top of one of the pieces, so it would seem we are supposed to believe that, either it broke and caused her to fall, or she slipped and it broke when she went down. But if the whole thing was staged, it might explain this.' Grace led Paget under the curve of the staircase and pointed upward. 'I found splinters from the broken crutch caught between the fifth step and the side support, and several more on the floor below the steps.

'Now, let's say that Susan was higher up the staircase than we thought – it doesn't matter in this case whether she was going up or coming down – and her crutch became wedged between the steps and broke. If she fell from there, there is no way she could have ended up where she was found, because the spiral is too tight. Unless, of course, she tumbled around the curve, but then she would be pretty banged up by the time she got to the bottom. Was she badly bruised?'

'Not that I'm aware of. The surgeon didn't mention it.'

'So, how did the splinters get here?' Grace asked rhetorically. 'A wooden crutch is not that easy to break. But if someone wanted to break one deliberately, all they would have to do is jam it between the back of these two steps, put their weight on the lower end of the crutch, and you have all the leverage necessary to snap the thing in two. I didn't know if it meant anything at the time, but I photographed it and bagged the splinters just in case.'

Paget nodded slowly. 'Then Mrs Marshall may not have been imagining things when she said she thought she saw someone in the shadows back here when she first entered the shop. Someone who slipped out of the back door in such a hurry that they didn't have time to close it properly. Which may be why he or she didn't have time to study the scene to make sure it looked right before they left – or to make sure that Susan was dead!'

'Bit of a hold-up on the warrants,' Ormside told Paget later that day. 'The super phoned down to say he's being questioned about why we need to go into the Johnson house and shop, since no one in those premises is suspected of a crime. I went over it with him about the dogs, and I *think* I was able to satisfy him, but it doesn't look as if we'll be getting all three warrants until the end of the day. Do you still want to have the teams ready to go when they do arrive? It will mean a hell of a lot of overtime, and I very much doubt if the super will authorize it.'

Paget shook his head. 'We'd never get authorization for the overtime, so you can tell everyone to stand down. I don't think Goodwin will be going anywhere, so we'll go in after she's left for work tomorrow morning.'

Thirty-Two

Much of the morning briefing session was taken up with the forthcoming execution of the search warrants, and the assignment of people to each location. Len Ormside – much to his surprise and consternation – was the designated leader of the team that would be searching the shop and living quarters in Bishop's Gate, while Tregalles would head the team searching Peggy Goodwin's flat in Caledonia Street.

Paget would wait until he'd heard back from the first two teams before leading his team into the Micro-Engineering Labs building to search Peggy Goodwin's office, and bring her in for questioning.

'So let's make sure that no one is allowed to let her know what is happening until we get there,' he concluded, 'and that applies particularly to Mr and Mrs Johnson. No phone calls in or out for them until we bring Goodwin in. You all know what we're looking for, so make sure you remember the rules, because I want everything to be done by the book. No short cuts. Any questions? Right, then, you'll be leaving here in fifteen minutes.'

'I haven't seen Molly this morning,' Tregalles said, looking around. 'Whose team is she on?'

'She's away today,' Ormside told him. 'She'll be back tomorrow.'

'A day off in the middle of the week when we're just about to wrap this up?' Tregalles said. 'How did she wangle that? Bit of pull with the boss, was it, since she seems to be the flavour of the month?'

'That's right,' Ormside said. 'Same as was done for you when you sat your sergeant's exam.'

'Molly's taking the *sergeant's* exam?' Tregalles spluttered. 'She never said anything about that to me.'

'Nor anyone else,' said Ormside. 'I had to know, of course, and so did Paget in order to assess her field experience and readiness for the practical aspects of the position if she passes the exam. Molly said she didn't want anyone else to know in case she found she wasn't ready for it. But she's been studying hard, and I'm sure she'll do well.'

Tregalles blew out his cheeks. 'So *that's* what's been going on,' he said. 'You might have *told* me, Len. I mean you must admit it did look a bit odd, and I couldn't help wondering why the boss kept taking her with him.'

'Thought he'd gone off you in favour of Molly, did you?'

''Course not!' Tregalles could feel his face reddening. Ormside had come just a little too close to the truth for comfort. 'It's just that I don't see why you couldn't have at least given me a hint.'

'I told you why. Molly asked me not to tell anyone, and I could see she was a little nervous about being under Paget's eagle eye, so I agreed. And I don't see why you're making such a big thing out of it, Tregalles.'

'I'm not.' The denial sounded feeble even to him. 'It's just that it took me by surprise, that's all.' Now that he knew what had been going on, he felt more than a little foolish about the way he'd allowed his imagination to run wild. Audrey had told him he was being silly, and she'd been right, and all he wanted to do now was drop the subject.

'Anyway, got to get the team together,' he said briskly, glad of any excuse to get away from the grizzled sergeant's probing eyes, while silently damning the man for keeping him in the dark. And enjoying it, he thought angrily. Well, chalk one up for the crafty old devil. There would be other days.

Muttering that it wouldn't do the reputation of the place a lot of good when people saw the police going through the place, the manager of the block of flats in Caledonia Street examined the search warrant closely before using his pass-key to open the door to Peggy Goodwin's flat.

'Just be thankful we're not in uniform,' Tregalles told him, and while the others went inside, he accompanied the manager back to his own flat, where he questioned him about Peggy Goodwin.

The manager's name was Lewis Corbett. He was a lean, middle-aged, wolfish-looking man with piercing eyes, and dyed black hair combed straight back. He'd been the manager there for almost ten years, he said, and claimed there wasn't much he didn't know about his tenants. His flat was on the ground floor next to the front entrance, where he could watch the comings and goings of the tenants from his front window.

'That's why I have my table where it is,' he explained. 'I have all my meals there. They're a pretty good lot, by and large, but I like to keep a friendly eye on them, so to speak.'

'What about Miss Goodwin?' Tregalles asked. 'What can you tell me about her?'

'Ah, now, there's a close one,' he said. 'Working all the time, she is, so I don't see much of her as a rule. Hardly ever goes out again once she's home. Why? What's she done?'

Tregalles didn't answer. Instead, he went to the window to take a look for himself. 'There must be a back door,' he observed. 'Aren't there lock-up garages at the back of the building?'

'That's right, but that back door is an emergency exit only. It's on the door in big letters plain as day. You can go out that way, but you can't come back in. It's a matter of security. That's why it's alarmed. See?' He pointed to a light on the wall just inside his own door. 'That light blinks when the door is open, and there's an alarm bell – well, more like a buzzer, really – in the stairwell. I'd know if anyone tried to use it – which they do the odd time if they have something big or heavy to bring in or take out – but that's all right as long as they let me know so I can turn the alarm off.'

'When was the last time that happened?' Tregalles asked.

Corbett thought back. 'Can't remember, exactly,' he said. 'I think it was around Christmas last year when number seventeen had a new bed delivered. The road was dug up out front for work on the water mains, so they had to bring it in the back.'

'Let's take a look at the door,' Tregalles said.

'Can if you want,' said Corbett, 'but there's not much to see.'

Corbett led the way to the back of the building and stopped in front of a heavy metal door. 'There, see?' he said. 'Emergency Exit. You just push down on the bar and it opens.' He demonstrated as he spoke, pushing hard on the bar. 'Heavy brute,' he muttered as the door swung open.

Tregalles didn't reply. He was listening, head on one side. 'Didn't you say an alarm goes off when you open the door?' he asked.

Corbett's heavy brows drew together in a frown as he closed the door and opened it again. 'That's funny,' he said. 'Never done that before. Bit of dirt in the contacts, I expect.'

'When did you last check if it was working?' the sergeant asked.

'It's been a while,' the man hedged. 'I mean it's not the sort of thing you do, is it? We've never had any trouble with it before.'

'How long ago is "a while"?'

The man screwed up his face, looked up at the mechanism at the top of the door, then shrugged. 'Probably not since number seventeen used it,' he admitted.

Tregalles nodded. 'I think we should take a closer look and find out exactly why that alarm isn't working,' he said. 'Because we may find that the light in your flat isn't going on either, which could mean that you wouldn't know if anyone has been in or out of here recently.'

Tregalles placed his hands against the door and pushed. It was, as Corbett said, a heavy door, spring loaded for automatic closing. He pushed harder.

'You have to use the bar . . .' Corbett began, then frowned as the door opened.

Tregalles pushed it wider, then stepped outside. 'Someone has taped the latch so it doesn't catch when the door is shut,' he said. 'And I suspect there is more than a bit of dirt between those contacts. In other words, Mr Corbett, anyone can come and go through here whenever they please without fear of being caught.'

The sign in the window said Closed. In fact none of the shops in Bishop's Gate opened until ten o'clock, so there were very few people about when Ormside led the team down the narrow passageway between the shop and the one next door to the back door of Mrs Johnson's card and gift shop.

He was still somewhat bemused as to why he was there at all, in spite of Paget's explanation. 'Goodwin's mother is in a wheelchair,' he'd said, 'and this is going to come as quite a shock to her, so I'd like someone who is closer to her age to lead in this case. Do you have a problem with that, Len?'

'Well, no,' he'd said, but the normally unflappable sergeant suddenly felt nervous; he hadn't been on active duty on the streets in years, preferring to sit in what he thought of as the centre of the web, controlling and directing operations from there. He'd tried to make a joke of it. 'I know we're short-staffed, but I don't think we're quite that desperate yet, are we, sir?'

'Look, Len,' Paget said patiently, 'we are going to have to tell her that her daughter is about to be arrested for two cold-blooded murders and possibly three. The woman is going to be devastated, and I don't know how her health is. She may even be frail, so I want someone there who understands that and will make allowances – at least up to a point.'

Ormside took a deep breath and knocked on the back door.

The man who opened the door was about sixty. Solidly built, he had a lean and weathered face, a receding hairline and a short beard. 'Yes,' he said in answer to Ormside's formal question, his name was Arthur Johnson, but his expression turned from one of mild curiosity to one of disbelief as Ormside told him who he was and why they were there.

'You want to do *what?*' Johnson demanded. 'You're really serious? You want to *search* this place? Why? What do you think is going on here? I think you've come to the wrong house, mate.' He stepped back and began to close the door.

Ormside braced his foot against the door. 'There is no mistake, Mr Johnson,' he said. 'We have reason to believe that we will find evidence here that will assist us with our enquiries into the death of Laura and Simon Holbrook. Now, please stand aside. I don't want to have to arrest you for obstruction.'

'What's going on there, Arthur?' A woman in a wheelchair came into sight behind the man. 'Who are these people? What do they want?'

'It's the police, love, and they say they have a warrant to search the house and shop. Something to do with Peg's boss and his wife being killed. I don't understand it at all. What's our house got to do with them two murders?'

Ormside moved forward, forcing Johnson to step back and allowing the rest of the team to move in and fan out through the rooms.

'You can't just come in here like that!' the woman screamed. 'This is our house; our shop. You can't go through!'

'I'm sorry, Mrs Johnson, but I'm afraid we can,' Ormside told her. 'It's not that we believe that you or your husband have done anything wrong, but I'm afraid the same can't be said for your daughter. We will be taking away every bit of clothing she may have left here, as well as anything belonging to her we deem relevant. I also need to look at the records of all the dogs you have kept here over the past three months. The breed, the dates they were here in your care, and the names and addresses of every owner.'

'I've never heard such a load of rubbish in my . . .' the woman began, but her words were cut off by the sound of several dogs barking at once. 'There, now! See what they've done? They've gone and upset the dogs.' She swung the wheelchair around and started toward the door, but Ormside grabbed the chair and swung it around so the woman was facing him.

'Look, Mrs Johnson,' he said quietly, 'I don't like this any more than you do, but this is a legal search, and unpleasant as it may be, it will be much easier on everyone if you will just let us do our job.'

'And what if I don't?' she snapped.

Ormside sighed deeply as he looked down at her. 'Then I'm afraid my instructions are to take you and your husband into custody and down to Charter Lane for further questioning to find out what it is you have to hide.'

'You wouldn't dare!'

Ormside shrugged. 'I would prefer not to,' he admitted, 'but I will if necessary.'

'Arthur?' She turned to her husband for support. 'Can't *you* do something to convince these people that they're barking up the wrong tree?'

'I don't think so, love,' he said quietly. 'I think the sergeant's right; there's no use fighting them. They have a warrant, so they'll get what they want whether we like it or not.'

Mrs Johnson threw up her hands. 'Useless!' she said bitterly. 'Might as well talk to the wall for all the good it does me to talk to you. That's my Peggy they're talking about. My *daughter*, in case it's slipped your mind. If I weren't stuck in this bloody chair . . .' She was shaking with rage as she turned on Ormside.

So much for the woman being frail, the sergeant thought.

'You'll find nothing!' she told him. 'Nothing! And you're all mad if you think Peg had anything to do with those deaths.' She glared at Ormside. 'Where is she now?'

'Being taken into custody,' Ormside told her.

'You'll be sorry for this,' the woman warned. 'Peggy's done nothing wrong.'

'In that case she'll be released,' Ormside said. The sergeant saw hope flare in her eyes. 'But I think it might be best if you don't count too heavily on that,' he added, not unkindly. 'I'm afraid the evidence against her is very strong indeed.'

Thirty-Three

If Peggy Goodwin was guilty of anything, it certainly didn't show in her demeanour as she faced Paget across the table. She'd remained silent, lips compressed as if physically holding in her anger throughout the journey in the police car to Charter Lane, but she'd objected strenuously to the Custody Office's questions, and had refused point blank to sign a copy of the custody record informing her of her rights. And she had remained silent from that point on until the recorder was set in motion, and she was asked to state her name.

'I'll do no such thing,' she flared. 'And as for this ridiculous charge, I think—'

'You have not been charged with anything as yet, Miss Goodwin,' Paget cut in coldly. 'You have been arrested on suspicion of murdering Laura Holbrook and Simon Holbrook, and you are here to answer questions regarding those murders. Your office, and your flat are being searched as we speak, as are the premises occupied by your mother in Bishop's Gate. You are entitled to have legal representation or someone of your choice present if you wish, but you are not leaving here until this interview is concluded to my satisfaction. Do I make myself clear, Miss Goodwin?'

'Yes,' she said with exaggerated weariness, 'you make yourself very clear, Chief Inspector, and I don't need representation, legal or otherwise, because I've done nothing wrong.'

'In that case, please state your full name for the record.'

'Margaret Diane Goodwin – alias *Peggy* Goodwin,' she added sarcastically.

'We're not here to play games, Miss Goodwin,' Paget warned. 'We are here to establish who killed two people.' He nodded to Tregalles, who pushed several clear plastic evidence bags across the table. Paget separated them and placed one in front of Peggy Goodwin. 'Miss Goodwin is being shown a set of keys, item number eleven of the contents of her handbag,' he said for the benefit of the tape. 'These are your keys, are they not, Miss Goodwin?'

Peggy shrugged. 'Yes, they are my keys, Chief Inspector,' she agreed with exaggerated weariness, 'but I don't see—'

'And this is the one,' he continued, pointing to a bronze-coloured key, 'you used to gain entry to the house the night Laura was killed. Right, Miss Goodwin?'

'Don't be ridiculous! I had nothing to do with Laura's death, and I have no idea what makes you think I did. Yes, I have a key to the house, but I've never had a reason to use it. And Simon didn't give it to me; Laura gave it to me when both she and Simon were going to be away on a business trip.'

'I thought it was Moira Ballantyne who had a key,' said Paget. 'Why would Laura give you one when Moira only lives three houses away?'

'That was for a totally different reason' Peggy said impatiently. 'Moira looked after the plants and the post, things like that. The key Laura gave me was for business reasons. Both she and Simon used to take work home with them, and Laura thought someone should have access to the house and her computer in case she had to call for information for one of her business meetings. There never was a need to use it, but that was Laura, always trying to cover any and every eventuality.'

'Have you ever been inside the Holbrooks' house?'

'Once or twice, yes.'

'When was the last time?'

'Last Christmas. They had an open house for the staff and a few friends.'

'Now, Simon Holbrook telephoned you from his mobile at 7.03 on the evening of Wednesday, March the fourth. Do you remember that?'

'Of course. Simon called to tell me that Laura was ill and he wanted me to call a couple of clients first thing in the morning to let them know she wouldn't be able to see them. I told you that before.'

'You did indeed,' Paget agreed. 'And what did you do after you hung up?'

'I told you that as well,' Peggy said irritably. 'Does it *matter* what I did?'

'Yes, I believe it does,' Paget told her. 'I think that when Simon phoned to ask you to let Laura's clients know that she wouldn't be able to see them next morning, you *thought* he was letting you know that Laura was in the house alone and vulnerable, while he had an ironclad alibi for the rest of the evening, with Trevor Ballantyne as his witness. An ideal time, you thought, to put into action the final phase of the plan the two of you had been working on since last February.

'The plan to kill Laura Holbrook.

'You went to the house, let yourself in with this key, then went upstairs and battered Laura to death. You took off her rings, went downstairs and proceeded to smash a few things to make it look as if it was the work of burglars, then used the murder weapon to pry the back door open to make it look like a forced entry. And then you went home.

'When Simon returned, and found Laura not only dead but battered beyond recognition, he was understandably appalled to the point where he was physically sick. And from that point on he was in trouble. He couldn't tell you that he'd been meeting with Henry Beaumont in Susan Chase's flat, and he couldn't rely on Trevor keeping quiet either, and that was when he began to panic.

'And that was when it all began to unravel, wasn't it, Miss Goodwin? You found out that Simon had been sleeping with Susan Chase while conning you into doing his dirty work for him, and somehow you learned about his secret dealings with Henry Beaumont – and that *was* the final straw, wasn't it, Miss Goodwin?'

'You are getting desperate, aren't you, Chief Inspector?' said Peggy contemptuously, 'because we both know who killed Laura. You had your killer here, probably in this very room only last week, but if this is the best you can do I'm not surprised you had to let her go. So, since I haven't been charged with anything, I have better things to do than sit here listening to your feeble attempts to cobble together some sort of case against me simply because you haven't been able to make your case against Susan Chase.'

'Sit down, Miss Goodwin,' Paget ordered as she started to rise. 'We haven't finished here.' He nodded to Tregalles, who picked up a large plastic bag from beside his chair and set it on the table. 'Miss Goodwin is being shown items of clothing,' he said. 'A tracksuit, dark blue, two-piece, well-worn; Reebok trainers, surgical gloves, and a clear plastic shower hat, all of which were recovered from a skip behind the Fairview Market in Caxton Road last Thursday, March the seventeenth, following the murder of Simon Holbrook earlier that day. Do you recognize these items of clothing, Miss Goodwin?'

The intake of breath when he opened the bag was so quickly controlled that both men would have missed it if they hadn't been watching closely. 'I don't know why you think I should,' she shrugged. 'Are they supposed to mean something to me?'

Tregalles slid a photograph across the table. 'This photograph was taken from your mother's album earlier today,' he said. 'It shows you wearing the tracksuit and trainers, while surrounded by dogs in the garden of your mother's house. The date on the back of the print is February the seventh of this year.'

Peggy's eyes glittered at the mention of her mother. 'You had no right to take things from my mother's house,' she breathed. 'No right at all. And there are all sorts of tracksuits like that around. That picture doesn't prove anything.'

'We'll see,' Paget said equably. 'You'll no doubt have noticed the dark stains on the clothes and shoes,' he continued. 'It's blood, Miss Goodwin. Simon Holbrook's blood, splattered on to your clothing when you stabbed him a number of times. And then there's the plastic shower hat. I'm sure you must have been sweating under that hat, because you left quite a few strands of hair inside when you took it off. You'll be familiar with what our labs can do with DNA testing these days, I'm sure, and I don't think we will have any trouble proving that those hairs belong to you.

'However, even if they don't, they still have the surgical gloves to work with, because you cut your little finger the other day, a paper cut – we were there when it happened, if you remember – and the dressing remained inside the glove when you tore it off and threw it in the bin. Oh, yes, and speaking of the bin, you had to hoist yourself up after you'd taken the gloves off to make sure everything had gone right down into the bin, and you left us a nice set of fingerprints on the metal.

'Anything you wish to say, Miss Goodwin?'

Peggy gave a shrug suggesting that what he was saying was of little concern to her. 'I know how desperate you must be to find someone guilty of killing Simon, so I have to assume all this was planted to make me look guilty. And if that is the best you can do, I'm not surprised you had to let Susan go, when you know as well as I do that she is the one who killed Simon.'

'Which is what you would like us to believe,' Paget told her, 'but there's more.' He turned the trainers over on their sides. 'If you look very closely, you will see fibres stuck to the bottom of the shoes, and tiny shards of glass embedded in the soles and heels. The fibres come from the carpet in Simon Holbrook's bedroom; the substance adhering to them is Simon Holbrook's blood, and the glass embedded in the shoes is identical to the glass recovered from a broken window in Susan Chase's car—'

'Which would suggest to any *reasonable* person,' Peggy cut in, 'that the trainers belong to Susan, and it was probably she who managed to get hold of those clothes to try to incriminate me.'

'Nice try,' Paget told her, 'but I prefer to think of it as the other way round. When you finally realized that Simon Holbrook had been conning you for years; that he was in fact sleeping with Susan Chase, and had been for months, you followed her, and when she left her car in Tavistock Road, you decided to plant evidence in the car – the rings you had torn from Laura Holbrook's fingers when you killed her.

'I'm sure you've noticed,' he continued, 'that the people in Tavistock Road pride themselves on their displays of early spring flowers, but it's not the place for someone with allergies, like yourself, is it? Was it a sudden fit of sneezing that caught you by surprise the night you smashed the window in Susan Chase's car and put the rings in the glovebox? I believe the tissue you used to wrap them in can be traced to you, Miss Goodwin.'

Peggy rolled her eyes as if she couldn't believe what she was hearing. 'So you found Laura's rings in Susan's car,' she said sarcastically. 'Did it not occur to your tiny minds that perhaps *Susan* put them there after killing Laura? She's been after Simon for years, and I suppose she thought that if she got rid of Laura he would turn to her. But Simon had no time for Susan. He told me himself that he wished he could find a way to get rid of her attentions, but he felt sorry for her and didn't want to hurt her feelings.'

'So sorry for her, in fact,' said Paget, 'that he had been sleeping with her at every opportunity long before his wife died?'

But Peggy shook her head. 'That,' she said emphatically, 'is a lie put about by Susan. She desperately wanted it to be true.'

'It is true and you know it,' Paget told her. 'He has been going away with Susan Chase or sleeping with her virtually every time his wife was away on business. And you know it's true because you were in the house while she was in Simon Holbrook's bed upstairs. Waiting to kill him for that very reason as well as for what he was about to do with you when he turned the company over to Drexler-Davies.'

Paget sounded almost sympathetic as he said, 'After all you have done for him throughout the years, including the ultimate demonstration of your devotion to him by planning and executing the murder of his wife. And a very clever plan it was, Miss Goodwin, breaking into people's homes while they were away – the homes of people who had confided in you when they came into the shop to buy a present or a card. But you left dog hair behind in several houses as well as in Laura Holbrook's bedroom when you killed her; dog hair that can be traced back to the dogs you helped your mother groom. And it was you who killed Simon because, after all you had done for him throughout the years, including ridding him of his wife, he was casting you aside for Susan Chase. Not only that, but he was quite prepared to see you pushed out of Holbrook Micro-Engineering Labs when he sold out to Drexler-Davies.'

'That's not true! Simon would never sell out to Drexler-Davies.'

'Oh, yes he would,' Paget told her. 'We have proof of that, and you would have been the loser – again. You have always been in love with Simon, haven't you, Miss Goodwin, but Simon was never in love with you, was he? He used you in the same way he used other women. He may have slept with you but he never loved you. Simon Holbrook used women and discarded them when he was tired of them or they were no longer useful to him. He used you to get his company up and running, but as soon as someone with better skills and more money came along, you were pushed aside.'

Paget looked puzzled as he shook his head. 'I don't understand how you could let him use you in that way. You are in many ways a very intelligent woman, but you seem to have a blind spot when it comes to Simon Holbrook. You didn't even get the message when he brought Laura Southern into the firm to take your place, then added insult to injury by expecting you to bring her up to speed. In fact you *still* didn't get the message when he went off and *married* the woman?'

Peggy's eyes glittered. 'You don't know what you're talking about,' she grated. 'Simon wasn't like that at all. Yes, women were attracted to him, and in Laura's case he was attracted to her. Laura was very clever, I'll grant her that, and Simon became infatuated with her. But that's all it was, infatuation, and by the time he realized that it was the company she wanted to control, and her interest in him was only for his talent as the key to the success of the company, it was too late to do much about it.'

'Except kill her,' said Paget quietly. 'And who better to get him to do it for him than the ever-faithful Peggy Goodwin? The woman who would do anything for him, especially if she thought he'd make good on his promise of marriage when the time was right.

'But the time would never be right, would it, Miss Goodwin? Because while he was persuading you to do his dirty work, he was bedding Susan Chase, and he made her exactly the same promise. She really believed he would marry her and they would go off together to Solihull once the deal was finalized with Drexler-Davies. Perhaps he meant it this time, but I doubt it even if things had worked out as he'd planned. But one thing I do know, after talking to Henry Beaumont, is that Simon was quite prepared to abandon you, because Beaumont had made it clear that you and others would be replaced by his own people. I suppose you could take some comfort from the fact that Simon did express regret at having to lose someone he described as "a secretary – a good one, but still just a secretary".'

'That's a lie!' she said savagely. Colour had slowly drained from Peggy's face as Paget made each point. 'Simon wasn't like that. You didn't know him as I did.'

Peggy paused to steady her breathing, but her voice shook as she continued. 'As for being in love with Simon, *yes*, I was in love with him, and he was in love with me. He only married Laura because we were desperate for the money she brought into the company, as well as the expertise to market our products. He discussed it with me, and I agreed it was the only way. Simon hated every minute he was married to her, but it was Susan who killed her, because she has always wanted Simon for herself. Susan hated Laura. Simon had nothing to do with Laura's death, and neither did I.

'As for this other business of merging with Drexler-Davies, that's nonsense. If it had been true, I would have been the first to know about it, because Simon discussed everything with me. Simon *needed* me. Apart from anything else, he would have had to keep me on, because I know more about that company that anyone in Beaumont's transition team.'

'Transition team? Interesting choice of words, Miss Goodwin, especially since you claim to know nothing about such a merger. But you did know, didn't you? Not because Simon told you, but because of this.'

Paget took a clear plastic evidence bag from his pocket and put it on the table. Inside was a small silver-coloured object no bigger than his little finger. 'I'm sure you'll recognize it,' he said, 'because it's a flash drive memory stick taken from your flat this morning. It contains copies of every email between Simon Holbrook and Henry Beaumont, and it has your fingerprints all over it. And the comments he makes about you, Miss Goodwin – not exactly flattering, are they? Not the sort of thing one expects from a lover.

'And that,' he concluded, 'was the final betrayal, wasn't it, Miss Goodwin?'

There were tears in Peggy's eyes, but they glittered with hatred as she said, 'You don't know *anything* about me and Simon——' only to be cut off by Tregalles.

'Sorry to interrupt, Miss Goodwin,' he said, 'but I would like to take a closer look at one of the keys on that ring.' He reached across the table to spread the keys inside the bag, and point to one of them – a longer, heavier key than the others. 'I've seen another one like that,' he said. 'I wondered why the key to Holbrook's back door was sitting on a shelf beside the door. But this explains it. That's the way you left the morning you killed him, isn't it, Miss Goodwin? You left the front door on the latch so that Janice West would go in and find the body, but you left by the back door because you didn't want to take the chance of someone seeing you with that black bag of clothing under the street lights at the front of the house. You locked the back door behind you with this key, leaving the second key on the shelf beside the door so we would think it had been locked from the inside, and the killer had left by the front door. That was your bike beside the back door, wasn't it? You rode home on it, stopping just long enough to drop the bloodstained clothing into a skip along the way. As a matter of fact I found the bike in your lock-up garage this morning, and the tyre tread matched perfectly.'

Peggy was shaking her head violently from side to side. 'I have never seen that key before in my life,' she declared. 'Someone must have put it there. Someone who——'

But Paget cut her off by saying, 'No one planted that key in your handbag, Miss Goodwin, as you well know, and I'm tired of listening to your lies and evasions.' He nodded to Tregalles, who took out his phone and entered two numbers as Paget continued.

'I believe that you and Simon Holbrook conspired to kill Laura Holbrook, and I believe that it was you who did the actual killing. I also believe that when you finally realized how he had used you to get rid of his wife, while carrying on a liaison with Susan Chase, and making a secret deal with Drexler-Davies, which would make you redundant, not only as an employee, but as a lover, you killed him and did everything in your power to incriminate Miss Chase.

'Margaret Diane Goodwin, I am charging you with the murders of Laura and Simon Holbrook. You are not obliged to say anything, but it may harm your defence if you do not mention, when questioned, something you wish to rely on later in court. Anything you do say may be given in evidence.'

The lines in Peggy's face might have been carved in granite as she slowly shook her head. 'You'll never prove any of this,' she began, but stopped when the door opened and a young woman entered the room and advanced to the table. Her name was Gwen, according to her name-tag, and she carried a small metal tray, partly covered by a cloth. 'Please open your mouth, Miss Goodwin,' she said. 'I need a swab for DNA purposes. It will only take a minute.'

Peggy Goodwin shot a malevolent glance at Paget as she got to her feet, then turned to face the young woman. 'And you can go to hell!' she grated as she snatched the tray from her hand and flung it straight at Paget.

'You should have seen it!' Tregalles said as he and Audrey sat down to a late dinner. 'It's all swollen around the eye. Blood was streaming down his face and all over his shirt, but he still didn't want to go to A&E to have it seen to. I finally managed to get him there, and it's a good thing I did, because it took four stitches to get it stopped. God! You should have seen that tray go! She just flicked it like a Frisbee. Wham! Caught him just above the eye.'

'He could have been blinded,' Audrey said reproachfully, 'but you sound as if you almost enjoyed seeing him bleed.'

''Course I didn't, love,' he said, lowering his voice. 'I didn't mean it to sound that way. It's just that, well, it was pretty spectacular.'

'So what were you doing, apart from watching him bleed all over his shirt?'

'Trying to get Peggy Goodwin calmed down,' he said. 'It's funny, but she'd pretty much kept it all together until Gwen came in to take a swab from her. But something must have snapped; I think she finally realized that she was going down for what she'd done, and she just lost it. Took all three of us on, fighting, kicking, screaming about Simon, how it was all Susan's fault and she should be dead as well. And you wouldn't believe how strong that woman is,' he continued. 'Tracy Woods was on the door, and she's no lightweight, but it took her and me and Gwen to wrestle Goodwin down. But she wouldn't give up even when we got the cuffs on her. She ripped Gwen's blouse, kicked me on both shins —'he paused to lift the legs of his trousers to display grazes and swellings that were turning a nice shade of blue — 'and she got a handful of Tracy's hair. Tracy was furious! You know how particular she is about her appearance. I thought she was going to kill Goodwin.

'Gwen never did get the swab. The way Goodwin was going on, there was no way she was going to try. After all that fighting we had to call the doctor in to examine Goodwin, so Gwen left it for him to get the swab. Fortunately, the tapes were still running, so she can't claim it was us who started it. Pity we don't have video in there, though,' he chuckled. 'It would've been better than championship wrestling on TV.'

Later, as they were getting ready for bed, Tregalles showed Audrey the bruises again. 'I'll be lucky if I can walk tomorrow morning,' he muttered.

'Oh, stop your moaning,' Audrey told him. 'Wear your blue shorts to work tomorrow. Go nicely with those legs, they would. You're lucky it was only your shins she kicked. Mr Paget could have lost an eye. It's a wonder . . . Aaahhh!' she gasped as Tregalles came up behind her and put his arms around her. 'Your hands are ice cold! Get them off me, you lecherous devil, and warm them somewhere else.'

'Sooner warm them where they are,' he told her. 'Like you said, it's lucky nothing else was damaged beside my shins. I hope you weren't planning on going to sleep for a while.'

Thirty-Four

Paget winced, squinting against the sun as they emerged from the court-room where Peggy Goodwin had been remanded in custody. The eyelid and the flesh around the eye was dark and swollen, and the eye itself was streaked with red and sensitive to sudden changes in light.

'We have to find the weapon,' he told Tregalles. 'I had a word with Starkie about Susan Chase's head wound, and he feels confident that it was made by the same weapon as the one that killed Laura Holbrook. And if that is the case, I want Goodwin charged with that assault as well.'

'Or murder if Chase doesn't make it,' Tregalles said soberly. 'The thing is, she could have hidden it where we're never likely to find it or thrown it away in a field or a ditch somewhere. It could be anywhere.'

'There are no fields or ditches between the flower shop and Goodwin's flat,' Paget pointed out, as they left the building and made their way to the car, 'and I'm betting she would get rid of it as soon as possible after leaving the shop. She wouldn't want to be caught with it in her posses-sion, so chances are she dumped it in the lane. She couldn't go up the lane, because the police were milling about, attending an attempted break-in, so I suggest you start by looking for the weapon at the lower end between the back of the shop and Tyndall Street.'

They found what they were looking for in one of the drains in the alley behind the Basket of Flowers. Tregalles could see it quite clearly on the screen even before the video snake they'd borrowed from the town touched bottom. Half submerged in a few inches of water, it had been impossible to see from above, even with the aid of a strong light.

'That's it!' the sergeant told the town engineer, who had been the one to suggest that they use a video snake in the first place. 'Now, the next thing is how do we recover it?'

'We fish for it with EMPART,' the man said. 'Electro-Magnetic Probe and Recovery Tool,' he explained. 'It's new. We just got it this year.

Shouldn't be a problem if we're careful and don't get it caught cross-ways in the pipe.'

'It's the murder weapon all right,' Tregalles told Paget, producing the evidence bag with a flourish. 'Found it in a drain behind the Basket of Flowers. And, brilliant detective that I am, I had a brainwave and pursued the matter further. I found out where it came from.'

The sergeant paused, as if waiting for applause, and for the first time that day, Paget found himself smiling. 'I can hardly wait,' he said, settling back in his seat. 'Tell me, where did it come from, Sergeant?'

Tregalles grinned. 'Thought you'd never ask,' he said. 'It's an old tyre lever,' he continued as he slid the bag on to Paget's desk, 'and it made me think of that mobile workshop Arthur Johnson runs from the back of Goodwin's mother's shop, so I took it round to ask him if he'd ever seen it before. Turns out he had; in fact it belonged to him.'

Now that he had Paget's full attention, Tregalles moved back and sat down. 'It's the largest one of a set of three he inherited, along with some other tools, from his father. They don't use them any more, of course, but he said he first realized it was missing around the middle of January, which ties in with when the burglary took place in Abbey Road.'

The smile left the sergeant's face. 'Shook him up pretty badly, I'm afraid,' he said. 'He didn't know what he was going to say to Goodwin's mother. He said she still refuses to believe that her daughter could kill anyone, and he didn't know how she would react when she found out that the murder weapon had come from his workshop.

'Anyway,' he said briskly, 'it ties Goodwin into the attack on Susan Chase, so they should be able to add that to the charges.' He stood up and picked up the bag. 'Any news on how Chase is doing?'

'As a matter of fact, Ormside just called to tell me that she's conscious, and they are cautiously optimistic that there will be no permanent damage to the brain. We won't be able to talk to her for a day or two, but all the signs are hopeful.

'Also, it appears that Peggy Goodwin must have done those burglaries herself, because according to Simon Holbrook's appointments diary, he was always with someone who could vouch for his whereabouts on the nights the burglaries occurred, and that as good as tells me that he and Peggy Goodwin planned this together. I don't know, but my guess is that it was Peggy who read about the Dunbar Road burglary, and decided to copy what they'd done. She used this tyre iron to pry the doors open and batter some of the furniture, and probably used a piece of pipe on other pieces to make us think two people were involved. And she carried that idea through by taking food away or making it look as if two people had stopped for a meal. And it worked – at least until she made the mistake of using the bloodied weapon to pry open the back door of Holbrook's house. As for the killing of Simon Holbrook, we have all the evidence we need, despite Goodwin's attempt to frame Chase. Forensic tells me that what we were supposed to believe were Chase's bloodied prints on the taps and wardrobe, were existing prints with Holbrook's blood smeared lightly over them. In fact, the prints were all but obliterated anyway.'

'Looks good, then,' Tregalles said. 'And I'm glad to hear that Susan Chase is going to be all right. Pretty woman, and she's had a rough time of it lately. Hope she makes it. Fingers crossed then, eh?'

Paget smiled. Tregalles had always had an eye for a pretty face, and he'd been quite smitten with Susan Chase from the very beginning.

'How'd you think you got on, yesterday?' Tregalles asked Molly, referring to the sergeant's exam.

'It's a tough exam, but I *think* I did all right,' she said. 'But whether I did well or not, at least the first part's over. As for the next step, only time will tell.'

'You could've told me you were going for it, you know,' he said. 'I mean it isn't all *that* long ago that I went through it myself, so I might have been able to give you a few pointers.'

Molly shook her head. 'It was nothing personal,' she told him, 'but you know what it's like round here if they know you're trying for something like that, especially if you're a woman. It's hard enough trying to compete as it is without having to put up with that while I was trying to study.'

'But I wouldn't have . . .' The sergeant's words trailed off and colour crept into his face when he saw the way Molly was looking at him. 'Yeah, well, I suppose I might have sort of teased you about it,' he conceded. 'Same as everyone else. Not that we would've meant it.'

'You never do,' said Molly, 'but you do it just the same, don't you? And the not so subtle put-downs get pretty tiresome after a while. I know,' she said as Tregalles started to protest, 'you may not be as bad as some, but it becomes a habit and you play off one another. Women are supposed to take the snide remarks as a joke, but it doesn't work the other way if we make remarks about you men, now does it, Sergeant?'

Later, as Tregalles stood in the kitchen doorway while Audrey was preparing dinner, he told her of the conversation. 'I didn't know what to say,' he ended. 'I mean Molly knows I respect her; she's a damned good copper, and I've always thought of her as a friend as well as a colleague, and I don't have any objection to her wanting to get ahead. All sorts of women do these days, and -'

'And you just proved her point,' Audrey cut in tersely as she turned to face him.

'I don't see how?'

'You don't even know you're doing it, do you, love?' Audrey wiped her hands on her apron. 'You just said, "all sorts of women do these days". You just set us apart right there. You talk of it as if it's something unusual; something to remark on, and something to make jokes about. Oh, I know, love,' she went on as he tried to break in, 'you don't do it deliberately, but it's there just the same, so I don't blame Molly one bit for not telling anyone. I wouldn't have told anyone either if I'd been in her shoes.'

'But I didn't mean anything by it,' Tregalles protested.

'So why say it, then, love?' A hint of a smile touched her lips. 'Try thinking of us as people. We really are, you know.'